DEATH FROM ABOVE

Suddenly Naran found herself uttering a sound of fear and warning, a flash of Sight causing the reaction. Something terrible was about to happen, but the heavy fog all around her talent kept her from Seeing exactly what.

A *"Crack!"* sounded from above the platform, the noise almost lost in the babble of comments and questions coming from all over the room. Naran quickly looked up, and her heart immediately began to thunder with terror. A large section of the ceiling directly above them had started to fall, so large a section that jumping out of the way would be impossible.

In a matter of seconds, they would all be crushed!

Also by
Sharon Green
From Avon Books/Eos

THE BLENDING
Book One: Convergence
Book Two: Competitions
Book Three: Challenges
Book Four: Betrayals
Book Five: Prophecy

Coming Soon in
THE BLENDING ENTHRONED
Book Two: Deceptions

INTRIGUES

Book One of THE BLENDING ENTHRONED

SHARON GREEN

An Imprint of HarperCollinsPublishers

EOS
An Imprint of HarperCollins*Publishers*
10 East 53rd Street
New York, New York 10022-5299

Copyright © 2000 by Sharon Green
Cover illustration by Tom Canty
ISBN: 0-380-81293-2
www.eosbooks.com

First Eos paperback printing: October 2000

Eos Trademark Reg. U.S. Pat. Off. and in Other Countries, Marca Registrada, Hecho en U.S.A.
HarperCollins® is a trademark of HarperCollins Publishers Inc.

Printed in the U.S.A.

10 9 8 7 6 5 4 3 2

FOR JON WEBB,
THE BEST ADOPTED SON ANYONE COULD WANT

INTRIGUES

HISTORY AND PROPHECY

... usually many things are lost to history simply because they were never recorded. During this period, however, we are fortunate to have the journal of Tamrissa Domon, third level High talent in Fire magic and one of the major figures during that period.

The journal begins with reminding us that that was still a time when the so-called nobility was powerful and therefore controlled everything in their reach. Although the vast majority of our citizenry had magical talent of some sort, only a handful of the people were permitted to use their talent. More detailed use of the various magical abilities of Earth, Water, Air, Fire, and Spirit were against the laws of the land, except under certain strictly controlled circumstances.

One such circumstance came during the time of a challenge. The empire was run by a single "Seated Blending," and every twenty-five years the competitions were held to choose a new Seated Blending. The nobility put forward their own candidates to stand against those of the "commoners," and although the empire had been ruled by noble Blendings for more than a century, the belief remained that a common Blending could well prevail at any time.

It was the time shortly before the latest competitions that Tamrissa Domon, Fire magic, Lorand Coll, Earth magic, Jovvi Hafford, Spirit magic, Vallant Ro, Water magic, and Rion Mardimil, Air magic, were brought together in Gan Garee, the empire's capital. According to Dama Domon's journal, the Five were less thrown together than deliberately combined. Members of the nobility were in charge of arranging the challengers, and the aim of their efforts, of course, was to produce the most ineffective challengers to their own candidates. Various difficulties among the common groups of five made the nobility believe that these people would never become effective Blendings.

In the case of *our* five "commoners," however, the nobility made a serious mistake. Each of them had been part of an odd occurrence before coming to Gan Garee, a fact noted by Guild watchers but not by the nobility. The Guild was a group comprised of people who had no talent of their own, but who were able to judge strength and kind of talent in others. Guild members were supposed to be firmly under the thumbs of the nobility, but there had been a "prophecy" concerning a "Chosen Blending" that would appear. The nobility watched for the Chosen to destroy them, but the Guild watched with the hope of deliverance.

The Five newcomers—Tamrissa, Lorand, Jovvi, Vallant, and Rion—were indeed formed into a challenging Blending. What they and the nobles in charge failed to realize was that one of the noble Blendings, slated to be defeated and destroyed during the competitions, had decided that *they* would be the Seated Blending. With that end in mind, they gave covert assistance to the common Blending meant to face the Blending which the nobles had already chosen to be the next Seated Blending.

This noble-chosen Blending was composed of Middle talents rather than High talents, people who were firmly under the control of those nobles actually running the empire. Tamrissa and her Blendingmates had been covertly drugged to make them easy prey for the chosen noble Blending, but with the help of the renegade noble Blending they were able to defeat the nobles' tools with ease.

In point of fact *all* of the noble Blendings but the renegades were destroyed in the first of the competitions. That left the nobility with the choice of giving assistance to their sole remaining candidates, or standing back to watch the Fivefold Throne being claimed by commoners. The nobility chose the lesser of the two evils, of course, and duplicity stole the last competition from Tamrissa and the others just as they were about to defeat the noble Blending.

Our Five should have been destroyed then, but arrogance turns caution into idiocy. The nobles simply separated the Five, intending to send most of them to join the ranks of the empire's army. The Gandistran empire was then in the process of covertly attempting to invade Astinda, a neighboring empire to the west. The renegade Five were Seated as the new ruling Blending, and our Five were sent off in different directions.

The new Seated Five began to consolidate their position by destroying their most dangerous "advisors" in large numbers. Most of the renegade Five were seriously unbalanced, and more and more it became clear to the remaining members of the nobility that they'd made a serious mistake allowing those people to be Seated. It was far too late to change matters, however, and the renegade Five considered themselves solidly Seated—until two unpalatable facts were brought to their attention.

The first fact was that the Blending that had almost defeated them *hadn't* been destroyed, and now had somehow escaped their capture to re-form into a Five. To make matters worse, the commoners had also somehow managed to free many of the enslaved members of the army, most of whom were either High talents or strong Middles. That force was now on its way back to Gan Garee, clearly intending to reclaim the Fivefold Throne.

The second dismaying fact was the imminent arrival of an avenging force from the empire of Astinda. The Gandistran armies had had the situation all their own way for quite some time, but now the Astindans had rallied and were defeating and destroying every segment of the Gandistran army they came across. Those nobles who were aware of the approach of the Astindan army began to demand that the Seated Blending go out and protect Gandistran interests—and their own necks—immediately, but that wasn't possible. The Seated Blending didn't dare to Blend again, not when two vital members were at each other's throats.

The "common" Five arrived in Gan Garee before the avenging army, and the renegade Five chose to face them individually. Once again the renegade Five tried to use unfair means to defeat their opponents, but this time the effort was useless. The renegades were defeated one by one, and when our Five stood completely victorious, they were told it would only be a short time before the Astindans arrived. The avenging army meant to level Gan Garee and destroy everyone in the city, and only our Five had a chance to defeat them.

But our Five also had a dilemma. The Astindan forces had come to avenge what was done to *their* country, which meant that destroying them would not have sat well with the Five even if destroying that army were possible. Our Five decided to try to stop the avengers instead of killing them, an act that would have been difficult under any circumstance. The one advantage our Five had was the newly discovered fact that Rion's beloved, Naran Whist, wasn't simply a Low talent in one of the aspects. Naran was the possessor of a sixth talent, Sight magic, which allowed her to see a short way into the future.

Desperation caused the Five to attempt Blending with Naran, an attempt that worked admirably. They were now a Six rather than a Five, and use of the additional talent allowed them to defeat the invading forces rather than killing them. Once victorious, our Six were able to negotiate a treaty with the Astindans, granting them all of the remaining members of the nobility as workers to perform the back-breaking task of repairing the destruction done to Astindan land.

But success, no matter how much difficulty there had been in achieving it, proved to be the easier part of the matter. Five was the accepted number of a Seated Blending, and now the people would need to become accustomed to the idea that there were six talents rather than five. And there was also the matter of those Guild members who insisted that our heroes were the Chosen Blending spoken of so long ago in the prophecies. At the same time it was suggested by others that the prophecies weren't true prophecy but simply a warning to the future, and yet five of the six had experienced *something* before traveling to Gan Garee that no one could explain.

Our Six were immersed in uncertainty, so what they did was . . .

I've discovered that writing in a journal is terribly habit-forming, and I'm not one who breaks habits easily. We defeated the Seated Five and came to terms with the invading Blendings from Astinda, but that just meant that our hardest jobs were still ahead of us. We could no longer deny the fact that we would be Seated as rulers of the empire, even if we still weren't terribly happy about the idea. A lot of changes had to be made, and with too many of those changes we were the only ones who would be able to accomplish them. Like letting the world know that we were the first Sixfold Blending . . . Adding the talent of Sight would not be like adding the balancing force of Spirit . . .

It wasn't necessary to have Sight magic to know that we would soon dampen the delight of many of those who now followed us. The question was, would the dampening go all the way to full drowning . . . ?

ONE

Naran Whist sipped quietly from her cup of tea as she watched and listened to the discussion going on among her Blendingmates in the house they continued, for the moment, to occupy. It was still a thrill to realize that she *was* a full member of the group, an experience she'd never before had in her life. She'd always thought of herself as a complete freak, but now she not only had people she belonged among completely, she'd discovered she wasn't quite as unique as she'd feared.

A private smile curved Naran's lips. A lot of people would have been delighted to find themselves to be unique, but that was only because they hadn't had *her* experience. Living all alone in a world filled with strangers, terrified that someone would find out just how different she really was . . . The time had been as far from pleasant as it was possible to imagine—

"What do *you* think, love?" Rion asked suddenly from beside her, his hand tightening gently around her own. "Do you See something that would affect our decision one way or the other?"

"I'm sorry, my love, but I'm afraid I was daydreaming a bit," Naran admitted with an apologetic glance for the others, her cheeks warming very faintly. "The wool-gathering kept me from hearing the last of what was said."

"You're entitled to be distracted at the very least, Naran," Jovvi told her at once with one of those beautiful smiles. "Finding out you're not alone in the world after all must be a delight, but almost an overwhelming one after so long a time of believing otherwise."

"And if anyone should know how that feels, I'm the one," Tamrissa said with understanding amusement. "It isn't fun to stand against the world all by yourself."

"Nor is it pleasant to be cut off from all the rest of humanity save for one solitary individual," Rion agreed with his own sweet smile. "I, too, have some idea of your feelings, my love, but not entirely. I was not left on my own at a very tender age."

"But Jovvi was, so she must have the best idea of what Naran went through," Lorand put in with clear commiseration for both of the women he mentioned. "I may not have gotten along completely well with my family, but I still felt myself a part of them."

"And I'm feelin' almost guilty," Vallant offered with an uncomfortable expression on his face. "Of all of us, I'm the only one who had a family he both loved and *wanted* to be a part of. With that in mind, *I'm* the odd one in this group."

"That's right, you are!" Tamrissa exclaimed with a wicked gleam in her eyes as she put a hand to Vallant's face. "My poor dear, the only one to be cursed with a loving family. How my heart goes out to you."

"Don't tease him, Tamrissa," Lorand scolded lightly with a chuckle as Vallant looked at her with narrowed eyes. "My family was fairly loving too, or would have been without the pressures put on my father by the nobility. If Vallant is odd, then I'm almost the same."

"Thank you, Lorand," Vallant said politely, pretending to be very formal while looking at Tamrissa coolly. "It obviously takes a gentleman to understand another gentleman's position. What a shame some *ladies* are bereft of all compassion for a man they've been *claimin'* to feel something for."

"Claiming?" Tamrissa echoed at once, that gleam still in her eyes. "*I* haven't made any claims like that, not as far as *I* can remember. Has anyone here heard me say anything like that?"

"No, not a soul," Jovvi answered with a laugh as Vallant mock-glared at Tamrissa. "But since we do need to make a decision, let's get back to what we were discussing. Naran, we were trying to decide whether to introduce the members of your link groups to our five-member Blendings, or to ask Dom Ardanis to send more of his people who might want to join a Blending. Everyone will need a wide choice, I think, so I'd like to hear your opinion."

"My opinion is that the question is more involved than that, and also less involved," Naran answered with a small laugh. "I know my response was no help at all, but that's because the situation is really two situations. May I explain?"

"No, Naran, absolutely not," Tamrissa answered dryly as everyone else nodded or urged Naran to continue with words of encouragement. "We *enjoy* being completely confused and in the dark."

"Now you're teasing Naran, Tamrissa," Lorand said with a good deal of surprise evident. "And it's just come to me that you've been doing a *lot* of teasing today. Has something happened to change your usual mood that the rest of us don't know about?"

"Jovvi says my new mood is relief at surviving after coming so close to dying," Tamrissa answered with a small, faintly embarrassed laugh. "She also said the new mood won't last forever, and before you know it I'll be back to my usual, sedately shy self. Won't that be a relief?"

"I'm still thinkin' about that," Vallant countered, making the rest of them chuckle. "Meanwhile, why don't we let Naran get on with explainin' what she means?"

"To begin with, there's a situation we've spoken about, but not really thought all the way through," Naran said before Tamrissa could distract everyone with more teasing. "You've already begun to show others how to Blend, but so far there are only a double handful of other Blendings besides ours. All the rest of our people are in link groups, which we needed for fighting purposes. When are the members of those link groups going to be allowed to form Blendings of their own?"

"You know, I never really stopped to think about that," Jovvi acknowledged, seemingly as surprised as the others. "But you do happen to be right, so we ought to discuss the point right now. Link groups can be formed by any five people with the same talent, but Blendings *should* have people who have some interest in each other. Until now, most of our followers haven't had the chance to get to know each other."

"So that means we need to throw a really big party," Tamrissa said, her frown of concentration showing Naran that the Fire magic user considered the matter a serious one. "We introduce everyone to everyone else, and then they can all look into forming Blendings. If something comes up where we need the tandem link groups, ten new Blendings will give us the link groups as easily as link groups alone."

"That's a good point," Lorand agreed with an equally thoughtful nod. "There's no real reason for our people not to form their own Blendings, but what about everyone else? How and when are we going to show the people in the rest of the empire how to Blend?"

"It isn't goin' to be done all at once, that's for sure," Vallant said, his expression faintly vexed. "We'll have to start with the people here in Gan Garee, and then send teachers to the other parts of the empire. By then we might know how to handle the problems that come up."

"I agree that we need to do it a little bit at a time," Jovvi said as Rion nodded, both of them looking as thoughtful as the others. "A party is a good idea, Tamma, and we ought to hold it in the palace when we move in. But that still doesn't answer our question about your peers, Naran. Will we just be inviting your link groups, or as many others as Dom Ardanis cares to send?"

"Jovvi, you won't need to *invite* anyone with Sight talent," Naran pointed out gently, matching her smile to the words. "If you feel you'd like to be formal you can issue general invitations, but those who will be joining Blendings already know where it will happen—and they'll be at the party."

"Obviously we all have adjustments to make in our thinking," Rion said ruefully as Jovvi closed her eyes, Tamrissa shook her head with a sigh, and Lorand and Vallant groaned. "It never occurred to me that your talent peers would already know that."

"It's fairly clear that we all should have known," Jovvi said with a headshake of self-annoyance. "And the way you mentioned Tamma's idea of a party . . . Am I correct in assuming that it was a strong possibility even before Tamma mentioned it?"

"It was a strong possibility then, but it's a near certainty now," Naran agreed, examining the shadows again even as she spoke. "We'll also be turning over this house to the people from Astinda fairly soon, to let them get on with processing the former nobles. Our being here is only slowing the processing."

"And it's time we relocated anyway," Tamrissa put in with a sigh of accepting the inevitable. "If we try to delay any longer, most of our 'followers' will get so frustrated that they'll haul us bodily to the palace and toss us in. If we're going to do this, we have to do it right."

"And we've already decided we're going to do it," Jovvi agreed with the same kind of sigh. "That means any more foot-dragging is just plain silly, so let's stop talking and start doing. Does anyone have a reason why we *shouldn't* go to the palace right now?"

No one did, which made Naran smile to herself. The shadows had already told her that the decision to go at once would most likely be made right now, but there was no need to mention that. Too much foreknowledge seemed to make people feel as though they were being manipulated by events rather than doing the manipulating themselves. Some events *did* force certain actions, but those actions were never the only options available. They were usually the *best* available, but some people still felt a need to choose second best.

Naran had no idea why that was, but when the others began to gather themselves together, she did the same. Something she did know was that her instruction on the best ways to use her talent would begin once they were settled in the palace. The thought filled her with more excitement than anyone else could possibly be feeling right now, which made her wish that everyone would *hurry* . . .

Jovvi waited beside Lorand as their horses were brought out of the stables, a million plans and necessities buzzing around in her head. It really didn't make much sense for them to hold off on taking up residence in the palace, and they'd decided to start things off right. Instead of using the coaches some of their followers had expected them to show themselves off in, their Blending would arrive at the palace on horseback. That informal an arrival should give the first hint that the new Seated Blending meant to institute changes . . .

"I wonder if anyone will realize why our 'escort' is so large," Lorand commented as he watched the horses being brought out. "Having our link groups with us probably won't excite much comment right now, but in a little while everyone will know who they are—and wonder why we feel we need the protection."

"If anyone asks, we'll tell them," Tamma put in, looking back over her shoulder at Lorand. "I seriously doubt if everyone with a grudge has already come at us, and I'd rather be safe than sorry. If anyone dislikes the idea of us wanting to protect ourselves, they can just look the other way to spare themselves the discomfort of seeing what we do."

"But we'll try not to put it quite that baldly," Jovvi said with a smile for Tamma's obviously fading teasing mood. "We'll be doing other things to protect ourselves, and some of those things will be more upsetting than having our link groups following us around."

"If we're goin' to be surrounded by armies of servants, I think we have a right to know where they stand," Vallant put in, his tone a bit more reasonable than Tamma's had been. "We need to have our Blendin' entity check those people, and for that Jovvi especially needs her link groups."

That was the first of the things to do on Jovvi's list as

soon as they got to the palace, and one Jovvi wasn't looking forward to. Invading people's privacy left a bad taste in her mouth, but there was no other choice. The usurping Blending had been poisoned more than once, and there was nothing to say that Eltrina Razas had been responsible for both occurrences.

"We're lucky there are so few servants left in the palace," Lorand said after nodding agreement with Vallant. "I'd just like to know what we're going to do if and when the former hordes try to return."

"Perhaps we ought to ask one or two of our other Blendings to oversee any additions to the palace staff," Rion suggested with the least bit of diffidence. "It won't be possible for us to do it all ourselves, after all, and the solution would help us a great deal if the members of the other Blendings aren't insulted by the request."

"That's a great idea, Rion, and I can't picture them getting insulted," Lorand said, suddenly brightening. "Those are people we've fought beside, after all, and interviewing the staff properly is something that will help keep us alive. On top of that, they can all use the practice at working in a Blending."

Everyone agreed, and then they separated to go to their respective horses. Once Jovvi was mounted, she waited until they were moving toward the road before she urged her mount close to Lorand's.

"I think Rion was afraid that his suggestion sounded too much like the way the nobility assigned tasks to underlings," Jovvi murmured to a partially attentive Lorand. "Your endorsement of the idea made him feel quite a lot better, so now it's *your* turn. What do *you* need to make you feel better?"

"If you're asking about what's bothering me, the answer isn't hard to put into words," Lorand replied, giving Jovvi the impression he groped for more than just what to say. "All those members of the former nobility deserve to be made to work for the Astindans, repairing the destruction they caused either actively or passively. The one thing I

haven't come to terms with, though, is also sending along
their children. I'm not sure that's right."

Jovvi hadn't missed seeing the crowds of people around
the house they'd appropriated, most of them the former
nobles of the empire. The rest were guardsmen from both
the empire and Astinda, and some of the former nobles
were still trying to assert their "rights."

One smaller group, though, contained children of various
ages, from young teenagers all the way down to infants in
arms. The vast majority of those infants were being held
by nurses, with only a single exception.

"I think I should have mentioned sooner that I've already
spoken to the Astindans about that very point," Jovvi said,
feeling a flash of guilt for having forgotten. "They really
are men and women of honor, and don't believe in condemning those who are guiltless. Children can't be considered a part of what was done to their country, so *these*
children are being examined with something else in mind:
whether or not they've been ruined beyond redemption by
the way they were raised."

"What do you mean by 'beyond redemption'?" Lorand
asked, his disturbance clearly lessened. "Those children
also aren't responsible for the way they were raised."

"Of course they're not responsible," Jovvi agreed. "But
you have to remember that most of them have been shaped
by that upbringing, and that majority will act just as their
parents have. Neither we nor the Astindans have a place
for people who think they were born to be deferred to and
pampered. The children who see themselves that way will
be put to work beside their parents, in the hope that they'll
outgrow the attitude."

"And the rest?" Lorand asked, his emotions perfectly
clear. He hated the idea of condemning children, and hated
even more not being able to argue the need. "Are they also
going to be put to work for the 'good of their characters'?"

"The others will be adopted by Astindans who lost their
own children to the madness of the invasion," Jovvi answered, wishing with all her heart that she was able to
ease Lorand's distress. But his strength had grown beyond

her ability to touch, so he would have to find his own easing . . . "Our people would have to make room for extra mouths to feed, and there would always be resentment against those children from *someone*. In Astinda their new parents will be told only that the children are orphans, so they now have a chance to be raised with love. And there *is* going to be an exception to the general rule. Did you see that one well-dressed young woman holding an infant?"

"How could I miss it?" Lorand asked, glancing over his shoulder at the group they'd passed. "She stood there glaring around at the world as if daring *anyone* to take the child she held."

"That's because she doesn't yet know she'll be the sole exception to having to give up her child," Jovvi told him, finally finding a reason to smile. "The main Astindan Blending has already examined her, and found that the usual attitudes of the nobility haven't taken well in her. She has very little respect or liking for the rest of her class, and she loves her child fiercely. She'll be sent out with the next group being taken to Astinda, but she'll be separated from the others almost at once. She hasn't been separated now for her own protection."

"Yes, the rest of those stiff-necked fools would blame *her* for the way she was treated, and would certainly consider her a traitor." Lorand nodded distractedly, his agreement clear. "So at least that's one saved, out of—how many?"

"There are a few others who also won't be forced to do the backbreaking work," Jovvi said, sighing over the same picture that Lorand now looked at inwardly. "Some of those people are more victim than noble, and the Astindans hope to find a way to reverse the way they were ruined. But as far as the rest goes . . . Lorand, we *have* to find a way to keep our own people and their children from turning into the same kind of parasites. If we don't think of something *now*, it's bound to happen."

"Yes, people do commit the worst horrors in the name of love, don't they," Lorand agreed with a matching sigh. "I wish I could say I knew exactly how to stop it, but I don't have the first clue. Hopefully something will come to one of us once we settle down into a routine."

Jovvi nodded and let the conversation drop, but her mind still worried at the need, along with a hundred others. There was so *much* that had to be done, all of it important if not downright crucial. Jovvi had been losing sleep over the worries, a lack that looked as though it would continue for a while . . .

The ride to the palace was uneventful. The day was a bit overcast, promising rain later, but Jovvi didn't ask Lorand about the rain. The temperature was still warm enough that the Astindans probably would make no effort to give the former nobles shelter from the rain, and Lorand didn't need *that* to worry over along with the rest. Lorand was a beautiful human being, and Jovvi sometimes felt that *he* was more aware of the suffering of others than she was.

"At least we won't have hordes of people waiting to attack us with demands," Lorand murmured as they drew rein in front of the main entrance to the palace. "The guardsmen we left here are still at their stations, so no one should be inside but the servants who were left after we faced the former Five."

"I've definitely learned to be grateful for small favors," Jovvi agreed, dismounting without waiting for anyone to help. "And for the fact that there are still stableboys here."

In point of fact there were a lot of stableboys, all rushing out to take the reins of their horses. Even so, not all of the horses would be taken to the stables at once, not with almost seventy-five people in their party.

"I thought ten boys would be enough," Vallant said after letting his reins be taken, looking around at the sudden flurry. "I left orders to have the boys be here when we arrived, but it looks like some of us are still goin' to be takin' care of our own horses."

"Some of the guardsmen are coming over to help," Lorand told Vallant with a smile of amusement. "And let me say how grateful I am that you dislike seeing to your own horse. I may be better at it than you are, but I don't like doing it any more than you do."

"Now that I know *how* to do it, I'm more than willing to let others have the honor," Tamma put in with her own amusement. "It's nice to know I can take care of myself if the need arises, but the rest of the time I prefer to be lazy."

"A perfect description of my own feelings," Rion agreed, voicing a small laugh as he took Naran's hand again. "I'm pleased no end that I'm able to look after myself, but prefer to leave exercising the talent for a time of need. And as soon as we've settled in, I even mean to learn how to cook."

Tamma immediately announced that she would join Rion in the cooking venture, and everyone, including members of the various link groups, put in their own opinions as they moved into the palace in a group. The guardsmen on duty remained at their posts outside, and the guardsmen they'd brought with them were off helping the stableboys with the horses.

The halls they walked through looked as deserted to Jovvi as they had the last time their Blending entered the palace. With very few servants and no guardsmen that was to be expected, of course, but Jovvi still disliked the . . . almost brooding atmosphere. Something would have to be done about that as quickly as—

Suddenly a man appeared out of a nearby doorway. The stranger held a long knife in each of his hands, and he screamed madly as he began to run in order to close the few steps between him and his chosen targets: Jovvi and her Blendingmates.

TWO

Rion saw the stranger charging at them, and immediately put a wall of hardened air between the attacker and his Blendingmates. At the same time the blades of the man's knives disappeared in a flash of very intense fire, and then the man himself crumpled to the marble floor.

"It's nice feelin' so well protected," Vallant commented dryly as he joined Rion and the others in stepping forward to inspect the now-unconscious attacker. It was fairly obvious that Tamrissa had destroyed the man's weapons and Lorand had put the man to sleep after Rion erected his wall of safety. "Naran didn't even have to warn us because the fool had no hope at all of succeedin'. Does anyone know who this man is, or what he has against us?"

"Apparently not," Jovvi answered for all of them after seeing nothing but headshaking. "But it won't be too hard to find out what his problem is, so let's bring him along with us. We'll also want to know if there are any more at home like him."

Some of the larger male members of the link groups came forward to carry the attacker, and it was a quieter procession that continued on into the palace. When they reached the area of meeting rooms just before the corridor diverged into the separate private wings, a small group of very disturbed servants was found waiting.

"Excellences, this is terrible!" one of the men said, wringing his hands as he stepped out ahead of the others. "We had no idea you were coming, so nothing is prepared for you, not even tea! Please forgive us our failure!"

"It's hardly your fault that we told no one we were coming," Rion soothed the man, not surprised that the servants were so agitated. "Your former masters might well have dismissed you for showing the terrible flaw of not being able to see the future, but happily we're not of their ilk. But before you run off to see to a million chores, please look at this man and tell us if you know him."

The servant, whose pathetic relief suggested that dismissal would have been the least he suffered at the hands of the previous Five, stepped forward to peer at the man Rion gestured to. A sharp intake of breath told Rion that the servant knew the unconscious man even before the servant spoke.

"Why, that's Feriun," the man exclaimed, his disturbance quickly returning. "He hasn't been among us long, but he's a very hard worker. What could have happened to him? Is he dead?"

"No, he's still among the livin'," Vallant said, glancing apologetically at Rion before taking over the servant's questioning. "Exactly when did he join the staff?"

"It was two or three days ago, Excellence," the man replied, causing Rion to exchange glances with Vallant and the others. "Not many of our people have come back yet, so he was put right to work. Have you any idea of what happened to the man?"

"We know exactly what happened to him," Tamrissa put in dryly, speaking in a way that Rion knew would keep the servant from asking the same question again. "Were any others added to the staff when this man Feriun was?"

"Yes, there were two others with him, Excellence," the servant answered at once, his eyes widening as he looked at Tamrissa. "One of the other two tends to avoid work more than do it, but we need the extra pair of hands too badly for the chief steward to dismiss him."

"Which of the magical talents do the three men fall under?" Naran asked abruptly, startling Rion along with everyone else. "Surely at least one of them has been seen exercising a talent, even one that happened to be weak?"

"Personally, I have no idea, my lady," the servant answered with raised brows before turning to look at the rest of the staff members still hovering behind him. "No, the others don't recall seeing them exercising talents either."

"No, Rion, don't correct him now," Naran whispered just as Rion was about to speak sharply to the servant for not addressing Naran as he had the rest of the Blending. "It isn't the right time."

Rion held his tongue as his love asked, but it was a near thing. He'd been about to instruct the servant that Naran was also to be addressed as "Excellence," but it was true that they hadn't yet made their announcement about the size and composition of their Blending. Rion felt annoyed at the need for silence, but then he realized what Naran's question could well mean.

"Thank you, Naran," Jovvi said, also clearly realizing the implications of the question—that the man and his friends could well be renegade Guild people. "We'll look into that as soon as we make ourselves comfortable." Then she turned to the servant. "Please have tea prepared for us and our guests. We'll be in the large meeting room."

The servant bowed his acknowledgment of the order, then turned and hurried the other staff members off to see to the wants of the new Five. He himself took up a hovering position, obviously ready to run in any direction should it be required of him. Jovvi led the way to the large meeting room they'd been in once before, and Rion joined everyone else in following her.

"All right, there's two things that need doin' right now," Vallant said once everyone was in the large room with the servant left outside the closed door. "We have to send some of our guardsmen to fetch High Master Mohr, and we have to check out the entire servin' staff of this place. Then we can wake up this man Feriun and find out what he's up to."

"Yes, I agree," Jovvi said as she took a chair and turned to Rion's love. "Naran, how certain are you that this man and his friends are renegade Guild members?"

"There's no certainty about the matter yet, but it's a very strong possibility," Naran responded as she obviously studied what only *her* eyes could see. "If it turns out to be true, it could be something of a problem."

"To say the least," Tamrissa commented dryly as she took her own chair. "We don't know how many of them there are, or what their aims and plans could be. I suggest we stop wasting time and try to find out."

The entire group agreed, so Jovvi waited until they'd all found chairs and then initiated the Blending. In heartbeats it was no longer Rion but the Blending entity who glanced over the situation before floating quickly out to the stables. Their guard escort hadn't yet unsaddled their horses, which made matters much easier for the entity. The leader of the guardsmen was given his orders about sending for High Master Mohr, and also told to bring the rest of his people into the palace when the messenger was sent. Then the entity was itself free to return to the palace.

There were a fairly large number of flesh forms in the immense structure, but each one needn't be examined individually when they were found in groups. The entity found it simplicity itself to take over the minds of the entire group at once, and then it spoke to those captive minds.

—*This entity would know of your loyalty to your new employers*— it put gently. —*Would you betray them for silver or gold, or possibly for political reasons?*—

Each flesh form in the first two groups quietly and truthfully denied any intention of ever planning betrayal, but the same did not hold true for one member of the third group.

"Of course I would betray them if I was given enough silver or gold," a female flesh form admitted freely, fear and caution both being denied her. "They're big-shots, aren't they, so why wouldn't I? Big-shots always push around the little people, so they deserve whatever they get."

The entity ordered the female flesh form to report to the meeting room where its own flesh forms were, released the others in the group, then continued on. Four others with the same attitude toward betrayal were found elsewhere and also sent to the meeting room, and then the entity located two male flesh forms who were different. There was not the least resistance to the entity when it took the two over, and the response of the first of them was immediate.

"Of course I would betray those interlopers," the flesh form admitted with pride, his companion nodding agreement. "The silver makes the situation sweeter, but I would betray those fakes even without being paid. They're pretending to be the Chosen Blending when they're not, and people need to know the truth."

"And they also ruined my relationship with members of the nobility," the second flesh form added with the shadow of anger. "I was well on the way to becoming a noble myself for all the help I gave, and now it will never happen. When they fall because of *my* efforts I'll have my revenge, but it still won't be complete. Nothing can repay me for what I've lost."

At one time the entity would have had little understanding of what the flesh forms meant, but now it understood all too well. It sent the two males to the meeting room with an inner sigh, released the others in the group, then resumed its chore. The completion of that chore took quite some time, but at last it was done and then it was Rion back again.

"Phew!" Jovvi said as she sprawled back in her chair. "That was some job, and for a moment I thought I'd need to draw strength from a link group or two. I'm really glad it's over, at least for the moment."

"You don't need a link group, you need a decent amount of rest," Lorand told her at once with a frown, leaving his own chair to move closer to hers and lean down. "You've been pushing yourself too hard with too little sleep, love, something I could feel much too clearly in the Blending. As soon as we finish what we're in the middle of, you have to take some time to get that rest."

"And in the meantime you *will* use one of your link groups," Tamrissa ordered, her tone much more stern than Lorand's had been. "For the first time in a long while I felt about three times stronger than you, which proves that Lorand isn't imagining things."

"Yes, yes, you're all perfectly right," Jovvi acknowledged as Rion joined the others in agreeing with what had been said. "I *am* tired and I *do* need rest, but I can't take the time until we're finished with this task. Have any of those people gotten here yet?"

Rion had already spoken quietly to a member of one of his link groups, and the man was on his way to the door to find the answer to Jovvi's question. The man, Eystren, put his head outside, looked around, then opened the door wider.

"The guardsmen are here, Jovvi, and so are some others," Eystren announced. "Which of them do you want first?"

"Let's have the guardsmen in first, and then that woman," Vallant said when Jovvi looked at him inquiringly. "The first woman, who doesn't have much likin' for 'big-shots.'"

"Yes, I'm curious about her as well," Rion agreed as Eystren took care of inviting in those who were wanted first. "I had the impression that she could well be the one who poisoned our predecessors."

"Yes, I got that definite impression," Naran agreed with a small shudder as she tightened her hold on Rion's hand. "And our tea is here."

Their guardsmen entered the room and immediately made way for the group of servants with two large tea services. Rion saw Lorand paying very close attention to what was being brought in, and a pair of moments later Lorand looked at all of them and nodded. That meant the tea and cups were safe to drink and use, so Rion rose and waited for the services to be set up. Then he poured cups of tea for Naran and himself before returning to his chair.

With everyone serving themselves it wasn't long before most of their people had tea to sip. Jovvi seemed to be drinking hers gratefully, and when she put the cup aside Rion had the impression that she'd also touched at least one of her link groups.

"Yes, that's definitely much better," Jovvi announced with a smile that made her look more like her usual self. "Now, let's have that woman in."

Vallant went with one of the guardsmen to find the woman they all wanted, and when the woman was brought in Vallant went back to his chair. The guardsman, however, stayed behind the woman, watching her carefully. The servant was a tall woman who carried more weight than she should, and she stood with her head up in a stance that Rion suspected was her usual one.

"All right, now you can speak to us a bit more freely," Jovvi said to the woman, whose gaze had lost the vague look of someone under the entity's control. "We'd like to know why you poisoned the former Seated Five. There has to be more to it than resentment."

"I don't know what you're talking about," the woman stated, all but looking down her nose at Jovvi. "I may be general kitchen mistress, but with five separate and individual staffs, I can't possibly know everything that goes on. I can't stop you from blaming me, but I'm *not* responsible."

"That's amazing," Lorand said as Jovvi made a sound of annoyance. "Almost everything she said is a lie, but she still expects us to take her at her word."

"She has a reason she hasn't mentioned," Jovvi told Lorand, then returned her attention to the woman. "You feel perfectly safe in spite of the fact that you've been found out, and I'd like to know why. Why aren't you worried about what will become of you?"

"There's nothing for me to worry *about*," the woman responded, her faint smile giving Rion the impression of vindictiveness. "We've all heard about your bunch, and how it's supposed to matter what people think of you. That's because you're peasants instead of nobles, and you don't want more trouble than you already have. If you start out by accusing innocent people of all sorts of crimes, you'll lose a lot of the support you need to stay where you are. I say I'm innocent, and if you try to argue that you'll have more trouble than the point is worth."

"I'm more in the mood to *do* than to argue," Tamrissa said, interrupting the mutter of outrage circulating among the people in the room, her tone coldly furious. "Let's see what roast cook is like."

A narrow ring of fire suddenly circled the woman, and

her exclamation of fear suggested that the fire was a good deal hotter than it looked.

"Only a fool believes everything she hears—and wants to believe is so," Jovvi told the woman, her own voice on the cold side. "You've probably already announced your innocence far and wide, relying on that to keep you safe from summary execution. What a shame for you that we don't believe in summary execution if it can be avoided, and in this case it can be. You'll stand trial in open court for what you've done, but my first question still hasn't been answered. Before the guardsmen take you away, tell me what made you do as you did."

"I was paid gold to eliminate those fools, and why shouldn't I have?" the woman answered without hesitation, showing that Jovvi had her under control again. The ring of fire abruptly disappeared, telling Rion that Tamrissa had seen what he had. "It isn't possible to explain to any of you how much better I am than you, how much better I am than *everyone*. Those puffed-up fools found out the truth, and so will the bunch of *you*."

"I'm happy to say that we already know that particular truth," Jovvi told her with a grimace. "Give me the name of the one who paid you that gold."

"See, you don't even know there was more than one," the woman answered with a sneer. "The first one was Edmin Ruhl, son of that fool Embisson Ruhl, and the second was Eltrina Razas. It was their *privilege* to pay me gold, and eventually things would have been turned the proper way around and *they* would have worked for *me*."

"I think it's fairly obvious that the woman is insane," Lorand said into the sudden silence after a brief hesitation. "Will the courts condemn someone who isn't entirely responsible?"

"I believe they'll first try to see if a physician can cure her," Rion replied when no one else offered an opinion. "If the attempt succeeds, the woman will be allowed to become a useful member of society. If it doesn't succeed, they'll most likely have her put down. Someone who kills for no true reason and without the least regret can't be allowed another chance to harm the innocent."

"No, they can't," Jovvi agreed with a sigh, and then she turned to the leader of their guard. "Seldon, please have two of your men take that woman to the court authorities to be charged with the attempted murder of the previous Seated Five. Also tell them we'd like to be informed of her eventual disposition."

"At once, Excellence," the man Seldon replied with a bow, and the guardsman behind the woman was quickly joined by a second guardsman. The two took the woman out of the room, and the fact that she began to shout out her outrage proved that Jovvi had released her again.

"I think we ought to wait until tomorrow to interview most of the rest of those servants," Lorand said, looking at Jovvi worriedly. "The only ones who can't wait are those two friends of our unconscious attacker over there. Are you able to do that much, love?"

"Easily," Jovvi reassured him with a smile and a touch of her hand to his. "Leaning on my link group is helping quite a lot, and there isn't that much left to do. I'm only tired, love, not completely drained. And I've just noticed that High Master Mohr has arrived. Vallant, can we have Dom Mohr and those two men in now?"

"I don't see why not," Vallant answered with a smile as he headed toward the door again, and then the smile faded. "Especially since I'm hopin' Dom Mohr can do somethin' about the situation."

Vallant stepped out of the room, and a moment later Lavrit Mohr, High Master of the Guild, walked in. Mohr was a tall, lean man who usually wore a pleasant expression, but at the moment he seemed perplexed.

"Good day to you, Excellences," Mohr greeted them, pausing to perform a small but respectful bow before continuing on into the room. "I hadn't thought you would be requiring a report from me quite this soon."

"We haven't asked you here for a report, Dom Mohr," Lorand told him with something of a smile. "I'm sure your people in the Guild are doing all they can to coordinate a renewal of the shipping of goods from all over the empire, but it *is* too soon to expect obvious and tangible results. We have another problem we need your help with."

Mohr parted his lips, probably to ask about the problem, but his words were interrupted by the arrival of the two suspected men. They were being guided into the room by guardsmen, and Vallant was at the head of the small parade. Mohr glanced at the men behind Vallant, then quickly looked at them again with a good deal more attention.

"Do you recognize them, Dom Mohr?" Jovvi asked gently as the tall man continued to stare at the newcomers. "There's a third member of the group, over there on that couch."

Mohr only glanced at the still-unconscious third man, but his face had paled and his lips had become a narrow line.

"No, I don't actually recognize any of them," Mohr said after an uncomfortable hesitation. "There's little doubt, though, that those two at least ought to be Guild men. I can't tell about the third man, not when he isn't conscious . . . What have they done?"

"The unconscious one attacked us with knives," Tamrissa answered promptly as always, but without her usual dryness. "We asked some questions and discovered that the attacker had been hired a few days ago with two friends, so we rounded up the friends. We thought you might like to help us question them."

"Yes, I would very much like to do so," Mohr replied, his tone having turned grim. "It disturbed me and the rest of my Guild members when some of our people refused to acknowledge you as the Chosen Blending, but forcing people to believe as we do isn't something we approve of. We simply let the dissenters go their own way, but if their way now includes physical attack . . . What can I do to help you?"

"We're going to question these men to find out if they came here on their own or were sent," Jovvi responded as she stirred in her chair. "If attacking us was their own idea, we can turn them over to the court system and let the proper authorities see to them. If they were sent, though, we need to know who sent them."

Mohr nodded to show his willingness to cooperate, so Jovvi touched Lorand's arm. Lorand also nodded before looking at the unconscious man, and a moment later the man was awake. Rion was prepared to pen their former attacker in a prison of hardened air, but Jovvi had control of the man so fast that other action became unnecessary.

"Please come over here and stand with your friends," Jovvi told the formerly unconscious man gently, and when he obeyed her she continued. "Tell us why you and those others took positions here in the palace as part of the staff."

"So that we could kill one or more of you, of course," the man answered immediately, the ghost of impatience behind his words. "The sooner you're no longer a Blending, the sooner things will go back to the way they were."

"Do you mean with the nobility in charge?" Jovvi asked in the same gentle voice. "Haven't you realized yet that the nobility will never be in charge again?"

"Please, do you think we're fools?" the man returned, now with faint disdain. "All you and your tools have done is gather up the deadwood among the nobility. The real powers left the city soon enough to avoid arrest and capture, and when they come back and take over again there will be more than enough room for those who help them to become nobles as well. We'll finally have what's been denied us for so long, the position of power we deserve."

"I see," Jovvi said as Mohr's lips tightened. "And is all this *your* idea, or did someone else let you share the dream?"

"Our leader shares everything with us, including the dream," the man answered, and a smile curved his lips as dedication began to gleam in his eyes. "As he says, the power will be there for the taking, and we'll be in the best position to do that taking."

"What's the name of this marvelous leader of yours?" Mohr demanded, clearly unable to remain silent any longer. "I'm curious about whether I know him."

"Of course you know him," the man replied, faintly disdainful again. "He's Holdis Ayl, your second in command."

Mohr looked so thunderstruck that one of the link members quickly pushed over a chair for him to sink into.

"Holdis," Mohr whispered after a very long moment, his face downright gray. "I thought he was my friend, and the one who would take over for me when I— How could he betray us like this?"

"He's not as much of a fool as you, and never has been," the former attacker answered, happily speaking his mind without hesitation. "He knows these peasants aren't chosen by anyone but the Guild, and if *he'd* been in complete charge those crippling rumors you started would never have been circulated. But he wasn't able to stop you in time, so he had to think of something else to do."

"Something else like murdering the only hope our empire has of surviving," Mohr growled, coming back to himself a good deal more quickly than Rion would have expected. "No, he isn't a fool like me, he's a deranged and mindless idiot. How many of you does he have under his thumb?"

"I don't know exactly how many of us there are, but we're the best in the Guild," the man replied proudly. "And not having *everyone* with us is to our benefit. There will only be so many titles to go around, after all."

"Titles," Mohr echoed with a sneer as he rose again to his feet. "Yes, you're perfect material to become one of the nobles. You never even stopped to wonder how long you would live if you did manage to kill one or more of this Blending. Are you really stupid enough to think that the survivors would have let you simply walk away?"

"They would have been too demoralized to act quickly enough to stop or hurt me," the man returned primly. "The point was explained to us carefully, so when I saw the bunch of them coming into the palace I grabbed my chance. But the element of surprise didn't work, so next time I'll have to try something else."

"Obviously, Ayl chose the most thickheaded members of the Guild as his dupes," Mohr said to Jovvi, his disgust perfectly plain. "If you'll lend me a few of your guardsmen, I'll have Ayl arrested and questioned at once."

"Have him brought here tomorrow so we can help with the questioning," Jovvi said to Mohr, at the same time nodding to Seldon that some of his guardsmen were to go with the High Master. "We don't want any of those dupes to do something that will ruin the Guild's new position. When people understand that they have their necessities again because of the Guild's help, very few will continue to think of your members as freaks."

"Thanks to *you*," Mohr said with a bow that was repeated for every member of their Blending. "If you like, we can have these three delivered to the authorities on the way to arrest my former second."

Jovvi agreed that that was a good idea, so in just a few moments the room was cleared of everyone but their Blending and the link groups.

"And now it's time for you to rest," Lorand said to Jovvi as he and most of the others stood. "I think we can all accommodate our link groups in our various wings, so that way we can all get some rest."

"But first I'm goin' to send for some of the other Blendin's," Vallant said as he stretched. "There's a lot to be done, and no reason for us to be doin' it completely on our own."

Everyone agreed with that as well, so they left the meeting room and led their respective link groups off toward their respective wings. All but Naran, Rion couldn't help thinking as he led his love into his own wing. But that would change as soon as possible, he vowed to himself. Naran *would* have her own wing of the palace just as the rest of the Blending did, even if she never did use it to sleep in . . .

"I'm afraid, my love, that we have a disappointment coming," Naran murmured as they walked. "That man Ayl . . . He isn't going to be there when they go to arrest him. Which means, of course, that we haven't seen the last of him and his followers."

Suddenly, Rion was no longer concerned about wings and places to sleep . . .

THREE

"Tomorrow we'll have to use *my* wing," Vallant heard Tamrissa say from where she walked along ahead of him. "I liked what I saw of it when we took my link groups in and got them settled."

"Yes, your wing wasn't bad at all," Vallant agreed, looking around critically as they moved. "This one can use a bit of fixin', mostly tonin' down the more garish items. Then we can set up a schedule and change off between the two wings."

"Speaking of schedules, I need some paper, a pen, and ink," Tamrissa said, pausing to look back at him. "Now that we've gotten *your* link groups settled in their own bedchambers, where do you think we can look for paper and the rest?"

"There's got to be a study of some kind among all these rooms," Vallant answered, still mildly in shock. There had been enough bedchambers so that all ten members of his link groups could have one of his or her own, with a number of extras left over. Palace accommodations obviously went far beyond the houses of even the wealthiest of ordinary people.

"Why don't you ring for a servant," Tamrissa suggested with a sigh while glancing around. "If we try to find the study ourselves, we could still be looking a year from now. And I'd enjoy having some tea when I start to make my list."

"Good idea," Vallant agreed as he moved to a bell pull.

"Two good ideas, in fact, since I could use some tea of my own. What kind of list do you plan on makin'?"

"I want to have that party tomorrow night," Tamrissa answered, moving closer to look up at Vallant. "We'll have to talk to the others, but I think we ought to invite everyone we can and then use the occasion to announce the fact that we're a six rather than a five. If they're going to change their minds about wanting us to be Seated, I'd like it to happen as soon as possible."

"Before we get too comfortable in this place," Vallant said with a nod, putting one hand to her arm. "That's another good idea, and here comes the result of your first suggestion."

Tamrissa turned to see what Vallant already had, a male servant hurrying along the hall toward them. The man looked nervous, and when he reached them he went down on one knee.

"Please excuse the delay in my answering your ring, Excellence," the man begged in a quivering voice, looking as though he was about to prostrate himself. "There are far too few servants left in the palace, and we had no idea you'd come into your wing—"

"It's all right, you don't have to make excuses," Vallant told the man quickly, interrupting what promised to be a very long monologue. "You weren't long in answerin' my ring. In my opinion, you were very prompt. I can imagine what you and the rest of the staff went through with those fools who called themselves nobles, but you won't have the same trouble with *us*. Stand up now and tell me if there's a room somewhere about that has a desk or two as well as paper, pens, and ink."

"Yes, Excellence, there certainly is," the man replied as he stood, his tone cautious and his expression wary. "Please follow me, and I'll show you where it is."

Vallant exchanged a rueful glance with Tamrissa as the man moved off in the direction he'd come from, the two of them following. It was obvious that the servant didn't quite believe his days of being treated like a slave were over, not after having served one very important noble and possibly even two. It would take time for the palace workers to learn the truth of what they'd been told; trying to convince them now would be a waste of breath and effort.

"Hopefully, this will meet with your approval, Excellence," the man said after walking to a door and throwing it open. "It's meant for the conducting of business matters."

Vallant stood aside as Tamrissa walked into the room past the bowing servant, and then he followed her to see what the room held. To the right was a very large, ornately carved darkwood desk with an equally large chair behind it, and to the left was a smaller desk probably meant for a secretary. Straight ahead were wide and beautiful windows, the dark red of their drapes echoed in the carpeting.

"Yes, this is precisely what I was lookin' for," Vallant told the servant as he only glanced at the rest of the soberly colored decorations of the room. "Now I'd like two more things, one of them bein' tea service for two. The other is more on the order of a question: Do you by any chance have a map showin' where everythin' is in this wing?"

"Yes, Excellence, there *is* a map of the wing, usually used to orient new servants," the man answered, a shadow of surprise hidden behind the words. "I haven't seen the map in a while, but I'll search for it and bring it as soon as I'm able. In the interim, your tea will be here in just a few moments."

"Good," Vallant said as he turned to smile at the man. "Thank you for your help."

The servant acknowledged Vallant's thanks with a bow that hid the man's wide-eyed surprise, and then he disappeared back up the hallway.

"I think you've shocked him badly," Tamrissa said with a chuckle as she turned and made for the smaller desk. "In his world, the strong and powerful don't say thank you."

"Knowin' our Blendin'mates, that's about to change permanently," Vallant said with his own chuckle as he headed for the windows. "Are you sure you don't want to use the big desk? I won't mind in the least."

"This is your wing, so you're entitled to use the bigger desk," Tamrissa replied, already seated in the chair and rummaging in the desk. "When we use *my* wing, then I'll—Ah! Here's paper and ink, and there are pens already on the desk. Hey, it's raining."

"It only just started," Vallant said, moving to the second window, which he opened, as he had the first. "Do you mind havin' the windows open?"

"Not as long as there isn't a chance someone will throw something at us," Tamrissa answered, her tone telling Vallant that she wasn't seriously worried. "What kind of view can there be anyway?"

"It's a nice view," Vallant said, feeling something of surprise. "These wings obviously radiate away from the palace proper, so there's grass and flowers and pathways down there in between. There are a couple of ways to get out there that I can see from here, and beyond the wings and a stretch of grass there's also a very high wall made of stone."

"Good," Tamrissa said, a glance showing Vallant that she now dipped a pen into a bottle of ink. "When it stops raining, we can enjoy the sunshine without being bothered. Let's see, what do I need first . . . ?"

Vallant smiled as he opened the third and fourth windows before going to his own desk. Tamrissa was so involved with planning for her party that it would take a serious attack against them to distract her. Vallant much preferred the thought of her distracted to the thought of them being attacked, so he searched his own desk rather than insisting that they share the pretty view. He and Tamrissa would have plenty of time to share things, and trying to rush the process would do no more than ruin it.

There was paper and ink in Vallant's desk too, as well as a selection of pens. One of those pens seemed to be made of gold, and Vallant shook his head as he chose a less ornate instrument to use. If he ever decided to impress someone silly, he now had the means to do it . . .

Vallant had only just started on his own list of things to do when a female servant appeared with the tea service he'd asked for. She rolled the service in on a cart, took it over to a table standing between Vallant's desk and the windows, and began to arrange things on the table. It was too familiar a process for Vallant to pay attention to, so he went back to making his list. The first thing he needed to do was get *all* their Blendings into the palace. If for no other reason, they deserved to be told first about Naran's place in the scheme of things . . .

"Your tea, Excellence," Vallant heard, causing him to look up. The woman—girl, really—had spoken in a low and sultry voice, a good match for her dark and sultry appearance. She was quite pretty if not downright beautiful, but the filled cup she offered wasn't proper.

"You should be offerin' the first cup to the lady," Vallant told the girl, nodding to Tamrissa where she sat writing at the other desk. "Where I come from ladies are *always* served first, and there's no reason not to reintroduce the practice *here*."

"As you wish, Excellence," the girl acknowledged with a smile added to her throaty voice. "But tea is all I'm able to offer the lady. You, though . . . It would be my great pleasure to offer *you* a lot more than tea."

The girl moved her body in so suggestive a way that Vallant had no doubt about what else she offered. It was so surprising to have the girl come on to him so strongly that he hesitated before answering, and the hesitation was misinterpreted.

"If you'll send the lady away, I can begin to show you exactly what I mean," the girl told him in a murmur, a hint of triumph gleaming in her dark eyes. "The lady is pretty enough, but I can please you much more than she ever could."

"I doubt that," Vallant said in a normal voice as he leaned back in his chair. "The lady isn't just pretty, and she isn't just a lady. She's another member of my Blendin', and someone who happens to be very important to me even beyond that. Give her that cup of tea, and then you can leave."

"Of course, Excellence," the girl acknowledged with an odd sort of smile. "I understand how that works, so I'll come back when the lady goes to her own wing."

"You're not understandin' me," Vallant said to the girl's back as she turned to give Tamrissa the cup of tea. Tamrissa's attention had also been taken from her writing, and the lady of Fire now inspected the serving girl with narrowed eyes. "There's nothin' 'that works' here, and the only time you'll come back will be to do some ordinary kind of servin'. Have I stated my position clearly enough?"

"You might also tell her that when I do go back to my own wing, you'll be going with me," Tamrissa put in as the cup of tea was set down in front of her. "Not to mention the fact that if I find her coming on to you again, she won't like what happens to her."

"She's probably just doin' what our predecessors wanted her to do," Vallant said hastily. The girl had frozen in the act of turning away from Tamrissa, her eyes wide and her face pale. "It will be a while before they all understand completely that we're not like the usual run of Seated Blendin's."

"Well, this one might get the idea a bit faster," Tamrissa said dryly as the frightened girl began to back toward the door. "She actually reached to the power a minute ago, but it's her bad luck that her talent is Fire. I don't know what she meant to do with her ability, but if I decide it was the *wrong* thing . . ."

The girl whimpered before turning to run, and a heartbeat later she was gone. Vallant heard her steps disappearing up the hall, and when they faded into complete silence he shook his head.

"I think we better make findin' new people to staff this place a top priority," he said to a still-annoyed Tamrissa. "The servants we have now may not be the sort to do us harm, but harm isn't the only thing we can do without."

"And some of those other things can *generate* harm, at least for the ones who try them," Tamrissa said, actually in agreement. "I can believe that those useless, so-called nobles cut a swath through the serving women, but I still don't like it. She could at least have waited to be asked."

"She was probably tryin' to get her bid in before any of the others," Vallant suggested with a sigh. "It happens to be a sad fact that the girl sharin' her master's bed is usually the last one to lose her job. Now I'm wonderin' if the male servants in *your* wing will do the same."

"If they know what's good for them, they better not," Tamrissa said, raising her head again to look directly at Vallant with a smile. "I have my own way of discouraging them, but I get the feeling that that isn't what they have to worry about."

"Very perceptive of you," Vallant responded in a murmur with a faint smile of his own. "I'm not a lady, so I don't have to worry about actin' ladylike. I think I'll have a cup of tea, and then see if any of the other Blendin's have arrived yet. We can get a lot of projects started, and then Jovvi will have less to worry about when she wakes up tomorrow."

"We'll probably have to tie her up before she understands that she doesn't have to do everything herself," Tamrissa said with a large and gusty sigh. "I don't know *what* we'd have to do to get her to realize that nothing at all will be accomplished if she collapses from exhaustion."

"We'll try showin' instead of tellin'," Vallant said as he rose from the desk. "If that doesn't work, we just may *have* to try tyin'. We'll talk to the others about it."

"Good idea," Tamrissa said before going back to her list. Vallant got his tea, then went back to his own list. They could get started with *some* of the things that needed to be done, but a number of the items on his list would have to wait until they were officially Seated. *If* they were Seated . . .

Lorand was investigating his discovery when the servant appeared in the doorway of the sitting room he'd found. The servant knew Lorand was aware of him, but no words came until Lorand looked up from the book he held.

"Please excuse the intrusion, Excellence, but a message has come from the Excellence Vallant," the servant said with a nervous bow. "He asks that if you aren't immersed in something vitally important, would you please join him in the outer meeting room. I've been instructed to tell you that the—the—other Blendings have arrived."

"Don't worry, you and everyone else will soon get used
to talking about Blendings in the plural rather than in the
singular," Lorand told the man with amusement, closing the
book he held. "In fact, you might even soon belong to a
Blending of your own. Would you like that?"

"I . . . find the situation impossible to imagine, Excellence," the servant replied, his eyes wide with the nervousness causing his hands to tremble. "Would—Would
something like that be—*required* of me?"

"Of course not," Lorand assured the man, rising to walk
to him and clap him gently on the shoulder. "No one will
be forced *into* a Blending any more than they'll be forced
not to join one. Things really will be changing for the better."

The man continued to look privately skeptical, so Lorand
dropped the subject and sent the servant to alert Jovvi's
link groups, which had been settled in her wing. Lorand
saw to gathering his own link groups, took one final look
at Jovvi where she slept in the main bedchamber of *his*
wing, then led the way to the meeting Vallant had called.
Lorand had used the help of his link groups to put Jovvi
to sleep, and it was a measure of her exhaustion that he'd
been able to do it—even with help. They'd all grown much
too strong to be able to touch one another, but Jovvi had
been pushing herself far too hard.

The meeting room was already full of people by the time
Lorand and his groups arrived, but it wasn't hard for him
to make his way through the throng to reach Vallant and
Rion.

"Jovvi is asleep, I take it," Rion said when Lorand
reached them. "If she weren't, she would surely have come
with you."

"Yes, she's asleep, and she'll stay that way until tomorrow morning," Lorand answered with a nod. "I made her
eat something first, so skipping tonight's meal won't hurt
her. Where are Naran and Tamrissa?"

"Vallant tells me that Tamrissa is deep into plans for
tomorrow night's party," Rion answered with a smile.

"Naran, on the other hand, has discovered that my wing has a bathing *room*, so it isn't necessary to go out to a bath *house*. She's currently taking a great deal of pleasure in soaking in warm water."

"And because the ladies' clothin' has been retrieved and fetched here, she'll have somethin' clean to wear when she comes out," Vallant put in with a small laugh. "It's lucky that Tamrissa hasn't found out about the bathin' room yet. Between that and her party list, we'd likely *never* see her."

"It seems that everyone has now arrived," Rion observed, and Lorand turned to see Jovvi's link groups coming in. "Would you like to begin this meeting, Vallant?"

"Yes, because we have a lot to do," Vallant responded, his tone pitched loud enough for everyone to hear. The small conversations quieted as everyone took seats, and Vallant nodded. "Thank you for givin' me your attention. The first thing we have to discuss is puttin' a Blendin' in charge of interviewin' people to staff this monster of a place. It won't be an easy job because we'll need hordes of servants—and we have to be on the lookout for renegade Guild members."

People exclaimed over that comment, so Vallant explained what had happened for those who hadn't been present for the attack and subsequent interview.

"When they went to arrest the man Ayl, they found he'd already gone to ground," Vallant concluded. "That means we can expect to trip over his people until we catch them all, so everyone stay alert. They may be after *our* Blendin', but some of them may decide that any High talent is fair game."

"Our Blending will do the interviewing," Wilant Gorl called from the middle of the room. "There are a lot of unemployed servants around now, so we should be able to take our pick. What do we do with the ones who don't measure up—and what do you consider not measuring up?"

"We don't want anyone who isn't capable of bein' loyal," Vallant answered with a nod to show that he'd been asked a good question. "That even means someone who's willin' to take silver or gold to look the other way. We need our people to be alert against intruders, because the guardsmen can't do it all. If they could, those three never would have gotten into the palace in the first place."

"I think it might also be a good idea to change the arrangement of who the servants report to," Lorand put in. "Jovvi mentioned something about having every group of five servants being known by sight to 'middle' supervisors. That way a strange face is noticed more quickly, and something can be done about it."

"We should be able to do that if we put the system in immediately," Wilant agreed with a thoughtful nod, after exchanging glances with his Blendingmates. "But you still haven't said what we do with the ones who don't measure up."

"Unless the person is seriously deranged, just turn him or her loose," Rion answered, giving the decision they'd all pretty much decided on earlier. "If they *are* seriously deranged, there are civil authorities to see to the matter. Once things settle down we can all make ourselves available to help them, but for now they'll have to cope on their own."

"That's because we're goin' to need another three Blendin's to supplement the posted guards," Vallant said, taking up the explanation. "Again, this will only be necessary until things settle down, but there's goin' to be a lot of craziness before that happens. We mean to have some High talents start to teach the people how to use their own talents properly."

"So soon?" someone asked in the middle of everyone's comments of surprise. "Shouldn't that wait until after you've been Seated?"

"We still aren't sure we *will* be Seated," Vallant answered after exchanging glances with Rion and Lorand. "There's somethin' you all need to be told, but we'll get to that in a little while. First you need to know that we're havin' a party tomorrow night, and we'll be invitin' everyone in the city who's part of or represents even a middle-sized group. All of *you* are also invited, so please pass the word to any of our people who couldn't make this meetin'."

"About time we had some fun," someone female in the

group called out, and the others all agreed with enthusiasm and laughter.

"Yes, it is, and in more ways than one," Vallant agreed with a grin and a chuckle of his own. "The next thing all you members of link groups need to think about is formin' Blendin's among you. Just because you're a member of a link group doesn't mean you can't also belong to a Blendin'."

There was a stunned silence then, but Lorand was glad to see more delighted surprise than shock. Then a babble of comments started, with one voice rising above the rest.

"We didn't think you'd be able to give up our help so soon," a man called out. "Are you sure you aren't rushing things?"

"You're right, we're *not* ready to give up the help of our link groups," Vallant said with a nod for the man. "But that doesn't mean you can't start lookin' around and maybe even gettin' together and startin' to practice. Once people know what they can and can't do with their talents, *they'll* be formin' Blendin's, so there's no reason for all of *you* to wait."

"And every reason not to," Rion added in a more serious way. "Until we have a solid core of Middle talent guardsmen trained to keep the peace, we'll need High talent people to prevent any accidental—or not so accidental—disasters. Some people are bound to get drunk on the Blending experience and do something foolish, and we'll be responsible for making that foolishness possible."

"So we'll also be responsible for keeping the damage to a minimum," Wilant Gorl said with a sigh and a nod. "It looks like interviewing servants really will be the easiest job any of us faces. But what's this about the possibility that you won't be Seated? If anyone thinks there's a stronger Blending around than yours, they can take *our* word that there isn't."

"Strength won't be the problem," Vallant said after exchanging glances with Rion and Lorand again. "Okay, it's time we told all of you somethin' you don't know about

us. We'll be announcin' it tomorrow night to everyone, but
you have the right to hear it first."

"What Vallant means is that we won't be a Seated Five,"
Rion said, taking up the explanation with something of a
smile. "You all know my lady Naran, but what you don't
know is that she isn't simply my lady. She's become part
of our Blending, a full part."

"You've doubled up on one of the aspects?" Wilant Gorl
asked incredulously. "How did you do that, and which aspect is it?"

"No, we haven't doubled up," Rion answered with a
small cough. "The truth of the matter is there's an aspect
no one has been aware of until now, and it's one that the
rest of you can also add to your Blendings. Naran has what
we call Sight magic, the ability to see a short way into the
future."

This time Lorand noticed that the stunned silence also
contained shock. It would have been nice to have Jovvi's
help to soothe everyone down, but in her absence words
would have to do.

"The people with Sight magic kept their existence a secret because the first Fivefold Blending tried to enslave
them," Lorand supplied, speaking gently and calmly.
"They've told us they *know* we won't do the same, so
they're finally coming out into public view. None of you
has met the members of Naran's link groups, but you might
want to take the time to do just that."

When Lorand gestured to the people sitting at the back
of the room, there was a small hesitation before everyone
turned around to look. Their mild distress and confusion
was met with friendly and merry smiles and waves from
the people in Naran's link groups, which went quite a long
way to calming people down.

"That's right, they're not three-headed monsters," Rion
said with a touch of amusement. "They're just as human
as the rest of us, and most of them are as willing to join a
Blending as Naran was. Is there anyone here who wants
nothing to do with them?"

"You've got to be joking," Wilant Gorl responded with

a snort after exchanging soft words with the members of his Blending. "This is the most exciting thing we've heard since we learned to Blend. Is the meeting over? We've got some introducing of ourselves to do."

"In a little while," Vallant answered with a laugh, obviously as relieved as Rion looked and Lorand felt. Most of the others had laughed aloud and agreed with Wilant, which made Lorand grateful to be among such open-minded people. If that had been Widdertown folk . . .

"I don't want anyone forgettin' about those jobs we need to have done," Vallant continued as he looked around at enthusiastic and impatient faces. "There will be more people with Sight magic at the party tomorrow night, so don't feel discouraged if you don't meet someone here who will fit into your Blendin'. And I'd like you all to consider movin' into the palace, at least for a while. We still have plenty of room, and it will save you the trouble of trekkin' on over here from wherever you're stayin'. But that means we'll need even more additions to the staff, so Wilant, don't get so involved in lookin' among Naran's link groups that you forget about lookin' for more staff."

"We'll get on that second thing," Wilant answered with a laugh, and then the meeting broke up with everyone standing and starting to crowd around those with Sight magic. Vallant watched them for a moment, then turned back to Rion and Lorand with a shake of his head.

"I have more items on that list I made, but we might as well save them for another time," Vallant said with a sigh. "I was hopin' they'd take the news well, but didn't realize they'd take it *so* well that they'd stop listenin'."

"It's just as well," Rion told Vallant with a chuckle. "We'll have to bring our ladies up to date on what was discussed, and this way we'll have less to report on."

"I think we'd better add one more item to the report anyway," Lorand said just as Vallant was about to agree with Rion. "I've found something in my wing that we all need to know about: There are journals written by members of Blendings from quite some time in the past. I haven't had the chance to read any of the journals, but I believe there are things discussed about Blendings that we might not yet know about."

"Now, *that's* a find," Vallant said after sounding a low whistle of surprise. "Are they journals done by Earth magic members?"

"Not entirely," Lorand said with a smile. "That means we all might want to institute a search in our libraries for similar volumes—as soon as we get more servants. If you'd all like to join me in my wing for dinner tonight, I'll be able to tell you if I've found anything in the journals I already have."

"We'll certainly be there," Rion answered, with Vallant nodding his agreement. "Speaking for myself, I'll enjoy my meal a good deal more if I know in advance that it's safe to eat. I drank the tea Naran and I sent for, but not without a certain amount of trepidation. If Naran hadn't assured me the tea was safe, I might have decided to do without it. I can't remember ever being this suspicious, even with that woman who pretended to be my mother encouraging my distrust."

"Paranoia is easy to understand in *this* place," Lorand assured a clearly worried Rion. "With the previous Five having been poisoned and the same thing almost done to *us*, it's a wonder we can even trust *ourselves*. But don't worry, we'll arrange things to keep us safe until the trouble all dies down."

"I hope so," Rion said, putting his hand to Lorand's arm in thanks for the reassurance. "I'd almost rather be back on the road and on my way to a confrontation with enemies."

Lorand joined Vallant in assuring Rion they felt almost the same way, and then they left the meeting room to those who were meeting people in a different way. Lorand's last thought as he walked out of the room was that he wasn't sure Rion hadn't had the right idea. Meeting an attack openly was a lot easier than worrying about who would next be trying to poison them or sneak up behind them with a knife . . .

FOUR

"Why are you still fussin' around?" Vallant asked me from where he lay completely relaxed on my bed. "I haven't seen you this nervous since we first met."

"I'm not nervous, exactly, just a bit harried," I explained, trying to give the conversation my attention. "My late husband always handled the details of any party he gave, and I was just another decoration added in. Now I have hundreds of people due in just a little while, and I'm not completely sure I've covered everything. What if I've overlooked something really important?"

"Then either the servants will take care of providin' it, or we'll do without it," Vallant answered with a smile as he sat up. "No one is goin' to make you leave the Blendin' if all the forks aren't properly lined up on the buffet table, so worryin' is a waste of time. I expected you to relax when you found out we'll have enough servants to do the servin'."

"That *was* good news," I agreed with a sigh, putting aside the list I studied to give Vallant something of a smile. "Wilant Gorl and his people have done a really great job in such a short time, going through and clearing that many applicants. Were they as careful as they were supposed to be?"

"They knew they had to be, so they got one of the other Blendin's to help," Vallant answered. He left the bed, then walked over to my chair to bend down and kiss my cheek.

"They went through hundreds of the people who turned up when they found out we were hirin', and eliminated the bad apples right from the start. They also found another of those renegade Guild people, and sent her to Jovvi for questionin'. Jovvi was feelin' like her old self this mornin' after all the sleepin' she did, but the woman she questioned didn't know where Ayl was."

"I would have been surprised if she did know," I said as I took Vallant's hand. "Holdis Ayl didn't strike me as a stupid man, and only a fool would send someone into our clutches when they knew where he was hiding. But he also should have known that the woman would be caught, so I wonder why he sent her."

"Either he was testin' the waters to see if we were too full of ourselves to take even basic precautions, or he's usin' her as a diversion." Vallant grimaced as he pulled over another chair to sit in, making no effort to release my hand. "I have no idea what he would want us diverted *from*, so I hope he's only testin' our precautions."

"But we can't count on it," I said with a weary nod. "We'll have to be really alert tonight, but at least his people can't come at us with unexpectedly strong talent. They have to use non-magical means, which all of us should be able to counter . . . Vallant, if we hired all that many people as servants, how are we going to pay them? *We* don't have vast fortunes of our own to call on until we find the funds meant to support this part of the government."

"Actually, we have all the funds we need," Vallant answered with real amusement, his free hand stroking my hair. "We set some of Ristor Ardanis's people on all the bankers, and it isn't possible to lie about whose gold is where when you're dealin' with Sight magic. We already have more than one vast fortune from all those former nobles at our disposal, and there's more to come."

"Oh, yes, I'd forgotten we did that even before we left that house we took over," I said, finding it impossible not to yawn. "A lot of that gold will go toward paying for the shipments of food and other necessities the Guild people have arranged for, but there ought to be enough left over to pay for help around *this* place."

"Yes, so it really is time for you to stop worryin'," Vallant said, this time using his free arm to pull me a bit closer. "And we still have a couple of hours before the party is due to start, so why don't we take some time for ourselves before I show you where the bathin' room is in this wing of yours."

"Bathing room?" I echoed, stopping short as I was about to kiss him. "We don't have to go outside to use a bath house because there's a bathing room right in this wing? Why didn't you tell me that sooner?"

"Because I didn't want to lose your attention to my greatest rival," Vallant grumbled, looking annoyed with himself. "If I didn't have such a big mouth, I wouldn't be sittin' here with two or three feet in it . . . Okay, let's go show you that bathin' room. Maybe you'll have some time for me afterward."

He got to his feet and pulled me up with him by the hand he still held, but I couldn't let it go at that. He'd been wonderfully patient the last two days while I gave all my attention to the party, and I wanted him to know how much I appreciated that.

"I don't see why we can't exchange some time *during* my bath," I murmured, leaning up to brush his lips with mine. "You haven't suddenly become too good to share some bathwater, have you?"

"I've always managed to force myself into sharin' a bath with you, so I guess I can do it again," he murmured back with a smile. "I hope you appreciate it when I make a sacrifice like this."

"Oh, absolutely," I assured him solemnly, ignoring the way his hand stroked down my back to pat my bottom. "And because you hate it so much, I'll bathe as fast as I possibly can. So which way is the water?"

"Come on and I'll show you," he said with a sigh, taking my hand again to lead off. I had the feeling he'd been hoping to divert me for a short time, and share my bath only afterward. Lovemaking was more comfortable in a bed than in a bathhouse, but I felt confident that we'd somehow manage to enjoy the time.

"Did you use your talent to locate the water, or were you given that map you wanted?" I asked as we walked along. "And have you heard whether Lorand discovered anything we need to know in those journals he found?"

"I did get the map, and all these wings are laid out in the same way," Vallant replied. "That makes findin' things easier, and I set a scribe to copyin' the map so we'd all have our own copies. Lorand hasn't mentioned findin' anythin' of importance in the journals yet, but he made a different discovery in the same room: a large stack of scribes' reports on the doin's of the previous Five."

"Does that mean someone had a sense of history?" I asked, glancing up at him with curiosity. "If so, the reports must be filled with comments about how great and clever those five people were."

"No, actually, Lorand said the reports looked like verbatim records of various meetin's and discussions," Vallant responded, his own expression filled with mild curiosity. "He hasn't gone through all of it yet, but he also located a stack of reports that had been very well hidden. If he hadn't noticed the presence of paper where no paper should have been, he said, those hidden reports would probably never have been found."

"Maybe we can give him a hand with reading all that tomorrow," I suggested, prodded by an odd and unexpected need. "I'd like to know more about those people who were here before us, and then maybe we'll understand why they did what they did."

"They did what they did because they wanted the power," Vallant answered with a shrug of dismissal. "The one I faced at the end, the Spirit magic user, didn't make a whole lot of noise, but he struck me as someone who was obsessed with the need to be in control. I've noticed over the years that those who need that badly to be in control usually suffered when others had the control."

"That's a point of view I can appreciate on a personal level," I said, making a face. "Whenever someone else was in control of my life, I ended up with pain. But if your theory is right, then *I* should want to run everything in sight and I don't. All I want is to be left alone by those who think they have a right to run my life."

"You're not showin' or feelin' the need to run things because you were able to learn the real lesson," Vallant said, sending me a smile filled with fond pride. "The only one a person has to be in control of is him- or herself, not the entire world. Bein' in control of yourself lets you say no to the ones who take advantage, and also lets you find a way to make the decision stick. But if you let fear take control instead . . ."

"Then you have to run the world in order to feel safe," I finished for him, following him through a doorway. Inside was a large and beautiful room with a marble bath rather than one made of wood, and the room even had windows. There were also a number of wide lounges and a few chairs that seemed to be made of cotton webbing, not to mention a bar, a place for a tea service, and a table probably meant for snacks.

"Those cabinets over there have towels and heavy cotton robes," Vallant said, pointing to our left. "Those things that look like vases at the edge of the bath are filled with soap, and there's only one thing missin' right now: nicely warmed water. The servants with Fire magic have been workin' on it, but they must be Lows because they haven't gotten very far. Tepid is all you have, but that's better than nothin'."

"It *is* better than nothing, but there's no reason to settle," I said, walking closer to the bath as Vallant closed the door behind us. "I should be able to give the servants a hand . . ."

There was an awful lot of water in that very large bath, and warming it posed something of a problem. Once the water was already warm it could be kept like that with only a small amount of effort from above, but the original warming needed to be done from below. I'd once forced bathing water to be warm with the help of other Highs in Fire magic, but right now there was just me and a lot of barely heated water. But there ought to be a way . . .

"Maybe that will do it," I muttered as an idea came to me. Those woven patterns we'd done so much with . . . One of them seemed to suggest that if it was changed just a little and spread out at the bottom of the bath beneath the water . . .

"Whoa!" Valiant exclaimed as heavy steam began to rise from the water. "Whatever you did, I'm guessin' it was a little too much. That water's hot enough now to boil us like potatoes."

"But I put barely any strength into it!" I protested, seeing that he wasn't joking. "I never expected it to get that hot that quickly, which has to mean the pattern variation I used is a *lot* more powerful than I thought."

"You varied one of the patterns you learned?" Valiant asked, now studying me rather than the water. "In what way did you vary it?"

"I . . . altered the method of braiding," I said, trying to put a new action into words. "Here, let me show you instead. This is the way the pattern was originally braided, and this is the way I changed it."

I used lengths of fire to illustrate what I meant, and when Valiant saw the altered pattern his brows rose high.

"If I'm followin' that correctly, I think I can alter one of my own patterns in the same way," he told me slowly. "The only thing I can't figure out is what I'd use the new pattern for."

"There's still so much we don't know that sometimes it makes me want to scream," I said, letting the fires I'd used to show the patterns disappear. "And now I can't even take a bath until that water cools down again. Me and my big ideas."

"I believe I can be a small amount of help with that," Valiant told my exasperation with a chuckle. "The situation just needs a bit of exchangin'."

I was about to ask what he was talking about when the steam rising from the water suddenly turned into ordinary eddies in the air. That meant the water was still hot, but not so hot that we'd be boiled.

"Judgin' how much ice to bring down from the upper air

was the hard part," Vallant said with a smile when I made a sound of pleased surprise. "Shall we see if I did it right?"

I gave him a quick kiss to show my agreement—and gratitude—and then began to get out of my clothes. He did the same, and a pair of moments later we entered the bath hand in hand. The water was only a little warmer than usual, something my tired body was able to appreciate quite a lot. I washed quickly and then soaked some, floating comfortably in Vallant's arms.

All right, so that was when I fell asleep. I'd been too busy working on the arrangements for the party to get a lot of ordinary sleep, but Vallant didn't have to leave waking me until it was time to dress. Sometimes I wonder about that man . . .

Jovvi entered the huge ballroom on Lorand's arm, her thoughts whirling with everything he'd recently shared with her. Some of it was just disturbing, but the rest needed to be also shared with the others.

"It looks like everyone Tamrissa invited decided to get here early," Lorand commented as they walked, nodding to those people he knew. "And for a last minute affair, we seem to have a really good turnout."

"Most of these city people would have preferred to die under torture rather than miss this party," Jovvi told him, also nodding. "They're the least bit intimidated by being in the midst of so many High and strong Middle talents, but an invitation to a ball at the palace is something they never expected to get. Even if they're never invited again, they'll still have *this* time to remember for the rest of their lives."

"You're still bothered by what you read," Lorand said, and there was more concern than questioning in his tone. "I'm beginning to be sorry that I located all those hidden scribes."

"Finding them was the only way to regain some privacy in our lives," Jovvi told him with a headshake, patting his arm. "What's really bothering me is the way that Earth magic user of those five people thought he'd made himself safe from their observation. He killed some of them and put others to sleep, and by doing that considered himself safe from discovery."

"He obviously had no idea that the scribes were all Spirit magic users and were closely linked," Lorand said with a sigh. "I still don't understand *how* they were linked, since it wasn't in groups of five or tandem tens, but every time he eliminated or neutralized one, another secretly took that one's place."

"And they recorded everything he said and did, including that . . . time with his parents," Jovvi added, fighting with all her strength to keep from being ill. "I'm really sorry I began to read that, but finding out about that special linking gives me something else than being sick to occupy my attention. It isn't hard to do once you know about it, but I have a feeling the linkage has a purpose other than the one it was put to."

"Doesn't everything?" Lorand asked with a grimace. "Every time we learn something new, it becomes very clear how much more we *don't* know. If it ever became possible to get my hands on the ones who first made using talent something to be kept secret . . . Well, let's just say that I would *not* be gentle with them."

"Let's also say that your violence would have mine to keep it company," Jovvi said, leaving Lorand in no doubt that she meant what she'd told him. "But we'd better save this discussion for another time. Some of our more exalted guests are beginning to make their way over to us."

Jovvi settled a pleasant smile on her face as Lorand glanced up to see who their social ambushers were. Lavrit Mohr was High Master of the Guild of those who were able to judge talent, although they had no talent of their own. He was there with his new second in command and some of his people, as was Ristor Ardanis, leader of those with Sight magic, along with some of *his* followers. Mohr and Ardanis hadn't been standing together because they hadn't yet been introduced, but that was one of the reasons for the party.

"Excellences, it's good to see you again," Mohr said with his usual bow when he reached Jovvi and Lorand. "I hope there will be time tonight for some of the city leaders to be introduced to you."

"That's one of the reasons we're all here," Lorand assured the man with his own pleasant smile. "We'll eventually want to meet everyone who is in charge of doing almost anything at all. It's time the credit for a job well done finally went to the people actually doing the work."

"You see, Dom Henris?" Mohr said to one of the men who had approached with him, his words almost gleeful. "I told you they were reasonable human beings rather than the puffed-up imitation nobles you were told they'd be."

"What's this?" Lorand asked with mild curiosity, and Jovvi added her own attention to the conversation. "Someone is calling us names *already*?"

"Just that fool Ayl and his misguided followers," Mohr answered in a way that wasn't quite as dismissive as he'd probably wanted it to be. "Excellences, allow me to present Dom Relton Henris, spokesman for the new shop owners consortium."

"It used to be the shop *workers* consortium," Dom Henris said with a self-conscious smile and bow. "We used to spend our time worrying about how to make ends meet, but now we have more pleasant topics to discuss—thanks to you and what you've done for us. When those rumors started to circulate about how you would become just like the nobles once you moved into the palace . . . Well, most of us started to worry again, I can tell you."

"I don't blame you for feeling that way," Jovvi told the man with one of her best smiles. "There seems to be something about being in charge that changes level-headed people into fools, but we're aware of the danger so we're deliberately resisting it. If anyone happens to see that starting to change, we're hoping they'll say so."

"At least by anonymous letter," Lorand added in a droll tone. "In someone else's place, I don't know if I'd be foolish enough to mention the point in person."

That comment made everyone around them laugh, which in turn eased a good deal of tension. Jovvi knew it was impossible to ease nervous people with words alone, but a well-timed joke or two did the job rather effectively. Lorand had said just the right thing, and if they'd been alone she would have kissed him for it.

"There's someone here you need to meet, Dom Mohr," Lorand continued when the laughter was done. "Once your people have regular shipments started on their way to this city again, we'll have to pay for them quickly so our suppliers have confidence in us. Dom Ristor Ardanis and his people have been given the job of locating the funds of former nobles, to be used to keep the city fed and supplied. Their efforts have already shown results, so we're ready for the first of the shipments."

Jovvi watched Mohr turn to take the hand Ristor Ardanis offered as he stepped forward, but the Guild High Master ended up shaking hands in a mechanical way. Mohr had begun to frown at the leader of those with Sight magic, a reaction Jovvi and Lorand had been expecting.

"It's a pleasure to meet someone who *provides* gold rather than takes it," Mohr said to Ardanis, trying to recapture his good mood as he studied the shorter, rounder man. "It may be indelicate of me to say this, but— May I ask which of the talents you have? I can't seem to reach through . . ."

"Your question is more understandable than indelicate," Ardanis assured Mohr with one of the warm, beaming smiles he was so good at producing. "There's a reason why you're unable to discern my talent, but I'm afraid that discussing the reason will spoil the surprise our new leaders have planned. They'll get to it as soon as everyone has arrived, so there's only a short time left to wait."

"Then it would be inexcusable of me to press the matter right now," Mohr said with a better smile, showing those without Jovvi's talent that the Guild's High Master had reacted to Ardanis the way most people did. "If the wait is *too* long I may die of curiosity, but other than that—"

"Excuse me," a brisk female voice interrupted, addressing Mohr. The woman who owned the voice was more than just brisk, and it was clear that she wasn't really asking to be excused for anything. Jovvi studied her with interest, noting that the self-confidence the woman showed would have looked more at home in an older person. The newcomer was no more than in her middle thirties, with a faintly pretty face and a good figure.

"Dama Zokill," Mohr said, momentarily looking startled and blank. "I wasn't expecting you quite this early . . ."

"I'm sure you weren't," the woman Zokill replied, her smile the sort that withered plant-life. "And possibly you weren't expecting me at all. By some odd happenstance my invitation to this gathering wasn't delivered until an hour ago, leaving me no choice but to show up in ordinary clothing rather than the finery everyone else here is displaying. But at least I *am* here, so now I would appreciate an introduction to the people you claim should be our new leaders."

"I'm not the one making the claim, Dama Zokill," Mohr tried to protest, glancing toward Jovvi and Lorand in embarrassment. "My Guild and I are in a position to know things others don't, and for that reason we support—"

"Yes, yes, I've already heard all that," the woman interrupted again, gesturing aside the explanation. "But as with most things I become involved with, I'll make up my own mind about just how fit your candidates are. Now, if you don't mind, I'd like to be introduced to these people."

"Yes, of course," Mohr muttered while Ristor Ardanis worked to hide his amusement. "Excellences, allow me to present Dama Rilna Zokill. Dama Zokill has become the representative of a group of women who—"

"Not just women, Dom Mohr," Zokill interrupted for the third time, actually speaking to Jovvi and Lorand rather than the man who had—reluctantly—introduced her. "I represent a large group of people, men as well as women, who feel that they haven't had the same opportunities in life that others have had. My people make up a good part of those who live in this city, and we'd like to know what you mean to do for *them*."

"First you'll have to tell us what kept those opportunities from your people," Jovvi responded pleasantly while Lorand seemed at a loss for words. "If we're talking about women who were passed over because they *are* women, I can understand the problem and will join with my Blend-ingmates to see that something is done to change matters. But if we're talking about people who sit back and make no effort, complaining about how life and other people just aren't fair, we won't be able to help you. We won't make people give up what they've struggled for just because you have a more persistently loud voice than they do."

"Well, you don't beat around the bush much, do you?" Zokill asked, studying Jovvi carefully. "Is the rest of your bunch just as outspoken?"

"Our lady of Spirit magic here is shy and retiring when compared to our lady of Fire," Lorand supplied with amusement that was hidden from everyone but Jovvi. "We men are proud of our ladies, though, and therefore tend to support the things they feel strongly about. Are your people willing to join the training program we'll be organizing?"

"Training program?" Zokill echoed, glancing narrow-eyed at Mohr. "I haven't heard about any training pro-gram."

"That's because *no one* has heard the details about it yet," Lorand said, saving Mohr from the woman's accu-sation. "We'll be assigning strong Middles to teach people how to make the most of their talents, and those who do well will be put to immediate use. Those who don't do well through no fault of their own will have other positions of-fered to them, but those who don't care to be bothered won't be catered to."

"And I have a question about your group aims regarding women," Jovvi said at once, giving Zokill time to do no more than open her mouth in response to what Lorand had told her. "Have any of your people looked into the situation of courtesans? I happen to know that a certain number of them aren't working as courtesans by choice. What provi-sion have you made to free the unwilling ones from what amounts to outright slavery?"

"If we're discussing women in difficulty, I have a ques-tion of my own," a new voice added. Tamrissa and Vallant had joined the group a moment earlier. "There are any num-ber of women who were forced into marriage with men who are beasts. If someone is doing something about women's problems in general, shouldn't something be done about *that?*"

"I—never expected any of you to be really interested," Zokill blurted, trying not to look at Tamrissa with awe. "You're Fire magic, I know, but you're so *strong* . . . I never knew there could be such a difference . . . Are you really willing to support my group . . . ?"

Tamrissa took over the discussion, so Jovvi used the opportunity to move a few steps away from the cluster. The Zokill woman had been filled with frustrated hostility when she first joined them, probably from having her cause constantly dismissed by the men around her. Now that the proposed new rulers were showing more than a slight interest she was ecstatic, not to mention well on the way to regarding Tamrissa with hero worship. Jovvi needed a break from all those intense emotions coming from a large number of people in the room, but standing alone for a moment or two was the best she could do. Returning to the peace and quiet of her wing was out of the question.

"How about something to drink?" Lorand murmured as he came up to put an arm around her. "You look like you could use *something* fortifying."

"You know me much too well," Jovvi returned with the smile that was for him alone, putting a hand to his chest. "Yes, I certainly could use something to drink, but just fruit punch or tea. This isn't the time for any of us to be even the least bit out of balance."

"Don't I know it," Lorand returned wryly, his own smile matching hers. "I never knew how easy it was to fall into the habit of fortifying yourself against constant stress on too often a basis. That means I'll be joining you in the punch or tea idea, and I'll also be right back."

Jovvi watched him move away toward the refreshment tables, now smiling to herself. Lorand wasn't aware of the fact that every servant in their immediate vicinity was watching to see if the new rulers needed or wanted anything, so his going *after* drinks was unnecessary. One gesture on his part would have had the drinks brought to *them,* but that was all right. Lorand—and the rest of them—would get used to constant pampering eventually, which would probably be a shame . . .

"Excuse me, Jovvi, but I must speak to you for a moment," a male voice said, and Jovvi turned to see a man she didn't know. He was tall, broad-shouldered, and very handsome, and the agitation inside him shouted itself to her senses.

"I'm Hargan Royd, a member of one of the Air magic link groups," the man went on in a rush. "I'm also terribly nervous, but I can't wait any longer to say what I need to. I think you're the most wonderful woman I've ever seen, and I really admire you." Then he took her hand with a soulful look. "And I'm also terribly in love with you."

The man Royd then kissed her hand before backing off with a bow and hurrying away. Jovvi stared after him with her brows high, but then she felt a small smile curve her lips. Strange men hadn't professed their love and admiration since she'd stopped being a courtesan, and the experience lifted her spirits in a way that a glass of wine couldn't have. The incident meant nothing, of course, except to give her a warm feeling . . .

"Here's your fruit punch," Lorand said as he returned with two crystal cups, offering one of them to her. "And I swear that some of these servants are annoyed with me because I was about to fill the cups myself. You'd think I was trying to steal something."

"In a manner of speaking, you *were* trying to steal something," Jovvi answered with amusement as she accepted the cup. "If we all start to do things for ourselves, we won't need so many servants. To some of these people you were trying to steal their job."

"I hope the training program gets results really fast," Lorand muttered, staring balefully at the servants moving around the room. "Once we expand the work force, most industries will flourish and new ones will grow up. Maybe then they'll stop treating us like cripples."

Jovvi smiled as she sipped her punch, making no effort to tell Lorand that he was indulging in wishful thinking.

Too many people considered it outrageous for rulers to fend for themselves, which might even turn out to be a good thing. A *little* pampering couldn't hurt anything, any more than a little admiration . . .

∾

FIVE

∾

Naran entered the ballroom on Rion's arm, carefully keeping her expression neutral. When Ristor Ardanis, leader of the hidden group with Sight magic, had spoken in glowing terms about her Blending's future reign, Naran had been delighted and relieved. But this morning she'd been able to see past that glowing picture, and the landscape didn't quite match. Yes, her Blending *would* make excellent rulers—if they ever managed to be Seated. There were so many shadows of other possible outcomes in the way that Naran couldn't tell for certain . . .

"Is something troubling you, my love?" Rion suddenly murmured as they walked toward the others. "You seem quiet nearly to the point of being withdrawn."

"I'm afraid that the last part of our announcements tonight won't be accepted with the same enthusiasm that the link groups and other Blendings showed," Naran told him with the best smile she felt able to produce. "I don't want you to be upset when that happens, my love, not when people always take the announcement of extreme change rather badly. There will be a lot of shock and protest before those around us grow used to the idea of there being a sixth talent, so you mustn't make a fuss."

"Is that why you made no mention of this difficulty

sooner?" Rion asked, typically looking and sounding more hurt than angry. "Because you feared I would make a 'fuss'?"

"No, it was because I didn't want to upset you sooner," Naran returned firmly, holding his gaze to make him know she spoke the truth. "What gives you pain does the same for me, my love, and I know you'll feel hurt when you think I'm being rejected as a part of our Blending. But those who speak against my kind will be frightened, Rion, and it takes time before fear can be conquered. Please, for my sake, give them that time before becoming angry and impatient."

"It remains a sad fact that I can refuse you nothing, my love," Rion said with a sigh that made Naran smile. "If it's patience you need, it's patience you will have, even if I have to grit my teeth against speaking. I had not imagined that you would ever ask something this difficult of me."

"I'm afraid I'm going to have to ask something a bit *more* difficult," Naran replied, knowing well enough that Rion teased her. "Our brothers also need to restrain themselves, so you must speak to them before we begin the announcements. They won't be pleased with what happens, but they'll exercise the same patience if *you* ask them to."

"I assume you mean to speak to our sisters at the same time," Rion said with another sigh, this one of resignation and full surrender. Naran had the impression that Rion had hoped Lorand and Vallant would be angry enough to do what he'd promised not to, and losing that option had brought Rion closer to real cooperation. "Jovvi will pose little or no problem, but Tamrissa is another matter."

"Actually, as far as I can tell, Tamrissa is the only one of us who is *supposed* to react differently," Naran said, feeling vexed. "Much of what I saw this morning is clouded, but when I practiced with my link groups I was able to get a clearer peek or two. I have the impression that those with my talent are trying to protect us by not letting me see many details of what's to come."

"Then it must be rather unpleasant but necessary," Rion

said, a musing expression now on his face. "What I wonder, though, is just who it's most necessary *for*."

"Yes, I've been wondering the same," Naran admitted with a bit of discomfort. "Those with Sight magic have had to stay hidden for so long that their need to be a full part of the outer world must be nearly overwhelming. I can understand being willing to pay any price to get what you need so badly, but I don't care for the thought that our sacrifice might be part of that price."

Rion made no response beyond a small frown, possibly remembering how the first Fivefold Blending had been sacrificed to keep the secret about Sight magic. It wasn't an incident to dwell on, but it also shouldn't be completely forgotten . . .

By that time they had reached the place where Jovvi and Lorand stood, a short distance from the small crowd near Tamrissa and Vallant. Rion, the dear, made no effort to hesitate in telling Lorand that he needed to ask a favor of him and Vallant. The two men moved on to where Vallant stood listening to Tamrissa's conversation, so Naran turned to Jovvi with a smile.

"Rion wasn't happy to hear that we would have trouble, but he agreed not to add to it," Naran told Jovvi in a murmur. "He also agreed to ask Lorand and Vallant not to make a fuss."

"I told you Rion would agree," Jovvi returned, adding her own smile. "And because it's Rion asking, Lorand and Vallant will also agree. Now all I have to do is hold my own temper, and we should be fine."

"If Tamrissa doesn't undo all the efforts of both of us," Naran responded with a sigh. "I still don't understand why she's the one meant to set the tone for us."

"Hopefully we'll find out once all the shouting is over." Jovvi's smile had warmed even more, and her touch to Naran's hand was just as warmly reassuring. "But whatever happens, at least we can face it together."

"That togetherness is what makes all the difference," Naran said, then she laughed self-consciously. "As though *you* need to have that truth pointed out. You know as well as I do what it means to be all alone in the world."

"I certainly do," Jovvi assured her with a better laugh. Naran could tell that Jovvi meant to add something to what she'd already said, but the pleasant background music abruptly stopped. The two of them joined everyone else in the room in turning to see what was going on.

Lavrit Mohr, his face flushed with pleasure over the larger role being allowed him and his Guild, stood near the now-silent orchestra with his arms raised for quiet. When he got that quiet, he sent a beaming smile to everyone.

"On behalf of the Chosen Blending, it's my honor to welcome you all here tonight," he announced happily. With the help of Air magic users setting up the proper resonances, his voice was heard easily all over the enormous room. "There are certain things the members of the Chosen Blending want you to know, so it's my pleasure to yield the floor to *them*."

There was a smattering of applause as Mohr yielded the raised orchestra platform instead of the floor, and Naran felt Jovvi touch her arm before Jovvi led the way toward the platform. Naran would have been willing to stand to one side apart from the others if the gesture would have done any good, but she knew well enough that it would be wasted effort. For that reason, she followed Jovvi without making the offer, the two of them reaching the platform a moment after their Blendingmates.

"They're all yours, love," Lorand said to Jovvi softly with a smile, Tamrissa, Rion, and Vallant obviously agreeing with him. "Maybe they'll swallow the medicine more willingly if you're the one who gives it to them."

"I doubt that, but I'm willing to try," Jovvi answered as Naran took her place beside Rion—and also took his hand. "I'll start with something smaller, since smaller things are easier to swallow."

When Lorand nodded with a smile and stepped back, Jovvi turned to face their audience.

"Good evening, everyone," Jovvi said, and Naran could feel the warmth and gentle friendliness flowing out of their Spirit magic member. "On behalf of my Blendingmates, I'd like to thank all of you for coming tonight. As you'll find out, the days of being 'ordered' to this palace or allowed the privilege of coming here are completely over. Pulling down the nobility would have been a waste of time if we simply adopted their method of doing things."

A murmur ran through the large crowd, mostly a sound of pleased agreement. An occasional frown creased a face here and there, undoubtedly produced by those who were firm believers in "tradition," but for the most part the news was received with approval.

"We'd also like to correct certain procedures started by the nobility to keep themselves in power," Jovvi continued to immediate silence. "There will no longer be any laws preventing people from using their talents in a positive way, meaning a way that doesn't hurt someone else. Teaching classes will be established for everyone, young and old alike, run by Middle and High practitioners who have been taught much of what their talents can do. The lessons should increase everyone's strength and control."

This time the murmuring held a note of underlying tension, but excitement rose above that. Using talent in anything but a minor way had been forbidden for so long that people were clearly nervous about acting differently. But the idea that they were about to learn something new and wonderful seemed to override most of their fears. Naran smiled to herself, knowing just how they felt.

"Also, once everyone has had a chance to make the most of the lessons, they'll be taught how to Blend," Jovvi said when most of the commenting had quieted again. "We've found nothing to suggest that people of all levels can't do what we have, so—"

There was suddenly such an uproar that Jovvi had to stop speaking. Naran noticed that some people were exclaiming in shocked delight, while others were exclaiming in shocked horror. It was difficult to tell which feeling prevailed, but then a sense of calm seemed to fill the room. Considering the number of people being affected, Naran knew that Jovvi must be using the help of her link groups to restore order.

"Please understand that no one will be *forced* to participate in any of this," Jovvi told everyone in the relative quiet she'd provided for herself. "Our aim is to make sure that the knowledge we've worked so hard to regain is never lost again through suppression. There will also no longer be a Seated High in any of the talents. Instead there will be a Convention of Highs, a group that will work to expand our present knowledge and to discover new uses for our talents. That should bring about the birth of new industries as well, so that our people will have more to do with their lives than ever before."

"How do you know there *are* new things to do with our talents?" someone in the audience called above the renewed clamor of voices. "If nothing can be found then people will be horribly disappointed, so isn't it better not to give them false hope?"

"If you're suggesting that we start to keep secrets again, then I strongly disagree," Jovvi returned, speaking to the man as others quieted in order to listen. "Chances are that's how the original nobility started their policy of suppression, supposedly for the 'benefit' of the people. And considering how little research has been done into our talents over the centuries, it's highly unlikely that nothing will be found. But even if nothing *is* found, at least the people will know we tried."

Comments and opinions began to be voiced all over the room again, and Tamrissa, who stood to Naran's left, made a soft sound of amusement.

"If this is how they take the smaller doses, I can't wait to see their reaction to the biggest one," Tamrissa murmured to Naran. "Either there won't be a sound for miles around, or we won't even be able to hear ourselves—"

Suddenly, Naran found herself uttering a sound of fear and warning, a flash of Sight causing the reaction. Something terrible was about to happen, but the heavy fog all around her talent kept her from seeing exactly what. Tamrissa lost her amusement and parted her lips to ask a question, but before the words could be spoken it became unnecessary to ask.

A heavy *Crack!* sounded from above the platform, the noise almost lost in the babble of comments and questions coming from all over the room. Naran quickly looked up, and her heart immediately began to thunder with terror. A large section of the ceiling directly above them had started to fall, so large a section that jumping out of the way would be impossible. In a matter of seconds they and most of the orchestra would be crushed!

But then Naran's fear dissolved as she became part of the Blending. Definitely a part of it but, oddly, still partially herself. The entity she was now a part of knew there was more than enough time to avert disaster, especially since one of its flesh forms had recently recalled some of the lost knowledge. A large pattern of fire flamed into being above them, as large as the section of ceiling rushing to meet it. When the two came together there was a . . . volcanic explosion rather than a simple consuming, an explosion that would have scattered white-hot shards in all directions.

The explosion, however, had been anticipated by the entity. Although the wall quickly erected was invisible, it was thick enough to contain the burning shards until they were completely consumed. No more than seconds passed before not even ash remained, and then it was Naran alone again. Shocked and frightened silence now reigned in the ballroom, with at least one exception.

"So *that's* what that pattern can be used for," Tamrissa commented happily, her voice unamplified but still ringingly loud in the silence. "And now that I know marble explodes when it burns, I'll be more careful next time."

Naran almost joined many of the people in the room in staring open-mouthed at Tamrissa, but then a verbal explosion came that drowned out everything else. Hysterics made up a good portion of the noise, and Naran thought seriously about joining the effort until Jovvi came up to pat her arm with a smile.

"Thank you for the usual timely warning, Naran," Jovvi said as Rion tightened an arm around Naran's shoulders. "I . . . attuned myself to you, so to speak, making sure that I'd know at once if your talent gave you any sort of hint about

danger. That let me initiate the Blending in order to take
care of the problem, which it did."

"At the moment I'm wonderin' what *caused* that particular problem," Vallant said in a growl as he looked at the
wreck of the ceiling. "And please don't anyone suggest it
was nothin' but an accident."

"Of course it wasn't an accident," Lorand put in with a
sound of ridicule, his own gaze still on the gaping hole
above them. "The smoothness of most of the edges around
that opening tells me that the marble was cut through, possibly from above, except for the four corners of the section.
Those were probably knocked out with sledges, definitely
from above, all of them at the same time. My guess is that
our friend Ayl is at it again."

"But how did his people get in without being caught?"
Tamrissa demanded, now looking highly incensed. "I
thought all new staff additions were being carefully
checked."

"There's a chance they got in as temporary workers,"
Jovvi said, her expression thoughtful. "That's the way *I*
would do it if temporary workers—and visitors—aren't being looked at as carefully."

"So the members of Ayl's group that we caught *were* a
diversion," Tamrissa said, glancing at Vallant. "Vallant said
they might be, and now we know what they were diverting
us from. But it must have taken them a long time to cut
through marble with hand tools."

"What choice did they have?" Vallant countered, his
mood staying dark. "They don't have talents to reach us
with, so they're usin' whatever else they can."

"And they obviously don't care about innocent lives,"
Lorand said with his own growl while looking around at
the members of the orchestra. "Those people would have
been killed right along with us, but there's something else
to consider. How did Ayl know we'd be standing here?"

"I think that's fairly obvious," Naran said when no one
else answered. "Since I know for a fact that the man Ayl
doesn't share *my* talent, he must still have supporters working with Dom Mohr. If Dom Mohr decided in advance to

use this orchestra platform and mentioned his intention aloud, that's all they would have needed."

"But this is hardly all that's in store for us," Rion put in. "I would suspect that we were being tested again by Dom Ardanis and his fellow Sight magic users, but saving the members of the orchestra as well as ourselves is too minor a matter. I suggest, though, that if we survive whatever else occurs, we have a word with Dom Ardanis about having too much faith in our ability. This could easily have turned out worse than it did."

"I agree," Jovvi said as everyone else nodded. "We may have been successful, but in my opinion that's cutting it much too close. But right now we'd better see what we can do about the chaos in here. Lorand, will you please do me the favor of lending your voice to begin with?"

Lorand agreed to the request without hesitation, but as Jovvi turned toward their audience again Naran couldn't help fretting. If this unexpected attack wasn't what her people had been trying to keep them from knowing about, what in the world could they be hiding?

"All right, let's settle down now," Lorand shouted, giving Jovvi the louder voice she'd asked for. "The danger should be completely over now, but we'll still make sure. Please stand where you are and don't try to distract those who are doing the investigating."

A mild babble came in answer, but Lorand ignored it to look around for some of their secondary Blendings. A number of the Blending members were standing together toward the back of the room on the right, but those people were obviously surrounding the members of two Blendings already seated on the floor. Two Blending entities were investigating the matter then, and without having had to be asked.

"This has to prove we're doing it right," Lorand said to a waiting Jovvi, his smile sincere. "Two of our lesser Blendings are already on the job, looking around for any more traps that might have been set. Letting our people think for themselves has obvious benefits."

"Having people who are wise enough to know when they're out of their depth also helps," Jovvi said with her own smile of amusement. "You run into trouble only when the ones involved don't know enough to step back out of the way of —"

"Excuse me, Excellencies," Lavrit Mohr interrupted, bustling over in great agitation. "I can't imagine how something like this could have happened, but I'd be pleased to have a few words with the people who are responsible for the upkeep of this palace. A faulty ceiling *has* to be considered their fault, and—"

"Dom Mohr, if you please," Lorand interrupted in turn, glancing around to be sure no one else could hear him. "The ceiling wasn't faulty, it was tampered with, and I think we both know who did the tampering. How long ago did you decide to use the orchestra platform as the place to call us up to?"

"Why . . . it was early yesterday, as soon as I was shown this room as the place where the gathering would be held," Mohr replied slowly, his expression now one of confusion. "You can't mean that one of the traitor's people was already in the palace and in a position to overhear me make that decision . . . ?"

"That would be stretching coincidence a bit too far, Dom Mohr," Jovvi told him gently with a shake of her head. "A more likely explanation is that some of Ayl's people are pretending to be *your* followers instead, which keeps them in a position to pass on anything important they might learn. I think you'd better consider having your people checked out by one of our associate Blendings."

Mohr, clearly shocked by what he'd been told, moved back down to the floor in an unsteady way. The man was seeing his organization crumbling to pieces around him, and Lorand felt a great deal of sympathy. Mohr had wanted his people to play a larger, more important role in life, but Ayl's efforts were ruining that for all the people in the Guild that Ayl had once been a part of.

"May I have your attention again, please," Jovvi said, raising her hands as her voice reverberated around the room once more. "I've just been informed by one of our associate Blendings that the rest of this room is safe, so there's no need for anyone to rush home. There's one more thing we'd like to tell you tonight, and then you can all get on with enjoying the dancing and refreshments."

There was an uncertain note in the murmurings now heard all across the room, but no one hurried toward the nearest exit. Lorand considered that a good sign, and Jovvi apparently agreed with him.

"I'm glad to see that you all seem willing to listen," Jovvi said to the crowd with one of her devastating smiles. "That shows how much wiser you are than the former nobility, all of whom would probably be back in their coaches by now. The final thing we need to tell you is a joyous occasion for us, since we, in your presence, will now be changing history like those people we've all learned about in school. We're delighted to tell you that fivefold Blendings are now a thing of the past, and we will be the first sixfold Blending."

Jovvi beamed around at the people in her audience, obviously trying to draw them into a positive response, but Lorand could see that the ploy wasn't working. Most people were staring wide-eyed and open-mouthed with shocked confusion, and those with more specific responses weren't smiling even a small bit.

"There can't *be* a sixfold Blending," Relton Henris, the spokesman for the small shop owners, finally stated from the front of the crowd. "There are only five talents, after all, and adding a null to your group accomplishes nothing. Trying to make that girl seem important when she really isn't is a waste of our time and your effort, so why don't we forget about it, eh? Buy the girl a new hat or something instead of trying to push her in where she doesn't belong."

"But that's just the point," Jovvi returned, completely unruffled, while everyone in Lorand's sight nodded agreement with what Henris had said. "There *aren't* only five talents, there are six, and it has now become time for everyone to know about it. Naran has Sight magic, which is the ability to see a short way into the future. It's thanks to *her* talent that we were able to come to terms with the invading Astindans."

This time *everyone's* jaw seemed to drop, and not a few of the faces owning those jaws also went pale. Dozens of eyes fastened themselves to Naran where she stood beside Rion, and many of the stares, oddly enough, were filled with fear rather than resentment.

"Why are so many of you frightened?" Jovvi suddenly asked, looking around with confusion of her own. "This is unexpected news, I know, but there's no call for fright."

"How about outrage and indignation?" Relton Henris snapped, one of his hands closed to a fist as he looked up at Jovvi. "No one has the right to know what I mean to do before I do it, no one! That obscene 'talent' invades my privacy worse than the nobility ever managed to do, and I won't have it! You get rid of that woman right now and we won't have to say anything more about it. If you don't . . ."

"If we don't, you'll . . . what?" a new voice put in, and then Tamrissa had come forward to stand beside Jovvi. The Fire magic user's gaze was colder than Lorand had ever seen it, except for when Tamrissa talked about her former husband or parents. "Who do you think you are to tell *us* what we will and won't do? If not for us you'd still be a slave, but you've had no trouble forgetting about that, have you?"

"There's a limit to how much a man can be expected to owe," Henris countered through his teeth, his face darkening. "My people and I are grateful for what was done for us, but not so grateful that we'll just hand over our privacy for the rest of our lives. We don't *want* a Blending with that Sight magic lording it over us, so you can just get rid of her—permanently."

"Does anyone disagree with that?" Tamrissa demanded, now looking around at the people in the audience. "Are you all so afraid of your own shadows—and think you're so important that we'd *bother* to see what you're going to do—that you insist on standing with *this* fool?"

One or two people, like Rilna Zokill, looked as if they

considered disagreeing with Henris, but no one said so aloud. Lorand joined Tamrissa in glancing around, but she gave up the effort first.

"So none of you has the stomach to disagree with the fool," Tamrissa concluded aloud, an odd smile now on her face. "And it's get rid of Naran or else, an ultimatum you all join in. All right, if that's the way you want it, it's fine with me. We'll take the 'or else.' "

"What are you talking about *now*?" Henris actually had the nerve to demand, sounding to Lorand like a noble addressing a drudge in his kitchen. "All you have to do is get rid of that woman, and then—"

"But we refuse to get rid of her," Tamrissa interrupted, deliberately stepping on the man's words. "If you people won't have a sixfold Blending running the empire and we refuse to revert to being a fivefold Blending, there's only one thing left to be done. We'll leave *your* palace first thing in the morning, to go on about our business as private citizens. You can run the empire yourselves."

Lorand would have sworn that the crowd reaction couldn't possibly be louder than it had been before, but now it was a pure bedlam. People screamed and yelled at whoever happened to be standing near them, and the only exception to all the noise came from those who stood on the platform. Lorand could see pained expressions on the faces of his Blendingmates, but not one of them stepped forward to disagree with Tamrissa.

"Now I know why this had to be left to Tamma," Jovvi murmured to Lorand while the noise continued. "I never would have had the nerve to say that and really mean it, but Tamma isn't bluffing. If they don't change their minds about Naran, Tamma expects us all to walk out."

"Oddly enough, I agree with Tamrissa," Lorand murmured back, faintly surprised at his own reaction. "My sense of duty keeps trying to insist that we *can't* walk out, but I'll do that sooner than refuse to support my sisters."

"The rest of us agree with you, of course, and that's what seems to be bothering our new people of standing." Jovvi's words were very soft as she nodded toward Henris and the others near him. "We're supposed to be frightened of losing what we worked so hard to gain, not all but throwing it back in the faces of those who—"

"You think we won't take you up on that?" Henris suddenly announced to Tamrissa over the din, his face quickly lighting with what he obviously considered a revelation. "Yes, that's it, you're trying to bluff us into doing what *you* want, but it isn't going to work. Your group isn't the only Blending around any longer, so if *you* walk out we can put one of *them* in your place. How's *that* for an or else?"

"Your plan is as stupid as I expected it to be," Tamrissa retorted with a snort, ignoring the smug victory on the man's face in a way that Lorand was having trouble duplicating. "Our associate Blendings are free to do as they please, but I seriously doubt if any of them is thick enough in the head to oblige you. They'd have to restrict themselves to staying a fivefold Blending when everyone else was free to expand, and instead of ruling the empire they would be working for *you*, which is what agreeing to your demands comes to. Now I think it's time that we left."

The smugness disappeared from Henris's expression as Lorand and the others began to follow Tamrissa off the platform. Unhappy discussions were still going on all over the room, but not in the back where the members of the other Blendings stood. Lorand had the impression that their associates were amused by the goings-on, but had no interest in joining in. They'd all seen too much fighting and danger to now be interested in playing politics.

"B-B-But Excellences, you're The Chosen!" Dom Mohr began to protest, as though he hadn't been able to believe what was going on until now. "The Chosen can't just pick up and walk away like—like—dissatisfied parlor maids!"

"It's *your* claim that we're Chosen, not ours," Tamrissa pointed out without hesitation, her tone pleasant but completely inflexible. "But who we are or are not happens to be completely beside the point. We risked ourselves to depose the nobility to save our own necks as well as yours, and now the chore is done. Ruling an empire is actually a much harder job, and now that the danger is over *you* people want to make it even worse by trying to run our lives to suit your own prejudices. Well, that's too bad about you because it isn't going to happen."

By turning away from Mohr, Tamrissa made it clear that she was through talking and ready to move on. Rather than stepping back to give her—and the rest of the Blending—a way through the crowd, Henris and his supporters moved closer instead. *They* weren't yet ready to end the argument, not when they hadn't gotten their way, and Lorand could see the stubborn set to their expressions. He was about to tell the fools just how big a mistake they were making when Tamrissa lost patience and made the point the most direct way.

"Yow!" Henris shouted along with his friends as they all jumped back; candle-sized flames had appeared under all their noses. No one had been hurt beyond being jostled, but Henris had turned red-faced with embarrassment.

"You had no right to do that, girl," Henris growled as he glared at the length of flame not far from him. "I think it's time someone taught you better manners."

Lorand had no idea what the man was talking about—until a fairly thick stream of water suddenly engulfed the length of flame closest to Henris. A matching smug expression on Henris's face made it clear who had supplied the water, but another point became even more clear: Henris had no idea who he was dealing with.

"Why is it always the biggest fool who decides to teach people things?" Tamrissa asked with a snort and a small headshake. "And a fool who's blind as well as stupid."

Henris frowned in confusion for only an instant before understanding what Tamrissa meant. Inside the stream of water the man had produced was a continuing glow, showing that Tamrissa's fire still burned in spite of the presence of the water meant to quench it. Henris ground his teeth and glared at the glow, but instead of dimming again the fire actually brightened.

"Don't be even more of a fool," Vallant told the man abruptly, stepping forward to touch Henris's arm. "You're no more than a Middle talent tryin' to play out of your league, and takin' in more of the power won't help you. Can't you feel the difference between us? How can you not know that we're Highs?"

"You *can't* be that much stronger, so it has to be some kind of trick," Henris ground out as he now glared at Vallant, his hands having turned to fists. "You five were in the right place at the right time, and ended up learning how to Blend. If any of the rest of us had been there instead it would have been *us* in your place now, so don't try to hand us any more lies. You're *not* special, so—"

Voices rose in immediate argument from all sides, some agreeing with Henris, some denying his stance. Lorand exchanged confused glances with his Blendingmates. How was it possible to deny the difference between Middle talent and High when a Middle talent could *feel* the greater strength in a High?

"Be quiet!" a voice suddenly shouted above the newest uproar. "All of you, be quiet and listen to this! We're not as through with bad news as you'd all like to believe!"

Lorand joined everyone else in turning to look at Dom Mohr, who had gotten back up onto the platform. Behind him stood a man who seemed to be out of breath, and Mohr's expression was pale and grim.

"No, Henris, keep your mouth closed!" Mohr snapped, pointing a finger at the man he addressed. "For once you'd better listen instead of flapping your mouth, because trouble is on its way again. My people in the east have sent word, and it isn't good. The army that was assigned to Gracely was obviously recalled, because it's now on its way back *here*. When it gets here, it will be working for the return of the nobility to power and the rest of us to the way things were."

"Then this bunch still has work to do," Henris said at once, gesturing toward Tamrissa and the rest of the Blending. "Once they get rid of those noble-loving troublemakers, we can all go back to discussing what was just interrupted."

"I have a better idea," Tamrissa said while Lorand stood

mute with outrage and the rest of the Blending reacted in other ways. "*You* take care of that army and save your own backside. As I've already said, we're out of here."

And with that they all pushed their way through the crowds and marched out of the room.

SIX

Edmin Ruhl paused in the entrance to the private garden to look around at the lovely day. The world he'd known and enjoyed all his life might be crumbling to nothing all about him, but at least the weather was decent . . .

"Edmin, do come and join us," Edmin's father, the former High Lord Embisson Ruhl, called from the chairs where he entertained a guest. "If, that is, you can spare the time from business."

"Unfortunately, Father, I have more time than business these days," Edmin responded with a faint, humorless smile as he joined the two men. "How nice to see you again, Lord Sembrin. I trust you and your family are well?"

"As well as can be expected, Lord Edmin," Sembrin Noll responded, standing to bow politely before sitting again. "I do wish I knew for certain what became of my brother Ephaim, but other than that my wife and I are as well as can be expected these days."

"Surely we all *know* what became of your brother," Edmin's father said to Noll as Edmin went to pour himself a cup of tea from the service. "Those interlopers did away with him, just as they did away with too many others of our peers. You were wise to leave Gan Garee when you did, before things really got bad."

"My wife insisted when she became convinced that I would be next," Noll said with faint amusement and something of a headshake. Sembrin Noll was just as imposing a man as his brother Ephaim had been, at least to look at. But where Ephaim Noll had shown his strength of character in the gaze he bent on others, Sembrin's gaze was no more than unintrusively mild. "I was about to return to Gan Garee when you and Edmin arrived here at Bastions, so it seemed wise to speak with you before returning to the city. I'm certainly glad I did."

"What I just learned from some of my people should make you more than simply glad," Edmin said with a sigh, taking one of the chairs. "Things are now even worse than they were when *we* left, which I hadn't really thought could happen. The first bit of news is, of course, that all five of the interlopers are dead."

"All five, you say," Edmin's father echoed thoughtfully as Lord Sembrin made noises of surprise. "Are there any details available about *how* they died?"

"My people made an effort to find out," Edmin replied, exchanging a glance with his father. The two of them knew that the false Five had been poisoned at *their* orders, or at least four of the five had been poisoned. The fifth had escaped through sheer luck, but it wouldn't do to mention those facts with someone else present. The interlopers might be dead, but their own positions were hardly so secure that they could afford to speak as they liked . . .

"Apparently the interlopers faced the peasant Five as individuals rather than as a Blending," Edmin went on after sipping at his tea. "It's been suggested that they knew they would lose if they fought again as a Blending, and so attempted to fight as individuals. The effort earned them nothing at all, and they were defeated individually. But oddly enough, they didn't die until *after* they lost at the confrontations. The peasants apparently had something other than death in mind for the ones who stole the Fivefold Throne from them."

"I wonder if the interlopers resorted to suicide," Lord Sembrin mused with a headshake. "Possibly they knew what fate awaited them at the hands of their enemies, and chose to avoid the need to face it. Or possibly they simply died from the poison you had them given."

Edmin joined his father in staring silently at Lord Sembrin, finding the man's pleasant smile and openly innocent expression disturbing. Great pains had been taken to keep the poisoning episode a private matter, and yet Sembrin now discussed it as though it were common knowledge . . .

"Oh, I do apologize for disturbing you," Sembrin said after a moment, his expression now one of faint distress as he looked back and forth between his hosts. "I was certain you understood that Ephaim learned most of what he knew about others from *me*. My strength has always been unearthing interesting happenings, and Ephaim's was using the knowledge to best advantage. We made a very effective team, just as effective as you and Lord Edmin, Lord Embisson, and I miss my brother quite a lot."

"I can certainly understand that," Edmin's father allowed with all his usual courtesy of manner. "Ephaim was most definitely a brother to be proud of, and *I'm* proud to say I considered myself his friend. But I *am* confused about one point here . . . If anyone knows what became of your brother, shouldn't you be the one?"

"I should be, but I'm not," Sembrin admitted with an expression suggesting total failure. "Ephaim was determined to control those people the way a Seated Blending is *supposed* to be controlled, and I'm afraid he underestimated them. Everyone thought he'd been partially successful—until his associates had various . . . accidents and incidents, and *he* disappeared completely. I began a search for him, of course, but wasn't able to discover even a single clue as to his whereabouts."

"He was undoubtedly forced to cover his tracks completely, most especially from those who knew him well," Edmin sympathized in his most sincere tone. "The interlopers *were* far stronger than they should have been, but . . . What gives you the idea that my father and I did anything at all to those people? And if you were way out here from the time your brother disappeared, how do you know whether anything was done to those people in the first place?"

"Oh, that's rather easy to explain," Sembrin replied with a small, almost embarrassed laugh. "I may have taken *myself* out of Gan Garee, but my people stayed behind. They continued to send me information for quite some time, but then the flow of information stopped rather abruptly. That was one of the reasons I considered returning to the city, but then you and your father arrived with word about what was happening. Now you have much more of an organization than I do, so please do go on with what you've learned. Do you by any chance know how the fifth member of the group might have been poisoned?"

"I'm fairly certain I do know," Edmin admitted, quickly making up his mind. "But first I must ask a question, Lord Sembrin. Am I mistaken in believing that your visit here today has more of a reason behind it than a simple courtesy call? Are you by any chance proposing an alliance?"

"Actually, I'm here with hat in hand," Sembrin replied, and this time his expression was open and serious. "You and Lord Embisson are among the very few really competent members of the nobility left, and I'd very much appreciate being allowed to join you in whatever plans you have for restoring things to the way they were. I *can* be of use to you without also being a danger because of excess ambition. My brother considered my lack of ambition to be one of my most endearing qualities."

Sembrin's smile filled with amusement, and Edmin couldn't help showing a smile of his own as he looked over at his father. Sembrin Noll was a very disarming individual who *could* be of use to them, but Edmin didn't know the man well enough to judge whether Sembrin might be more dangerous than useful. Edmin's father also smiled, but with decision rather than doubt.

"Yes, Lord Sembrin, I heard your brother say that about your lack of ambition more than once," Embisson commented, most likely for Edmin's benefit. "We would be honored to have you join us, most especially if you're able to add gold to the effort as well as your very capable talents."

"Gold for the hiring of more men as guardsmen," Sembrin said with a thoughtful nod. "Yes, I can contribute my share to that effort, which should keep us in control of this area at the very least. And there are others of us not far from here who can be talked into making their own contribution to the common effort. They think they can assure their safety by simply keeping their heads down, and they need to be disabused of so foolish a notion."

Edmin exchanged another glance with his father, trying not to show how impressed he was. For someone who no longer had an organization to gather intelligence, Sembrin still knew far more than Edmin would have expected. The fifty new guardsmen who had been quietly hired shouldn't have been known to Sembrin, but he also seemed to know about the additional fifty they hadn't yet concluded a deal with. This was definitely a man they wanted on *their* side . . .

"If you'll give us the names and locations of those of our peers you just mentioned, we'll be glad to pay them a visit," Edmin assured their new associate. "Now, as to what happened to the fifth member of the interlopers, I believe he was poisoned by Lady Eltrina Razas."

"Ah, then she *was* successful," Sembrin exclaimed with an odd sort of amusement. "I'd come to the conclusion that the woman was too obsessed to actually accomplish anything, but apparently I was wrong. May I ask what leads you to believe that the poisoning was accomplished through Lady Eltrina's efforts?"

"Aside from the fact that she spurned leaving the city with us in order to remain and continue her efforts?" Edmin said with another faint smile. "I have, in addition to that, the report of an agent who returned to my service after seeing how matters ended up in the city. The fifth of the interlopers *was* poisoned, and she nearly accomplished the same with the five peasants. She'd apparently taken a position as a servant in the palace, and when her final poisoning effort didn't work, she attacked the five with a knife."

"Which couldn't possibly have gotten her anything but caught," Lord Sembrin said with a nod. "She would have done better biding her time, but those who are obsessed are seldom rational. May I ask what particular happening in the city caused your agent to return to your service?"

"The happening was rather traumatic for my agent, as he'd hoped to sell his services to one of my peers," Edmin said, speaking also to his father, who hadn't yet heard the news. "It seems that the avenging force from Astinda was stopped by the five peasants and their followers, probably due to an agreement that was made. The agreement saw every noble left in the city placed under arrest, and then processed like animals at a slaughterhouse in order for them to be sent to Astinda. Once they reach Astinda they'll be put to work as slaves, cleaning up the devastation created there by our armies."

"You're joking," Lord Sembrin said with a small laugh of disbelief while Lord Embisson turned absolutely pale. "Those of our peers left in the city may not be terribly bright, but they're still full members of the nobility. Those peasants wouldn't have *dared* to do something like *that* . . ."

"Not only did they dare, but they acted without hesitation," Edmin assured his listeners bitterly. "They took people of the highest quality and put them under arrest, and then the Astindans did something to them to keep them from escaping again. The Astindans invaded our empire with an army consisting of Blendings rather than simple link groups, and it's those Blendings that are doing the dirty work. And on top of that, those five peasants have created their own multiple Blendings."

"Those fools!" Lord Embisson exploded, his face now darkened with outrage. "We've worked for centuries to keep the peasants of the empire under control, and they throw away all that effort in a matter of weeks! How do they expect to rule an empire where others have the same ability they do? If the peasants are able to protect *them-*

selves, why would they need a Seated Blending to do the protecting *for* them?"

"Obviously they have no real understanding of the proper way to rule," Lord Sembrin said with a disapproving shake of his head. "But that very lack of understanding could well be their downfall. If there are *multiple* Blendings available as Lord Edmin's agent reported, we should be able to find at least one that's willing to do things our way in order to be Seated themselves. Once they've been made to see the light, they'll be able to eliminate their competition from the safety of anonymity. Then there will be only one Blending again, and it will be to their advantage to keep it like that."

"Yes, of course, you're perfectly right," Lord Embisson agreed as he regained control of his temper with a bit of difficulty. "The doings of the interlopers certainly outraged me, but in fine they were members of *our* class. To think that mere peasants would have the colossal nerve to do even worse! Well, as you say, their naivete will turn out to be their undoing. We'll have to start inquiries at once to find the perfect tools, but we won't be saddled with them for long. As soon as they've returned things to normal in the empire, we'll replace them with people of true quality— and less potent ability."

"And I would advise against resurrecting the practice of challenges every twenty-five years," Edmin put in, looking back and forth between the other two men. "Instead we can simply have the ruling Blending retire, and another take its place. If the peasants dislike the idea, they'll have to learn to live with it."

"Yes, I agree," Lord Sembrin said with a thoughtful nod. "The sop given the peasants turned out to be our undoing, so we'd be fools to reinstitute the practice. And the five peasants may have even done us a favor. Our ranks really were becoming filled with deadwood, and Ephaim was constantly complaining about being pestered by those who had gold and property but nothing of ability to contribute to the general effort. That deadwood is now gone, and we'll be able to start over again with those who are actually able to accomplish something."

"I hadn't considered that, but again I think you're right," Lord Embisson said, echoing Lord Sembrin's nod. "This is a priceless opportunity, and we must take advantage of every aspect of it. Once we're in control again, we'll take steps to avoid the mistakes made by those who came before us."

"I don't mean to change subjects, but there are two other things you may not know as yet," Lord Sembrin put in slowly. "The first item is of lesser importance, but really should be counted among our assets. My wife and I have two houseguests, her aunt and cousin. Her aunt is of no consequence, of course, but her cousin is Rimen Howser, who did rather well for himself before the troubles."

"He also worked for the interlopers," Edmin pointed out coldly. "My agent filled me in on that, and also the fact that he disappeared rather abruptly. If you're suggesting that we allow him to join us, I'm afraid I must disagree."

"Please hear me out," Lord Sembrin said with a sober expression, holding up one hand in Edmin's direction. "It's true that Rimen worked for the interlopers, but he offered his services at the suggestion of the group he was a member of. They were determined to rid themselves of the interlopers, but needed someone on the inside to keep them informed of the interlopers' doings. He may have worked for them, but what he really worked for was their downfall."

"And the group was headed by Grall Razas before he died," Lord Embisson put in before Edmin could voice further doubts. "Yes, I'd heard about that, and with all the other things we were involved with, Edmin, I simply forgot to mention it. Are you saying, Lord Sembrin, that Howser walked away when he saw that things were falling apart?"

"Actually, Rimen was carried away," Sembrin said with a grimace that negated any thought of amusement. "At first that Spirit magic user, Arstin, seemed to be in charge of the interlopers, and Rimen's ability was put to proper use. Then it was suddenly the Earth magic user, Delin Moord, who was in charge, and Rimen allowed his . . . prejudices to overcome his good judgment. Moord told Rimen that he would immediately be made a High Lord if he collected the gold due Moord from the peasants, and Rimen actually tried to do that collecting. He ended up beaten so badly that he nearly found it impossible to get home, and his mother was frantic. But she did manage to get him to a healer, and then she took him out of the city. He's now recovering at my place."

"If he recovers quickly enough, we should be able to find a place for him," Lord Embisson said with a nod. "What was the other thing you thought we should know?"

"It's come to my attention that the interlopers must have ordered home the Gracely army," Sembrin answered with something of a smile. "I make that assumption for the reason that the army in question is on its way back to Gan Garee and will soon pass through this very neighborhood."

"Really," Edmin murmured. "I was under the impression that the Gracely army had been sent to the west."

"Either they received other orders, or the leaders of the army decided to make their stand in defense of Gan Garee," Sembrin replied with a shrug. "Whatever the reason, we'll soon have an army of our own to use as soon as they're told that their superiors in the city are no longer in a position to make use of them. I suggest we send a messenger to them, inviting the officers to sit down with us for a meal and a discussion. Would you rather receive them here or at my place?"

"Neither," Lord Embisson said at once, an instant before Edmin would have said the same. "Using them for our own purposes is an excellent idea, but there's no need to burden them with too much knowledge. We'll find a house that isn't being used right now, and that's where we'll meet them. Then, if one of them happens to be captured by the enemy, he won't be able to reveal our true locations."

"And those of us going to the meeting ought to be masked," Edmin added. "There are members of our peer group running that army, and we don't want to be recognized and remembered. Until we're back in control, the key to our survival will be discretion in all things."

"And I never thought of that," Sembrin said with a rueful smile and shake of his head. "As I said, making use of the information I gather isn't my strong point. Shall I let you know when the army gets close enough that a messenger won't be days about delivering his message?"

"Yes, do," Lord Embisson agreed with his own smile. "We'll get right to choosing an appropriate meeting place, so we'll be ready when they get here. And don't forget that we'll need that list of our peers who expect to be able to hide their heads in the sand waiting for things to return to normal."

"I'll prepare the list, and have one of my servants bring it to you tonight," Sembrin said as he rose from his chair to bow. "Lord Embisson, Lord Edmin, you both have my thanks for allowing me to join your efforts. You have my word that you won't regret the generosity."

"Oh, I'm quite certain of *that*," Lord Embisson agreed amiably, remaining seated as Edmin rose to return the bow of courtesy. "Please do feel free to visit here again as often as necessary."

Sembrin repeated his bow, and then Edmin saw him into the house and to the front door, where the man's carriage waited. Once Sembrin was gone, Edmin retraced his steps to the private garden his father hadn't yet left.

"I consider that a very profitable visit," Lord Embisson commented as Edmin reclaimed his previous chair. "The man obviously still has sources of information that haven't been lost, and we'll be able to make good use of him and them."

"And yet I wonder if Noll can be fully trusted," Edmin said, paying close attention to what his father's response would be. "Despite all that open friendliness, he *is* the brother of Ephaim Noll."

"My dear Edmin, *no* one can be fully trusted but the two of *us*," Lord Embisson pointed out with an amusement that brought Edmin a great deal of relief. "Noll may hope for a position that gives him a say over empire policy once we're back in control, but there's no need for us to go overboard. We'll be the ones to have the say, and he'll have to satisfy himself with simply being associated with us."

"Just as he was associated with his brother," Edmin said

with a satisfied nod. "We'll use him in the same way, and simply give him enough gold and property to satisfy him."

"Yes, that should take care of the matter," Lord Embisson agreed comfortably before reaching for his tea. "Now let's discuss where we'll hold that meeting with the officers of the army."

Edmin composed himself for the discussion, briefly reflecting on how pleased he was that his father seemed as sharp as he'd always been. Together they would certainly succeed in their planning, especially if other useful tools happened to present themselves . . .

When Lord Sembrin Noll arrived home, he immediately went to search out his wife. He found Bensia in her sitting room with a book, which she put aside as soon as she saw him.

"How did it go, my dear?" she asked with one of her marvelous, warming smiles. "Did they take you at your word?"

"Of course they did," Sembrin answered with his own smile as he sat at the side of the lounge she lay on. "It isn't as if they know me as well as Ephaim did, and even he never doubted my lack of ambition."

"But Ephaim also never noted the fact that you're not the only one in the family," Bensia said with a small, very amused laugh. "These two new allies of ours will work very hard to get themselves to the height of power, intending to keep it solely to themselves. What a shock they'll have when they find *me* there ahead of them."

"In the place you deserve more than they do," Sembrin murmured as he kissed her hand. "You deserve everything and anything you want, and I'm the one privileged to get it for you. I'm the luckiest man alive."

"And I'm the luckiest woman alive, having a man of your abilities dedicated to helping her," Bensia murmured back, putting her book aside so that she might lean forward and exchange a kiss with him. "I've also had a few words with cousin Rimen, and as soon as he's back on his feet he'll be adding *his* efforts to ours."

"He saw the truth, then," Sembrin said with a satisfied nod. "It was the old guard among our peers who kept him from becoming a High Lord, and who also kept him from doing as he pleased with the peasants. Putting him in charge of the . . . animals, as he calls the peasants, will keep those people from ever becoming a problem again."

"Yes, and while he pretends to work for Lord Embisson and Lord Edmin, he'll really be working for us," Bensia said, her smile filled with her own satisfaction. "Not one of those fools who used to run things understands that eliminating High talents is a criminal waste. If you put them under your complete control instead while they're still children, you have their abject and unswerving devotion once they're grown. And you also have their ability to use as *you* see fit."

" 'Waste not, want not,' as the old saying goes," Sembrin agreed with a laugh. "If we'd had those High talents supporting us instead of Low talent guardsmen, we'd still be back where we belong. And speaking of children, where are ours?"

"They're busy practicing," Bensia told him with a chuckle. "My aunt Faella is an excellent example of the old nobility, petulant, constantly whining, and the next thing to mindless. When the children are able to make her do anything they please without her noticing that they're manipulating her, they'll know they can do the same with any of the others who are left. They'll be invaluable to us as a means of keeping our former peers in line when we take over."

"It's too bad there are only four of them," Sembrin teased the way he usually did. "If we'd had the proper foresight, we would have produced twice their number."

"You must remember, my dear, that we're still not too old," Bensia teased back with that smile that always tingled deep inside him. "Why don't we take a short while and see what we can accomplish."

She reached forward to touch his face before kissing him again, and Sembrin was instantly ready for her. She was still the most beautiful woman he'd ever seen, and he really did consider himself the luckiest man alive that she'd married him. If she wanted to run the empire, that was perfectly all right with him. She would have his support and assistance to the day he died.

Sembrin moved closer to take Bensia in his arms, the way she moved against him saying that she, too, was ready for lovemaking. As often as they made love, it was odd that they *hadn't* had more than the four children. But when her hand touched him intimately, he forgot all about oddness and gave his full attention to nothing but her. He would kill for her or die for her; using those who thought they were using him was really the easiest of it . . .

Bensia stoked her husband's desire briefly before rising from the lounge and leading him toward the bedchamber. Rather than protesting as he once might have done, he followed her eagerly and docilely to the place she most preferred to make love. She'd looked around carefully for a long while before she'd chosen Sembrin Noll as her husband, and she'd never regretted the decision. They'd been almost ready to make their move when disaster struck, but that had been a setback, not a defeat. She had more than a few plans for the empire once she was in control, and that aim could still be achieved. They just had to be even more careful than they'd been . . .

Sembrin worked quickly to help her out of her clothing, having no idea that her Spirit magic encouraged him to behave exactly as she wanted him to. He also had no idea that they'd had no more than four children because she'd decided she wanted no more and had taken precautions. Sembrin was very old-fashioned when it came to limiting a family size, believing that a woman ought to have as many children as her husband cared to give her. It was the one point she had to slide past him rather than control, but that was perfectly all right. It was the only flaw he had, and one that was easily handled.

It was no more than a moment before Sembrin joined her in bed, and then they began to enjoy each other. It was never hard to encourage him when she felt the need rising, and he was always more than adequate.

But once the empire was safely in her hands, she really would have to start sampling the abilities of other men . . .

SEVEN

Zirdon Tal, very important person in the empire of Gracely and the capital city of Liandia, allowed the servant to rinse his hands in the scented water, after which he gave a second servant the privilege of drying his hands again. Both servants were nearly beside themselves with awed delight, of course, a reaction which still made Zirdon smile. They were like small children in their innocent enjoyment, and it gave the Fire magic user a warm feeling to watch them in their happiness.

A crystal bell rang just outside the lounging room, telling Zirdon that one of his upper servants needed to see him. Since he wasn't engaged in anything that couldn't be interrupted, Zirdon nodded to the servant holding another crystal bell. That servant answered the first ring with another, and the door opened to admit Leesto, Zirdon's chief servant. Leesto was as short and thin as most chief servants were, and equally weak in talent. The man scurried into the room without raising his eyes to his master, fell to his knees, then touched his head to the carpeting.

"Please excuse the interruption, Exalted One, but a visitor has arrived begging audience with you," Leesto said, his head raised from the carpeting but his gaze still lowered.

"The Honorable Sheedra Kam would know if you are receiving callers."

"Yes, I think I *am* in the mood for a visitor," Zirdon decided aloud with a smile. "Show the lady in, Leesto, if you please."

"At once, Exalted One," Leesto quickly acknowledged, rising to his feet before bowing. The bow was as deep and respectful as it was supposed to be, and then the small man backed out of Zirdon's presence. Once the door was closed he would raise his gaze again, but not until there wasn't the least chance of his actually laying eyes on Zirdon. If he had, it really would have been too bad.

That particular lounging room wasn't too far toward the back of the house, so it wasn't long before the crystal bell rang again. When Zirdon allowed the second ring, Leesto opened the door and bowed Sheedra Kam into the room. The door was quickly closed behind the woman, and then Zirdon was able to give Sheedra his complete attention.

Attention which she fully deserved. Sheedra was one of the most beautiful women in the empire of Gracely, a fact Zirdon had researched personally. Her hair was a shining and lustrous black, and today she wore a small hat in red to match her gown, a hat with lace and a modest amount of feathers. The gown had more lace and no feathers, but did a marvelous job showing off Sheedra's small waist and rounded bosom. She paused to give him a bit of a curtsey, and then her radiant smile came forth as she approached the chair his wave had gestured her to.

"I'm delighted that you were able to see me, my dear," Sheedra said as she allowed a servant to seat her. "I have a very great favor to ask, and if I'd had to wait I would have been terribly distressed."

"Well, we certainly don't want you distressed," Zirdon said as he took her hand before raising it to his lips. "If you'll tell me what you need this time, I'll see if I can arrange it."

"But of course you can arrange it," Sheedra replied with a small laugh, making no attempt to free her hand. "Not only are you the major talent in your Blending, but you're also a member of the strongest coalition in the assembly. If *you* can't do something, then it simply can't be done by anyone."

"Modesty forbids me to agree, but nothing forces me to argue," Zirdon said with his own laugh as he moved a bit closer to his lovely visitor. "Tell me what favor you've come to ask."

"It was horribly humiliating," Sheedra said with a head-shake, just as though he'd understand exactly what she meant. "Riskor Marvis and his wife Teedri had their quarterly reception, but I wasn't invited! You can't possibly imagine how devastated I was."

"Riskor Marvis," Zirdon murmured, finding the name faintly familiar. It took a moment or two, but finally he remembered. "Ah, yes, those dreadfully boring people you were telling me about the last time you called. They're one step away from gaining the title of Honorable, you said, and once they gain the title you were thinking of giving it up yourself. Why in the world would you *want* to go to one of their receptions?"

"My dear man, don't you know who *goes* to their receptions?" Sheedra exclaimed. "Half the members of the coalitions in the assembly, that's who. With that in mind I would have agreed to add my presence to their silly gathering, but they didn't ask me! That's why I want you to ruin them."

"Ruin them," Zirdon echoed a second time, reflecting that he should have known. Many beautiful women had minds to match, but Sheedra's exceptional beauty seemed to have been paid for in something other than coin.

"Yes, that's right, ruin them," Sheedra agreed happily, as though she'd just asked him to join her for lunch. "I know you can do it, so please say yes."

Zirdon felt the urge to heave a greater sigh than usual. In point of fact he *could* have ruined the man no matter *what* his position was in the city, but the matter was hardly that simple. If the man had connections to even a small number of coalition members, it might not be the best idea politically to move against him. He would have had to investigate carefully, and frankly that was just too much trouble.

"Well, of course I'll ruin them for you, my sweet," Zirdon said almost at once, his hesitation covered by the way he'd raised her hand to his lips again. "Naturally I'll expect a favor in return, but you won't find that *too* objectionable, will you?"

"Oh, now, you aren't going to ask what you did the last time, are you?" Sheedra put coyly with the hint of a pout. "I don't mind in the least sharing *your* bed, but some of those others you gave me to were *quite* objectionable. My mother said I should have made my position clear in the beginning, so that's what I'm doing now: making my position clear at once."

"My dear, sweet child, your position is more than clear," Zirdon replied with a laugh. "You've come to ask a favor, but everything has its price. If you want that favor badly enough, you'll be required to meet that price."

Sheedra's pout grew more pronounced as her brows drew together in a delightful frown of thought, and Zirdon left her to it. She knew as well as anyone that he had no need to do her a "favor" in order to have her in *his* bed. All he had to do, as he'd done any number of times, was voice his desire for her. She was brought to his house at once by her father, and Zirdon kept her as long as he pleased.

But when she came to ask for something she wanted, he then had the opportunity to . . . bind some of his supporters a bit more closely. As soon as he'd first indicated his interest in her, he'd made Sheedra unavailable to the rest of his class. The only way any of them could have the girl was through *him*, and the price for her use was the need to back him in the assembly. Some of his peers had hesitated to pay that price, but others were far too taken with her charms to consider the cost.

And a number of those who had hesitated at first were now wavering. They, like him, could have any woman they wanted, so they weren't used to being denied. That very denial seemed to stimulate them to greater desire, enhancing Sheedra's already potent charms. For powerful men they were far too much under the rule of their physical desires, a condition Zirdon never hesitated to take advantage of. He, himself, would never think of falling to the same failing, which made the situation rather amusing.

Sheedra moved in her chair as she continued to consider her options, something else that amused Zirdon. It wasn't possible for the girl to refuse his demand, not if she wanted what she'd come here for, but it would take a number of minutes for her to realize that. She had no choice but to agree, but, unfortunately for the dear girl, her agreement would not bring her the end she desired.

Zirdon meant to use his Blending to make her forget exactly what she'd asked for, at the same time giving her the definite impression that she'd had full satisfaction. It was an annoyance that the law required her agreement to anything but his own personal use of her, but when one had a Blending to be the major talent of, the annoyance was easily seen to. Zirdon had been thinking of using the Blending to bring her to him, but the cooperative darling had come all on her own.

"Are you sure that *that* has to be your price?" Sheedra suddenly asked, a sullen annoyance faint in her voice. "One of those men you gave me to last time made me do all sorts of disgusting things, and another struck me repeatedly on my bottom before putting me to normal use. It was all very undignified, and I disliked it quite a lot."

"I regret that the time was so terrible for you, but I'm afraid I must stand firm," Zirdon replied, again hiding amusement. The girl had failed to mention how strongly she'd responded after being so horribly put-upon, strongly enough that the men involved were eager to have a second opportunity with her. "If you'd really rather not agree, we can simply forget about the entire matter. Your favor won't get done, but that won't be so awful, will it?"

"Yes, it *would* be awful," she disagreed, but then her frown disappeared behind a sigh. "Oh, all right, I'll pay your price. But there won't be as *many* as there were last time, please say there won't be."

"Of course there won't be," Zirdon assured her after her

grudging agreement, his amusement increasing. In point of fact there would be quite a few more, but that was something else she would not remember afterward. He also had one or two servants to reward, servants who spent their time in other households than his own . . .

"Well, at least that's something," she allowed with a sniff, then made herself more comfortable in the chair before looking at him with her head to one side. "Now that the most important question has been taken care of, I have another that's made me very curious. When your man came to find out who was calling, he never once looked at my face. I had to tell him who I was, and that was rather annoying. Is something wrong with him?"

"No, actually, something is finally right," Zirdon told her with a smile as he gestured for tea to be served. "Leesto had a habit of staring at me, as though trying to guess what I might be thinking, and I found it extremely annoying. He also didn't show anyone the proper respect, bowing even to me in a way that suggested he'd probably gotten above himself. So I had him beaten soundly to show exactly what his position really is, and then I promised to have his eyes taken out if I ever found his gaze resting on me again. Apparently he finds it easier to keep his gaze from everyone as well as from me."

"Well, I don't like it," Sheedra said, accepting a cup of tea from one of the servants. Another had brought a cup to Zirdon, and he sipped from it immediately. Just once his tea had been hotter than he cared for, but certainly not a second time.

"Can't you insist that your man look at everyone *but* you?" Sheedra continued after sipping at her own tea. "That might make things more difficult for him, but at least then he won't be so annoying."

"I've been considering doing that very thing," Zirdon admitted, reaching for her hand again. "If Leesto slips I'll have to have his eyes taken out, of course, but then the fault will be his and my visitors won't find themselves annoyed. I should make up my mind in another day or two, but at the moment there's something I'm much more interested in. Unfortunately there isn't much time, as an assembly meeting has been called for later this afternoon."

"You mean you want me *now*?" Sheedra asked, as though she'd never considered the possibility. "But you didn't send for me, I came on my own."

"Yes you did, my sweet, but seeing you has given me the urge to taste you," Zirdon explained patiently. "The last two times you came without being sent for, I was engaged in important business and couldn't indulge myself. But don't you remember that the time before that wasn't the same?"

"Oh, yes, it wasn't, was it?" Sheedra granted with a vague look in her lovely eyes. "That was weeks ago, so I'd nearly forgotten. But I have an appointment in a little while that I really can't miss. Some of my friends and I have heard that that new eating parlor has incredibly good food, and we've decided to find out for ourselves. I told everyone I'd be there, so I can't possibly show up late or not at all."

"Of course you can," Zirdon disagreed, putting his teacup aside and taking hers before standing and drawing her up to her feet. "You'll be with *me*, after all, and that should increase your standing among your friends a good deal more than joining them in an eating parlor, don't you think?"

"Why, yes, it will," she answered with a revelation that suggested the point had never occurred to her before, which it may well not have. "You're perfectly right, Zirdon, just as you always are. But you're not in *that* much of a hurry, are you? The longer I'm here, the better it should look."

"I'll have you back again tomorrow, and keep you overnight," Zirdon promised, gesturing to one of his servants to begin undressing her. He would enjoy her right there, on the wide and armless lounge he kept in the room for the purpose, and then he would send her on her way. He really did need to attend that meeting, and there was no reason to be late when he could have the woman any time he pleased. *She* might not end up completely satisfied but he certainly would, and that was the important thing . . .

*   *   *

Antrie Lorimon looked at her visitor with her brows raised, but the man didn't seem to be impressed. He shook his head in annoyance and gestured with one big hand.

"Please don't pretend to be surprised by what I just told you," Cleemor Gardan said in his usual growl. "You know as well as I do that Zirdon Tal expects to have the entire assembly in the palm of his hand someday soon, so we might as well mention the fact aloud. Refraining from speaking the words won't keep him from making every effort to complete his plans."

"But speaking the words aloud *can* lose us the support of those who don't know Zirdon as well as we do," Antrie pointed out mildly. "You're not a novice in the game of politics, Cleemor, so why do you insist on acting like one?"

"What I'm acting like is a worried man, Antrie, and that's because I *am* one," Cleemor corrected with a shake of his head. "I just found out that Zirdon has somehow acquired two more members for his coalition, and that gives him a total of seven votes. One more and he outnumbers *us*, three more and he has the necessary two-thirds to do anything he pleases."

"Cleemor, you really must calm down," Antrie scolded gently and softly. They sat outside in her garden and ought to be able to see anyone trying to eavesdrop, but certain happenings still managed to find their way to the wrong ears. "You're acting like a Fire magic talent instead of someone who has Air magic just as I do. If you'll get control of yourself, I'll tell you exactly how Zirdon got those additional two members."

"You know how he did it?" Cleemor demanded loudly before he controlled himself. "I apologize for that, my dear, but you startled me. My people have been trying to find out, but they haven't learned a thing."

"That's because Zirdon is guarding himself against your efforts, and also because you're a man," Antrie returned with a small part of the amusement she felt. "Zirdon tends to underestimate *me*, and his victims aren't too shame-faced to let *my* people find out the truth. My people aren't other men who might laugh, after all."

"Yes, I know your people are women, even if I *don't* know who they are," Cleemor commented dryly. "So what was it that they learned?"

"Apparently Zirdon is using Sheedra Kam to entice certain of our assembly members," Antrie said with a shake of her head. "The girl might have the intelligence of a shoe, but the rest of her attributes seem to make up for the lack. Ever since Zirdon claimed her first, quite a lot of the men in the assembly have been reportedly sitting on the edge of their chairs, so to speak."

"And now Zirdon makes it possible for them to take seat elsewhere," Cleemor growled, his broad face wearing a disgusted look. "I can't believe they'd give up their autonomy just to tumble a piece of fluff like Sheedra Kam."

"That's because you have a woman you're in love with," Antrie pointed out, still keeping her comments mild. "Most of the others don't, so they're vulnerable to the looks of a girl who can't be had except through someone else's permission. But it isn't really anything to worry about, as that particular tool of Zirdon's is about to be taken out of his hands."

"Excuse me?" Cleemor asked, abruptly pulled out of the fuming anger he'd been submerged in. "What do you mean, he's about to lose the girl? What could you possibly have done aside from arranging her death?"

"Why kill the girl when you can have her married off instead?" Antrie asked, now showing a bit more of her amusement. "Zirdon's claim on her will no longer be valid once her engagement is announced, and that's due to be done later today. The young man is from a rather influential family and is downright handsome, but he also hasn't a brain in his head or anything to speak of in the way of talent. That's why Sheedra isn't yet married, by the way. Her talent is so weak that suitors have been conspicuous by their absence despite her looks. Her intended was in the same position with girls refusing *his* suit, but now both sets of parents agree that the match is perfect."

"And I'll wager none of them knows that *you're* the one responsible for the perfection," Cleemor said with a delighted laugh. "I should have remembered that you find cold-blooded murder distasteful."

"It's distasteful only when it's completely unnecessary," Antrie corrected with a smile. "I won't say I didn't have the help of my Blending in arranging matters so tidily, but the situation was a perfect one to take advantage of. This way the only resentment and antipathy will come from Zirdon, who already dislikes and resents us."

"A reaction like that from him couldn't make me happier," Cleemor commented with his own smile. "Far too often, it's been the other way about. Now all we need is more luck than usual in the monthly testings. The Middle talents of Zirdon's Blending—and those of his closest allies—are still stronger than the ones in our own Blendings. If we can find members stronger than his, our positions will be much more favorable."

"Assuming we continue to retain those positions," Antrie felt it necessary to point out. "I'm told that we'll be facing some formidable contenders this coming quarter, young Highs who have been dreaming all their adult lives of becoming the major talent in an assembly Blending. I'm also told that even Zirdon isn't feeling quite as comfortable as he used to."

"That could be because those . . . accidents last quarter are being guarded against now," Cleemor said with a mirthless laugh. "It was impossible not to notice that an entire group of very promising Highs in Fire magic drowned when that excursion boat sank, but no one can point the finger of proof at Zirdon. The same, of course, goes for the unexpected illness which struck down that group of Spirit magic users."

"Even though Zirdon's two strongest supporters have Spirit magic," Antrie agreed. "Yes, it does look as if he's trying to maintain himself in power using something other than talent, but I'm not quite convinced he's as guilty as he seems. It isn't beyond him to kill all those young Highs, but I can't dismiss the feeling that he would have been more . . . subtle."

"I hadn't thought of that," Cleemor said, and this time it

was *his* brows that were raised. "But if Zirdon isn't responsible for those contrived accidents and we aren't, then who could it be?"

"Someone out to displace the leadership of both of our coalitions," Antrie replied with a shrug. "If people come around to believing that Zirdon is the guilty party, then he'll be removed from his place by superior force. Once he's gone beyond recalling, it could be pointed out that the 'accidents' weren't subtle enough for Zirdon to have been guilty."

"And then *you'll* be the one the people go after, for having framed Zirdon," Cleemor growled with a headshake. "Yes, I can see it happening, even if it goes the other way about. People become convinced that Zirdon is being framed, so they go after his strongest rival. Once you're well out of the way, the suggestion is made that Zirdon was responsible after all but acted in a way that made *you* look guilty. That would take care of *him*, and then whoever is really behind all this would be free to take over completely. So what are we going to do about it?"

"There's not much we *can* do until we find out who's behind the attempt," Antrie told him, trying not to show how annoyed she'd become. "My people haven't been able to find out a thing, and although I have a suspect or two I can't confirm the suspicions. All I can do is watch my back, and I suggest that you do the same."

"As if I'm not already doing that," Cleemor returned sourly. "I feel like a fool for not having doubted Zirdon's guilt even for a moment, and as soon as I get home I'll get my people started on an investigation. Maybe they can turn up something that everyone else has missed."

"I sincerely hope they can," Antrie agreed as she watched Cleemor finish his tea in a single swallow and then stand. " 'The enemy who faces you is never as dangerous as the one who creeps up from behind,' an old saying but a very true one."

"Unfortunately yes," Cleemor growled as he bowed. "I'll see you later at the meeting, of course."

"Of course," Antrie confirmed. "You didn't think I'd take to hiding out, did you?"

"Of course not," Cleemor returned dryly. "I can't in any way picture you *being* that accommodating, even if there were High talents waiting for you in ambush every foot of the way. I never thought I'd worry more about a woman's safety than my own, but now I have two women I worry about. I'm seriously considering refusing to meet another female for the rest of my life."

Antrie chuckled as he bowed again, and then she watched the man as he headed for the walk that circled her house to where his carriage waited in the drive. He disappeared from sight without looking back even once, a clear indication of how disturbed he was.

"Well, he has a good deal of company in being disturbed," Antrie murmured, no longer amused. Cleemor was the first of her allies that she'd shared her suspicions with, but he certainly would not be the last. It had become perfectly clear that there was a new player in the game, someone who had to be identified as quickly as possible before the question became moot.

"I wonder who the newcomer will go after first, me or Zirdon?" Antrie wondered aloud as she reached for her teacup. She wasn't as unworried as she'd led Cleemor to believe, but showing a lack of confidence would cause her to lose her allies so fast it would make everyone's head swim. Assembly politics wasn't a game for the faint of heart, and she had enough counts against her simply from being a woman. Men still outnumbered women in the assembly, and many of those men still discounted women completely.

And that circumstance suggested the new player might be a woman. Antrie sipped at her tea slowly, hoping it didn't prove to be so. Men in the empire of Gracely might be ignorant about how dangerous women could be, but Antrie wasn't. Women were much more dangerous than men, especially a woman who had hidden herself behind the screen of male prejudice. That could be why Antrie's people hadn't found anything yet . . .

"But we'd better find something soon," Antrie muttered

as she returned her teacup to the hand table beside her chair. "*Before* whoever it is makes a move we can't counter . . ."

Not a pleasant thought, Antrie acknowledged silently as she got to her feet. But there was still that meeting to attend, one she couldn't afford to miss. It was an unscheduled meeting, and there was always a reason for ones like that. Too bad she *couldn't* hide out . . .

EIGHT

Ebro Syant sat at the desk in his study, considering his plans. He was a short, overweight man with ordinary brown hair and dull brown eyes, a High's strength in Earth magic his only redeeming feature. His peers in the assembly considered him a mouse of a man and not terribly bright, and that was the best camouflage he could possibly have. As the major talent in his Blending he ruled with an iron fist, but no one beyond his Blendingmates knew that and *they* weren't about to tell anyone. Couldn't have even if they'd wanted to . . .

A smile curved Ebro's lips at that thought, along with another just as amusing. He always covered his tracks carefully when he acted out of character, but he'd discovered that it wasn't necessary to make people *forget* what he'd done as long as they weren't able to talk about it. Afterward Ebro was able to watch those people as others dismissed him as unimportant, enjoying the way his victims squirmed about wishing they could tell the truth about him.

But they couldn't tell the truth, not under any circumstance, which assured Ebro's continuing amusement as well as his safety—with the ones who survived, that is.

"That foolish girl," Ebro murmured, shaking his head with a sound of annoyance. He'd claimed her as he'd had every right to do, and she'd come to his bed showing all the disdain a really beautiful woman always felt toward a short, stupid, pillow of a man. He'd then used his Blending to take over her mind and will, allowing her awareness of what was done to her without also allowing her the will to refuse. She *had* struggled, of course, just the way he wanted her to, but her struggles had been a waste of effort. She'd been allowed to struggle, but not to free herself.

Ebro had enjoyed himself with the girl as often as possible, knowing the second time he summoned her that she'd tried to tell someone about what he'd done. The effort would have made her heart beat wildly as she choked on the words she would have spoken, and only giving up the effort would have returned her to normal. Her faint pallor and slight unsteadiness had told him the story, and he'd scolded her gently about not trying the same thing again before he'd taken his enjoyment.

At first the lovely little dear had been certain that her torment would soon be ended when she became engaged to be married. She had three suitors vying for her hand, and her father was about to decide whose suit to accept. When the first suitor withdrew his suit, the girl was completely unsuspecting. When the second withdrew, she became concerned and faintly suspicious. When the third and last withdrew, the girl finally understood that Ebro had no intention of allowing her to escape him.

So the stupid little fool committed suicide by refusing to stop trying to tell people what was happening. Ebro had pretended to be devastated by her death, but in full truth he'd been extremely annoyed. The girl had not only denied him the pleasure of *her* use, but now Ebro had to be extremely careful not to cause a second such incident. One tragedy is easily overlooked, but two of the same kind brings suspicion from the worst possible quarters.

"And it isn't yet time to let them know who's standing in the shadows," Ebro murmured, again examining his plans mentally to search out the least and smallest flaw. "My greatest weakness is arrogance, and although I've learned to guard against it I must remain ever vigilant. It would never do to let people in on the secret too soon."

No, that would certainly never do, Ebro thought as he left his chair and walked to one of the large windows his study boasted. If there was any lesson he'd learned well in life, that was the one. His parents had doted on him because of his quick mind when he'd been a small child, but once it became obvious that he would be short and his body would run to slight obesity, their doting turned to scorn. The way he looked became *his* fault, and his father's disappointment turned into tormenting at every opportunity.

Ebro had found himself furious at being treated like that, and when it became clear that the situation would never reverse itself he began his plans to get even. He was a mere teenager at the time and a small one at that, but his mind proved itself larger and stronger than those around him. He gained his revenge against his father, making the stupid man look as foolish as he really was, but then arrogance caused Ebro to make the biggest mistake of his life. He came out and *told* his father who was responsible for the man's embarrassment.

Even now Ebro automatically put his right hand to his left shoulder, unfading memory bringing back the unbearable pain of the beating he'd been given. His father had been rabidly furious, and the riding crop he'd used on Ebro's back had ended up covered with blood. Ebro had quickly lost consciousness during the beating, but he awoke to find that that hadn't stopped his father. Ebro's back was a mass of raw meat, and his parents had even refused to call a healer. They didn't want *anyone* to know that Ebro had been the one responsible for their difficulties . . .

So Ebro had had to heal slowly, on his own without the aid of a healer. His ability in Earth magic had helped to a certain extent, but he'd been little more than a child, completely untrained in healing and not yet at his full strength. He'd been able to keep the wounds on his back from becoming infected, but he hadn't even been able to dull all the pain. It had seemed like forever before he was even able to breathe normally without hurting terribly . . .

"But I did learn a lesson from that," Ebro murmured to the lovely day outside his window. "My parents eventually talked themselves into believing that I'd been 'lucky' when I'd embarrassed them, and had possibly even taken credit that wasn't due me. Years later, when my father was financially ruined, it was perfectly clear that his greatest business rival was to blame. Neither of my parents even glanced in my direction . . ."

Another smile turned Ebro's lips, a smile that remained for a time. When Ebro displaced the former major talent of his Blending and took the man's place in the assembly, his parents had actually come to beg his financial help. He'd given that help immediately, of course, but for some reason nothing his father did lifted him and his wife out of the poverty they hated so much. It was almost as though some agency worked against the man to keep him no more than a step or two above the condition of beggar . . .

A knock came at his study door, so Ebro quickly swallowed his amusement and called out permission to enter. Many of his peers in the assembly used bells to indicate and allow entry, but that would have meant having a servant near him at all times. There were too many occasions when Ebro needed to be alone, so he pretended to be too lumpish to take up the practice.

"Exalted One, you asked to be told when it was time to leave for the assembly meeting," his chief servant announced with a bow once he'd opened the door. "It's nearly that time, and your carriage awaits you at the front of the house."

"Tell my driver that I'll be right down," Ebro directed after a slight hesitation, as though he'd forgotten having given the order and wasn't quite sure how to reply. The servant bowed himself out and closed the door again, leaving Ebro to smile as he went to his bedchamber to change clothes. Even his servants considered him a nonentity, and that was just the way he wanted it.

Changing into a fresh shirt and adding a coat didn't take

long, and then Ebro went down to his carriage. The driver helped him inside, then drove him to the assembly building in the middle of the city. Ebro's house, on its small estate, wasn't far from the building, and neither were the houses of the other assembly members. The arrangement made attending meetings convenient for the major talents of each Blending.

As usual, Ebro arrived neither too early nor too late. No one noticed him as he puffed his way inside to his assigned seat and writing ledge and gratefully sat down. The leader of the coalition he'd long ago formed a loose association with, Zirdon Tal, was already there, standing with his strongest supporters. Tal was a large, well-built man with lightish hair and eyes, his regular features turning his face into one that attracted women and encouraged friendship in men. Tal had even pretended to be friendly toward the lumpish Ebro Syant, but the attempt hadn't lasted beyond Ebro's agreement to the association with Tal.

Ebro looked around as he caught his breath, quickly locating Tal's major opponent in the assembly, Antrie Lorimon. The woman was small, dark, and rather pretty, with a smoothness of manner that never insulted anyone. No one else seemed to have noticed the look in the woman's brown eyes, the same look Ebro saw in his own when he dropped the pretense of being a nonentity in private. Antrie Lorimon was highly intelligent and very much a force to be reckoned with, despite the fact that she allowed Cleemor Gardan to do most of the talking for their coalition.

A low buzz of conversation tinged with anticipation rolled about the large, round meeting room as it filled to its capacity of fifteen major attendees and their advisors. Ordinary citizens also filled many of the places behind the circle of seats reserved for the assembly members. The interest of the ordinary people ranged from simple curiosity to a hope that something would be said to give those individuals an edge over business rivals. The remaining members of each Blending were, of course, left in the residence of the major talents they worked with. If their presence became necessary, they could always be sent for.

Once the last assembly member arrived, a man named Frode Mismin moved to the center of the room and held up his hands to request quiet. Mismin was the head of the assembly's special investigations branch, and had the power to convene the assembly when something of national importance happened. The man's ugly, square-cut face wore a sober expression, which did more to quiet everyone than his gesture.

"I've had word from a number of my agents in our neighboring empire of Gandistra," Mismin said as everyone still standing began to settle into a seat. "Things have changed there in a way you all need to hear about."

People exchanged glances with their brows raised, but no one was foolish enough to demand answers they would soon be given.

"Thank you," Mismin said, referring to the close attention he was now being paid. "As you all know, the nobility in Gandistra intended to again Seat their own choice of a Blending, as they've been doing for the last century or so. The effort started out well enough, but their chosen Blending was destroyed in the first round of challenges, so they had to settle for the sole remaining noble Blending. They reluctantly helped that five to win over the common Blending they faced—which was about to best the noble Blending—but they lived to regret their decision. Or should I say, most of them *didn't* live to regret it."

A soft murmur eddied through the room, one Ebro would have contributed to if he hadn't been watching himself as closely as he usually did. The nobles in Gandistra were being decimated? What would that do to their long-standing policies of expansion?

"The new noble Blending was Seated, but that didn't last very long," Mismin continued into instant silence. "The common Blending that had nearly defeated them had been separated rather than killed, a stupid move on the part of stupid people. The members of that common Blending reunited, recruited a large number of supporters, and eventually returned to defeat the noble Blending."

"Where did their supporters come from?" Cleemor Gar-

dan asked, pretending that the question was his rather than
Antrie Lorimon's. "Were they ordinary people that the five
simply came across?"

"Not quite," Mismin responded, his tone rather dry.
"They freed members of the Gandistran army, both members not yet in the army and those who were fleeing from
the forces in Astinda. It seems that Astinda had finally gotten around to replying to the invasion of their country."

"So Gandistra and Astinda are now openly at war," Zirdon Tal put in with his usual smooth friendliness. "That's
an occasion for celebration here in Gracely if I ever heard
one."

"Celebration would be premature, Exalted One," Mismin
said at once, throwing cold water on everyone's newborn
excitement. "The common Blending first defeated the
Seated noble five, then went on to somehow make peace
with the Astindans bent on revenge. The common Blending's people gathered up all members of the nobility still
left in Gan Garee, and the Astindans are now in the process
of taking those former nobles back to Astinda to work to
reclaim the decimated land there."

"It's a shame there won't be war between those two, but
so far I see no reason for your gloominess, Frode," Tal
commented with a smile to take all possible sting from his
words. "The common Blending will rid themselves of hated
nobility the easy way, and once they're Seated they'll form
their own nobility. Matters there will continue on just as
they always have."

"I'm afraid not, Exalted One," Mismin said with a slow
shake of his head. "To begin with, my people have reported
that the common Blending has already allowed other
Blendings to be formed. From now on there won't be just
a single Blending in Gandistra, and on top of that the commoners apparently intend to train *all* their people in the
use of their various talents. From our point of view, they
couldn't have done worse if they'd tried."

This time the comments and exclamations were far
louder than mere murmurs, and even Ebro cursed under his
breath. The restrictions in Gandistra against the use of talent

had been a great source of comfort to the citizens and leaders of Gracely, and now those restrictions were about to end. This couldn't possibly have happened at a worse time, and Ebro had to struggle so hard to keep from showing his true feelings that he almost missed the next question.

"Excuse me, Frode, but what about the 'invading army' sent here to Gracely?" Antrie Lorimon asked, not bothering to put the question through Cleemor Gardan. "Have they been forgotten about in all the confusion, I hope?"

"No such luck, Exalted One," Mismin answered with a grimace. "That Seated noble Blending ordered the army home before the Blending was defeated, and the army was on its way and out of reach before anyone knew what was happening. The army was supposed to head west, I'm told, but the nobles leading the army decided their duty lay in 'defending Gan Garee.' In other words, they were hurrying home to defend their own property and fortunes."

"Well, that isn't likely to hurt us in any way," Tal decided aloud after a moment. "No one in that army knows what we did to them, so they can't accidentally mention it at the wrong time to the wrong people. Once they get back to Gan Garee, they'll either be destroyed or else take charge. Either condition will suit us nicely, but we do have a decision or two to make. If the commoners win again, shall we send a furious delegation demanding reparations for the damage done our property, or a nervous delegation all but begging for a peace treaty?"

Other members of the assembly began to make audible comments then, but Ebro listened with only half an ear. He'd meant to make his move against Zirdon Tal and Antrie Lorimon in a little while, but now a postponement would be necessary. Inexperienced replacements of the two leaders would be easier for *him* to handle, but then the coalitions would be far too likely to stand together in the face of the Gandistra problem. Ebro needed the coalition members squabbling and trying to stab each other in the back, not cooperating against a possible common enemy.

Keeping nothing but the usual dull, blank expression on his face, Ebro reluctantly leaned back to listen to what was being suggested as the best way to approach the new leaders of Gandistra. When his own plans worked out, the approach would no longer be even a small problem. But first his own plans had to work out, and as much as he detested the delay he would simply have to accept it . . .

Cleemor Gardan walked out of the assembly building with a very silent Antrie Lorimon. He'd known Antrie long enough to recognize the signs, so he waited until they were all but walking alone before speaking.

"All right, what have I missed *this* time?" Cleemor murmured, trying to keep his usual growl from traveling to the closest ears. "Something is bothering you badly, but I don't know what it can be."

"Actually, there are two things bothering me," Antrie admitted with a sigh, glancing up at him. He always felt too large and blocky beside the small, delicate, and graceful woman, but his size never seemed to disturb *her*. "You heard what Frode said, just as I did. That common Blending took supporters from intended and actual members of their army."

"Yes, I did hear that," Cleemor agreed cautiously. "What about it?"

"Two things about it," Antrie responded, her expression remaining more than sober. "The first point is something I'm sure you know, but have probably forgotten. In Gandistra, the challenging Blendings were all made up of High talents even though the Seated Blending never had anything but Middles."

"But—that means the common Blending now in control is composed of all Highs," Cleemor protested, suddenly alarmed. "The rest of *our* Blendings are just strong Middles, and that puts us at a very great disadvantage."

"More than that," Antrie added with a sigh. "Their followers also have to be Highs, since they were people meant to be added to their army. There's no doubt that the army sent *here* was mostly Highs with some strong Middles, all but their leaders, of course. That makes the situation considerably worse than Zirdon obviously considers it."

"So what sort of delegation to send is the least of our worries," Cleemor said, forcing himself not to exclaim aloud. "What we really need to do is think of a way to keep those people out of Gracely, or come up with a way to deal with them if they don't stay out. We may also have to exchange the Middle members of our Blendings for actual Highs."

"Taking Highs into our Blendings will never work," Antrie disagreed with a headshake. "Every High dreams of facing one of us and winning a place in the assembly for themselves, and it happens often enough that newcomers aren't discouraged. How many of them do you think will give up that dream? Enough to fill out a full fifteen Blendings? I really don't think so, and if all Blendings can't be filled out, no one can allow any of them to be."

"No, not when that one High Blending would probably try at once to take over," Cleemor agreed with a sigh. "No one in the assembly would be willing to take the chance, so that option is a dead issue. It seems that our only other choice is to make sure that the new rulers of Gandistra never set foot in Gracely."

"That may not be possible," Antrie said, the continuing worry in her eyes disturbing Cleemor even more. "That common Blending didn't destroy the members of the army they encountered, it freed them to be followers. If it does the same with the members of the army that was *here*, it could conceivably learn something we don't want Gandistra to know."

"Yes, and we can thank Zirdon for that," Cleemor growled, no longer caring if anyone heard him. "What we did was *his* brilliant idea, an idea he forced through when most of the rest of us wanted to destroy that army. Now we're faced with the consequences of that action, but Zirdon won't be the only one harmed because of them."

"I'm sorry I didn't oppose him more strongly," Antrie said with her own sigh. "The main reason I didn't was that he had a very valid point. If we destroyed the army, as soon as the nobles in Gan Garee found out they would have sent a larger, stronger force. That was a foregone conclusion, so the best idea seemed to be to let the army send back reports of success while in reality it did absolutely nothing. If we'd known that the nobles would soon be too concerned with saving their necks to send anyone at all— But we didn't know, so I don't see what else we could have done."

"Well, now we have to come up with an else," Cleemor said. "And it had better be really good, or we might find ourselves in quite a lot of trouble. The only luck we've had in this whole mess is that we've only firmed up our plans to invade Gandistra, and haven't yet put them into practice."

"I doubt if that will help us if the new rulers of that empire find out about the plans," Antrie pointed out dryly as she stopped not far from the waiting line of carriages. "Everyone here in Liandia knows about those plans, which means that *someone* will say the wrong thing at the wrong time. Even accepting an embassy from Gandistra will probably end in disaster."

"So we'll have to tell the others about this as soon as possible," Cleemor grumbled. "But we'd better start with our own people first, or they'll begin to believe we're keeping secrets from them."

"No, they already believe we're keeping secrets," Antrie corrected dryly. "This would just confirm that belief. If you'll take care of informing our supporters, I'll be the one to explain it to the entire assembly tomorrow during the meeting Zirdon called. He expects to discuss what sort of delegation to send to Gandistra, and won't look good when it's pointed out how much of the critical picture he's missed."

"And he'll look even worse when it's a lowly woman doing the pointing out," Cleemor added with a chuckle. "Between that and his loss of Sheedra Kam as a toy to be loaned out, we ought to pick up at least two or three of his current supporters."

"I'm hoping for four, which will reduce him to being no more than a nuisance," Antrie said very softly while making sure that no one overheard her. "We can't afford to have serious opposition at a time like this, not when our positions and possibly even our lives are at stake. Let's not forget what that common Blending did to rid itself of the nobles. If we aren't very, very careful, the same thing could happen to us."

"I'll be sure to mention that when I speak to our people," Cleemor promised, suddenly feeling the least bit pale. "I'll caution them all not to say a word until we get to the meeting tomorrow, and then the impact of the revelation won't be softened. And I'll also have my people look around for whoever might be after you and Zirdon both. We need to know who that is as soon as humanly possible."

"To keep them from acting at the worst time for all of us," Antrie agreed with a nod. "I've already set my own people on the problem, so hopefully we'll learn *something*. And soon enough to avert disaster. Give my love to your wife, Cleemor, and we'll speak again tomorrow before the meeting."

Cleemor bowed as he watched Antrie walk away toward her carriage, but his thoughts were filled with worry, both for himself and his beloved wife Tenia. Something had to be done to keep all of them from going down in ruin, but at the moment not a single plan came to mind. Well, if it became necessary, he wasn't above arranging the deaths of two or more members of that common Blending they'd been discussing. What good that would do, Cleemor didn't know, but as he walked to his own carriage he silently admitted that he also didn't care.

Doing something was better than doing nothing, especially if it meant the possible protection of the woman Cleemor loved more than life itself . . .

NINE

"Are you sure we're doing the right thing?" Lorand asked, not only me but everyone else in the Blending as well. "I mean, just walking out like this?"

"If we don't, we might as well put the slave chains on ourselves instead of waiting for *them* to do it," I pointed out, trying not to sound too impatient and short tempered. "I didn't risk my life time and time again just to end.up working under the thumb of a fool. We'd be doing things *his* way, not ours, and we'd probably be better off with the nobles."

We'd gathered in my wing of the palace this morning, and now that breakfast was over we were getting ready to leave. We'd all packed up some of our clothing, and would send for the rest of it once we were settled back into my house.

"She's right, love," Jovvi told Lorand gently with a hand to his arm. "I know how you feel about walking away from your responsibilities, but Relton Henris has made it impossible for us to stay. As Tamma said, if we did stay we'd be doing things Henris's way rather than ours."

"And besides bein' a fool, the man has too many blind spots," Vallant put in from next to me. "Thinkin' there's no real difference between Middle talents and Highs is dangerous as well as stupid, and knowin' that about him tells me he's stupid about other things as well."

"And it seems that we're *supposed* to do this," Naran added, her expression as sympathetic as it usually was. "At this point we really have no other viable choice, not if we're going to make a true difference. If we allow any restrictions on us, we'll spend our time arguing rather than doing."

"All right, I surrender," Lorand admitted with both hands held up, palms out. "I can see that even Rion agrees with you, so in this instance my feelings must be wrong. And I have to agree that our staying won't help if we aren't allowed to continue on as *we* see fit."

"Not to mention the fact that they think they can keep Naran from being a part of our Blending," I finished up as I stood. "I'll *never* allow something like that, and besides, I've always wanted to be an outlaw."

"An outlaw?" Rion echoed with brows high as he and the others followed my example and got to their feet. "Why in the world would you think we would end up being outlaws?"

"It stands to reason," I explained patiently, pausing on the way to where I'd left my one piece of luggage. "If someone Henris and his cronies approve of gets to run things, having Naran with us won't be the only thing they'll declare illegal. Training people in the proper use of magic will also be disallowed, because whoever takes over won't be able to control things if it isn't. But spreading the word about how to use magic properly is necessary, so I'll continue to do it no matter what. The rest of you will probably do the same, and that will make us outlaws."

"Now I see," Lorand said ruefully as Rion sighed and simply nodded. "I've never had the urge to be an outlaw, but it looks like it will end up being my ultimate career choice. Will they just lock us up, or decide in the end to execute us?"

"They'll be too busy with the riots to spend much attention on *us*," Naran commented, and the way she stared into empty air said she wasn't simply guessing. "If they try to take over in our place and do things according to their own beliefs and desires, they'll tear the whole empire apart starting with Gan Garee. But that's just one possibility among many, so don't think it *has* to come to be."

"And no, we can't do anything to change their minds if

we stay here," I said as Lorand opened his mouth again.
"As long as they think we'll handle things until they can
wear us down into agreeing with their demands, they won't
make a single effort to change their stance. That army heading in this direction is probably the best thing that could
have happened right now."

"It will put things in perspective for them," Vallant said
as he picked up my bag as well as his own. "Right now
they're seein' runnin' things as nothin' but handin' out orders. When they find out how much more there is, they just
might start seein' reason."

"I hope they see it soon enough to keep that army from
walking in and taking over for the nobles again," Lorand
muttered as he picked up Jovvi's bag in addition to his own.
"If they don't, it will just make things harder for *us*."

"If necessary, we'll step in before that happens," Jovvi
assured him with a smile. "Our associate Blendings know
we won't go to unreasonable extremes while this disagreement is going on, so they won't offer Henris a way out of
the dilemma by agreeing to help."

"Look, I really do know all this, so I apologize for making you all say it," Lorand blurted, looking around at us
with unhappiness clear in his eyes. "It's just that . . ."

"It's just that you're too decent a person not to protest a
little," I finished when he let his words trail off, moving
close to lean up and kiss his cheek. "We know that, love,
so don't let it bother you. And now it's time we got going."

Rion had claimed his and Naran's luggage, so I led the
way out of my wing toward the palace entrance. Or the
exit, as it happened to be. The servants in my wing had
stared at us with confusion in their eyes, but they hadn't
said anything and made no attempt to stop us. The same,
however, didn't hold true for the crowd we found waiting
in the public part of the palace. Everyone from the city
who had been at the party the night before seemed to be
there, along with a few people extra.

"There, you see?" Lavrit Mohr exclaimed even as he
sketched a bow in our direction, the Guild High Master
standing at the front of the crowd. "I told you they meant

what they said last night and really would leave. Obviously you're wrong again, Henris."

"Just because they're carrying luggage doesn't mean they intend to leave," Henris came back, stubbornness in the set of his broad shoulders. "As a matter of fact, I'll bet those bags are all empty."

"Guess again," Vallant said as I bristled, stepping forward before I could. "Daylight hasn't made you any less of a fool, Henris, and fools always need to be shown the error of their ways."

And with that he dropped my bag on Henris's feet, making the shop owners consortium head howl and stumble back. Everyone else in the crowd laughed with true amusement, and that made Henris furious.

"Obviously you knew I was going to say that about the bags, so you all made sure to pack them," he snarled, sending a quick glare at Naran before returning his attention to Vallant. "I still say you're just bluffing, trying to force us into giving you permission to invade our private lives. That's not going to happen, so you might as well take that stuff back where it belongs and get on with doing what you're supposed to. That army is getting closer to us by the minute, and it's your job to stop it."

"It *would* be our job if we were the head of this empire," Vallant countered, holding the fool's gaze while others in the crowd muttered uneasily. "You've been makin' it clear that you consider *yourself* the head of the empire, so *you* take care of that army. We have private lives to get on with."

"But you can't just walk out on us," Rilna Zokill, the woman representing the disenfranchised, protested. "You know well enough that *we* can't do anything against that army, so it has to be you or one of the other Blendings. Some of us have already spoken to members of the other Blendings, but they refuse to do so much as listen. They said we have to straighten this out with *you*."

"That's because they all know we're strongest," I told the woman, doing nothing to hide my sense of satisfaction. "In this empire the strongest Blending has always ruled, and there's more to the circumstance than mere law. If you ever manage to become a member of a Blending yourself, you'll find out what I mean. But don't count on ever being part of a Blending if that fool Henris is allowed to take charge. The first thing he'll do is limit the practice and use of magic just the way the nobles did."

"But that's nonsense," Zokill said as the muttering came again from those in the crowd. "We've already been denied our abilities far too long, and Dom Henris would never—"

She broke off when she saw the expression on Henris's face, a mixture of anger and embarrassment. It was clear that Henris *did* intend that the practice and use of magic be limited, and once he realized that the matter was no longer his own little secret, he puffed himself up and tried to defend his position.

"It won't be anything *like* what the nobles did," he said, looking around at the crowd at the same time. "Just for now there will be too many other problems to take care of, so using magic more will just have to wait awhile. It won't be forever, just until things settle down, and then we'll have classes and everything."

"That's undoubtedly what the original members of the nobility said," Rion put in, letting his disgust show clearly. "What they really meant was they wanted time to form a strong enough guard force to make people toe *their* line, and that's probably what *you* mean as well. And even if it isn't, who are you going to get to run all those classes?"

"It won't be hard at all to get people to run classes," Henris blustered, carefully ignoring the first part of what Rion had said. "There are lots of people who are strong enough, and I may even run one of the classes myself."

"You?" Vallant challenged with a sound of scorn. "What could *you* teach people, aside from the nonsense you've been spoutin' last night and today? How much trainin' were *you* put through by the nobles callin' themselves Adepts?"

"I don't *need* any other training, because I've been training myself over the years," Henris growled, glaring angrily at Vallant. "There isn't anyone I know who's stronger in

Water magic than I am, and that certainly includes *you*! Why don't we step outside so I can prove what I say."

"You just proved the exact opposite," Vallant told him with a snort. "You want to go outside because there's too little moisture in the air in here for you, but I don't have that problem. If you're all that good, let's see how easy you find stoppin' *me*."

For an instant no one understood what Vallant meant, but then Henris cried out and we saw that all his clothing was suddenly dripping wet. Henris was furious, of course, especially when the people behind him started to laugh, and I could almost see him reaching for the power. If he hadn't been opened to the power before, the way most of the untrained tended to be, it was no wonder he thought he was all that strong. He hadn't been able to compare himself to someone with real strength . . .

"No, this isn't possible!" Henris shouted, still dripping wet. "For some reason I can't remove the water! It has to be a trick, that's what, it has to—"

His words broke off as he suddenly looked up to stare at Vallant, his mouth open and a look of shock on his face. It seemed hard to believe, but apparently Henris hadn't paid full attention to Vallant as my Blendingmate used the power. Right now, though, Vallant had every bit of the attention Henris was able to give, and the annoying man's mouth moved without any words coming out.

"I think you now have a better understandin' of what the difference between a High talent and a Middle talent is," Vallant told the shocked man dryly. "Why don't you try holdin' on to that water instead, while I work to get rid of it."

Henris nodded woodenly, but a moment later his clothing was as dry as it had been when he'd first arrived. Henris moaned as though in extreme pain, and Lavrit Mohr patted his shoulder.

"Don't be upset, Dom Henris," Mohr consoled him, his tone sympathetic. "You're certainly a very strong Middle, but the Excellence Vallant is a very strong High. In point of fact, as I've said more than once, the strongest High in

Water magic we've ever come across. There's nothing to be ashamed about in losing to him."

Henris stood with his head down and his eyes closed, the pallor of his skin telling the whole story. His entire world had been turned around and his beliefs shattered, and for the moment at least he no longer had what to say.

"You could have done a bit better against me if you knew which of the patterns to use," Vallant said to the man, as if they were still in the middle of a conversation. "But you've had no way of learnin' the patterns, and that's part of the whole problem. Too much has been lost because the people in power wanted to keep themselves safe by keepin' everyone else in ignorance."

"Their biggest mistake wasn't in keeping things secret," a thin man behind Henris commented, his expression calm but his eyes showing a sly greasiness. "Their foolishness was in not keeping and practicing all that knowledge themselves, which would have saved it from being lost. I think there are enough of us here to make sure it isn't lost a second time."

"It isn't going to happen that way," Jovvi said just as calmly, taking her turn at speaking before me. "You've just maneuvered almost everyone here into wanting to be part of the select group that knows and does things everyone else doesn't, but it isn't ever going to be like that. We'll teach what we know to everyone, not to a small group of those who consider themselves superior."

"Which you and your puppets don't happen to be," Naran added, her gaze unfocused again. "You're trying to push those you have control of into making themselves the leaders of the empire, but even if you do manage to accomplish it you and they won't last longer than weeks in power. You'll all go down in the riots you cause when you fail to handle the first serious challenge to your claims of leadership."

I noticed half a dozen faces in the crowd go pale, and Henris raised his head again with a frown. Naran had called the thin man's associates puppets, which probably meant he had Spirit magic. From Henris's expression, he had just realized that he was being used rather than leading on his own.

"No, don't bother trying to take control of them again," Jovvi said to the thin man with faint amusement. "Right now I'm shielding them, and in another minute or two you won't be able to use your talent to influence anyone ever again. But someone is really going to have to be on the alert for people like you, who force others into doing their dirty work. You cause far too much bother."

The thin man started to look furious—with intense fear shading the emotion, but then his expression smoothed out again. All slyness disappeared from his eyes, and he was left with a placidness that seemed to go down to the very center of him.

"Yes, that's much better," I commented with my own amusement. "And there really *has* been too much bother this morning, so let's put an end to it. Our horses should be saddled and waiting by now."

"No, you can't do that," Henris protested with one hand held up toward us. The man appeared to be a bit disjointed, but even if his heavy confidence was gone his brashness still seemed intact. "You can't just walk away and leave us helpless, we refuse to allow it. You have to do your job first, and then maybe—"

"*You* refuse to allow it?" I echoed, suddenly drowning in indignation. "Just who do you think you are, and who do you imagine you're talking to? If we were nobles you'd be on your knees begging, even if we were no stronger than you are yourself! But in your mind we're *commoners* and therefore unimportant, so you think you can say anything you please to us. Not once have we gotten even so much as a bow of courtesy from any of you, but you still expect us to go out and risk our lives for you again because you've decided it's our *job*. Well, it's *not* our job, because we've already handed in our resignation and because what you're asking for isn't part of a job but a position. Either we're in charge or we're not, and you've made it perfectly clear that in your opinion we're not. With that in mind, get out of my way before I *move* you out of my way."

"No, she's right," Rilna Zokill said in a loud voice as Henris and a number of others began to babble out their protests, turning to look at the crowd. "Would we have had the nerve to talk to a noble Blending the way we've been talking to *them?* I think we all know the answer to that, and the reason we've imposed on them so freely is that we all know them to be decent people. Instead of destroying us or taking us over as they could so easily have done, they argued with us. Now they're tired of arguing, so we're about to lose the best thing that's happened to this empire in more than a hundred years. I was a fool to go along with the rest of you, but I won't be a fool any longer."

With that she turned away from the crowd, glanced at the six of us, then very deliberately performed a deep and more than respectful curtsey.

"Excellences, on behalf of the people I represent, I humbly ask you to stay and be our leaders," she said, her head down and her body still in the curtsey. "I apologize sincerely for the foolishness I've shown, and I promise not to ever do the same again."

Many of the men in the crowd—and the sprinkling of women—looked shocked at that, but a moment later there were people pushing forward to add their own bows and curtsies. It took a short while, but with a handful of exceptions everyone in the crowd did the same. Even Relton Henris finally added a grudging bow, and no one said a word about there being terms and conditions. The handful of exceptions stalked off without looking back, and Jovvi stepped closer to me with a smile.

"Some of them aren't happy about the decision, but they're all in agreement," she murmured as she patted my arm. "We now have a *position* rather than a job, and it's all thanks to you. I think we can go back to our wings now."

"After I tell them one more thing," I murmured back, then raised my voice. "All right, we'll stay, but on one condition. You have to arrange for our immediate Seating as a sixfold Blending, but you can let people know that the Seating is only temporary. A year from now we'll be holding the challenges again, which ought to give everyone who's interested the chance to join a Blending and get in some practice. The winners of the challenges will be Seated on a permanent basis, but for five years instead of twenty-five. There will also be other changes, but we'll tell you about them some other time."

A few of the people who had straightened looked like they wanted to argue or ask questions, but for the most part they were too surprised over what they'd already heard. Aside from muttering to some of the people around him, Relton Henris actually kept his mouth closed, and the only one who looked completely delighted was Lavrit Mohr.

"Thank you, Excellences," he said with his own bow and a wide smile. "Everything you do strengthens my belief that you are indeed the Chosen Blending. Before long, everyone will share in that truth."

"I'd rather share some details about that army comin' from the east," Vallant put in dryly. "If we'll be goin' after them, we need to know as much as your people can tell us."

"I'll put a report together as quickly as possible, Excellence," Mohr agreed, giving Vallant a bow of his own. "I'll try to have it done by sometime this afternoon."

"When you come back, tell the guards to interrupt us even if we're in the middle of something," Lorand instructed Mohr, the first words he'd spoken in quite some time. "We'll tell them the same, so there won't be a delay in your reaching us."

"As you say, Excellence," Mohr agreed, also bowing to Lorand before he turned and hurried away. All that bowing was faintly annoying, but it had finally come through to me that if you didn't insist on being shown *some* deference, people tended to think they could walk all over you. That made the bowing necessary, but we'd have to see if there was something we could do to limit the practice.

"Since we're staying, we now have the time to go over all those transcripts and records I found in my wing," Lorand said to the rest of us, strong relief in his dark and pretty eyes. "Unless someone has something to do that's more important?"

"Now that our visitors are leavin', we ought to *take* the time," Vallant said after glancing at the slowly retreating backs of the people who had so recently made up the crowd. Most of them were talking or arguing softly with the people around them, but they *were* going. "Since we'll be leavin' soon, there's no knowin' when we'll have another chance."

Leaving to face that army from the east, he meant. We all knew we ought to have very little trouble stopping that army, but as we turned to follow Lorand back to his wing I wondered how much difference there would be between "ought to" and what we did have.

TEN

Lorand watched as the others, one by one, finished reading the transcripts he'd found. Under other circumstances he would probably have been wondering how his Blending-mates were taking what they'd read, but this time their expressions were eloquent.

"Those people were really horrible," Tamrissa said as she turned over the final page of the transcript she'd been reading, her pretty face troubled. "But I think I can almost understand how that Earth magic user felt about his parents, and that bothers me."

"Don't let it disturb you *too* badly," Jovvi told her at once, full understanding in her beautiful eyes. "That man was so badly twisted by what he'd gone through that he couldn't really act as a fully responsible human being. You may get pleasure out of thwarting your parents' plans, but that's not the same as what *he* did."

"And you *are* a fully responsible human being, otherwise the rest of us would know it," Naran pointed out in a gentle way. "Do I have to remind *you* how much Blending does to really let you get to know your Blendingmates?"

Tamrissa shook her head with a weak smile as she leaned into the comforting arm Vallant had put around her. Their Fire magic user was as strong as possible in her talent, but Lorand knew that she was far from also being what most people considered tough.

"Their Spirit magic user also seemed odd in some way," Rion put in, obviously trying to change the subject. "At first he struck me as being the only rational one in the group, but he did have that habit of talking to himself out loud when he was alone."

"I noticed that as well, and I have a theory," Jovvi said with a sigh, shifting in the chair she'd taken. "He used his grandmother's help in putting the three members of his Blending under control, but I think that *he* was under control as well. When his grandmother died the control began to unravel, making him unstable and unsure of what was happening. I have a feeling he wasn't talking to himself, Rion. I think he was reporting to his grandmother."

"What bothers *me* most about all this is a feelin' I've gotten," Vallant said as he shook his head. "Jovvi, am I wrong to believe that most if not all of those people would have been more like what's considered normal if they hadn't gone through all those horrors while growin' up?"

"There's no way to tell for certain, but I tend to have the same belief," Jovvi said, confirming Lorand's own feelings in the matter. "That's why I'm more anxious than ever to find a way to protect all children, especially those of our closest followers. A lot of our people will end up being wealthy, and the offspring of the wealthy tend to go to extremes to avoid the boredom of a life without struggle."

"And extremes too often include hurting even more children," Rion said with a nod as he rose to go to the tea service. "I still haven't thought of anything myself, but I refuse to believe that the effort is hopeless."

Lorand found the fact that no one answered or commented aloud depressing, since he hadn't thought of any answers either.

"I've been reading one of the journals I found," Lorand said into the silence, attempting his own change of subject. "The man lived about a hundred and fifty years ago, and his bitterest complaint was that his Blending didn't get to practice enough together. He was sure their entity couldn't do half of what was possible a hundred years earlier, but the Blending's 'advisors' constantly told them not to Blend unless it was absolutely necessary. The advisors claimed that their Blending made people uneasy, and doing something like that wasn't wise."

"Right, and we know who they were makin' most uneasy," Vallant commented dryly. "Those noble advisors couldn't have all the control they wanted if the Seated Five Blended, so they spent a lot of time discouragin' the practice. That's a point everyone in this job ought to know about."

"For now *we're* the ones who need to know about it, and we do," Tamrissa told him with a smile. "So far we haven't done too badly keeping ourselves from being limited, but we can't let people make us think we're being unreasonable. We have to—"

A knock on the study door interrupted Tamrissa's words. When Lorand called out permission to enter, they all saw a guardsman behind the servant who opened the door.

"Your pardon, Excellences, but the man Lavrit Mohr has arrived," the guardsman reported without stepping into the room. "Will you see him now, or do you prefer that he wait?"

"No, we'll see him now," Lorand told the guardsman, the others suddenly as attentive as he, himself, felt. "We've been waiting for his report."

The guardsman nodded and turned to his right to gesture, and Lavrit Mohr hurried to the doorway. He stopped to bow as usual before he walked in, but the door wasn't closed immediately behind him. A higher-ranking guardsman suddenly appeared behind the servant, and when Vallant saw the man he got up and went to speak to him.

"Why don't you help yourself to a cup of tea, Dom Mohr," Lorand invited while Vallant listened to what the new guardsman had to say. "We should be able to take your report in a minute or two."

Mohr smiled his thanks while adding another bow, his glance going to Vallant and the murmured conversation before he turned to the tea service. It would be foolish to have Mohr begin his report before Vallant could hear it as well, and even beyond that Lorand was curious about what Vallant was being told. By the time Mohr had his tea and had been convinced that sitting down wasn't a breach of some higher law, Vallant ended his conversation and came to rejoin them while the servant closed the door.

"That was somethin' you all need to hear," Vallant said as he reclaimed his place beside Tamrissa. "The guard captain tells me that two women were caught tryin' to add themselves to the servin' staff, and they made a real fuss before they were arrested and taken away. A little while later one of the servant supervisors saw a man he didn't recognize, and it turned out that none of the other supervisors knew him either. The man was quiet and a hard worker, and under normal circumstances would never have been noticed."

"So the women expected to be caught, and they made a fuss to cover the arrival of the man," Jovvi said with an understanding nod. "What did the guard do with them?"

"They were turned over to civil authorities to be questioned, just as we ordered," Vallant answered. "The judges will question them under puredan, and if they know anythin' about where Ayl and his followers are, the judges will find out."

"It's unlikely any of them knows a thing or they wouldn't have been sent," Tamrissa put in with clear annoyance. "I just hope the judges don't find out it's some group other than Ayl's."

"Bite your tongue," Lorand told Tamrissa firmly as the

others looked startled. "We have enough to occupy us without needing another organized force determined to get rid of us. Vallant, was the servant supervisor who spotted the man rewarded the way he or she was supposed to be?"

"The supervisor was given the five silver coins as soon as the man was arrested," Vallant answered with a chuckle. "The captain told me the servants didn't really believe they would get anythin' beyond a pat on the head if that, and seein' all that silver almost made them fall over in shock. Now everybody is lookin' at everybody else, and the next time someone tries sneakin' in they'll probably be caught as soon as they show their face. But I apologize for makin' Dom Mohr wait to give his report. We're all eager to hear what you have to say, Dom Mohr, so please go ahead."

"Thank you, Excellence, but I didn't really mind waiting," Mohr answered quietly, disturbance clear in his eyes. "Considering who those people probably were, I feel more guilty than put-upon. And if you haven't yet been told, your people found almost a dozen supporters of Ayl still pretending to be loyal supporters of the Guild. They were also handed over to the authorities, but so far their questioners haven't gotten anything beyond a few locations where messages were meant to be left."

"If our people used their heads and are watchin' those locations, we may end up learnin' a lot more," Vallant told the man with clear sympathy. "But right now I'd like to know what you found out about that army."

"My people have reported that it's approximately ten days' march from Gan Garee," Mohr replied. "There are four officers and a large number of . . . prods, I believe they're called, and the fighting force itself numbers over four hundred."

"That could well be two armies combined into one," Lorand said. "But I think I read in one of the transcripts that they were ordered to the west to stop the invading Astindans. Why are they now on their way here instead?"

"With nobles in charge of them, I'm not surprised that they're coming here instead," Rion put in with a look of disdain. "Those nobles will have property in Gan Garee that they'll want to protect, and they're not likely to be very practiced at obeying orders. Their own wishes and desires will always come first, even if that's the worst thing they could do."

"So we do have time before we need to ride out to face them," Jovvi said, her expression thoughtful as her finger tapped her lips. "We'll be able to move much faster than that many people, and we'll have to discuss how large our own force ought to be."

"My people have discovered something else as well," Mohr said before a tangential discussion could be started. "It seems that a substantial number of the former nobility escaped before the troubles, and they're now more or less hiding out on various estates. My people tried to start the same sort of movement in the smaller towns that we did here, but it didn't work. The nobles employ a very large number of servants, too large for the limited means of the towns to help support. In addition to that, the nobles have been recruiting their own guard forces, and the townspeople are afraid of what will happen if they try to revolt."

"They're right to be afraid," Naran said, her expression grim as she shook her head. "One of the things that made the changes here possible was the depletion of the guard force. If the nobles have recruited guardsmen in any sort of number, the townspeople would be very much at risk. Killing a few people at random and destroying a small number of houses would bring the rest of the town back into line at once."

"So we have more than just an army to worry about," Lorand said with a sigh. "I knew it was too good to be true."

"That just means we don't have quite as much time as I thought," Jovvi said, and oddly enough she seemed to be holding back laughter. The rest of the group laughed aloud without bothering to hold it back, and even Mohr showed a smile. "Yes, my love, what you said was funny, because most people don't consider themselves lucky to be facing nothing more than an army."

"And the funniest part of it is that I saw it exactly the

same way," Tamrissa put in around her chuckling. "Do you think we've changed just a little over the past weeks?"

"Not me," Vallant denied at once, amusement still dancing in his light eyes. "I'm the same humble, lovable, highly talented man I always was. Did I remember to mention humble?"

"At least we don't have to go into all this alone," Jovvi said with a smile as everyone else laughed again. "We can take some of the Astindans with us, and afterward they'll have more workers to take back to their country."

"I second that," Tamrissa said at once. "Supplying them workers to rebuild their country is one thing. Having to capture those workers and then finding a way to deliver them is something else entirely. I think we have enough to do on our schedule."

"It seems that your schedule has just been added to, Excellence," Mohr put in with a small, pleased smile. "Your Seating ceremony has been scheduled for tomorrow morning, and everyone in the city has been invited to attend. The notices have been going up on announcement boards most of the day."

"It looks like those people are *really* anxious to get us going after the approaching army," Tamrissa commented, wrinkling her nose. "Or else they're hoping that riots will start when we announce that we're a six rather than a five. Or am I being too suspicious of those dear, sweet people?"

"Believing that they've all had a complete change of heart would be foolish on our part," Jovvi said with a small shake of her head. "Part of me thinks I *am* being too suspicious, but the rest of me remembers that most of the people in the crowd this morning were swept along when Rilna Zokill curtsied to us and a few others followed her example. Some of them must have regretted going along once they had time to think."

"You know, I'm getting very tired of this," Tamrissa said, no longer in the least amused. "I think I'm going to ask for a show of hands tomorrow before we go through that ceremony. If enough people raise their hands to show that they don't want us as leaders of this empire, we can walk away before we commit ourselves too far. I believe I've mentioned how much I hate to be where I'm not really wanted."

"I agree with Tamrissa," Rion said at once. "This back and forth is making me dizzy, and I also dislike being where I'm not wanted. Our lives would be a good deal less complicated if we took ourselves off to some private part of the world."

"But you can't," Lavrit Mohr blurted, looking from one to another of the group with sudden desperation. "You're the Chosen Blending, and it's your *destiny* to rule! Why do you keep talking about leaving?"

"Possibly because we don't enjoy wasting our time," Tamrissa told him, her exasperation making her tone a good deal sharper than Lorand's would have been. "I think we all understand that there's never going to be unanimous agreement among the people we have to deal with. But letting ourselves be Seated and then spending years arguing in order to get anything done isn't *my* idea of how to run an empire. If it's yours, then I say we let them Seat *you.*"

"Not to mention the fact that we still aren't completely convinced about being Chosen," Rion added, his tone no softer than Tamrissa's. "That point, however, is neither here nor there. If we really aren't the Chosen of the Prophesies, then we won't end up in charge even if we decide we want to be. It's just that lately I've felt an . . . understanding for some of the methods used by the nobility, and that disgusts me. If the only way to accomplish anything is to crush everyone ruthlessly underfoot, then I'm definitely in favor of walking away."

"What we're trying to say, Dom Mohr, is that we're ordinary people, not nobles raised to rule," Jovvi put in, but *her* tone was gentle with compassion. "Possibly it would have been better if we *had* been nobles, as many of our supposed followers would be less likely to argue with us. And we would have a better idea of how rulers are supposed to behave. Apparently *our* behavior encourages disagreement."

"There's also a fact that all those people aren't considerin'," Vallant said, almost as gently as Jovvi. "If we really wanted to be Seated above all other things, those people would have a chance to bargain for what they think they want. But we aren't particularly eager to start workin' our backsides off for nit-pickers, so if they push us too hard we really will walk away."

"But if we do stay, we'll need an intermediary," Naran contributed, surprising Lorand until he saw that distracted look in her eyes. "The person—or people—we name can do any necessary listening, arguing, and persuading in our place, leaving us free to do the important things."

"Now, *that's* an idea I like," Lorand had to put in, finally finding something he could support wholeheartedly. "High Master Mohr, here, for instance, has the patience needed to listen to people without exploding, and Dama Zokill would be perfect to handle those who shouldn't be shown patience. That way staying won't mean our being driven crazy."

"Well, that *might* work," Tamrissa grudged while everyone else considered the matter with pleased surprise. "Then, if someone does happen to come up with a good idea, it won't be lost behind all the bad ones. Yes, I think I can go along with that—assuming we can get all those pests to also go along with it."

"Once we're actually Seated, we shouldn't have much trouble putting the idea into practice," Jovvi said, a thoughtful finger to her lips. "Right now we're 'unofficial,' so to speak, but after the ceremony everyone will see us differently. Yes, I think the idea will work."

"The least we can do is try," Rion allowed, his arm around Naran again. "If the plan doesn't work, then we can discuss the matter and decide what must be done."

"And even if it doesn't work, we'll only have to put up with the nonsense for a year," Vallant pointed out. "After that the competitions will be held again, and if the people have been givin' us too much of a hard time we don't have to enter them."

"But right now we have plans that need to be made," Jovvi pointed out. "Is there anything else you need to tell us, Dom Mohr? If not, there must be tasks that need *your* attention as well."

"Yes, Excellence, there certainly are, and I have nothing to add right now," Mohr answered with evident relief, quickly getting to his feet to bow. "If I learn anything new from my people, I'll either send word or bring it. In any event, it will be my pleasure to see all of you tomorrow, at the Seating ceremony."

"Just where is the ceremony supposed to be held?" Tamrissa asked before Mohr could bow a final time and leave. "We were . . . otherwise engaged or out of the city when the usurpers were Seated, and I, at least, wasn't born for the one before that."

"The ceremony will be held in the amphitheater, so everyone in the city can attend if they wish," Mohr told her with raised brows. "Are you saying that no one sent word of the location of the place you're supposed to be tomorrow? If *you* don't show up, there won't *be* a ceremony."

"It's possible that word just hasn't reached us yet," Jovvi said, soothing the man's sudden and obvious suspicion. "And you have to remember that almost everyone already knows where the ceremony will be, so not mentioning it could be an oversight."

"And you'll have an escort, who will certainly know your destination," Mohr conceded with a nod and a sigh. "I'm afraid I'm beginning to fall victim to the state of mind that sees dark plots everywhere, which means I do need to leave. There are enough real plots about to occupy us all."

And with that Mohr bowed only once then quickly left the room. Lorand watched until Mohr was gone, and then he shook his head.

"If Dom Mohr isn't careful, he'll worry himself into true illness," Lorand commented as he looked back at the rest of the group. "He's pushing himself too hard, and there's a tension inside him that's doing damage."

"He considers himself responsible for Holdis Ayl's actions, I think," Jovvi added with a sigh. "And he also seems to be afraid that we'll suddenly begin to blame him and his true followers for what that splinter group is doing. He's spent many years dreaming of getting full acceptance for himself and his people, and now, when the accomplishment is within his grasp, it could be snatched away forever."

"Snatched away by a bunch of fools who think they could have become nobles, or who have talked themselves into deciding they're the only ones who can stop the 'false' Chosen." Tamrissa's tone held the shadow of impatience, but behind the shadow Lorand could hear true disturbance. "I think the first thing we need to do is check the amphitheater for any surprises Ayl and his people have planned. If they didn't fail to take advantage of that party, they won't ignore something as important as the Seating ceremony."

"What I can see of the ceremony is on the odd side," Naran contributed, apparently aware of the fact that everyone had turned to her even though her attention was again elsewhere. "There are so many possibilities surrounding the event that they're almost crowding each other out, and some of them are obscured by the number of shadows. I think I'm going to have to get a bit . . . insistent about increasing the lessons from my peers. I was told I'd be fully trained once we were here in the palace, but so far I've only had three sessions which weren't particularly helpful."

"I'm willin' to bet that even rantin' and ravin' won't get you anywhere," Vallant put in thoughtfully after finishing the tea in his cup. "There seems to be a lot of things your people don't want us knowin' about in advance, like what Tamrissa did last night at the party. When she said we were leavin', Dom Mohr was almost in shock, but Ristor Ardanis never lost that jolly smile of his. He knew all about it, and probably knew we wouldn't be leavin' after all. What we need is for our Blendin' entity to take a few good looks around that amphitheater, startin' right now."

"Starting after I visit the comfort facility," Tamrissa said as she quickly got to her feet. "I've had too much tea today to ignore the need."

It turned out that Tamrissa wasn't the only one with the same need, so a few minutes passed before everyone was ready. Lorand took the opportunity to tell the servants and guardsmen that they weren't to be disturbed, waited until

Tamrissa had alerted their link groups just in case they were needed, and then he felt Jovvi initiate the Blending.

But this time the blending wasn't as it had been in the past. Lorand wasn't simply a submerged part of the entity; instead, his awareness continued on, and it was the Lorand entity that floated above the bodies of his flesh forms. The Lorand entity was pleased to be in existence again, and he knew precisely where he was meant to go. This time, however, his destination was one that was well known to all of his flesh forms, therefore was a roundabout journeying unnecessary.

With that awareness, the Lorand entity simply translated himself to the place called amphitheater. No time elapsed in the doing, of course, and it immediately became clear that searching would also be unnecessary. A number of flesh forms showing not the least amount of talent were busily working in the amphitheater, their attention on more than one project.

A wide stand made of wood had been erected in the middle of the sand of the amphitheater, a platform meant to hold quite a few flesh forms. Some of the flesh forms now present were spreading around large amounts of the substance known as hilsom powder, carefully mixing the powder into the sand all about and under the platform. At the same time other flesh forms were working to weaken the wood of the platform, clearly so that the structure would collapse after a short time under the weight of those who stood on it.

The Lorand entity then floated to other locations about the amphitheater where other flesh forms were, at first not understanding what it was that they so carefully hid. Then the Lorand entity recognized the weapon called bow, accompanied by the missiles called arrows which the weapon threw over long distances. Bows and arrows were being hidden inside niches carved out of the rock of the seats, thin sections of rock standing by to be inserted in the niches. With the sections of rock in place, the seats would look untouched under any but the most attentive examination.

The Lorand entity considered those various doings, then firmly took over the minds of the scattered flesh forms.

—*This will be the last time you perform an act of this sort*— the Lorand entity told the flesh forms, making the thought an order rather than a suggestion. —*You will, however, make no attempt to sever ties with the organization to which you belong. Instead, you will make all reasonable efforts to discover the location of the leader or leaders of the organization. When you succeed you will seek out the captain of the palace guard, and tell that flesh form everything you have learned.*—

The flesh forms in the Lorand entity's control acknowledged their instructions, then went back to the tasks they were in the middle of. The Lorand entity took one last look about, marking the locations where the weapons were being hidden, and then Lorand was an individual again.

"I don't believe the nerve of those people!" Tamrissa exclaimed at once, highly indignant. "And why isn't that place being guarded against exactly what they're doing?"

"I suppose it isn't being guarded because no one gave orders to *have* it guarded," Jovvi suggested, her expression odd. "But isn't anyone going to comment on what *we* did? In the beginning, I mean, to get to the amphitheater."

"Yes, that was rather strange, to say the least," Rion said, accommodating her with his own wide-eyed expression. "I had no idea that our entity could just . . . decide to be somewhere and then be there instantly. Am I correct in assuming that this hasn't happened before for the reason that we've never before known exactly where we were going?"

"That or we weren't before *ready* to do it," Vallant put in, his own expression delighted. "It's nice knowin' the doin' is possible, but I don't see it helpin' us much against that army."

"Because we don't know the area where we'll be facing the army," Jovvi agreed with a nod. "But whatever we did to perform that little trick will be of great help when we do know where we're going. If you haven't noticed, it wasn't necessary to draw strength from our link groups to go all the way to the amphitheater and back."

"I think there's something else the rest of you haven't noticed," Lorand was finally able to say. Talk about being shaken . . . ! "This time the entity was me, or I was the entity. That's never happened before, and I'm not sure I like it."

"It *is* rather disconcerting," Naran agreed with a sympathetic smile. "It happened to me last night, during the trouble at the party, and if we hadn't been in the middle of so much else I would probably have been somewhat upset."

"When it happened to me in Widdertown, there was also too much going on for me to do more than mention it," Tamrissa told Lorand with the same sort of supportive smile. "I haven't really thought about it since, but I don't remember it being all *that* bad."

"I found it downright pleasant," Vallant said as Rion murmured something of the same. "We were in Collin' Green and were about to be attacked at the time, and that was all I could think about."

"And my experience with it was during the confrontation with the Blendings from Astinda," Jovvi said, closing the circle. "The experience was unexpected, but I didn't find it particularly disturbing. Maybe that was because we almost lost Tamma . . . Was it really that bad for you, my love?"

"Well, maybe not bad exactly," Lorand conceded, the unsettling feeling of the experience beginning to fade. "I suppose the unexpectedness of it was what got me the most. Does this mean we've all now had a taste of the same thing? Apparently so, and that means the next question is: What comes next?"

"I can answer that," Tamrissa responded as she got up and headed for the tea service. "First we get to swallow a good deal more of this tea while we decide which of the strong Middles are going to start the first round of training classes while we're gone. Then we'll tell the people we've decided on that they're nominated, after which we'll tell the captain of our guard to expect one or more informers' reports on the whereabouts of that man Ayl. Then we'll talk about how many changes of clothing to take with us when we leave the city, and then we'll discuss which of the associated Blendings to take as well. We'll also have to think about how many link groups to take and the number of guardsmen, if any, and how many Astindans. Then I'll get to burn up every last speck of that hilsom powder spread into the sand in the arena, while one of you others assigns guards to watch those seats in the stands where the bows were hidden. Once all that is done, we'll have the time to wonder what, if anything, comes next in our experiences with the entity."

Lorand's groan joined those from everyone else, a unanimous reaction to the long list of chores they had in front of them. Someone else would just have answered Lorand's question by pointing out that they had very little time to worry about a next happening with the entity that might not even come about. Leave it to Tamrissa to be different, not to mention horribly detailed . . .

ELEVEN

Rion looked around at his brothers and sisters when they all met in the public area of the palace the next morning. The night of the party all the ladies had been beautifully gowned, including Naran, who had borrowed a gown from either Tamrissa or Jovvi. He and his brothers had been equally splendid in pastel-colored trousers and coats with complementary shirts, their clothing produced much faster by a small army of tailors.

This morning, however, he and his brothers had chosen more soberly colored clothing, Vallant in blue with a white shirt, Lorand in brown with a pale yellow shirt, and Rion himself in gray with a light blue shirt. Naran had dressed in a new frock that had just been made for her, the material an eye-teasing shade that shifted from color to color as the light touched it in different ways. Tamrissa's gown was an emphatic red trimmed with gold, a combination that seemed neither muted nor blazing. Jovvi, beside Tamrissa in a gentle off-white with pale blue and pale green trim, somehow managed to keep from being blotted out by Tamrissa's gown color.

"Good morning, everyone," Jovvi announced as she looked around, pretending they hadn't seen each other yet this morning. "It seems that all of us are ready to go and face the music."

"As long as they understand that I'll be doing my own dance step no matter *what* music they play," Tamrissa said with more amusement than argumentativeness. "I think we all look marvelous, and the people who made this clothing for us deserve a bonus. And I think I'm going to love wearing riding dresses. What about you, Naran?"

"Oh, I agree completely," Naran replied with her own amusement as she stroked a hand down the material of her gown. "This will be much more comfortable than riding in an ordinary gown, and we have Jovvi to thank for telling us about it."

"Are you ladies certain you won't change your minds?" Rion asked again, just as he had when they'd met earlier for breakfast—and a second examination of the amphitheater. "Arriving at the ceremony in coaches *will* give us a small amount of standing in the eyes of most of the people. Arriving mounted on horses won't accomplish the same thing at all."

"But it *will* let everyone know that we aren't the same sort of Blending they've gotten used to," Tamrissa pointed out, just as she had earlier. "The sooner they understand *that* point really well, the better off we'll be."

"I know you think we women are being disaccommodated for no reason, Rion, but it isn't so," Jovvi said, putting a gentle hand to his arm. "It *is* necessary to make this particular point, and I've learned to *prefer* riding a horse to riding in a coach. Tamma and Naran feel just the same about it, so please don't worry that our dignity is being damaged."

"You see, love, I told you the others felt the way I do," Naran chided Rion gently as he sighed and gave up his stance. "Everything will be fine, and better than fine."

Rion exchanged glances with Lorand and Vallant, their expressions telling him that he hadn't had a prayer of changing the minds of the ladies. He'd known the same, but he'd still had to try. He'd been able to throw off most of what he'd been taught while growing up with the woman who had claimed to be his mother, but treating women in the proper way wasn't part of what had been discarded. Nor would it ever be, if *he* had anything to say about the matter . . .

The hovering servants were finally able to begin accompanying them when Jovvi and Lorand moved off up the corridor that led to the palace entrance. Rion waited until Tamrissa and Vallant had followed before bringing up the rear with Naran, his misgivings submerged rather than erased. He hadn't argued for his point of view as strongly as he could have, most especially not when the discussion first began.

The morning began with a surprise when Vallant and Tamrissa suddenly appeared in Rion's wing, but not through the usual route. Vallant had been studying the map he'd gotten from his servants, and somehow had discovered a secret underground corridor that linked all the wings. The corridor had been heavy with dust, showing that it hadn't been used in quite some time, but that hadn't stopped them all from using it to reach Lorand's wing. Jovvi had been there when they'd arrived, and they'd all had a very pleasant breakfast in Lorand's dining room as they praised Vallant's cleverness.

But Rion hadn't done more than echo what everyone else said, his mind far too distracted with private thoughts. He'd had a dream last night, an odd and oddly disturbing one, and he'd been trying to bring back enough details of the dream to let him understand it. There had been something about being part of the Blending entity, a now-familiar situation that shouldn't have been disturbing in the least. But there had also been something else, and that was what Rion couldn't quite remember . . .

"Have you decided to walk instead of ride, my love?" Naran asked, bringing Rion abruptly back to the world around him. A single glance showed that Naran and the others were already outside and mounted, and only he stood staring rather than doing.

"Possibly I *should* walk, my love, to teach me not to let my mind wander," Rion responded with a smile that was a bit shame-faced. "I apologize for making everyone wait, and I'll be with you in an instant."

He turned to his own horse then, and once he was settled in his saddle he could see that their escort of guardsmen was also ready. But Jovvi, rather than joining the others in heading for the palace gates, moved her horse close to his.

"Rion, something seems to be bothering you," Jovvi said softly as their mounts moved along with the others. "Is there anything I can help with?"

"Not really," Rion told her with the best smile he could produce, leaning over to pat her hand in thanks. "I've been trying to remember the dream I had last night, but my memory isn't cooperating. It's very frustrating."

"Yes, I know how that goes," Jovvi agreed with relief clear in her lovely smile. "You feel as though you have the answer to every question in the world, if only you could remember it. I've experienced the same myself more than once."

"Well, this is the first time I've gone through it, and I'd be quite satisfied to have it be the last," Rion assured her, making a deliberate effort to pull away from pointless distraction. "And later we must discuss again the matter of how we attend public functions. Tamrissa's point does need to be made, but at the same time we really must be aware of the prejudices of others. If we want to be treated as leaders of the empire, we must begin to act like leaders."

"I . . . think you may have a valid point of your own," Jovvi allowed slowly after a moment of thought before bringing her gaze back to him. "We'll definitely have to discuss it more thoroughly later."

Rion nodded, then gave his attention to their surroundings as they all rode through the gates opened by the guardsmen stationed there. Outside the gates there was a respectable number of people on both sides of the road, ordinary people who stared open-mouthed as they watched the party leaving the palace grounds. They'd probably hoped to get a glimpse of their new leaders as the coaches passed, and were more than a little surprised when there *were* no coaches.

That thought annoyed Rion a bit, but it was more a matter of self-annoyance. Tamrissa *did* have a point about letting people know they would be different as a Blending, but there should have been some acceptable compromise that would have done little or no harm to the image of the position. If he had ignored that foolish dream and put his mind to the problem . . .

The next moment Rion became aware of something odd in the air about them, a faint . . . acrid sharpness in a handful of places that shouldn't have been there. He had no idea what it could be, but seeing Lorand stiffen in his saddle made it clear that quick action would be necessary. With the speed of thought Rion thickened the air around the members of their entire procession, and his effort was only just in time.

Rounded, cloudy jars were suddenly hurled in their direction from the handful of places he'd noticed a moment earlier, jars that brought the sharp smell tainting the air immediately closer. The missiles were aimed at the six people leading the procession, and the jars cracked open when they came in contact with the invisible but solid wall of air. The contents of the jars splashed back in the direction of the watching crowds, and there were outcries of pain as those who had hurled the jars scrambled to escape the area.

"Catch as many of those back-stabbers as you can!" Vallant shouted to the guardsmen escort, pointing to the running men. "Just don't hurt anybody innocent while you're doin' it."

"Vallant, quick, help me!" Lorand shouted as he dismounted and headed for the nearest person screaming in pain. "Those wax jars held etching acid, and these people have to have it washed off them as fast as possible."

Vallant nodded as he also dismounted, and a heartbeat later there were torrents of water pouring over the seven people who had been splashed with the acid. Rion had already dissolved his wall, of course, and he watched all around as Lorand went from victim to victim, healing their burns as best he could. The guardsmen left in their escort were frantic, of course, babbling something about how the Excellences had to get themselves to safety, but not one of their six paid attention to the advice.

"I think I'm beginning to be really furious," Naran said in what was an actual growl, a tone which startled Rion. "I should have foreseen this, but my Sight is still being interfered with. What's *wrong* with those people?"

"Obviously we're still being tested," Tamrissa said in a matching growl from her place to Naran's left, clearly understanding that the people Naran meant were those with her ability. "They don't seem to care *how* many innocent bystanders get hurt as long as they find out whatever it is they're still curious about. I think I'll have a short talk with Dom Ristor Ardanis the next time I see him."

Tamrissa sat her horse as she glared about, obviously looking for someone to take her anger out on. Jovvi had joined Lorand to help ease the wounded, and everyone else in the modestly sized crowd seemed to be unusually silent. Two of those who had thrown jars were in the midst of being dragged toward the palace gates for the duty guardsmen to see to. The rest—and the guardsmen chasing them—had disappeared, and Rion silently wished the pursuers good luck. Fanatics were a danger to everyone, and needed to be caught and stopped as quickly as possible.

It took a few moments of intense effort before the wounded were no longer screaming in pain. All seven of the victims, five men and two women, sat together on the ground with friends or family hovering nervously near, and even their color had returned almost to normal. Lorand *was* an excellent healer, and when he finally stepped back from the last of those who needed his attention an odd thing happened.

The silence that had been thick with all sorts of overtones and undertones was suddenly broken as people began to cheer. The cheering intensified as clapping and foot-stamping was added, and a heavy man with a big smile on his face stepped forward from the smaller group around the victims.

"I wouldn't have believed it if I hadn't seen it myself," the man said loudly in more educated accents than Rion would have expected from the look of him. "We've actually got a Blending that cares more about ordinary people than they do about themselves. You really shouldn't have stopped to help, not with crazies out to get you, but we're all very glad you did. For what you did to ease my wife and son—and everyone else—you have my deepest thanks."

Quite a lot of people seemed to have heard the man, for the crowd cheered even more loudly after he finished speaking. Lorand, Jovvi, and Vallant were smiling as they remounted their horses, and when Lorand looked in his direction Rion knew what he wanted.

"Please, thanks aren't necessary," Lorand told everyone with one hand held up, his voice amplified through Rion's efforts with the air. "These people were hurt because of us, so just riding off wasn't possible."

"It woulda been more'n possible fer th' nobles," someone shouted, and the comment was echoed by many voices. "Yer folks like *us*, real folks, an' about time we got ya."

That second comment was cheered even more loudly, so Lorand simply smiled again, waved, and then led off up the road. Rion and everyone else followed, the guardsmen finally looking a bit more relieved. The cheering people got happily out of their way, and in just a few minutes they'd left the scene of the attack behind.

"I hate it when people have backup plans," Tamrissa grumbled from where she rode beside Vallant, just ahead of Rion and Naran. Her anger hadn't lessened much, and

Rion suspected that the cheering had added to her temper. Those people had been so sincerely grateful . . .

"Yes, it wasn't logical havin' them attack now, when we're headin' for their more involved trap," Vallant agreed with a headshake. "We've got to stop those fools before someone gets really hurt."

"One of those men would have lost his sight if not for us," Lorand said from where he and Jovvi rode ahead of Tamrissa and Vallant. "That's hurt enough as far as *I'm* concerned."

"Which means we really do need to find a way to stop this sniping," Jovvi turned around to say in agreement. "Let's put our minds to it as soon as the ceremony is over."

No one disagreed with that, so they continued on to the amphitheater in silence. Rion racked his brain trying to think of a way to apprehend that miscreant Ayl, but they reached the amphitheater and he hadn't thought of a single idea. There were small crowds here as well, so Rion shielded them all again until they'd ridden through one of the wide doors leading to the interior of the amphitheater.

"That attack could well have been a distraction, meant to make us think we're safe now," Vallant said just before they all began to dismount. "I know we checked this place again this mornin', but let's still be alert and really careful. If they arranged one distraction, there could be more."

Rion considered that good advice, as did the others, so they were all extremely alert when they began to walk toward the people waiting for them. Lavrit Mohr stood with a group of men and women who weren't all familiar, but ranged around and behind those people were the Blending's link groups and associate Blendings. That made Rion feel fractionally better, but not entirely.

"Excellences, please excuse the observation, but you're late," the man Mohr exclaimed as they neared, stepping out in front of his companions. "Is everything all right?"

"It wasn't, but we took care of it," Tamrissa answered for all of them, her tone still far from friendly. "Is there any chance at all that someone with Fire magic is in the mood to offer a challenge?"

As his sister deliberately looked around with those words, Rion could see flinching in all directions. The members of Tamrissa's link groups—and the Fire magic users of the other Blendings—began to study the high ceiling above them with complete attention, and the gesture wasn't lost on those who *didn't* have Fire magic.

"With all due respect, Excellence, we don't seem to have anyone with suicidal urges in our group," a man they didn't know commented, trying to hide amusement. He was a rather large man, burly with dark hair and light eyes, and his clothing was on the shabby side despite the fact that he sounded like a scholar. "I'm Tolten Meerk, and I'll be conducting the Seating ceremony."

"Meerk," Jovvi echoed as Tamrissa's attention turned sharply to the man. "Were you by any chance related to Alsin Meerk?"

"He was my brother," Tolten Meerk replied, a sad smile now turning his mouth. "I was told that he lost his life bravely, defending your lady of Fire, and I appreciate having that memory of him. He always seemed determined to give his life in *some* cause or other, and I'm just glad that he found a worthy one."

"Please understand that we share your grief," Jovvi told him gently, stepping forward to put a hand to the man's arm. "Alsin was a close associate and a good friend, and we all miss him quite a lot. So what will we have to do during the ceremony?"

"Not all that much," Meerk answered. "I'll present you to the people, and ask if there are any challenges to your being Seated. Since there *won't* be any, you'll all sit in the chairs that have been put on the platform for symbolism. After that the people will cheer, and then we can all go home."

"Obviously, the public Seatin' ceremony was nothin' but a time-wastin' formality for the nobility," Vallant commented with a shake of his head. "We'll have to see about changin' that, startin' with the ceremony next year. If the people have to live under a Blendin's rule, they ought to be able to feel that they had a hand in makin' it happen."

"What ceremony next year?" Meerk asked, glancing around with narrowed eyes. "Did someone tell you that you'll have to go through this again in a year's time? That doesn't happen to be true, not when a reign is supposed to last for twenty-five years."

"Dom Meerk, the idea is ours," Jovvi told the man soothingly, adding one of her loveliest smiles. "The competitions have been controlled for so very long that we now want to add as much fairness as possible. We're putting off the next competitions for a year, so that any Blending that wants to participate will have a chance to practice and grow strong. Only under those circumstances will the Seated Blending truly be representative of everyone."

"And you can also tell everyone that classes in the use of talent will be started immediately," Tamrissa added, her tone no longer quite so belligerent. "In a few weeks, once everyone has had a chance to attend those classes, the people who are interested will then be taught how to Blend. Even if they're in no position to compete in the challenges, they'll still be taught."

"Either you're more than very sure of yourselves, or you're the answer to our prayers," Meerk said, looking around at each of them, his expression odd. "I sincerely hope it's the latter, but in any event it's time we got on with the ceremony. Ah . . . may I ask why all those other people who apparently know you are here? They aren't part of the group from the city, I'm sure, and there's really no place for them in the ceremony."

"Then I suggest we make a place for them," Rion couldn't help putting in. "Those are the people who made it possible for us to survive long enough to reach this point in time. Their suffering has earned them the best place we can provide, so we would appreciate your help in creating that place."

"The ceremony would hardly be complete without them there," Jovvi added as the others all nodded their agreement. "A word or two on our behalf indicating our appreciation would certainly be enough. Our full thanks will be shown them in a private, more fitting way."

"As you wish," Meerk concurred, with the calm that seemed to be a part of him. "The representatives of the city groups will join us on the platform, but only as witnesses. Is that all right?"

"That's fine," Lorand agreed for all of them. "Now I think we've kept those people out there waiting long enough."

"But that doesn't go for everyone out there," Tamrissa said under her breath as people began to move in all directions. "It would not bother me in the least if Ayl's idiots died of old age waiting. But I do want to see the look on their faces when they find out what we did."

Rion smiled at Tamrissa's comment, understanding exactly what she meant. Ayl's people had weakened the platform so that when their Blending sat in the heavy chairs which would be provided for their use, the platform would collapse. The collapse was meant to throw some if not all of them onto the hilsom powder-laced sand, and then, presumably, the men with bows in the stands would find it possible to murder them.

But that morning their Blending entity had taken possession of the watchers left by Ayl, and had used the men to reinforce the platform against collapse after destroying every speck of hilsom powder. Then the entity had made the men forget what they'd done before allowing them to return to their posts. The men would report that everything was as it had been left by those working the day before, but anyone waiting for the collapse—and a general loss of talent—would be sadly disappointed.

"No, I'm afraid that *can't* be left for another time," Rion heard Lorand saying to Meerk, the two men having already reached the wide doorway leading to the sands. "If you can't find another chair like those five, take them away and bring out *any* six chairs. If you can't find six chairs that are the same, then we'll all stand for the Seating ceremony."

"But I was told that you'd agreed to hold off with doing something that will upset everyone," Meerk persisted, his tone disturbed. "It's really too late for you to change your minds again, so—"

"You're missing the point," Lorand interrupted as the remaining members of the Blending reached the doorway. "We never changed our minds to begin with, so whoever told you that we had was lying. Please make whatever arrangements you have to about the chairs, and then we'll want to know who gave you that false information."

By then Rion was able to see that only five chairs had been placed on the platform in the middle of the sand. The sole thing that kept him from exploding in anger was the fact that Lorand had already made their position absolutely clear, and was also clearly holding down his own anger. For that reason Rion controlled himself as Meerk called over a young man who was probably his assistant. Meerk gave the young man rapid instructions, and when his assistant dashed off at a run, Meerk turned back to Lorand.

"There are additional chairs of the same sort stored on the side of the amphitheater that used to be used by the nobles," Meerk informed them all with continuing calm. "We'll have another chair out there in just a few minutes, and then we'll be able to begin."

"And the name of the person who told you that we'd changed our minds about how many of us would be Seated?" Lorand asked, the question downright curt. "I'm not asking just for form's sake, or because I mean to go through all sorts of accusation scenes. We made our stance perfectly clear to everyone, but someone still wants to do things his or her own way. We'll have enough trouble with problems that can't be avoided. There's no need to add someone who wants to rule in our place without first challenging and defeating us. Now please give me that name."

"I'm afraid I don't know the man's name, and I don't even see him here any longer," Meerk responded after turning to study the group of city leaders. "He was a thin man of average height, and he spoke with such casual authority that there seemed to be no reason to disbelieve him. He also suggested that if you changed your mind again, just a little coaxing would change it back."

"Are you sure that Relton Henris had nothing to do with it?" Tamrissa asked Meerk, her annoyance having returned. "Only some thin man who isn't here any longer?"

"No, I can honestly say that Relton Henris had nothing to do with the matter," Meerk assured her, adding a warm smile. "It's fairly obvious that the man is unhappy about something, but he never mentioned what that something might be. And now, if you'll excuse me, I'll supervise the placing of that sixth chair."

It was just possible to see, across the sand and behind the chairs already on the platform, that the doors on the other side of the amphitheater were being opened. Meerk performed a small bow before striding off toward the platform, and the buzz of noise from the thousands of people in the stands broke off for a moment. Everyone seemed to be watching as Meerk made for the platform, and when he reached it the crowd noticed that there were three men struggling with the chair they'd just carried outside. That observation renewed the babble of conversation, only a bit more intensified.

"Meerk was lying," Jovvi said softly to Lorand, her voice reaching only the six of them. "Did you notice that as well?"

"Yes, it so happens I did," Lorand admitted, his gaze on the man they discussed where he stood on the platform. "He does know who told him that story, but he won't give the name to *us*. But I'm certain it wasn't Henris."

"So we have yet another player in this game," Vallant said with something of a sigh. "Callin' Meerk on the lie probably won't do any good, and if we insist or force him to tell us, we'll most likely just make another enemy. There was a time when I really hated the idea of controllin' everyone around us, but now . . ."

"Now it's starting to look like the best way to save our sanity," Tamrissa agreed with her own sigh. "It's a good thing for these people that we have more self-control than that."

"For the moment," Lorand said, his headshake obviously filled with annoyance and frustration. "How much self-control we'll have left after the ceremony is over remains to be seen."

And that, unfortunately, was a sentiment Rion had no trouble understanding fully.

TWELVE

It wasn't very long at all before the sixth chair was placed on the platform, the noise from the stands getting louder by the minute. Tolten Meerk ignored the waves of questions and comments, giving all his attention to having the newest chair properly placed, and then he sent his assistants away and just stood waiting.

"I have a feeling I'm not going to like this man as well as I did his brother," I muttered, the annoyance I'd been feeling all along increasing again. "He's all but demanding that we come out *now* because *he* thinks it's more than time we did."

"It's amazing how close you've come to interpreting his feelings without having Spirit magic," Jovvi commented from beside me. "He seems to have decided not to 'waste' any more time, so he's not going to be coming back in here. And he's also trying to avoid being questioned again."

"I flatly refuse to dance to that man's tune," Rion stated, and I had the impression that he was almost as annoyed as I'd gotten. "No matter how much work we have waiting for us, I'd rather waste an hour standing right here doing nothing than walk out at *his* command."

"I'm surprised at my lack of patience, but I feel just the same," Lorand put in, his expression filled with exasperation rather than surprise. "I'm getting very tired of everyone around us trying to make us do things *their* way."

"Either by tellin' us or tryin' to lead us," Vallant put in just before he stepped out into the path of the group of city leaders accompanied by Lavrit Mohr. "Excuse me, folks, but where do you think you're goin'?"

"Why, we're going out to join Dom Meerk on the platform, Excellence," Mohr answered for all of them, his expression showing confusion. "Isn't the ceremony about to start?"

"Not quite yet, so why don't you and the others hold on for a bit," Vallant answered, and then he turned back to *our* group to speak in a murmur. "Refusin' to go along with that man out there may look childish, but that's the only thing I'm in the mood for. So how are we goin' to do it?"

"Let's go over and tell the link groups and other Blendings what's happening," I suggested. "That should waste a few minutes, and then we can all stroll out together."

"And we can't let Dom Meerk speak for us," Naran said suddenly as the others were agreeing with my suggestion. "If we do, things won't go well at all."

"Which means another tradition bein' thrown out," Vallant said with a shrug. "It's a terrible shame, but I think I can live with it. Let's go talk to the link groups and other Blendin's."

Our people were murmuring among themselves, and when we walked over to where they were standing each link group or Blending sent someone to meet us. We explained about Meerk's behavior to this smaller group, and a lot of them looked scandalized on our behalf.

"So we'd like all of you to range yourselves around the city leaders, and we'll all go out together," Jovvi finished. "I'm fairly certain that we're supposed to walk out alone, but we haven't quite earned that great honor yet. If and when we ever accomplish something entirely alone, then we can think about it."

"As far as everyone *I* know is concerned, you've earned anything you care to claim," a woman from one of the link groups said with a smile. "I wasn't with our army long, but even half the time would have been much *too* long. You're the ones who got me out of that, made me feel like a human being again, and gave me something to do that more than needed doing. I now have my dignity back, and I'm all for anything that gives *you* the same gift."

"Everyone in *my* Blending thinks you're all crazy for putting up with even a small part of that nonsense they've been pestering you with," Wilant Gorl stated without showing a smile. "Those people are doing it because they have no real idea what you're capable of, but that's beside the point. If you're finally tired of going along with that garbage, we're behind you."

Everyone else in the group made noises of agreement with both stated opinions, which was an incredible relief. It made me remember that there actually *were* people in the world who saw things the way we did.

"Thank you all," Jovvi said with her own smile as she looked around. "We value your good opinion and hope we'll never do anything to lose it, but we really should get things moving now. If you'll bring everyone else up to date on what's happening, we may get home before nightfall."

People chuckled, but the group did break up to do as Jovvi had asked. The rest of us walked over to where the city leaders waited near the opened doors, and Jovvi smiled at *them* as well.

"Thank you for your patience, my friends," she said, looking around at them. "Everyone will be ready to go in just a few more minutes, and then we'll all walk out together. Our being here was a joint effort, after all, so that's the way we'll present it."

"And there's been another small change in plans," I put in. "We've decided that having Dom Meerk speak for us would be much too pompous, so I'll speak. We intended to explain that when Dom Meerk came back in, but since he hasn't come back he'll have to find it out when it happens."

"As you wish, Excellences," Mohr said with a bow as some of those around him looked disturbed. "This is, after all, *your* Seating ceremony, so it ought to be conducted the way you want it to go. The nobles certainly did it in *their* own way, and they did nothing to earn having their say."

"When people have opinions about something, they tend to think that what they approve of is the only right way to do that thing." Lorand now took over, his tone gentle and friendly. "Everyone should have the right to his or her opinion, but they must also understand that what's fitting for them isn't necessarily just as fitting for others."

"In other words, we'll be doin' what *we* consider fittin' for a while," Vallant added in the same friendly way. "If, for one reason or another, our ideas don't work out, we're willin' to change them for somethin' that does work. We're tryin' to be reasonable, but that doesn't mean we're easy to push around."

"There are those who don't understand the difference between reasonable and biddable," Rion put in, taking his turn, but not sounding quite as friendly. "We appreciate the fact that many people want to see us succeed by doing the proper things, but their definition of proper and ours don't quite agree. As my brothers have said, for the time being *we'll* be doing the defining."

The city people looked like a group of children who had been taken to task by their elders. Some of them shuffled in place, others wore disconcerted expressions, and still others sighed a bit. Not one of them, though, made the extremely unwise decision to argue, not even Relton Henris.

"And now the rest of our people seem to be ready, so we can get on with the ceremony," Jovvi said after glancing back. "Please follow us."

Jovvi walked to the doors and waited until the rest of us were lined up on either side of her, and then we all walked out together. The group of city people followed behind us, and ranged behind *them* were the link groups and other Blendings. Naran's link groups usually tended to stay together and off to themselves. Today, though, a number of them were walking with some of the other Blendings, and everyone involved looked pleased with the change.

Stepping out into the bright sunlight after being inside in the dimness was hard on the eyes, but once the adjustment was made I could look around at an arrangement I hadn't expected but should have. The chairs on the platform faced our side of the amphitheater, and everyone seated in the tiers was crowded into places where they could see the front of those chairs. At first I wondered how they'd found enough room, and then the truth came to me. There was enough room because there weren't any nobles who had to be accommodated.

As soon as we appeared the crowd began to cheer, the noise increasing as the rest of our people came out behind us. Tolten Meerk still stood on the platform all by himself, and the way he held himself suggested that his calm was only on the surface. I would have put gold on the fact that he was raging inside, hating the way we hadn't obeyed his unspoken command to come out sooner. I had no idea what his problem was, but my mood refused to let me worry about it.

By the time we reached the platform, the crowd noise was close to deafening. I felt tempted to look around for the guardsmen, wearing ordinary clothing, who'd been stationed in the stands, but that would have been a waste of time. I already knew they were in places near those hidden bows, handily available to catch the people who were assigned to use the weapons. With all the losses to his ranks that Ayl had lately sustained, he was hopefully close to running out of people to use. Hopefully . . .

The sand was annoying to walk through, but we'd done it before with a lot less confidence and company. During our approach Meerk had been . . . gathering himself, I suppose you could say, and when we finally reached him he gestured with his right arm.

"The members of the Blending are to stand to my right, with the city leaders behind them," he directed without hesitation, raising his voice to be heard over the crowd noise. "I'm afraid there isn't room on the platform for all those others."

"Those *others* will be ranging themselves *around* the platform, so don't worry about it," I told the man as we all stepped up to his level. "It's unfortunate that you chose not to come back inside after getting the sixth chair put in place, or you would have heard the latest. We've decided that the Seated Blending ought to speak to the people directly rather than through someone else, to keep people from thinking we consider ourselves too good to notice the unimportant peasants. That means we appreciate your efforts on our behalf, but we'll take over now."

"You most certainly won't," Meerk said with a small laugh, as if he thought I'd been joking. "There has to be *someone* to present you to the people, and I'm that someone. Presenting yourselves is completely out of the question."

"And why would *that* be, Dom Meerk?" Naran asked in a soft voice, studying the man intently. "Possibly for the reason that the man presenting the new Seated Blending is tacitly accepted as the leader of all the Blending's other supporters? The simple act of presenting us will give you an enormous amount of prestige and power, eliminating the need to struggle for position."

"And even beyond that, the presentation will let you say whatever you care to, won't it?" Jovvi added while Meerk paled and stared at Naran. "You intend to make yourself the one everyone else has to go through in order to reach *us*, supposedly to keep us from being bothered by time-wasting nonsense. You expect to surround us with your cronies, and cut us off from anyone who doesn't go through *your* very proper channels."

"In case you haven't yet gotten the picture, that isn't going to happen." I felt more disgusted than I had in quite a while. "We aren't going to let *anyone* make themselves the new nobility, not when we've only just gotten rid of the old ones. Your brother ran from guardsmen with us, fought beside us, and died for one of us, Dom Meerk. What have *you* done to earn even half the power you want?"

"What I did was spend most of my time bowing to those useless nobles when I was ten times better than the best of them!" Meerk retorted, his complexion now dark with anger. "I lived a lie waiting for them to be brought down, and now it's *my* turn! I can make this empire run more smoothly than it ever has, with everyone in the proper place and doing what they're supposed to. I *can* make it happen, and I *will*!"

And with that he turned away from us, raising his arms as though asking the audience for silence so that he might speak. How he meant to make himself heard without the help of Highs in Air magic I have no idea, but the question became moot. Jovvi looked at him, and suddenly all the frenzy in his actions disappeared into true calm and serenity. He lowered his arms and stepped back away from the edge of the platform, and Jovvi shook her head.

"Doing nothing but waiting for someone else to change things entitles you to the same nothing, Dom Meerk," Jovvi told the man softly. "You can't let other people make the effort and sacrifice, and then step in and take over just because you think you deserve to. That's the way the nobility thought, and a million people could have died because of that mindless outlook. If you think we'll give it a second chance to destroy us, you're completely insane. Now go and stand behind the others where you belong."

Meerk turned and walked toward where the city leaders were standing and looking shaken, moving behind them as he'd been told to do. Once again we were faced with people who knew little or nothing of what we could do, a truth Wilant Gorl had pointed out a short time earlier. Well, hopefully that would soon change.

"You ladies are making the rest of us feel superfluous," Lorand teased. "Rion, Vallant, and I are thinking about taking a nap while you finish up the rest of this."

"I know you older folk *need* to nap, but try to hold off for a short while," I countered while Jovvi and Naran chuckled. "Those people in the stands with the hidden weapons haven't made a move yet, and it's time for me to make that speech. Are you ready to help me, Rion?"

"My link groups will also be helping, Tamrissa," Rion answered with his own amusement. "This place is the least bit bigger than the ballroom we had the party in."

"Yes, the *least* bit bigger," I echoed in a mutter, making myself walk to the edge of the platform. The crowds seemed to have grown even larger somehow, and they'd been quieting down ever since Meerk held his arms up. Now they were all but completely silent, waiting to hear what I had to say. Speaking up when angry has never been a problem for me, but I couldn't help noticing that anger is never around when you really need it.

"Hello," I began in a weak way, hearing the word echo to every corner of the amphitheater. "Thank you for coming today."

The sudden roar of delighted voices was accompanied by thunderous applause, a reaction that was encouraging in spite of being rather startling. A glance back showed all my Blendingmates smiling, so I held my hands up and in a moment or two I had silence again.

"There are a number of things we have to tell you before we actually get to the Seating ceremony," I continued, finding it slightly easier to get the words out. "The first thing, I think, ought to be the fact that we'll only be Seated for a year. Next year the competitions will be held again, and the winners will be Seated for five years instead of twenty-five. Making people wait half a lifetime to compete for the place of strongest Blending just isn't fair."

This time the applause was composed of surprise and startlement, but it was also strong and supportive. Most people obviously thought we'd just continue on with what the nobility had started, and were clearly finding themselves pleased that that wasn't so. I just hoped they'd continue to be pleased—with everything.

"The next thing you have to know about is the training classes that will start tomorrow," I said once I had enough quiet. "Centers are being opened throughout the city today, and anyone who wants their talent trained can go to one of the centers and register. Classes will be filled on a first-come, first-served basis, but don't be upset if you aren't in one of the first classes. The initial training won't take more than a few days, and then new classes will be started. That will continue until everyone who wants the training has gotten it, but no one will be *forced* to take it. If you're not interested, then you're not."

There was applause again, but only a smattering as most people seemed more interested in commenting to the people next to them. It was hard to tell what the comments were about, but I decided not to let that distract me. There were more things to tell them before we would all be able to go home.

"Once everyone who wants to be trained *is* trained, we'll go on to the next step," I said, and the ripple of talk died down to a bit of muttering. "Those people who want to learn how to be part of a Blending will be shown the way, preferably with others whom they feel they can get along with. You don't want to be part of a Blending with just anyone, not when the association is closer than anything you can imagine."

The crowd noise rose almost to its original roar, and most of the people I could see looked downright shocked. We'd been hoping that word of our intentions would spread, but obviously it hadn't spread nearly far enough.

"The leader of our empire is supposed to be the *strongest* Blending, not the only one," I said, and somehow Rion and his link groups made my voice loud enough to be heard over the noise. "There will also be minor competitions during the year, to let people know how strong they are in comparison to others, and to give them chances to practice. When the real competitions are held a year from now, everyone will know that the Blendings competing really are the best of the best."

The comments and exclamations coming from all around now sounded as if they were filled with excitement, and the shock I'd seen a minute ago had changed to expressions ranging from wild elation to deep worry. More people seemed to be pleased than worried, though, definitely a positive sign.

"Please try to calm down," I finally said when the uproar refused to end, my voice echoing all over the amphitheater. "There are still a few more things to say, and I'd like to get to them."

"Wait, wait just a minute," a voice called as a man left his place to walk a short distance onto the sand. It should have been impossible to hear the man, but somehow his voice managed to reach us.

"He's a Middle talent in Air magic, and has a few other Middle talents helping him," Rion said from where he stood, a faint smile on his face. "They're not using the proper pattern, of course, but their effort is quite credible. Do we want to hear what he has to say?"

"Of course we do," Jovvi said at once, looking around at the rest of us. "We need to know what people think, people who aren't appointed leaders as well as those who are. Does anyone disagree?"

"Of course not," I said, as the rest of our Blendingmates smiled or shook a head. "If he says he hates our ideas and everyone else here agrees with him, we can go home that much sooner."

"Then for that reason, if no other, I'll give him a hand," Rion said, returning his attention to the man. From what I could see the man was dressed in simple clothing, clean but not very new. He was of average height and build, but his hair was light and his face was on the square side.

"All right, I'm waiting," I told the man, and the noise died down just a little. "What did you want to say?"

"I wanted to say—" he began, the words chopping off when the volume of them surprised their speaker. It took a moment or two for the man to recover, but then he smiled wryly.

"Thank you for that," he said as he gestured with one hand, obviously referring to the fact that everyone could now hear him. "I don't know why I was surprised, but I guess I'm no more used to being treated like I'm actually worth something than anyone else here."

There were a lot of garbled comments made by the crowd at that, but all the comments clearly agreed with him.

"What I want to say first is something not everyone here may have heard about," the man continued after a moment. "Friends, on their way here, our new Blending was attacked by some crazies who threw etching acid at them. The acid didn't reach them, of course, but it did splash quite a few people who were watching them go by. The guard escort wanted the Blending to ride away to someplace safe, but they refused. Instead they got off their horses and tended the hurt, and people who would have been blinded or scarred are now going to be all right."

Here and there exclamations of surprise sounded, but for the most part the crowd seemed to know all about our little mishap. The others and I exchanged glances of surprise over how the story had managed to get there and spread so quickly, but we weren't given a chance to ask.

"Now we're told that we'll be given the chance to do something none of us had even dared to dream about," the man went on. His attention was on those of us on the platform, but his words seemed to be addressed to everyone in the amphitheater. "I'm tempted to think I'm dreaming, but if I am then a lot of other people are having the same dream. I don't know what we did to deserve you people, but whatever it is I hope we never stop doing it."

Pandemonium broke loose, and the man who had spoken just stood there smiling at us while everyone cheered and screamed out their agreement. I felt tempted to simply accept that approval and enjoy it, but I knew all too well how quickly approval could turn into condemnation. My parents had been delighted with how well I learned to act like a lady, but their approval disappeared when I began to act in a way they hadn't told me I could . . .

"I think you'd better hear the rest of what I have to say before you decide how happy you are to have us here," I said when the cheering and shouting finally died down. "We're going to do something else that hasn't been done before, and your city leaders aren't very pleased with that something. You'll do well to hear about it before you say something you may regret."

"Unless you're planning to murder all of us, I can't see myself changing my mind," the man said while a concerned buzz circled the crowd like bees considering the benefits of a rampage. "Go ahead and say what you have to, and then we'll see."

"Yes, we will, won't we?" I agreed with the faintest of smiles. "All right, here it is. You've probably been won-

dering why there are six chairs on this platform instead of
five, so here's the answer. We have a sixth member of our
Blending, a full, useful member with a talent called Sight
magic, which you haven't heard about before. Some of our
associated Blendings have also taken the same kind of
sixth, but that doesn't matter. We've decided that either
we'll be Seated as a Six or we won't be Seated at all, and
that decision is yours."

This time there was a moment or two of silence before
the buzz began again, wilder than before. The noise rose
to a true roar, and after a short time the man on the sand
shook his head.

"Wait a minute, everybody, wait just a minute," he said,
holding up his arms toward the crowd. "I never expected
to hear anything like that either, especially the last part of
what she said. There are going to be six of them no matter
what, but if we decide that what they're doing is wrong
they won't be *our* six. Is that what you want? To find someone not as good as them, not as good to *us*, just as long as
they're five instead of six? For myself, I don't care if there
are ten or a dozen of them, as long as they keep on making
my dreams come true. So what do the rest of you think?
Do we want them to walk away?"

"No!" the crowd roared, taken up and carried away on
the words the man had spoken. "No, no, no!"

Other people said other things as well, but for the moment it was perfectly clear what the general opinion was.

"So there you have it," the man on the sand said, his
smile now filled with satisfaction. "There are a lot of
damned fools in this city, but most of them seem to have
stayed home today. We want you Seated no matter what
your number is."

"It looks like we have our decision," Jovvi murmured
while I stood there trying to think of what to say. I'd been
sure everyone would turn against us, but now . . . "Tamma,
tell them we accept, at least for the year we promised."

"If that's what you want, you have it," I said after taking
a deep breath. "But if you change your minds once you get
home, don't worry about it. This Seating is only for a year,

just as I said to begin with. And now let's get *to* the Seating."

The cheering rose to deafening proportions as we turned and headed for the chairs on the platform, the group of city leaders—wearing a variety of expressions—stepping aside to let us do it. Lavrit Mohr stood there beaming with pleasure and pride, but Ristor Ardanis, the leader of those with Sight magic who was so happy with us, was nowhere to be seen. We each took a chair and sat, and I couldn't help noticing how expensively made but shabby those chairs were.

The wood surrounding the back of the chair, as well as the arms and the legs, were all intricately carved with representations of the five previously known talents, and the padded back and seat was of red velvet. It came to me that the chairs were very old, and the extra one must have been a spare. It would never do if one of a new noble Blending had to stand because his or her chair had collapsed at the last moment . . .

That, of course, was when Naran's indrawn breath reminded me about the people waiting to murder us. It must have infuriated them that the platform refused to collapse and send us down into the hilsom powder they still thought was in the sand, but fury didn't make them change their plans. When I looked up into the tiers of seats where one of the bows had been hidden, I could see that it wasn't hidden any longer. A man stood holding it with an arrow nocked, and I could even see the choking anger on his face.

A single, sweeping glance told me that the other bowmen were also preparing to loose, so it was time to try the new trick we'd thought of. That morning our Blending entity had . . . marked the bows and arrows with a touch of my talent, somehow linking the weapons and their missiles to my Fire ability. I had no idea how the trick had been done, but even as I sat there looking up into the tiers, I could feel those bows and arrows as clearly as I felt the power I used.

So without wasting another moment, I sent my fires to the places that had been marked, along spiderweb-thin and invisible trails in the air. The bows, along with the arrows in their strings, flared up in bright, burning flames that instantly turned the weapons to ash. Most of the men screamed at the pain they felt from the small amount of burning I'd allowed to reach their hands, this time marking *them* for the guardsmen who quickly headed in their direction. One of the men managed to loose an arrow an instant before I touched his weapon, but the arrow only climbed a short way up its arc before taking on the appearance of a backward-falling star.

We watched as the guardsmen began to arrest the would-be assassins, most of whom struggled to free themselves. Then, abruptly, the prisoners stopped struggling and tried to shrink back behind the guardsmen. The change was caused by the growls and snarls coming from almost everyone in the tiers, people who had just realized that another attack had been launched against their new leaders.

"Is that likely to get out of hand?" Lorand asked as he stared at the same scene I did, most likely speaking to Jovvi. "If that crowd loses control, there won't be anything left of those bowmen."

"Far worse is the near certainty that there would also be nothing left of the guardsmen," Jovvi answered heavily. "Mobs tend to have very little control once they form, and anyone trying to stop them becomes an enemy. Tamma, you speak to them while my link groups and I go to work."

"Stop where you are!" I shouted as I got to my feet, my voice reverberating all around the amphitheater. "Those cowards have been placed under arrest, and they'll go to trial for what they tried to do. If you make any attempt to take the law into your own hands, you'll be doing just what *they* were trying. Is that what you want? To be murderers like them?"

Half the crowd began to argue bitterly with what I'd said, but the other half paused in the slow movement they'd started toward the assassins. They glanced around at each other as though seeking support, and the guardsmen wisely used the hesitation to drag their prisoners out of easy sight and reach. Once the targets for their anger were gone, the crowd lost a lot of the tension that had moved through them like small chains of lightning. No one seemed particularly happy about it, but the objects of their aborted vengeance had disappeared so the monster called mob never appeared.

But that must have been one of the most unusual Seating ceremonies ever to be held.

THIRTEEN

Lord Belvis Drean, nearly to the end of his strength, accepted the extended hand offering to help him up into the wagon. The hand belonged to some minor noble whose name he had never bothered to learn, and under ordinary circumstances Lord Belvis would never have allowed the man to so much as come close, not to speak of touching him.

But circumstances had turned into ongoing nightmare, and nothing remained ordinary or usual. Lord Belvis stumbled over to the nearest unoccupied piece of wagon floorboard and collapsed, paying no attention to the way the man who had helped him dropped off the wagon to walk behind it. The man had obviously already had his rest period, and now made room for those who hadn't.

"This is completely intolerable," an exhausted voice near Lord Belvis said, speaking the words he, himself, had been thinking. "There *has* to be a way to end this nightmare for good and all, but no one seems to be looking for it. How are we to be returned to our proper places if no one looks for the way?"

"I agree," Lord Belvis managed to get out as he regained some breath, his back against the hard wooden side board of the wagon. "And if it takes much longer, I'll have some very sharp words to say to those in charge."

"When are you fools going to wake up to the real world?" a harsh younger voice demanded from a short distance away. "The only ones in charge are the Astindans, and they won't do anything but make our lot harder."

Lord Belvis opened his eyes with a frown, seeing first the man who had spoken first. That man, like Lord Belvis, was clearly a noble in his middle years, looking just as tired. Like Lord Belvis, the man's body and face showed sagging traces of the weight he'd lost during this forced march. The pace set by the Astindans was much too fast, and the food given the prisoners was far too little and tasteless.

The second man, however, seemed another matter entirely. The man was at least ten years Lord Belvis's junior and a good head taller, and the rigors of the forced march seemed to have hardened rather than weakened him. In fact the man looked more like a peasant than nobility, which observation made Lord Belvis sniff.

"Don't speak of things you know nothing about, boy," Lord Belvis told the younger man, who stared at him with a light-eyed, very intense gaze. "We may be in the Astindans' capture right now, but that can't possibly go on forever. Our ancestors were in charge of this empire for more generations than you have years, and that means we'll soon be in charge again. No other outcome is possible."

The older man who had spoken nodded his agreement, but the lowborn-looking young man rudely made a sound of scorn.

"If I didn't know better, I'd think the Astindans forced you to believe that," the young man countered with heavy ridicule. "But all the Astindans did was make us obey all their orders and resist falling into suicidal depression. And come to think of it, maybe that's the answer. The only way you pampered fools can keep from giving up is to believe that you'll be rescued, so you talk about 'those in charge' finding 'a way out.' Obviously it's beyond you to understand that escaping is impossible because we've been ordered not to even try. No matter how badly we want to."

The last of the boy's words were muttered rather than spoken, and the other man who had spoken simply closed his eyes and began to weep. Lord Belvis also felt the distinct urge to weep, but was kept from doing so by the last remnants of pride. He was a powerful lord, after all, and the powerful made others weep. They didn't indulge in foolish hysterics themselves . . .

Belvis, no longer a lord, began to sob, as did a few others in the wagon with him. He had no true idea why they had all come to such a pass, but it would have been a great kindness if he could have lain down and died. But that particular kindness had been denied all of them, and the shedding of tears was only a small comfort allowed in its place.

Even as the tears flowed down his disgustingly bearded cheeks and face, Belvis made sure to let his body relax. He would soon be walking again, and would then require all the rest he'd managed to get . . .

Kail Engreath, youngest son of High Lord Mergen Engreath, pretended he saw nothing of the crying going on all around him. Instead he looked up past the small bit of awning over the wagon to study the very blue sky, a continuing indication of the nice weather they'd had since leaving Gan Garee. The only problem was, his Water magic told him that the nice weather was about to come to an end and they'd soon be walking the road in cold, pouring rain.

The usual surge of anger flashed through Kail, a small part of the fury he'd been filled with ever since he and his family had been arrested. Kail's father and two older brothers had refused to believe something like that could actually happen to *them*, and they'd wasted miles of breath trying to tell the guardsmen that they were making a mistake. Only Kail had understood immediately that it wasn't a mistake on the part of the guardsmen, just on *their* part. They'd expected the world to continue on forever in the same way it had always gone, paying no attention at all to who the new "leaders" of the empire were.

Kail had actually tried to warn his father when Delin Moord and Kambil Arstin and the others were about to be Seated, but High Lord Mergen Engreath had had no patience for what he'd seen as the foolish fantasies of his youngest son. He'd felt that just because Kail hadn't gotten along with the other two young men was no reason to make a fuss about seeing them Seated. After all, they *were* nobles rather than low-class peasants . . .

The internal clock activated in Kail by the Astindans suddenly began to pulse, telling him it was time to leave the wagon. Kail got immediately to his feet and made his way to the end of the wagon, then offered a hand to the woman who walked close. Her own internal clock had told her that it was time to rest, so he helped her into the wagon and then hopped off before resuming his place in the lines following the slowly moving vehicle.

"I'm glad you're back," Renton Frosh said from a few paces ahead of Kail, his thinning face a good deal less florid than usual. "I really don't think I'm going to make it to my next rest period, Kail. If I collapse, will you keep people from walking over my prostrate body?"

"Actually, Renton, I've been thinking about *urging* them to walk all over you," Kail responded, his mood lightening the least little bit. "That way you'll start to feel right at home again."

"Won't I ever," Renton agreed with a short laugh. "In actual fact I'm beginning to feel better than I ever have in my life, which is a horrendous joke. As a noble I was overweight and miserable, but as a slave I'm feeling marvelous? I'm afraid there's something definitely wrong there."

"There are a lot of things wrong with this situation, and that's only the most minor part of it," Kail returned in a growl, anger burning inside him again. "It wasn't my fault or yours that the throne was stolen from those five peasants, so why do *we* have to pay for it along with those whose fault it really was? If they're all that interested in justice, where is the justice in this?"

"I heard them answer that question," Renton said, no longer quite looking at Kail. "They said that some of us may not have actively done anything to cause the problems, but we also did nothing to stop them. In their view that makes us just as guilty as those who were actively involved in starting the war with Astinda, so we've been given the same punishment. And weren't you about to take over a rather important post in the government?"

Kail didn't answer the question, and not only because Renton already knew the answer. Yes, Kail had been about to take over a governmental post, but only because his father had insisted. The man previously holding the post had died of old age, and his own sons had found positions elsewhere in the government years ago. High Lord Mergen Engreath had pulled a large number of strings in order to get the post for his youngest son, the only one in their family who didn't yet perform a "responsible function."

Kail hadn't wanted the position, not when he'd been far more interested in being part of a small group that was trying to think up new uses for all aspects of magic. Most of the few people in the group were sneered at by anyone who learned of what they were doing, the sneerers suggesting that the group members would do better as peasants than members of the ruling class. It was considered bad manners even to mention magical ability; actually trying to work with magic simply wasn't done.

So Kail hadn't had the courage to tell his father that he preferred the company of his group to the company of those in the government. His father was an important man in the government, so anything said against the others could also be said against his father—and no one, not even his son, would be permitted to speak against Mergen Engreath.

"It wasn't my choice *or* my fault," Kail muttered, his anger turning sullen. He couldn't have stood up to his father alone, not without being tossed out, and where would he have gone? To one of his sisters and her husband, a husband who was just as eager a part of the government as his father was? It wasn't fair, it simply wasn't fair . . .

A scream sounded near the wagon ahead of theirs, the kind of scream you would hear when a child threw a tantrum. Renton leaned out of his line to see what had caused the noise, and then he turned to Kail with a grimace.

"It's just that Mardimil witch again," Renton told him with a huge sigh. "They can make her walk with the rest of us and eat with the rest of us, but apparently keeping her from throwing a tantrum when she's forced to leave the wagon is beyond them. I really do think she's worse than our fathers."

"Or at least as bad," Kail agreed, no longer looking over his shoulder before saying that. Families had been firmly separated before they left the city, which made the situation less than a complete horror for Kail. "But that other woman does seem to take a great deal of pleasure in seeing the Mardimil woman being treated like the rest of us. There must be something between them that we don't know about."

"That other woman is Eltrina Razas," Renton supplied, as usual knowing the names of almost everyone. "She had something to do with the competitions, I understand, and the Mardimil woman's son is one of the peasant group that defeated the Seated Blending. I don't quite understand how he *became* a member of that group, but the Mardimil woman was brought to the palace by the Five toward the end of their time because of that fact."

"Renton, did you know any of that Five?" Kail asked slowly, suddenly needing to confirm his own impressions. "Like Delin Moord or Kambil Arstin?"

"I more or less knew all of them," Renton admitted after a short hesitation. "The girl, Selendi Vas, was very interested in my older brother for a time, and then suddenly she wasn't interested at all. Homin Weil seemed to live his life in constant terror, and Bron Kallan was an overgrown spoiled brat. As for the other two . . . they frightened me, but for different reasons."

"Moord struck me as being completely out of his mind despite that charm he always projected," Kail said, nodding to show his agreement. "Arstin was . . . easygoing, friendly, and never threatening, but there was always *something* about him that made me want to leave the room when he walked in. His father tried to get him a good position in the government, I heard, but apparently there were others who felt about him the way we did. And they're the ones our vaunted leaders allowed to be Seated. If they'd had the kind of 'accident' that happened to more people than anyone will admit, I wonder how things would have turned out."

"If they'd had that 'accident,' it would have been the peasant Five who were Seated," Renton pointed out, his tone weary. "Since no one in a position to do anything about it would have allowed something like that, things couldn't have turned out any differently than they did. Many of the Advisors said they'd rather die than allow peasants on the Fivefold Throne, and oddly enough that's just what happened."

Yes, they died, Kail thought as he noticed the clouds starting to roll in. *Most of the people responsible for Seating that Five are dead, but they're the lucky ones. The rest of us* aren't *dead, at least not yet . . .*

High Lord Embisson Ruhl chose a chair and sat while Edmin looked about the house where they would meet with the leaders of the Gracely army. Embisson had already inspected the house even before he'd had some of his servants clean it up, and it was small but perfect. Its furnishings proved to be almost new under the sheets and dust covering them, all the services and decorations were in exquisite taste, and the stables outside were large enough to accommodate a great many horses.

"The servants almost have our meal ready." Edmin reappeared to announce this in his quiet, understated way. "Lord Sembrin is just now arriving, and hopefully our guests won't be far behind him. I'm hungrier than I expected to be."

"And the meal promises to be excellent," Embisson agreed as he shifted in the chair. "Since we no longer eat such a full meal at luncheon, I find my anticipation just as keen. Do the servants understand about wearing their masks?"

"They'll put the masks on as soon as we catch sight of

our guests, and won't remove them again until we give them permission to do so," Edmin responded as he walked to the tea service. "The man we have on watch at the road should give us plenty of warning, so we'll be able to don our own masks in good time. Would you like a cup of tea, Father?"

"If you don't mind," Embisson agreed again, finding the chair he sat in too comfortable to rise from. "I'm still the least bit weary from all those 'courtesy' visits we paid our peers in the area, but running all over the countryside was worth the effort. We'll be able to make very good use of the gold we collected."

"I've already begun to make use of it," Edmin responded as he turned from the tea service with two cups in his hands and a faint smile on his face. "That second group of fifty new guardsmen is now ours, and I'm in the process of locating even more groups outside this area. In the end we should have a force of more than three hundred men to return to the city with us."

"Excuse the intrusion, my lords," a servant said suddenly from the doorway behind Embisson as the High Lord took his teacup. "Lord Sembrin Noll is now approaching the front door. Shall I show him in immediately?"

"Yes, do, Rachers," Edmin told the man, and then after a brief pause continued with a somewhat wider smile. "You weren't able to see that, Father, but Rachers is already wearing his mask. Isn't it nice to have servants about who worry about being dismissed from their positions?"

"Dismissal will be the least of the worries of any servant who shows his or her face," Embisson murmured after making sure that Rachers really was gone. "I want there to be nothing whatsoever to link us to this meeting, just in case the worst happens. If the face of one of the servants is seen, you must make sure that he or she is never seen again."

"As you wish, Father," Edmin agreed in a murmur after sipping at his tea, making no effort to choose a chair of his own. "It's always better to be safe than sorry . . . Ah, and how are you today, Lord Sembrin?"

"I'm quite well, Lord Edmin," Sembrin Noll replied as he passed the escorting servant to enter the room. With clear courtesy, Noll waited until he stood where Embisson could see him without twisting around before performing a polite bow. "Good day, Lord Embisson. I trust you've recovered from the rigors of all your travels? You must have almost doubled the list of names I supplied."

"That I did, Lord Sembrin," Embisson admitted with a chuckle for the knowledge deliberately shown by the man. "I see you've been busy rebuilding your organization."

"A necessary effort if you and Lord Edmin are to be successful," Noll conceded with his own smile, but then his amusement faded. "Would you care to hear the latest while we await the arrival of our lunch guests?"

"From your expression I'm tempted to say no," Embisson observed, studying the man carefully. "That, however, would be complete foolishness, so please tell us what has disturbed you while you pour yourself a cup of tea."

"I'm also tempted to pour something stronger than a cup of tea," Noll responded with a sigh. "Unfortunately, this isn't the time to be under the influence of drink, so tea will have to do. I received word this morning that the peasants have been Seated, but the matter wasn't handled in quite the way we expected."

"How many ways are there to handle a Seating ceremony?" Edmin asked as he also watched the man. "Surely even peasants are able to follow the example they saw only a short time ago when the interlopers were Seated."

"I'm told that most of the peasants were prepared to do just that," Noll said over his shoulder as he filled a cup from the tea service. "What they were *unprepared* for was the desires of those to be Seated. To begin with, the Fivefold Throne is now the Sixfold Throne."

Embisson tried to think of something to say to that, but a sudden, distant memory insisted on rising. There were old writings, dating back to the time of the first Fivefold Blending, writings that suggested there might be more than five talents. Embisson had dismissed the veiled hints as nothing more than imagination run wild, just as everyone with sense had dismissed them. Now, though . . .

"How can there be more than one of each talent in a Blending?" Edmin demanded as Noll turned away from the tea service. "There *can't* be, so the peasants must be taking advantage of their position to elevate an outsider. That means we have an excellent point of attack against them, one that even the other peasants will sympathize with."

"I'm afraid not, Lord Edmin," Noll disagreed with a sigh as he moved to a chair and sat. Edmin chose his own chair, his face creased into a frown. "One of the now-Seated group explained that there's another talent called Sight magic, and they were successful at including that new talent into the Blending. The addition was what let them get the better of the Astindan invaders, and the peasants in the audience actually accepted the explanation—and the changed circumstances."

"They've accepted it for the moment," Embisson corrected as Edmin's expression changed to one of shock. The matter was highly disturbing, but Embisson's own mind had rallied quickly enough to let him think again. "Once we're back in the city, we can stress how disrespectful it is to change what's been done for so many years. We would also do well, I think, to start a rumor that there really is no such thing as a sixth talent, and the peasants were lied to. There are always a large number of peasants around who are willing to believe the worst about others, and they can rally even more support against the new Seated Blending."

"Lord Embisson, I fear that the matter won't be that easily seen to," Noll said solemnly with another sigh. "There's more involved than I've yet mentioned. The peasants were also told that classes would begin immediately, to train anyone interested in the proper use of his or her talent. Once the training is over, the peasants have been promised that they'll also be taught how to Blend."

"Those people really *are* fools," Edmin exclaimed, back to looking shocked again. "How do they expect to maintain control—and their position—if everyone can do the same as they? Are they *trying* to have themselves displaced?"

"Apparently they're trying to do exactly that," Noll agreed, his bewilderment clear. "One of the first things they announced was that their Seating would only be for a year, when new competitions would be held. They maintain that the throne belongs to the *strongest* Blending, not the first one managing to be Seated, and in a year's time those who want to compete will have had enough practice to do so."

"I don't believe this," Embisson blurted, suddenly delighted. "Lord Sembrin, are you absolutely certain that you've been given correct information? I find it hard to believe that those peasants have actually given us our victory."

"I find that just as hard to believe," Noll commented much too dryly. "I'm absolutely certain of the information I've been given, but I'm afraid I don't see anything of our victory in it."

"Perhaps that's because you haven't considered how much confusion and uncertainty such a stance creates," Embisson told the man with a smile, seeing that Edmin also needed the explanation. "If things in the city were settled and calm, we would have our hands full with trying to take over again. But when furor and confusion reign, it's much more difficult to notice the subtle doings of others. With the very thoughtful help of those peasants, we should be in position to take over again before anyone even knows we're there."

"You're saying that we'll need to move more quickly than we'd originally planned," Edmin concluded aloud with a thoughtful nod. "Yes, I can see that now, and I certainly agree. I'll do all I can to hurry that matter of hiring additional guardsmen."

"There's one area not far from here that you've somehow overlooked, Lord Edmin," Noll informed them, apparently encouraged by what Embisson had said. "It's the settlement called Reed Springs on the other side of Margintown. A band of would-be outlaws and raiders has gathered there, lording it over the immediate environs and supposedly making plans to expand its area of influence. I'm told they mean to take advantage of the confusion in Gan Garee to advance themselves, and I think if they're offered enough gold they'll join our enterprise."

"Then I'll just have to offer them enough gold," Edmin said with the faint smile that told Embisson of his vast amusement. "I appreciate the assistance, Lord Sembrin, and hope you'll continue to supply it whenever you find that I'm . . . overlooking something."

Noll raised his teacup with a smile that indicated his agreement to do just that, but the air of general amusement was pierced by the appearance of the servant Rachers.

"Your pardon, my lords, but word has just come that your guests are very near," the man announced briskly. "If you would care to prepare yourselves, I'll make certain that the servants are also notified."

"Yes, do that, Rachers," Edmin ordered, putting aside his teacup and rising from his chair. Edmin had put his and Embisson's masks on the table with the tea service, and now went to fetch them. Noll, on the other hand, had *his* mask in his inner coat pocket, and now withdrew it after also putting down his teacup. The mask, like the ones brought by Embisson and Edmin, was more than a simple domino. Sewed to its bottom was a length of thick black veil, an addition meant to cover the wearer's entire face. Once again Embisson meant to take no chances about being recognized.

From the speed with which their guests arrived, Embisson had the impression that they, too, were looking forward to the meal. Rachers showed the four of them into the sitting room without speaking, then withdrew just as silently. Embisson felt relieved that he didn't know any of the four personally, but it was time to begin the meeting.

"We've come to bid you welcome to the area, my lords," Embisson said with a bow after standing. "Would you care to introduce yourselves?"

"I'm Lord Henich Rengan," the man in the lead snapped, his tone more than brusque. "What nonsense *is* this?"

Henich Rengan was a large man, larger even than Embisson although not as old. Hefty was the best word to describe his appearance, both in body and in face. His body strained the material of his elegant uniform, and his wide and square-jawed face was just short of being florid. Rengan was obviously a man who lived to be in charge, of everything around him and as many as possible of the things that weren't.

"I'm afraid that 'nonsense' isn't the proper word, Lord Henich," Embisson replied, keeping his own voice low and roughening it a bit. " 'Precaution' would be more fitting, which is what these masks can be considered. You'll understand more fully when we fill you in on what's been happening. Would you care to introduce your officers as well?"

"Possibly later," Rengan stated, drawing himself up. "Right now I'd like to hear why supposed lords of this empire are hiding their identity from another of the same. And the reason had better be good."

"Nothing about this situation is good," Embisson replied dryly, then gestured to the chairs near his that had been prepared for the visitors. "If you'll take seats, I'll begin the explanation of recent events until lunch is ready. It shouldn't be long before we're able to go to table."

Rengan hesitated an instant, but then he nodded curtly and stomped toward one of the chairs. His officers followed, and Embisson examined them as they passed. The one closest to Rengan was as expressionless as he, clearly the man's next in command. He was a fairly tall man with an air of knowing what he was about, but the other two weren't the same. The first, with light red hair, strolled along as though bored by the proceedings, and the second, with brown hair, moved as though hoping no one would notice him.

"All right, you can begin now," Rengan announced once he and the second man were seated. The other two had only just reached their chairs, but Rengan seemed oblivious—or uncaring. "What are all these not-good happenings that call for your being masked?"

Embisson began a succinct—and carefully edited—description of recent events, and aside from occasional exclamations and muttered curses he wasn't interrupted. He had

just completed his summation when Edmin signaled that
Rachers had appeared to silently announce lunch, so the
High Lord got to his feet.

"While you're digesting what I just told you, we can all
begin digesting our meal," Embisson suggested. "If you and
your men will follow me, Lord Henich?"

"If I were a softer man, my appetite would be ruined by
now," Rengan muttered as he rose more slowly. "It's difficult to understand how the rabble were allowed to get the
upper hand."

"For the most part it was due to the actions of those
interlopers who were Seated," Embisson explained as he
slowly led the way to the dining room. "They stripped the
city of guardsmen in an effort to recapture the peasants who
were such a threat to them, leaving our peers almost un-
protected. When the rabble realized what an advantage
they'd been given, they jumped to make the most of it."

"What about the armies of the west?" Rengan's second,
who still hadn't been identified, put in with disturbance.
"Surely at least one of *them* could have dealt with the peasants."

"As I said, most of the armies sent to Astinda were destroyed by the force the Astindans finally managed to put
together," Embisson lied blandly. "But some of the segments of those armies were taken over by the now-Seated
peasants, using who-knows-what kind of underhanded
methods. You'll have to make sure that the same thing
doesn't happen to portions of your own force."

"Those miserable peasants won't get the *chance* to do
the same to my force," Rengan assured Embisson with a
growl as he was gestured to the chair at Embisson's right
hand. "Are you certain that they won't accompany whatever force they send against us? I want the pleasure of
getting my hands on them as soon as possible."

"The reports we've gotten say that the new leaders have
told their people they'll be coming against you, but I seriously doubt that they will." Embisson's assurance to the
man was filled with his own belief as he took his seat at
the table. "Their places on the throne are barely established,

so they aren't likely to leave the city and give their enemies a chance to work against them. They'll undoubtedly find a reason at the last minute to send others in their place, others they consider expendable."

"That's disappointing, but not terribly so," Rengan said as he gave his attention to his salad. "Now that I've stopped to think about it, I'll first have the enjoyment of wiping out whatever force they send against me. Then I'll have the very great pleasure of hauling that rabble out of the palace and hanging them beside the gates."

"And after your victory, it will be our pleasure to show you more lavish hospitality than you now receive," Embisson told him, all but dismissing the fairly lavish meal now being brought out. "Then my associates and I will make for the city first, to prepare the way for you and your forces."

"Excuse me, sir, but there's something I still don't understand," Rengan's second, who wasn't paying quite as much attention to the food, put in. "If you consider our victory so certain, why are you and your servants masked? Being identified as allies of a victorious force should further your cause, not harm it."

"Under other circumstances you would be completely correct," Embisson informed the man without hesitation, having prepared for the question. "We do expect you to be fully victorious, but there have already been too many unexpected twists of fate involved in this matter. If some underhanded trick defeats part of your force and one of you along with it, we'll still be an unknown factor to our enemies. And believe me, we'll do our best to avenge whatever part of your force may be lost—and restore your freedom once Gan Garee is in our hands again."

"Which can't happen too soon to suit *me*," Rengan muttered around a mouthful of food, pausing in stuffing his face to send Embisson a glare as he also swallowed the excuse. "We'll have a lot of hangings before this is over, so many that the rabble will come to believe that traitors grow on trees. My word on that."

And that was the last of it for the rest of the meal. The

food was just as good as Embisson had expected it to be, and he did his own part making it disappear. The army leaders ate so much that Embisson wondered what they were forced to eat on the march, then dismissed the question. The uncertainty of army life, even for its leaders, was such that Embisson had made sure to dissuade Edmin when that worthy had considered asking for a commission. That life had nothing whatsoever to commend it to a true gentleman . . .

"Well, that's that," Sembrin Noll said once the four men had ridden away from the house again. "And isn't it typical of Lord Henich Rengan not to introduce his companions at all?"

"I've never met the man before," Edmin said as he removed his mask with an expression of relief. "What have you heard about him, Lord Sembrin?"

"Only that he's a complete martinet, and no one is allowed to put himself forward while in the man's presence," Noll said, also quickly removing his mask. "The only partial exception to that is his son Vodan, the young man who followed him most closely. The others were two of his younger sons, whose names I can't quite recall at the moment."

"So he's made it a family affair," Embisson said, shedding his mask as happily as Edmin had. "I hope that encourages him to do his utmost best against the force the peasants send to confront him. If we have to go to Gan Garee without the backing of his army, we'll be in a less secure position than I care for. Although we'll still most certainly go."

"While we're waiting, we really must decide whether to hope for something," Noll said slowly as he gazed at Embisson. "You told Rengan that the Seated peasants would not be coming against them, but that might be an untruth. My agent informed me that there's an excellent chance they *would* lead their countering force, and that's my dilemma. Where would we *rather* have the six of them? In Gan Garee when we get there, on hand to counter our moves, or out here, spending all their attention on Rengan's army? I can't quite decide."

Embisson exchanged a glance with Edmin, but that didn't help. He was certain that the Seated peasants would stay in the city, but *he* couldn't quite decide whether he liked that idea either . . .

FOURTEEN

"Good morning, Tal," Olskin Dinno greeted Zirdon in his usual rumble. Dinno was a High in Earth magic, a large, bulky man with dark hair and light eyes who had supported Zirdon in the assembly for quite some time. He waited for Zirdon beside Zirdon's seat in the assembly room, and the Fire magic user smiled as warmly as possible at his follower.

"Well, it certainly is morning, Dinno," Zirdon agreed, trying to sound less than sourly displeased. "Have you decided yet which side of the issue I've raised that you'll be supporting?"

"You seem very much out of sorts this morning, Tal," Dinno observed calmly as he ignored Zirdon's question. "Has something happened to upset you?"

Dinno always looked so placid and bovine that Zirdon constantly found himself surprised when the man showed his keen powers of observation. This time, however, Zirdon felt more annoyed than surprised.

"It's nothing for you to be concerned about, Dinno," Zirdon replied after the briefest of hesitations. "I'm just out of sorts because that young lady I chose, Sheedra Kam, was officially engaged to be married last night. She was so pleasant a companion that I'll be hard put to find someone to replace her."

"I'm fairly certain you haven't yet told some of our colleagues about your loss," Dinno commented, an odd expression in his light eyes. "A number of them seemed almost as pleased by your claim on the girl as you were. And I'm sure it *won't* be easy to find a replacement for her that the others will feel the same about."

Zirdon stared at the man for a moment without answering, then decided to be prudent and look away again. Dinno shouldn't have known how Sheedra Kam was being used to strengthen Zirdon's major coalition, but Dinno had a minor coalition of his own. So far Dinno and his friends had supported Zirdon's stance in the assembly, but Zirdon wasn't fool enough to think that pushing the man would go unnoticed by him. Dinno was too intelligent by half, and so far Zirdon hadn't found a way to bind the man tightly. A pity he wasn't as vulnerable to a pretty face and body as some of the others were . . .

"Ah, I think we're ready to begin." Dinno's rumble brought Zirdon back to where he stood. "Everyone seems to be here now, and most have even taken their seats. I think I'll do the same."

Dinno performed a small bow and walked away, leaving Zirdon to glance around to see that everyone *was* in place. They were all waiting for *him* to begin the meeting he'd called the day before, which lightened Zirdon's mood to a large extent. He did so enjoy having everyone hanging on his every word . . .

"Good morning, all," Zirdon announced cheerfully after stepping away from his seat, putting out of his mind for the moment what he would say to the men waiting to be told when they might have Sheedra to themselves. "Just to remind you, we're here today to decide whether to demand reparations from the new Gandistran government for the 'destruction' caused by their army, or to meekly—and quickly—offer them an alliance. Who would like to speak first, and on behalf of which option?"

"I'd like to speak first," Antrie Lorimon said at once, surprising Zirdon and silencing the handful of others who had been about to respond. "If, that is, you don't mind, Zirdon. I won't take long."

The woman had risen to her feet and had ended her request with a smile, leaving Zirdon no choice whatsoever. She had graciously—and clearly—left the granting of permission up to *him*, and refusal would have made him look like a complete boor. Zirdon would have been happier sending her back to her sewing where she belonged, but instead he showed his own charming smile and bowed.

"By all means, Antrie, we would all be delighted to have you speak first," Zirdon responded smoothly. "But please do be brief, as we have important matters to resolve here today."

Zirdon smiled to himself as he returned to his place and sat, pleased with the way he'd trivialized whatever the woman chose to say. She'd been given permission to speak first, but then the *men* of the assembly would get on with "important matters"—a category *her* thoughts would not fall into.

"You're quite right, Zirdon," Antrie said in her sweet and gentle voice as she stepped out to the middle of the floor. "We do have important matters to discuss today, and the questions you've raised don't enter into it at all. The first thing the members of this assembly need to be told is that the new Gandistran ruling Blending is composed of all High talents. We no longer have weak Middle figureheads to contend with."

Exclamations of shock sounded all over the room, coming even from the seats of the citizens observing the meeting as well as from the members of Zirdon's coalition. That point should have been obvious, but somehow Zirdon and his people had missed it. But Antrie's people weren't looking shocked or surprised, which meant they already knew what she was going to say.

"No, Zirdon, don't interrupt right now," Antrie said as Zirdon was about to stand and take over the meeting again. "There's a good deal more that needs mentioning before everyone knows exactly what problems we have before us. A second point of importance is that the new Gandistran Blending didn't destroy the other armies sent against it. They freed the members of those armies, and then recruited the High talents to their own cause. That means there's an excellent chance they'll do the same with the army which was *here*."

This time the exclamations were quite a bit louder and more disturbed, and Zirdon knew how the others felt. He'd been about to order Antrie to resume her seat, but sudden shock kept him from moving or speaking. Making the nobles leading that army believe a fantasy had been *his* idea, one he'd made sure everyone gave him full credit for. Now the idea had turned into catastrophe, and it was far too late to put the blame for it onto someone else.

"How much of a chance do you think there is that all those Highs will come here to Liandia?" Olskin Dinno asked Antrie in his deep rumble, his tone filled with a concern that was clearly shared by everyone else. "And if they do come, how do you propose we face them?"

"If you mean confront them, the simple answer is we can't," Antrie returned calmly and reasonably. "The Highest Aspect may send a miracle and keep those people out of Gracely, but if we count on that happening we're absolute fools who deserve whatever happens to us. We have to assume that the new Seated Blending will take over the Highs in the army that was here just the way they did with other armies. If they find out that the nobles leading the army were tampered with they *will* come here, so we have to be ready for them. If they don't find out, we won't be any the worse off for having devised a contingency plan."

"But that's ridiculous!" Zirdon blurted in protest, too upset to keep the words back. "I know we were told that they took over and freed the Highs in other armies, but that has to be nothing more than a—a—misunderstanding or a deliberate lie. It isn't possible for five Highs to take over dozens and hundreds of other Highs, and even if it were, these Highs that were here don't know anything."

"But their noble officers do," Antrie pointed out with

continuing calm that underscored Zirdon's distress. "If the Highs and strong Middles of the army are taken over, their officers can be captured rather than killed. That means captured and *questioned*, something any of us would do with them. Gandistra has just narrowly escaped a war with Astinda, so they'll make very sure they're not about to have one with us. They won't simply shrug and take themselves back to Gan Garee."

Quite a few people began to talk then, most doing nothing more than voicing their own distress. Zirdon's frantic thoughts darted in all directions as he sought a way out of the predicaments, both Gracely's and his own. Saving the empire was all well and good, but what about *his* position in it? Antrie Lorimon had taken over *his* meeting, and no one was figuratively patting her on the head and telling her to sit down.

Zirdon's racing mind came to an idea, and he seized it immediately. It would regain his control of the meeting even if it *did* show the strength of his position prematurely. He'd meant to show that strength in a different way, but there was no sense in having power if you didn't use it when you needed it.

"People, please!" Zirdon called out after standing and taking a step forward. "Give me your attention for a moment." The frenzied babble died down, and Zirdon smiled his most charming smile. "These issues that were just raised are much too important to consider without serious prior discussion, which they haven't had. I propose that we adjourn this meeting for a short time to hold that discussion, and reconvene in two hours. A show of hands in agreement with my proposal should suffice in place of a formal vote."

Zirdon smiled pleasantly at Antrie Lorimon, wanting to see her expression when three of the members of her coalition abandoned her. Those three members would give him the ten votes he needed to have the final say over *anything* the assembly considered, making him the most powerful man in the empire. The Lorimon chit gazed back at him with her own faint smile, not yet aware of how thoroughly

she'd been bested, so Zirdon turned his gaze to a count of
the votes. *That* would show her . . .

The smile died on Zirdon's face as he saw something he
didn't believe, and frantically he looked around again.
There were only two hands raised around the circle of assembly seats, and one of them, belonging to the man Ebro
something or other, seemed more tentative than certain. Not
only didn't Zirdon have the support of three of Lorimon's
people, four members of his own coalition had abandoned
him! How was that possible?

The flat-eyed stare coming from Olskin Dinno told Zirdon part of the story. Dinno had apparently increased the
number of his minor coalition to four, and now he'd taken
all of them out of Zirdon's camp. But what about the others,
the three supporters of Lorimon who were supposed to support *him* instead?

Glancing from one to the other of the three men brought
Zirdon to instant fury. The three were staring at him with
dark vindictiveness, and there could only be one reason for
the attitude. Zirdon had promised them Sheedra Kam's use
in return for their support, and somehow they already knew
he was no longer able to make good on the promise. It was
the same hold he'd had on the members of Dinno's minor
coalition, and they *all* knew . . .

Antrie Lorimon's smile hadn't widened even by so much
as a breath, but Zirdon knew without a doubt that she stood
there laughing at him. *She* had to be responsible for this
disaster, for stealing from him the position that should have
been his and relegating him to the place of a very minor
coalition leader. Only three votes! What was he supposed
to do with only three votes?

There was *nothing* he could do with only three votes,
but that would change. As Zirdon quietly sat down again
he vowed to himself that the situation would change back
again even if he had to burn Antrie Lorimon to cinders!

Cleemor Gardan kept his expression neutral, but on the
inside he laughed gleefully. Zirdon Tal had been completely humiliated, and it would be quite a while before he

regained any of his power. The man now sat in his seat and glowered around, having no idea that he was too stupid to use power properly. If he'd gained control of the assembly their empire would probably have been doomed, but Cleemor had made sure that *that* became impossible. Telling everyone of Tal's loss of Sheedra Kam had more than done the job. If Tal hadn't been an incompetent fool, he would have found a stronger tie than the use of a pretty girl to bind his people to him.

"Please, my friends, let's discuss this problem in a way we can all follow," Antrie said, raising her sweet voice only a bit. "I'll start us off by saying that we can't expect to *fight* the Gandistrans, and not just because the idea of open fighting is distasteful to most of us. Our empire has fifteen Blendings represented by this assembly, but the fact that our Blendings outnumber theirs doesn't matter. They have far too many High talents acting together, and a miscalculation through overconfidence on our part could mean disaster."

"Then what do you propose we do?" Olskin Dinno, formerly a fairly staunch supporter of the fool Zirdon, asked in a more than reasonable way. "Do we send a contingent of our own Highs to refuse them entry to Liandia? If they're more interested in peace than war with their neighbors, they just might not press the point."

"Yes, you're right," Antrie granted him in that cool and gracious way of hers. "There's every chance they would *not* enter the city if we forbade it, but I'm afraid that that would scarcely solve our problem. Our refusal would let them know we have something to hide, and if they had any intelligence at all they would then quietly send in people to find out what that something was. *You* tell *me*, Olskin. Would they have much trouble discovering what our intentions toward them were?"

"Unfortunately not," Dinno agreed with a sigh. "By making sure that our intentions had the approval of everyone in the city, we *told* everyone in the city what we meant to do. At the time I wasn't certain that that was the wisest course of action, but I never expected to learn we were wrong in *this* particular way."

Dinno only glanced in Zirdon Tal's direction, but other members of the assembly glared at the Fire magic user. Tal had been the one to talk everyone into "sharing" their plans to invade and conquer Gandistra with the populace, supposedly to gain their understanding agreement. Cleemor privately believed that the gesture had been a ploy on Tal's part to let the man reap all the credit when their plans worked, but now the effort had backfired on him. The mistake was typical of the fool's lack of imagination . . .

"Well, it's too late to take back the information, and it's certainly too late to reconsider," Antrie said, her tone now soothing and sympathetic. And, of course, she made no mention of the fact that she had been against letting everyone know what they meant to do. "So we can't insist that the Gandistrans stay out of our city and we can't give them free access to it, but there's one thing we *can* do. If we invite them in and treat them as *very* important people, we ought to be able to keep them from coming in close contact with the populace."

"And in the meantime we spread the word," Cleemor added into the low and thoughtful buzz of comments, speaking the suggestion that really was his. "This time we *do* have to tell everyone about what's going on, and make sure that the people understand what's at stake here. If *we* go down because someone speaks out of turn, there's a very good chance that everyone in the city will go with us. We can't be everywhere to make sure that people keep their mouths closed, but our citizenry *is* everywhere. It will be everyone's job to watch his or her neighbor."

"I hate the need to make everyone watch everyone else, but I honestly see no other way to handle the matter." Antrie spoke quietly, responding to the frowns clear on a number of faces. "And it shouldn't be for very long anyway. Once we've been able to sound out this new Seated Blending, we can make up some story about how a previous faction in the assembly tried to force our empire into war. We, of course, wanted nothing to do with something like that, and we struggled hard to displace that terrible faction. Now that we've accomplished our aim, we'll be able to offer peace and friendship instead."

Some members of the assembly chuckled at that, and others lost much of their expressions of distaste. If Tal's smooth charm had swayed people to support his point of view, Antrie was at least as adept at doing the same—but with more imagination. People began to relax all over the room, and a smattering of applause came from the ordinary people watching the proceedings.

"Does anyone have any other suggestions about what we might do?" Antrie put after a moment or two as she looked around. "Our planning is by no means finalized, so any and all suggestions will be welcome. If you can't think of anything at the moment, don't hesitate to get in touch with us when you do get an idea. We certainly want to hear from you, and we won't do anything at all without the full knowledge and consent of this assembly. Let's think about it for a day or two, and then we'll meet again."

The immediate murmur of agreement came through clearly, and Cleemor chuckled to himself as he stood and stretched. Antrie had kept saying "we" to soothe the indignation of some of their more stiff-necked male colleagues. If she'd even hinted that she was in charge of their coalition the fools would have balked, immediately refusing to ally themselves with people led by a woman. By using the word "we," Antrie had suggested that there were really men in charge, and she simply spoke for them. As well as the woman knew and handled people, she should have been a Spirit magic user rather than Air magic . . .

"So how do you think it went?" Antrie murmured once she had walked over to him. "We have most of them following our lead now, but will we keep them long enough to save ourselves?"

"We should, if we don't run into something unexpected," Cleemor murmured in return as he glanced around. "Zirdon looks positively murderous, but I'm willing to bet that he has no clear plan to dig himself out of the pit we've thrown him into. If he can't think of anything to help himself—

and he probably won't—I would not put it past him to attack you physically in some sneaking, behind-the-back way."

"I've already considered that," Antrie said with a smile, then gestured with one graceful hand. "Let's walk out to the carriages before we continue this conversation."

Considering the fact that people seemed to be moving around in all directions, Cleemor agreed at once. Keeping their voices down would hardly make their conversation private if others happened to be standing near enough to catch a few words. Cleemor offered his arm, and Antrie took it with another smile. Once they were outside and strolling along one of the walks that broke up the expanse of lawn in front of the assembly building, however, Antrie's smile faded to nothing.

"I decided it might be best if I worked with the other members of my Blending on personal protection," Antrie said with a sigh when it was clear that no one else walked near them. "There is now a . . . thin layer of hardened air all around me, and nothing but fresh air should be able to get through it. We molded it tightly to my entire body and head, so it shouldn't be noticeable. Are *you* able to discern it?"

Cleemor reached for the power with a frown, and once he'd opened to it and used his ability he was able to see just the hint of what she'd done.

"If you hadn't told me the layer was there, I would have dismissed the very faint indications of displacement," Cleemor admitted after a moment. "I'm pleased that you're finally doing something positive to protect yourself, rather than relying on being ignored."

"After this morning, I'm not likely to be ignored as much as I would like," Antrie told him ruefully as they continued to stroll. "Zirdon certainly knows who ruined his plans to make himself supreme leader of the assembly, and he's really nothing but a large, overindulged child. He'll sulk for a little while, and then he might well decide to 'get even.' That's why I'd like to ask *you* to protect yourself in the same way I have."

"Me?" Cleemor said in surprise, about to protest the need, but then he thought better of the reaction. "All right, yes, you're probably right. Zirdon knows how close we are, just as everyone in the assembly does. If something happens to me you'll be left as 'nothing but a woman,' and Zirdon might then be able to take back control."

"At the very least he'd try, so I do appreciate your agreement," Antrie told him with the sparkle of mischief in her beautiful eyes. "If you'd refused to protect yourself and then had died, I would have been very vexed with you."

"Not as vexed as Tenia would have been," Cleemor countered with a chuckle. "My lovely wife is very firm about how well I'm to take care of myself, and even dead I would *not* want to have the two of you angry with me. I have the definite feeling I'd know all about that anger, and be made to regret it."

"That's very wise of you, my dear," Antrie said, but then her amusement disappeared again. "Have your people had any luck with identifying our hidden enemy? It's no longer likely that Zirdon will be his or her first target, and that's another reason for us to protect ourselves. If we let ourselves become flushed with victory, we could well be handing over the game."

"And that's something we really don't want to do," Cleemor agreed, heaving a sigh. "No, my people haven't had any luck yet. How about yours?"

"My ladies have found the same nothing," Antrie said, frustration now peeking out of her eyes. "But I've given them a suggestion you might want to pass on to your own people. Instead of trying to find out who the enemy *is*, it might be easier in this instance to eliminate those it *can't* be. At worst we'll be left with only two or three suspects, and at best we could conceivably be left with only one."

"That's a good idea, but I have one suggestion," Cleemor said with sudden enthusiasm. "It would be a waste of time and effort for our people to investigate the same suspects, so let's divide the list. With you, me, and Zirdon already eliminated there are twelve assembly members left, meaning six for each group."

"Yes, we could do that, but you must caution your people just as I have," Antrie said with a slow, thoughtful nod. "No one can be eliminated without a concrete reason to back up the elimination, no matter what those doing the investigating *believe*. I'd rather have multiple suspects than pass by the guilty party because he or she doesn't *look* guilty."

"That's more than reasonable," Cleemor agreed again, rubbing his face as he considered the matter. "I'll pass along the word, and hopefully in a day or two we'll have only one or two people to worry about instead of twelve. Are you going to the competitions this afternoon for our Blendingmates? Your protection might not stand up properly if one of your Blending members is defeated."

"I've thought of that, so I'm definitely going to the competitions later," Antrie told him as she stopped near her carriage. "This competition couldn't have come at a worse time, but there's no help for it. I'm hoping that my Blendingmates are strong enough to successfully defend their places, as I'd hate to have to start over with a new member or members just at *this* time."

"Not now, and not when—rather than if—the five from Gandistra show up," Cleemor growled, more bothered than annoyed. The monthly competitions among Middle talents for places in the fifteen Blendings couldn't possibly be suspended or even delayed, but Cleemor certainly wished they could be. Things were getting far more complicated than he had a taste for . . .

FIFTEEN

Ebro Syant wasn't a happy man, despite the fairly nice weather they had for the competitions. Too many things had happened to affect his plans, and now in addition to everything else it was time for another competition.

This section of the park was reserved for the competitions, and fifteen comfortable chairs had again been placed around a fairly large circle of grass where the competitions took place. Behind each of the fifteen chairs were four smaller ones, now filled with the Middle talent members of each Blending. A short distance behind the four chairs were rows and lines of benches for spectators, and the fact that they were well filled wasn't to Ebro's taste. Competitions for Middle places in a Blending weren't as important as the ones for major talent, but even these ought to be held somewhere private. Once *he* began to run the assembly, things would quickly change . . .

But he wasn't yet in a position *to* run the assembly, and remembering that for the hundredth time almost made him move in his chair with annoyance. Just a few more days and he would have eliminated that Lorimon woman and Cleemor Gardan, leaving behind indications that Zirdon Tal was responsible for the deed. Tal would have been quickly put down, and then there would have been no one in Ebro's way to full control of the assembly and empire. He might have had to work through that man Olskin Dinno, but he, Ebro Syant, would have been in complete control. But now . . .

191

"It's almost time for *your* people to compete, Exalted One," some official of the competitions appeared to say, pulling Ebro from the depths of his thoughts. "I'm sure they'll do just as well as those talents who have competed before them."

"Yes, I'm sure they will," Ebro agreed with his best vague expression, smiling in the man's direction. "Thank you for letting me know."

The official bowed with his own smile and then moved away, reacting to Ebro's act the way most people did. That official would tell himself he was superior to Ebro in every way but where talent was concerned, and for that reason would dismiss Ebro completely. It was the way Ebro wanted it, but this afternoon the necessity was more galling than usual. If it wasn't absolutely essential to hide his brilliance . . .

But it *was* essential, since those who were short and heavy weren't permitted to be brilliant. In order to be tolerated by the tall, pretty people he had to be considered a nonentity, otherwise they would quickly do something to get rid of him. Or worse, they would hurt him until he crawled away to find a corner in which to die. He refused to let that happen, so he *had* to find a way to be in charge.

Polite but approving applause came from the benches all around, drawing Ebro's attention to the last competition. Antrie Lorimon's Blendingmates had retained their positions earlier, as had Cleemor Gardan's. One of the other assembly major talents had lost two members of his old Blending, and now Zirdon Tal had lost one of *his*. Tal looked completely unconcerned where he sat in his chair, but Ebro knew that Tal had to be seething on the inside. It was always such a bother when a new Middle talent had to be brought into one's Blending, and Tal didn't need any additional problems at the moment.

Just as Ebro didn't need more. It would probably be possible to stay with his previous plan to eliminate Lorimon and Gardan, but now Tal had an excellent, very visible motive to do away with the two. If *too* much evidence was left pointing to Tal, people might become suspicious and decide that Tal was being blamed for something he hadn't done. If too little evidence was left, Tal might be able to talk himself out of being found guilty. Not to mention the fact that he, Ebro, still had to investigate what Lorimon had told them about the situation with Gandistra. If Lorimon, Gardan, and Tal were taken out of the picture right now, would there be time to establish full control before that High Blending appeared?

Ebro was pulled out of his thoughts again, this time by the movement of the members of his Blending rising from their chairs. It was time for the four of them to defend their positions, and they walked out to the center of the circle with casual confidence. All four of them were really very strong for Middle talents, so it wasn't terribly likely that they would be displaced.

A servant stood with a glass and a pitcher of something that ought to be cold and sweet, so Ebro gestured her over. The servant had been stationed near him by the officials running the competitions, but Ebro still examined the girl briefly as she poured his drink. If he decided he wanted her, he could find a way to get her. But the sweet and friendly smile she offered along with the filled glass showed Ebro that she wasn't his type despite her pretty face and attractive figure.

In the very short time Ebro had been distracted, the first of the four competitions had been set to begin. Ebro's Fire magic user stood ten paces from his challenger, both of them waiting for permission to start. The two were probably fairly equal in talent, so it wasn't talent they used to compete with but manipulation of the power itself. It was possible to be strong in talent and still hesitant in dealing with the power, which would naturally affect the user's ability. One could be born with an orator's ability, but the talent would be useless if the person was afraid to speak aloud.

An official rang a small copper bell, and the two Fire magic talents bent a fractional distance toward each other. It wasn't possible for those of other talents to perceive anything concrete even if it *was* the power being used, but it wasn't long before the results of the contest itself were visible. Ebro's Fire magic user was forced back two full steps, and the girl who had challenged him stood victorious.

Ebro needed to use every bit of control he possessed to keep from cursing under his breath. Even that small a response would have been out of character, but what reaction could have been more natural? On top of everything else, he now had a new member to add to—and condition for—his Blending. One problem after another . . .

During the next few minutes Ebro went from extremely annoyed to furiously angry. He'd made sure that the members of his Blending couldn't speak out against him on any subject at all without committing suicide the way that girl had, but they'd found a way to escape him. One after another they'd all lost their competitions, which had to mean they'd found a way to plot against him. To consider the losses a coincidence would have been mindless, and Ebro was as far from that as humanly possible.

But gibbering insanity wasn't that far off, and Ebro had to fight harder than ever before to keep himself from killing those four turncoats. But he *couldn't* kill them, not without bringing himself to the attention of those who might see through his pretense, something he couldn't afford to let happen. Had the four known his hands would be so thoroughly tied? Had they counted on his need for secrecy to keep them safe after they betrayed him?

Ebro knew that the answer to those questions was probably yes, that his former Blendingmates *had* known the truth. Hatred for those people seeped out of Ebro's very blood to poison his entire being, and afterward he had no idea how he managed to control himself. Now, at a time when he needed to be free to consider his moves against his greatest rivals in the assembly, he had to waste time bringing new Blending members under his control.

But he would *not* be under unreasonable constraint forever. Ebro smiled faintly to himself, forcing his hatred to understand that those tall and pretty fools who used to be his Blendingmates would also not remain safe forever. As soon as people no longer had their attention on four unimportant, former Blending members, those four would find just how long his reach was. The knowledge would only be with them a short while, but during that short while they would wish they had never even *thought* about betraying and deserting him, they surely would . . .

Lodria Angar considered herself the best among the group of women who were Antrie Lorimon's eyes and ears. For that reason Lodria got herself into the position of being the appointed servant of Ebro Syant at the competitions. Syant was one of those whom Lodria's group had been asked to investigate, and as soon as Lodria turned her attention to the man she began to wonder about him. Everyone seemed to consider Syant a complete nonentity despite the strength of his talent, and that attitude was odd in itself.

So, when a closer inspection was called for, Lodria became Syant's servant for the afternoon. A personal servant was *supposed* to watch his or her Exalted One closely to see if he or she needed something, and that made her staring at the man expected and required behavior rather than noticeable rudeness. And it turned out to be a good thing she was there . . .

Sixty people stood one at a time in the grass circle to answer a challenge, but the contests never lasted more than a minute or two. For that reason it wasn't quite forever before Lodria was freed from her position as servant by Syant's leaving, it only felt like forever. She returned to the serving tent to hand over the pitcher and glass she was responsible for, made sure to collect her payment for the afternoon, and then left the park.

Lodria started back toward the small house she shared with her sisters, but as soon as she was certain there was no one about to see her, she headed for Antrie Lorimon's house instead. A small side gate leading onto the property was opened at Lodria's knock, and as soon as no one was able to see her Lodria picked up her skirts and ran as fast as possible to the house.

Happily, Antrie sat alone in her study working on some papers. Lodria made certain of that by peeking through the keyhole, and only then did she straighten again and knock.

"Exalted One, I found your enemy!" Lodria blurted as soon as she opened the door after being given permission to enter. "Of course, I did start out being suspicious, and my suspicions were confirmed. It's definitely him."

"Lodria, calm down," Antrie directed with amusement as she gestured to a chair. "At the same time you can also *sit* down, and then start from the beginning."

"I'm sorry, Antrie, but having to wait to tell you all about what I saw has turned me into a scatterbrain," Lodria apologized after closing the study door firmly. "To begin with, the man I'm talking about is Ebro Syant. I've suspected for some time that he isn't what he seems, and this afternoon I got confirmation."

Lodria was at the chair by then, so she sank down onto it while Antrie considered what had been said, her brows raised in surprised thought. As a Middle talent who had been displaced from a Blending, Lodria had thought all interest had gone from her life along with her former position. When Antrie Lorimon had quietly approached her and asked if she were interested in doing something unusual, the world had brightened again . . .

"I'm ashamed to say that I never even considered Ebro Syant," Antrie admitted after a moment, now leaning back in her chair. "I took the man at face value, and never thought about what might lie beneath the surface. What happened that confirmed your suspicions of him?"

"Well, at first he was just as lumpish and dull-looking as always," Lodria answered with a wave of her hand. "You know, paying little or no attention to what went on around him? Yes, well, then his Blendingmates were called to answer the challenges, and when the first one lost I thought Syant would growl out loud like an animal. But he didn't, and instead went back to looking lumpish, but this time on purpose. Do you understand what I mean?"

"Yes, I think I do," Antrie agreed. "At first the lumpishness looked natural, but afterward it didn't."

"Exactly," Lodria confirmed, moving around in her chair. "There was always the chance I was imagining things, so I watched him very carefully after that—even though I didn't have to. When the second, third, and fourth members of his Blending lost their challenges, I thought Syant would explode into little pieces."

"*All* the members of his Blending lost their places?" Antrie echoed as she suddenly sat forward again. "That will teach me not to pay attention to what I foolishly think of as unimportant. I've never heard of something like that happening before, and the fact that it's happened now leads me to believe that there's nothing of coincidence involved. If all of them lost their places, then they *wanted* to lose."

"Why would anyone want to lose their place in a Blending?" Lodria demanded, shocked into speaking almost harshly. "Once you know what Blending is like, losing it means losing part of your soul. How could anyone do that on purpose?"

"The answer to that question has to be a very painful one," Antrie responded with a flash of sympathy. "If there's something about being in the Blending that's completely intolerable, then your only option is to leave that Blending. I hate to think how bad it had to be for all four of them to take that same, horrible way out."

"But why didn't they tell people what was going on instead?" Lodria asked, the words begging for understanding. "Why did they have to throw away what they'd earned instead? Wouldn't the assembly have paid attention if all four of them complained together?"

"The assembly would have investigated at the very least, so your objection is a good one," Antrie said, now looking thoughtful again. "They *should* have gotten together to protest whatever was bothering them, so why didn't they? Why didn't they just— Oh, no! Ebro Syant's talent is Earth magic."

"So is mine," Lodria responded with a shrug of confusion. "What does that have to do with— No, you can't be thinking that he did something to *keep* them from telling people what the problem was. They were his *Blending-mates*!"

"And he's a High talent," Antrie pointed out as she rose from her chair and turned to a row of beautifully carved cabinets ranged against the wall behind her desk. "If he took them by surprise one at a time, they would have been helpless against him. And I've just remembered an odd report I was given a while ago, about the girl Ebro claimed not long after he won his place as major talent. I dismissed the report at the time, just as everyone who knew about it did, but now . . ."

Antrie's silence had a grim overtone as she began to search, and Lodria fought to keep from being physically ill. The thought of misusing a talent, especially a High talent, was sickening, and Lodria couldn't picture anyone evil enough to do it.

"Yes, here it is," Antrie said as she pulled out a thin stack of papers from one of the cabinet drawers. "Ebro was supposedly crushed when the girl died, and he hasn't yet chosen another to take her place. But the girl choked to death apparently trying to say something, a something everyone assumed was a plea for help against whatever was causing her to choke."

"What she was really trying to say was probably something against Ebro," Lodria agreed with a shudder, her eyes closed against a sight that wasn't actually before her. "He arranged things so that the girl would choke to death if she tried to speak out, but she tried anyway. Why would she do something that was nothing less than committing suicide?"

"I can only guess, and would really rather not know the complete answer," Antrie said with a sigh. "It's fairly obvious that whatever Ebro Syant did to her, death was more acceptable than going through it again. And there's a good chance that he forced the rest of his Blending to help him. If he hadn't, there would have been no reason for him to silence them as well."

"Exalted One, you have to do something about this," Lodria suddenly found herself begging, fear making her voice tremble as she reverted to the formality Antrie never required in private. "When I brought that man a drink this afternoon, he . . . *looked* at me. If he decides to claim another girl . . ."

Lodria couldn't complete the thought, but Antrie's grim expression said she didn't have to.

"Yes, something definitely has to be done, but we need proof rather than speculation," Antrie agreed with a brusque nod. "We have to be able to give the assembly details of what was done, and the only ones who can do that are the members of Syant's former Blending."

"But how can they do that?" Lodria objected as Antrie rose again to walk to a bell cord and pull it. "If they try to speak, they'll die the way that girl did."

"Not if they're freed first," Antrie countered, now walking toward the study's door. "You stay here for now, Lodria, and once my Blending and I have gone you can leave without notice as usual. I'll let you know what happens as soon as possible. And thank you for being bright enough to see through Syant's disguise."

Lodria watched the woman smile before leaving the room and closing the door behind her. Lodria had twisted around to watch Antrie leave, and now she straightened again to slump in the chair. Antrie had promised to tell her what happened and the woman would keep her promise, but Lodria wasn't certain she *wanted* to know . . .

It didn't take long for Antrie Lorimon to gather her Blending, but locating the former members of Ebro Syant's Blending was another matter entirely. It was late afternoon when Antrie and the others began the search, but it had long since become full dark before the search was over. And, toward the end, it was their Blending entity that had done the work. The four people Antrie wanted to talk to had dropped out of sight, not surprising in view of their very real danger, but Antrie's Blending entity had managed to track them down.

"Yes, this is the place," Cristi Imgard, the Earth magic member of their group, confirmed as they all studied the run-down, darkened shack in front of them. "It looks deserted, but there are four people inside."

"Four very frightened people," Regin Seldid, their Spirit magic member, qualified. "If we don't calm and reassure them before bursting inside, they could well take off in four different directions."

"And then we'll be all night locating them again," Silta Marne, Water magic, summed up with a groan. "By all means, let's calm them down first."

Hilsho Adran, their Fire magic member, chuckled along with his brothers Cristi and Regin, but as usual said nothing of his own. Hilsho didn't believe in speaking unless he had something of real importance to say, but that didn't affect his ability with Fire magic. Silta, on the other hand, usually made up for his silence with comments that weren't always clearly thought out, but this time Antrie agreed with her.

"Yes, chasing them all night is not something I want to do either," Antrie told them softly. "Regin, will you please initiate the Blending again?"

Regin nodded his agreement with a smile, and a moment later it was the Antrie entity that floated toward the shack. Entering through a wall wasn't difficult at all, and the deep darkness inside didn't keep the Antrie entity from perceiving the four flesh forms arranged on blankets. They seemed to be prepared for sleep, but none of them had yet found that state of lessened awareness.

—This entity is a friend, and its flesh forms have come to aid you— the Antrie entity said into all four minds at once. *—You have been cruelly treated, but reversing your difficulty is far from impossible.—*

"Oh, yes, please help us!" one of the female flesh forms begged as the others, one female and two male, all exclaimed aloud. "But how did you know we *needed* help?"

—That will be explained by this entity's flesh forms when they enter— the Antrie entity responded. *—For the moment, freeing you is of primary concern.—*

The four flesh forms agreed eagerly, therefore the Antrie entity examined them with its Earth magic segment. The shift in perception was faintly awkward, but that particular shift was usual and did nothing to hinder the Antrie entity's efficiency. The insubstantial mechanism linking certain speech to the ability to breathe was perfectly clear, and removing the mechanism was only slightly difficult. Once it was gone, Antrie was an individual again. Regin had dissolved the Blending so that they might all go inside the shack, which they did as soon as they'd all taken a deep breath.

Opening the door into the shack was a bit disturbing. The entity hadn't appreciated the fact that the hovel had a dirt floor and no furniture whatsoever, but in the light of the lamp that had just been lit the hovel's lacks were perfectly clear. And the terrible smell hovering just at the edge of awareness . . .

"Can you tell us now how you knew we needed help?" the girl who had just lit the lamp asked as she turned away from it to face the newcomers. "You're Antrie Lorimon, I know, but we've come across you before and you never noticed our predicament any more than anyone else."

"Your brave and clever gamble brought your plight to our attention," Antrie told the girl with a smile, also looking at the others with the same approval. "I really do apologize for not noticing earlier, but there are times when all of us are blind to what's right in front of our faces. Will you tell us now why you were silenced like that?"

"We were silenced so that we'd be helpless to speak out against that monster," the girl said bitterly, putting one hand to her head. "If we didn't do what he told us to we would have died in terrible pain, and we couldn't even overcome him when we Blended. He was too strong for us to get around his precautions."

"What he forced us to do was put those poor girls under our control," one of the men said heavily. "The first one deliberately caused herself to die rather than let him savage her again, and that kept the monster from claiming another girl openly. But that didn't keep him from using us to force girls from the lowest class to come to the house secretly, so that he could do as he pleased with them and no one the wiser. One of the girls even died from his . . . 'attentions,' and when the body was found there wasn't the smallest clue that he'd been involved."

"But most of those poor victims are still alive," the girl said with a sob, taking up the narrative again. "They have to live with the knowledge that he can force them to come to him at any time, and I don't understand why they haven't gone insane. I nearly went insane just thinking about it!"

Antrie knew that Regin was surely soothing the girl's torment, but that didn't keep her from going to the girl and taking her in her arms. The poor thing clung to Antrie as she cried and shuddered, and that made Antrie almost rabid with fury. Ebro Syant, that pitiful excuse for a human being, had damaged enough lives. It was more than time the favor was returned to him, tripled and squared!

∞

SIXTEEN

∞

Ebro Syant would have been totally annoyed as he walked into the assembly hall if he weren't also rather curious. He hadn't found the opportunity to take control of any of the members of his new Blending yesterday afternoon when they'd followed him back to his residence. They were so pleased with having won to their positions that they held a party for friends and relatives, and the party had gone on quite late. So he'd decided to work on the four the first thing this morning, but now he'd been summoned to an emergency meeting of the assembly.

As Ebro made his colorless way to his seat in the circle, he wondered if the emergency had to do with those Gandistrans. That was the most likely explanation, but people weren't standing in frantic clutches, worrying out loud. Most of the assembly members looked calm to the point of indifference, with only two or three murmuring to the person in a neighboring seat. None of them looked *his* way, of course, but that was usual and exactly what he wanted.

Oddly enough, Ebro found that he was the last one to arrive. As he took his seat he scolded himself on the matter of sloppiness, as those who arrived last were always noted and remembered. This time he seemed to have gotten away with it, but next time would surely be different. If his plans were to have any chance of succeeding, the smallest details had to be—

"We're here this morning for a very important reason," a voice suddenly broke into Ebro's thoughts. It was Cleemor Gardan who spoke, and he both sounded and looked rather grim. "It's been discovered that one of our members has been taking advantage of his position by using his abilities and those of his Blendingmates to victimize ordinary people, which is completely intolerable. Such a practice is an abomination, and the one indulging himself so must be punished."

The people watching the proceedings began to mutter among themselves, shock and outrage coloring the sound. Ebro glanced over at Zirdon Tal, seeing that the man was the least bit pale. Tal had been using his Blending to influence that Sheedra Kam bit, the girl he'd bartered to further his political ambitions, and now he seemed to have been found out. It would be interesting to see what the assembly did to punish Tal, but other than that Ebro was more than annoyed. With Tal out of the picture, Ebro's plans would have to be completely revamped . . .

"The guilty party is being accused by a number of his victims," Gardan went on in that same grim way. "The ordinary people so misused have been found and assured that they're now safe, but most of them are incapable of pointing the finger of accusation. Two, however, have the courage to appear before us, along with those who have the greatest knowledge of what the abomination consisted of. I now call them forth to give us their testimony."

Ebro was in the midst of wondering who else Tal had victimized when the witnesses began to be escorted in by guardsmen. The blood in Ebro's veins turned cold when he saw the former members of his own Blending, followed by two of the meaningless fluffs he'd taken for his enjoyment. But that couldn't be, it *had* to be Zirdon Tal they were about to accuse—!

"This matter was brought to our attention when all four of Ebro Syant's Blendingmates 'lost' their challenges," Gardan continued while Ebro's mind clanged with shock and fear. "Such a thing had never happened before, and when we sought out the former members of his Blending to learn why it had happened this time, we learned something else as well. Ebro Syant had used his Earth magic on his own Blendingmates, linking their lives to their continuing silence about what they were being forced to do. Once we freed them from constraint, we were told of the whole, sickening matter in detail."

Terror made Ebro try to reach the four turncoats who had betrayed him so vilely, but for some reason it wasn't possible to touch them in any way at all. The same went for the bits of fluff he'd given the honor of pleasing him, so Ebro immediately decided to try something else. If Gardan suddenly collapsed before actual charges were leveled, there would be enough confusion that Ebro would find it possible to slip away before anyone noticed.

But when Ebro reached to Gardan instead, the man's vitals seemed to be hidden behind an impenetrable barrier! Ebro pounded on that barrier in frenzy for a moment, and then he was abruptly back inside himself completely, as though something had blocked his connection to the power! Ebro jerked erect and stretched his hand out, mindlessly trying to touch the power physically, but his hand came in contact with something invisible instead that didn't let him move more than a single step in any direction.

"Ebro Syant, know that you're being restrained from using your ability by your former High practitioner brothers in Earth magic," Gardan intoned so menacingly that Ebro shivered from the words alone. "You've also been surrounded by an invisible wall of hardened air, so escape from the just deserts due you isn't possible. Do you have any words to say on your own behalf, in answer to the accusations made by those who now stand before us?"

"It isn't true!" Ebro screamed, wild and nearly mindless with fear. "I didn't do *anything*, not anything at all! They're all lying because they know you'll believe them! I'm short and fat, and people will believe *anything* about someone like me!"

"Do you take us for fools?" Gardan asked with faint indignation after glancing to one side of the room. "Our Spirit magic users have verified the truth of what the witnesses had to say, and now they've verified the fact that *you* are lying. Is that all you have to say for yourself?"

"It wasn't my fault!" Ebro blurted, his hatred exploding to the surface. "You're all the same, you tall and beautiful people, all the same! Every one of you laughed at me behind my back and ignored me to my face because I wasn't attractive enough to be accepted as one of you! I'm short and fat, and that's a crime you people never offer a pardon for. Why *shouldn't* I have done as I pleased to get even for that? I had the right!"

"You had no right to harm innocent people because of your own mind sickness," Gardan ground out. "If you'd ever bothered to look around yourself, you would have seen that you're not the only one in this assembly who isn't tall and slender. But your peers in body shape know how unimportant surface appearance is, so it has never become a problem for them. What problem *you* have is of your own making, something else only you are responsible for."

That was a bald-faced lie, and Gardan must have known it as well as Ebro did. But Gardan was posturing for an audience, pretending to be innocent in order to make *him* look as guilty as possible. Well, if that was the way they wanted it, saying anything else would be a waste of breath. For that reason Ebro simply sat down again, waiting for them to banish him or do whatever else they considered a fitting punishment. He would survive just as he had once before, and as soon as they no longer watched him it would be *his* turn to hand out some punishments.

"Apparently you have nothing else to say," Gardan observed aloud to Ebro after a moment. "Your silence indicates that there are no extenuating circumstances to account for your actions, no acceptable reasons to excuse them. In view of this, I now ask for a vote on the matter of your guilt. Those who consider this man guilty as charged will now please raise their hands."

It came as no surprise to Ebro when, one after another, every member of the assembly raised a hand. They'd always been against him, all those marvelously popular people, and now they'd been given the chance to rid themselves of him. They quickly jumped at the chance, and once Gardan had seen that total agreement he turned his attention to their victim again.

"Ebro Syant, you've been found guilty by your peers of engaging in abominable activities," Gardan intoned, again bringing Ebro the urge to shiver. "There is only one fitting punishment for such an act, and that punishment will be applied immediately. And, as a body, the assembly asks the citizens of this empire to forgive us for having allowed this to happen in the first place."

Gardan nodded then, and Ebro had only an instant to wonder what the man might be talking about. The next heartbeat Ebro felt a stabbing flash of pain, so intense that he nearly cried out. But the duration of the pain was so short that it was gone before he could react, and then there was nothing.

"It's done," Gardan said after glancing to one side again. "Ebro Syant, High practitioner in Earth magic, misused his gift to the detriment of others. For that reason Ebro Syant's gift has been taken away, so that it will never be misused again. Justice has been done."

A mutter rose from the seats filled by spectators, a sound that was only faintly tinged with the puzzled confusion Ebro felt himself. It was all over, and they hadn't even exiled him? If that was Gardan's idea of justice having been done, Ebro wasn't about to argue. And they hadn't even ejected him from the assembly . . . !

Ebro felt the urge to smile as the members of the assembly rose from their seats and turned to talk to the people nearest them. The whole accusation thing was obviously over, and now people were getting ready to leave. No one at all was watching *him*, so Ebro considered it the perfect time to get a little of his own back from at least one of those four turncoats who had betrayed him. A small heart attack, or possibly even a stroke would do nicely . . .

Ebro reached for the power, certain that he was no longer being blocked from it, but for some reason he couldn't quite get a proper grip. He knew the power was there and un-blocked, right beyond his fingertips, but he couldn't . . . quite . . .

Terror touched Ebro again, this time freezing him where he sat. What had Gardan said about the gift being taken away? Tears filled Ebro's eyes as he tried again and again to reach the power, but he just couldn't do it. The beautiful people hadn't exiled him, no, they'd done far worse. They'd somehow taken away his ability to do Earth magic, and now he was nothing more than a complete cripple.

Now all he had left in his life was the brilliance of his mind . . .

Zirdon Tal sat in his study with only one servant to see to his needs, his nerves too ragged to allow any others around him. His hands were wrapped about his teacup so that he might share its warmth, but the icy center of his being remained untouched. It had been all he'd been able to do to keep control of himself in the assembly hall . . .

That fat little fool, Zirdon thought as he sipped at the tea he held. *Who would have imagined that* Ebro Syant *would be the one to be found out and maimed? If they hadn't told me beforehand what was going on, I probably would have broken down in the middle of that . . . horror.*

Another swallow of tea kept Zirdon from moaning aloud, but it was a near thing. *He* had used his Blending to influence that silly girl he'd been dangling in front of those assembly members interested in her, and it was more than possible that at least one of the men suspected what he'd done. If one of them ever accused *him* of misusing his position, Zirdon knew he'd never be able to face the re-sulting punishment. Syant's ability had been burned out at the source, leaving the man as less than the lowest of the Lows.

Zirdon couldn't hold back a whimper this time, not to mention how his hands shook. He'd come so terribly, terribly close . . .

That was when he heard the tinkle of a bell outside his door, a sound that meant someone wanted to see him. For an instant he was furiously angry that his servants would ignore his orders that he wasn't to be disturbed. Then it came to him in a rush that he *wouldn't* have been disturbed under normal circumstances, so someone of importance must have come to see him. And he had to see that someone, if for no other reason than to show how guiltless he was . . .

"Ring a permission for entrance," Zirdon told his servant as he forced himself into unconcern and his usual negligent pose. At least he had enough practice doing *that* . . .

And then the door opened, shocking him out of the pose and making him sit bolt upright. The one coming in was Ebro Syant, the fool who had gotten himself crippled and thrown out of the assembly!

"What are *you* doing here?" Zirdon demanded, on his feet before he realized he wanted to stand. "Get out of my house at once, and don't ever come back!"

"We have something of importance to discuss," Syant replied calmly, more . . . forceful personality behind the words than Zirdon had ever seen before. "I'm not leaving until I have my say, and I know you'll want to make your own comments. If you really don't mind making those comments in front of that servant, then let him stay. It isn't *my* neck."

"What if I simply have you thrown out?" Zirdon countered, outraged over being given orders in his own home but also wary. No one had ever suspected the man of doing anything he shouldn't have, which meant he was clever . . .

"Yes, you could have me thrown out," Syant granted, but the small man didn't seem terribly disturbed over the possibility. "If you do, though, I'll go and have my say to Cleemor Gardan. Gardan probably won't believe me until he asks certain questions of certain members of the assembly, but then he'll have no choice about believing. I think you know what will happen after *that*."

Zirdon felt as though all his blood was about to drain out of his face, and he clamped down hard on the feeling. The servant was still in the room, and *looking* guilty was almost as bad as admitting the guilt out loud.

"But speaking to Gardan would be horribly hard for you, I know," Zirdon said after a moment, fighting to sound concerned and kindly. "We've never been friends, Syant, but after what was done to you the least *I* can do is listen to what you have to say. All right, you may leave us alone."

"At your command, Exalted One," the servant acknowledged at once with a bow, knowing Zirdon's last words had been for him. After the bow the man hurried out of the room, closing the door behind him.

"You're being very wise," Syant said softly once they were alone. "They didn't hesitate a moment to violate the very essence of me, and they won't hesitate any longer over doing the same to you."

"I have no idea what you're talking about," Zirdon told the distasteful little man with a grimace. "I'm innocent of any wrongdoing, and there certainly aren't all sorts of people lined up to accuse me—the way there were to accuse *you*."

"A few simple words can change that," Syant disagreed with a faint smile, walking to a chair and sitting without waiting to be invited. "Most of your former associates think that that Sheedra Kam bit let herself be used just to please you. What do you think they'd say—along with the girl's father—if they found out you'd used your Blending to make her more amenable and cooperative? Do you expect they'd laugh and consider it a marvelous joke?"

"How dare you suggest something like that?" Zirdon demanded, fighting to be outraged rather than terrified as he looked down at Syant. "It was *your* Blending that stood together to accuse you. Mine would never do the same, most especially since the accusation would be a lie."

"You do that very well, but not well enough to negate

the facts," Syant observed, his manner still utterly calm as he looked up at Zirdon. "I made it my business to be aware of everything done by other members of the assembly, and finding out about *your* little hobby wasn't difficult at all. I'll wager anything you name that the Kam girl has no idea of the actual number of men you gave her to, and when she finds out she'll be furious. She *is* that kind, you know, the kind who works to get even after getting mad."

It was all Zirdon could do to walk the step or two necessary to bring him back to his chair. The nasty little slime knew *everything*, and Zirdon had to use sitting down to keep himself from showing that fact on his face. He took a long moment to pull himself together, then he looked straight at his visitor again.

"I deny everything you've said, but arguing the point isn't worth the time it will waste," he told Syant without beating around the bush. "What do you want?"

"Something you'll find abhorrent, but will have to learn to live with," Syant answered at once, a chilling expression in those flat, dead eyes. "I haven't yet made my plans in full, but when I do and I've gotten in touch with you again, I expect you to obey any orders you're given without hesitation. If you don't, you'll go down right along with that lapdog Gardan and his precious mistress Lorimon."

Zirdon, about to vehemently refuse to obey *anyone's* orders, paused when he heard the rest of what Syant had said. So the man meant to take down Cleemor Gardan and Antrie Lorimon, did he? An action of that sort would bring Syant nothing but satisfaction over vengeance taken, but it could well bring a good deal more to *him*. Zirdon was still a member of the assembly while Syant was not, and with Gardan and Lorimon out of the way there would be little or nothing to keep Zirdon from forming a two-thirds coalition at the very least.

"If you're against Gardan and Lorimon, you certainly have *my* support," Zirdon said after the pause, voicing an admission that would have surprised no one. "After the way they stole away my supporters in the assembly, I haven't the least amount of sympathy for them. If it's my cooperation you want, you'll definitely have it."

"That's very kind of you, Tal," Syant stated with a nasty edge to his tone and smile as he stood. "Just keep in mind the fact that kindness isn't really the thing causing all that cooperation. Oh, and I really ought to mention that killing me won't solve your problem, only make it infinitely worse. I've written out what I know about you and left the document with someone who is utterly trustworthy. In the case of my sudden death or disappearance, that document will be opened and read."

Zirdon paled a little before he had control of himself again. For some reason it hadn't occurred to him to dispose of Syant, but the thought would certainly have come at *some* time. Now the idea was completely beyond consideration, something Syant's vindictive smile showed the miserable man already knew.

"That was something you needed to be told, but don't let it disturb you unduly," Syant said, pausing on his way to the door to turn back to Zirdon. "You have a good deal to gain by . . . cooperating with me, so let your thoughts dwell on *that* truth. If you behave in the way I require of you, you need have no fear of losing even more. Don't forget to tell your people to admit me at once when I return. They still think of me as an Exalted One, but they'll soon learn better and I don't want to be kept waiting on your doorstep. Do you understand?"

How could I fail to understand? Zirdon growled in his thoughts before nodding stiffly in answer to the question. Syant was hardly likely to be pleased with even that small a rebellion, and antagonizing the man would be foolish.

"Good," Syant said with a nod, almost nothing left of his smile. "If you support me faithfully in this, we'll both benefit tremendously. Keep to that thought, and everything will be just fine."

Syant nodded before going the rest of the way to the door, and a moment later he was gone. Zirdon sat back and reached for the teacup he couldn't remember having put down, his thoughts in a whirlwind of confusion. He seemed to be trapped into helping Syant whether he wanted to or not, and the vast benefits he expected to reap were already looking more dangerous to obtain than he cared for.

But he'd been given very little choice in the matter. Zirdon sipped the now-cool tea as he racked his brain for a way out of the mess, but there didn't seem to be one. If he didn't go along with Syant, *he* could end up just as maimed as the stupid little fat man.

A shudder passed through Zirdon at that realization, and he gulped down the rest of the tea then rose shakily to refill his cup. There was no sense in being nervous, not when there was nothing anyone could do to change the situation, but his mind seemed reluctant to accept that comfortable truth at least for the moment. Later it would hopefully be different, but right now he had to hold his cup with both hands to keep from spilling the tea on himself . . .

Ebro Syant let his hired coach carry him away from Zirdon Tal's house and back toward where he'd left his own coach. As soon as the vehicle began to move, Ebro leaned back and made himself as comfortable as possible. It wasn't likely that he would ever be completely comfortable again, most especially not with Tal being the only tool he could use to exact his vengeance. The man did know how to play cool and innocent even in the face of evidence proving his guilt, but that didn't make him any less of a fool.

Without stopping to think about it, Ebro tried to touch the horses pulling the coach in an effort to make them move faster. He *was* in a hurry, but asking the driver to pick up the pace would do too much to make the man remember him—and where he'd been taken. It took a moment or two of nothing happening to remind Ebro that his talent was gone, and the stab of pain and rage he felt was almost too sharp to control. But he *had* to control himself, so he quickly turned his mind to something else.

Yes, Zirdon Tal was a fool, all right, even more so than he had expected the man to be. If *he* had been in Tal's place, doing away with someone threatening him would have been his first thought. Ebro had been waiting for a sign to show that the idea had occurred to Tal, but nothing of the sort had appeared. That was why *he* had mentioned the point, to keep Tal from later thinking of it on his own and acting before considering the matter carefully. Tal was an idiot as well as a fool, and dealing with idiots was extremely dangerous.

But Ebro knew he had been given no choice, and possibly the matter would turn out to be much safer than he expected. Again, if he'd been in Tal's place, he would have used his Blending to find out who that damning document had been left with. He would then have given Tal instructions to retrieve the document, made certain that no others existed once it was retrieved, and then it would have been completely safe to make his attempted blackmailer simply disappear.

And, in this case, Tal would have discovered that there *was* no written accusation against him. Ebro had seen no reason to bother with something that could be retrieved so easily, but now there was every reason to go through with it. If the idiot ever forced himself to use his Blending, the effort of writing an accusation would end up wasted, but the fool's talent was Fire magic, not Earth magic. Tal could never silence his Blending the way *he* had, and so would probably end up compromised anyway.

The street was filled with far too many people to suit Ebro, but there was nothing he could do about it beyond moving to the middle of the coach seat. That would make him more difficult to notice without also making it look as if he were hiding, the necessary balance that was now required. And it would just be for a handful of minutes more. They were almost to the dining parlor where he had asked to be taken.

Once the coach reached the dining parlor, Ebro paid off the driver and then entered. He had no intention of stopping for a full meal, not now when his appetite had been destroyed along with his talent. But he did need to be inside the parlor until the hired coach was no longer in the area, something that should be accomplished rather quickly. Ebro ordered a cup of tea and a slice of sugar loaf, nibbled at the cake for appearance's sake, but finished the tea completely. That fool hadn't even thought to offer refreshment . . .

Ebro paid his bill and walked outside slowly, having made sure that two or three groups of people had left before him. It was highly unlikely that none of the three groups would require a coach, which turned out to be so. The coach he'd hired was nowhere in sight, which let him walk around the block to where he'd left his own coach.

His driver sat waiting patiently, just as he was supposed to have done. Ebro told the man to take him home, then climbed into the coach. The seats were much more comfortable than those in the hired coach, and Ebro leaned back near the right-hand window as the coach began to move. Ebro hadn't yet returned home this morning, finding it easier to think while the coach took him all over the city. His thinking had been extremely productive, but now it was time to continue his thinking in more comfortable surroundings.

It wasn't long before the coach pulled into the drive of his house, but the sight of the activity there pulled Ebro out of his reverie immediately. The servants were carrying out various boxes and setting them near the drive, just as if the boxes contained trash for pickup and burning. But the house didn't *have* that much trash, not when he couldn't abide clutter . . .

"What *is* all this?" Ebro demanded once the coach had stopped near the boxes, gaining the attention of two of the servants. "Have you fools been saving up trash rather than moving your lazy hides when it was time to put it out? If so, you won't find me in the least pleased."

"Why would we care whether or not *you* were pleased?" one of the servants, a man named Frarin, asked with an actual sneer. "You don't live here any longer, and these are your personal belongings. I'm supposed to tell you that you can use the coach one more time to move these things to wherever you'll be living, but after that you're on your own."

Ebro froze in the act of opening the coach door, fighting

not to show how devastated he felt. It hadn't really come through to him that he was no longer a member of the assembly, even though no one had said it in so many words. He was also no longer the major talent of a Blending, and the house belonged to whoever was chosen to take his former place.

Tears tried to well up in Ebro's eyes as he closed the coach door and sat back again, but he refused to give *anyone* the satisfaction of seeing how deeply he'd been touched. They could have waited at least one day to throw him out of the place he'd called home for so long, but he was no longer of any consequence so they *hadn't* waited. He now had to find someplace to live, a task he'd need a decent amount of gold for. But if they'd taken back his house, they'd surely cut him off from the funds that used to be his by right . . .

Ebro sat stiffly and watched the very few boxes being loaded onto the coach. Those boxes couldn't possibly hold anything beyond some of his clothing and a handful of personal possessions, which obviously didn't include any of the artwork and beautiful accessories he'd bought for the house. Those would stay *with* the house, while he—

A burning lump blocked Ebro's throat, but it didn't stop him from thinking. He didn't yet know where he *would* go, but it certainly would *not* be Tal's house. Tal was his secret weapon, the tool he would use to destroy those who had hurt him so badly. It would happen, Ebro swore to himself, it would happen even if vengeance was the last thing he accomplished!

SEVENTEEN

Honrita Grohl stood third in one of the lines at the new "center," a place that was really a newly opened shop that sold nothing. Even at that early an hour there were quite a few other people in line, people who, like Honrita, were eager to have their talents trained. And after the training, maybe even finding a Blending to be part of . . .

Honrita felt a shiver go through her that was half delight and half fear. She had always wanted to *do* something with her talent, but for every moment of her twenty-nine years people had told her how bad using talent was. She'd listened to them, of course, her upbringing allowed her to do nothing else, but she'd always felt . . . incomplete, somehow. But now things had changed in a way she'd only dreamt about . . .

"Name and aspect, please," a voice said, and Honrita came back to where she stood to find that she was now at the head of the line. The man seated behind the table smiled at her encouragingly, but she couldn't keep her answering smile from being tremulous.

"My name is Honrita Grohl and my aspect is Spirit magic," Honrita replied in a whispered rush as her fingers pulled at one another. "Even if I have to wait, I'd still like to be in one of the classes."

"As early as you've gotten here, you'll probably be in one of the first classes," the man said after writing on the

216

paper in front of him. "Are you free during the day, or do you need one of the evening classes?"

"Oh, no, I can't attend during the day!" Honrita protested, her insides in a sudden flurry. "I work during the day as a seamstress, but did you say something about evening classes?"

"Yes, there are evening classes for those who have to work," the man told her in a kindly way. "Is there anything to keep you from starting *this* evening?"

"No, there's nothing to keep me from starting tonight," Honrita answered, her emotions trying to surge out of her control. "Where do I go, and how much will it cost?"

"You report back here at six tonight, and it won't cost you anything," the man responded with a wide smile, probably because Honrita had started to glow. "We're using the gold left behind by the nobility to pay for these classes, which is only fair. After all, they're the ones who kept people from using their abilities for so long. Take this paper and go over to the side of the room, where people are waiting under the signs of the different aspects. Go to the Spirit magic sign, and the people there will tell you how strong or weak your talent is. But don't worry if you're considered weak. You'll still be trained as far as possible."

"Thank you," Honrita whispered, taking the paper the man had written on and turning to her right. It was all she could do not to clutch the paper as she walked to the line with the sign of Spirit magic above the two people sitting there, where she hesitated. No one else stood in line, so she would have to be first . . .

"Good morning," the man sitting there said with a smile, and the woman beside him smiled as well. "I think that paper is supposed to be given to me."

"Oh, yes, of course," Honrita said quickly, feeling a bit foolish as she handed over the paper. She also felt less nervous, which was a true blessing.

"You'll have to open to the power if we're to rate your strength," the woman told her in a kindly way. "Don't be afraid, it's perfectly legal now and in fact required."

"I'm sorry, I don't know why I'm so foolish today,"

Honrita apologized with a small laugh. "Of course I have to open to the power. I'll do it now."

After all those years of being told not to, opening to the power was something of a chore. But Honrita did it anyway, and was immediately startled. Most of the people in the shop—center—were at least as nervous as she was, and some were in worse case. But the two people sitting behind this new table weren't nervous, they were as pleasant and friendly as they appeared. And for some reason they also seemed impressed.

"Well, that's a pleasant surprise," the man said, looking up at her from where he sat. "She's a good, strong Middle talent."

"More than that, she's a third level Middle talent," the woman said with brows high. "That means you're the strongest a Middle talent can be, dear. How did you keep from being sent with other strong Middles to fight in the army?"

"Oh, no one ever really looks at me twice," Honrita said, a truth that wasn't as painful as she usually found it to be. "A noble came once and talked to me for a moment or two, and then he went away and didn't come back . . . But *I'm* not all that strong, not compared to *him* . . ."

By then Honrita stood with her mouth open, staring at the man. His talent . . . towered above hers, so wide and deep and strong that Honrita felt powerless beside him. How could her meager efforts possibly compare to *that?*

"No, now, you can't compare yourself to *me*," the man said quickly, and Honrita felt herself being calmed. "I'm not only a High talent, I've been through training as well. Once you finish your training—with other Middle talents— you'll have a truer picture of relative strengths. You'll probably find that you're stronger than most of the people around you, so you *will* try to not let that go to your head, won't you?"

Honrita laughed softly with the man, knowing—really *knowing*—that he simply teased her gently. That sort of knowledge made all the difference in how a person felt, to know that the gentle teasing had no malice behind it. If only she could know that all the time . . .

"I would recommend that you keep a touch on the power for as long as you can," the man said after writing something on the paper Honrita had given him. "You'll find it tiring at first, but after a while the tiredness will go away. And tonight you'll be told that eventually you won't be *able* to release the power, but that's a perfectly natural step in your development so don't worry about it. We'll see you tonight, then?"

Honrita knew she was being gently sent on her way, and it was a good thing. She had to be at work, and tardiness was frowned on. She thanked the two people with the best smile she'd ever been able to manage, turned away from the table—and stopped dead to stare with her mouth open.

Two people had come into the shop, and now stood to one side of the doorway looking around. The man was tall and broad-shouldered and handsome, but the woman wasn't simply beautiful. She was also even stronger in Spirit magic than the man at the table was, which seemed impossible.

"Leave it to Lorand and Jovvi to come see how things are going," the man at the table behind Honrita said with amusement he actually felt. "If the people of this empire let them and the others go after a year, they all need their heads examined."

Honrita tried not to gasp, but it was a lost cause. The two people near the doorway were two of the Seated Blending, and they'd come in person to make sure everything was going properly! It was the most marvelous thing Honrita had ever seen, and she stood staring while the two people walked around and talked to those who sat behind the tables. They also spoke a word or two to some of those who had come to register for the classes, and as they walked toward the door again, the woman smiled at Honrita and patted her hand in passing.

It was at least a minute before Honrita was able to do something other than stand and stare with vacant mind. By then the two beautiful people were gone, but every applicant in the center was abuzz with excitement and awe. The man next to Honrita babbled something with a big smile on his face, and Honrita nodded her agreement with her own smile. Being agreed with was what the man needed, and understanding what he'd said was unnecessary.

But then Honrita realized that what *she* needed was to get to work, and that at once. She looked about as she hurried out of the office, but the two unexpected visitors seemed to be gone. They must have come in a coach, she realized, and increased her pace even as she wished *she* had one. But all she had was her feet, and they couldn't possibly move fast enough. She'd never before been even tardy to work, but today she would be out and out late.

Honrita should have been out of breath by the time she reached the shop where she worked, but circumstance had kept that from happening. She'd been able to feel the emotions of everyone she passed in the street, and the fact that their emotions didn't, for the most part, match their expressions and/or actions had slowed her pace with confusion. She'd never realized that so many people hid their real selves behind behavior that didn't match at all . . .

"Well, good afternoon," a cold and distant voice said, pulling Honrita out of introspection. "How good of you to decide to join us."

It was Dama Listern, of course, the woman who owned the dress shop where Honrita worked as a seamstress. Dama Listern was a tall, handsome woman who catered to those in the city who had gold but weren't of the nobility, and her shop was never patronized by those of the lower classes. Honrita should have been flushed with embarrassment and all but incapable of speech, but instead she offered a timid smile.

"Dama Listern, you won't believe it but I saw two of the Seated Blending," Honrita blurted, somehow knowing it was the right thing to say. "They actually stopped and talked to ordinary people, and the woman patted my hand. I've never been so excited and overwhelmed in my life!"

"Well, no wonder," Dama Listern exclaimed with brows high, no longer cold and distant. "How could you *not* be excited and overwhelmed? Seeing even two of the six . . .

You do know there are six now, rather than five? I was at the Seating ceremony yesterday, but I don't think you were. Do you know which two they were?"

"Someone said they were . . . were Jovvi and Lorand, I believe," Honrita answered, gently encouraging Dama Listern's new mood. "Did I get the names right?"

"Yes, you certainly did," Dama Listern told her with a smile and a pat on the shoulder. "Spirit magic and Earth magic they are, and I find myself quite envious. I would have given much to be as close to them as you were."

"I wish you *had* been there," Honrita confessed with a small, breathless laugh. "I just stood there gaping like a fool, but you would have found it possible to speak like an intelligent human being."

"Well, some of us do have more self-possession than others," Dama Listern allowed with a pleased laugh, then she patted Honrita's shoulder again. "You'd best get to work now, before we begin to fall behind. These days we need to keep every order we get."

"Yes, Dama," Honrita agreed with a small curtsey, then hastily made her way to the back of the shop. All the others were hard at work, of course, but Dama Wislet put down her sewing and stood to confront Honrita.

"I'm sure Dama Listern has already seen to exacting a price for your inexcusable lateness, woman," Dama Wislet said, every inch the head seamstress. "If this ever happens again, you can expect to be dismissed instantly. Is that clear?"

"Yes, Dama Wislet," Honrita whispered with a curtsey, her head deferentially down. The older woman nodded once and turned back to her work, allowing Honrita to hurry to her own place. The embroidery on the hem of the skirt she'd been working on was almost done, but Honrita quickly went to work before she allowed her thoughts freedom.

Dama Wislet had never had a friendly word for anyone in the shop, and all the girls thought that that was due to the woman considering herself to be too far above the ordinary workers for her to bother with them. Now Honrita seemed to have learned better, as the older woman was filled with fear and bitterness. It was fear that kept Dama Wislet aloof from everyone, an emotion that seemed somehow linked with the bitterness.

Honrita sighed for the woman's carefully hidden pain, and couldn't keep from soothing Dama Wislet a bit before giving her complete attention to the embroidery. She also had to release the power for a while, but silently vowed to keep the rest time as short as possible. She'd never known there were so many people who needed soothing at the very least, and she didn't mind doing them that favor. Maybe, after the training, she'd be able to do even more than that . . .

Driffin Codsent entered the shop the way he entered most places, furtively and with an eye out for guardsmen. He was of average size—if a bit thin—with average brown hair and eyes and very ordinary features. Most people never noticed him, which was just the way he wanted it. If no one noticed him, his description couldn't be given to anyone in authority.

There were a lot of people in the shop, but Driffin couldn't see anything being offered for sale. And yet people were on line in front of others who sat behind tables, so *something* had to be going on. If they were giving away silver or even copper or maybe food chits, Driffin was very interested. If they were offering jobs, his interest would quickly disappear.

One line seemed shorter than the others, so Driffin put himself on it without any fuss. Just as he resigned himself to something of a wait, the line abruptly moved up. The man ahead of him now stood at the table, and Driffin heard the man being asked his name and talent. The man answered without hesitation, and then was asked whether he preferred days or evenings. The man's answer of evenings sounded very relieved, as though he'd been afraid he'd be told something else. Then the man was given a slip of paper and told to move to the appropriate line to the right, and it became Driffin's turn.

"Name and talent, please?" the woman seated behind the table asked with a smile. "And don't look so worried. I won't take the name and use it myself."

" 'Course you ain't gonna," Driffin said with a laugh that had been surprised out of him. "I just been wonderin' why this place looks s'different. Most places I been, they's do th' runnin' don't know nothin' 'bout smilin'."

"That's because everything used to be run by the nobles," the woman said with her own laugh. "If I had to work for one of *them*, I wouldn't do much smiling either. So, what's your name and talent?"

"I'm Lisso Varn, an' m'talent's Earth magic," Driffin answered smoothly, using the made-up name without hesitation. "You like that there comb'nation?"

"Oh, I love it," the woman answered while she wrote on a piece of paper on the table in front of her. "And which do you like the idea of better, Lisso Varn, a class during the day or one at night?"

"I kinda work nights, so I gotta go with daytime," Driffin answered, wishing he knew what kind of classes she meant. For the time he'd been in school, he'd enjoyed himself in a way . . .

"Daytime it is," the woman agreed, writing again, and then she lifted the paper and held it out toward Driffin. "Take this to the Earth magic line by the side wall, and they'll tell you what to do next. Good luck."

"Yeah, thanks," Driffin muttered, taking the paper and getting out of the way of the next person on line. The woman behind the table had obviously already dismissed him, and curiosity had begun to burn inside him anyway. What in the name of chaos was going *on* here?

A woman stood in line by the table in front of the Earth magic symbol, but she walked away even as Driffin approached. This time there were two men seated behind the table, and the one on the right smiled faintly and held out his hand.

"Good," the man said when Driffin handed over the paper he'd been given. "All right, Lisso, we need to find out your talent strength so we'll know your standing in the class. Open fully to the power, please."

Driffin knew his stare at the man was filled with shock, but there was nothing he could do to change that. Didn't the fool know it was against the law to use talent anywhere but behind closed doors?

"No, it's perfectly all right," the man said with a warmer, more comforting smile, apparently reading Driffin's mind. "People aren't forbidden to use their talent any longer, and if we don't know how strong you are normally, how will we know if you make progress in the training class? If you make *enough* progress and you have the strength to go with it, you might even be offered a job training others."

"Damn," Driffin muttered under his breath, keeping his eyes from widening by sheer willpower. Those rumors about the new Seated Blending changing things had to be true, then. Driffin hadn't believed anything but the people in power would change, but it looked like he'd been wrong. And by sheer luck, he'd stumbled on a way to take advantage of the new arrangement . . .

But all that hesitation he now showed could well make the men in front of him suspicious, so Driffin quickly opened himself to the power. It was something he'd been doing in private for about twenty-five years now, ever since he'd been five, and both of the men in front of him smiled in approval.

"That looks like a solid Middle talent to me," the man who had been doing all the talking said, turning his head to the man beside him. "What do *you* think?"

"I think 'solid' is a less than adequate description," the second man said with clear amusement. "He seems to be trying to present himself in a . . . downplayed sort of way, but he's definitely a third level Middle."

"Well, good," the first man said in surprise, turning raised brows to Driffin. "We can use all the third level Middles we can get. But how did you avoid getting grabbed up by the nobility along with everyone else?"

"Those fools din't know nothin'," Driffin assured the man, remembering his role just in time. "They couldn'a found—well, they din't find *me*. But *you* ain't no Middle."

"No, I'm a High, and I wish we'd met a lot sooner," the man said with wry amusement. "I would have enjoyed learning how to keep the nobility from finding *me*, something I wasn't able to do on my own. But you're set now to start the first class, so be back here at two this afternoon. That should let you get some sleep after your night's work, to give you a better chance in class. Good luck."

Driffin nodded his thanks and walked away, so deep in his thoughts that he forgot to move furtively. Unless he was completely mistaken, he'd just been given the chance of a lifetime. He'd have to look around carefully, but if he couldn't find *some* way to take advantage of this unexpected break, he'd give up his old life and take an honest job. Not that there was much chance of *that* happening . . .

Before Driffin had taken many steps outside the shop, he was back to showing the world nothing it could use against him. He shuffled his way home in his usual inconspicuous manner, really looking at the old warehouse for the first time in a very long while. The place appeared to be ready to fall down, and that was due only in part to its "disguise."

The wood of the building was painted some long-faded and peeling color, the front doors looked flimsy and ready to fall in, and what windows weren't boarded up were too filthy to see through. Driffin had been careful to keep the warehouse looking like that, and to completely disguise the rebuilding he'd done. When a place seemed ready to collapse, there weren't many about who tried to take it away from you. That's not to say that no one had ever tried, but very soon now all that ought to be changing.

Shuffling around to the back of the warehouse brought Driffin to the only door that had an actual working lock. The front doors just looked to be feeble, and anyone trying to open them was meant to think they were warped closed. Pushing and kicking would cause some of the wood to rattle, but the stronger, braced wood inside would keep the doors firmly shut. Other doors around the sides were sealed closed on the inside and boarded up on the outside. The single working back door also had a bar on the inside, to be dropped into its brackets in times of emergency.

Using the key he carried hidden in his shoe heel, Driffin let himself into the warehouse and then quickly relocked the door behind him. There wasn't a sound from the heavy shadows looming all about, but Driffin didn't need light to know what the shadows hid.

"It's all right, it's just me," he called softly, making sure his voice would not carry outside. "Is everything all right?"

"Yeah, no problem," Tildis Lammin answered, stepping out to join Driffin in the dim light coming through the small and filthy window not far from the door. The boy carried a cudgel just the way he was supposed to, just the way the other boys in the shadows did. "We ain't had— We *haven't* had anyone come near the place all morning. Why are you back so early?"

"I'm back because I stumbled into an incredible piece of luck," Driffin answered, smiling to himself. Tildis, like the other boys and girls Driffin looked after, had started out speaking as badly as street kids usually did. Now the boy was almost as good as Driffin at hiding his street accent when he had to, or, to be more precise, when he *wanted* to. There were times when survival meant sounding as low-class and ignorant as possible, and other times when eating depended on sounding completely different.

"Do you remember all those rumors we heard about the new Seated Blending?" Driffin asked as he slowly walked more deeply into the building, speaking to the other boys in the shadows as well. "We laughed when people said things would be different, but we were the ones who were wrong. The new Blending has people setting up classes to train us in using our talent, to make us stronger than we are normally."

"So that they can make better use of us afterward?" Tildis said with a snort of ridicule as the other boys formed a loose circle around them. "Do they really think we're *that* stupid?"

"We're going to pretend we *are* that stupid," Driffin said with a smile of approval for the boy's very proper outlook. "We're going to be all innocent and trusting while we let them train us, we're going to find out as much as we can about what they mean to do with us afterward, and then we're going to disappear and make use of what we learned—about everything. There's got to be gold in this somewhere for them, and I want a good chunk of that gold to be ours."

"So where do we sign up?" Tildis asked with a laugh, the other boys chuckling their agreement. "I'm ready to cooperate."

"You and the others are ready for school," Driffin corrected dryly, glancing around at the eager group. "*I've* already signed up for the first class, and I'll find out how to get the rest of you signed up as well. In the meantime, you all have a duty to this family to learn as much as you can before you take yourself out of the reach of the gold-grabbers. The more we know, the more useful we'll all be."

One or two of the boys began to grumble at that, but Driffin just smiled. Not everyone was made for taking advantage of school learning, but he insisted that they all try. He hadn't been very eager for school himself at one time, at least until he realized just what was being offered . . .

The boys knew themselves that it was time to leave for school, so they went to put away their cudgels and collect the girls. By ones and twos they would all leave by the back door, and Tildis would lock and bar the door after them. Once they were gone Tildis would leave by the secret way, and afterward would pretend that he'd gone out a hidden window. It didn't pay to have too many people know about your secrets, not when some people just couldn't keep from telling what they knew if silver or threats were offered . . .

Driffin sighed as he walked toward his private part of the warehouse. He'd rescued Tildis from the streets just as the boy's drunken father had tried to reclaim him, knowing from personal experience what the boy was going through. It had taken some time to gain Tildis's trust, but once he had he knew the boy himself could be trusted as far as anyone could be.

But then circumstance—and Tildis—had made Driffin

start to pick up the other kids, all of whom needed looking after. Before he knew it Driffin had a larger family than the one he'd originally come from, all of them looking to *him* for guidance and support. It hadn't been easy for Driffin— or for them—to survive, but for some of the kids who had been out on the street it would have been impossible. And the kids did brighten Driffin's world, even if he felt he couldn't trust *all* of them. In this world, some people were always stronger than others.

Stronger. Driffin smiled bitterly as he reached his private area of the warehouse and silently let himself into the bed-chamber. Idresia lay asleep in the bed, her labored breathing making it sound as if she ran instead of slept, but Driffin had already done all he could for her. There was something inside her that didn't work quite right, but he had no idea how to fix that something. Maybe this was another thing those classes could help him with. If they did, he would give eternal thanks to the Highest Aspect . . .

Tears formed themselves in Driffin's eyes, and for once he made no effort to stop them. Idresia was the woman he'd fallen in love with, for her courage, for her humor, and for the love she gave in return. He really wanted to tell her about the good fortune he'd had, but she'd started to have so much trouble getting to sleep that he didn't dare wake her. She needed the sleep desperately if she was to survive, and she *had* to survive. If she didn't . . .

If she didn't then he might not survive either, but there were too many people depending on him. If she died then he might not be able to follow after her, and the thought of being left all alone added soundless sobs to the tears trailing down Driffin's face. He *would* figure out something to help Idresia, he *had* to!

EIGHTEEN

Jovvi dismounted with Lorand at the palace, and gave the reins of her horse to the stableboy who hurried over. Lorand did the same, and then they were free to enter the palace. Happily, their guard captain was nowhere in sight, which ought to mean he had no idea that she and Lorand had gone out without an escort.

"I think we may be home free," Lorand murmured as he also looked around, apparently reading her thoughts. "As long as no one knows we went out alone, we ought to get away without a scolding."

"I've been spending some time trying to understand why some people are willing to do just about anything to be in our position," Jovvi answered with a sigh. "Everyone expects us to do things *their* way, and we can't even go out alone without sneaking out. Talk about being treated like a prisoner."

"But at least we've found a way around one corner of the coverage," Lorand said with a little-boy grin. "Or at least *you* found the way, and it works really well. Now we have to decide whether to tell the others."

"Since our escape method can't be used without *me*, I don't see why we *can't* tell the others," Jovvi pointed out. "I'd be willing to oblige them, but there isn't that much time left before we leave the city. Tamma may hate me for not taking her along this morning, but the indignation shouldn't last more than a moment or two."

"Probably not, since we'll all be getting out from under

in just a little while," Lorand agreed with a nod. "If there wasn't an army heading for the city, I wonder what it would take to get us out of here in the same way."

"It's going to take a change in standard policy, and outright battle would probably be easier," Jovvi answered, resisting the urge to sigh again. "Unlike those who used to be called Seated Blending, our group can take care of itself under most circumstances even without Blending. And since we don't have the urge to stand high above the common masses, keeping ourselves away from ordinary people is nonsensical."

"Not to mention the fact that standing aloof is just asking for trouble," Lorand pointed out, still looking around as they hurried up the corridor. "That man Tolten Meerk can't possibly be the only one with the urge to take advantage, and the next one may not be so obvious about it. We have to stay in touch with everything, or before we know it we'll be back to having a ruling nobility."

"At least Wilant Gorl and his Blending have been warned about that," Jovvi said, doing her own checking of the rooms to either side of the corridor. Most of them were empty, and those that weren't seemed to contain cleaning people. "I really do want to get away from this city for a while, but I also hate the idea of leaving just when our new projects are getting started. If we get back to find them ruined in some way . . ."

"If we get back to find our projects ruined, Wilant Gorl and his people will either be dead or in hiding," Lorand pointed out dryly. "Every one of them knows how we feel about the training classes and the new placement agency that should be opening in a few days. If we come back to find that the projects aren't running smoothly, the ones responsible for making trouble will have to face *us*."

"Or, to be more accurate, they'll have to face Tamma," Jovvi said with a laugh. "Since I can't think of anyone who knows her who's willing to do that, I have the suspicion that our projects will go smoothly no matter *what* anyone has to do to make it happen."

"Yes, you and I are pushovers, but Tamrissa isn't," Lorand said with his own laugh. "And if, by any stretch of the imagination, she happens to need help, Vallant isn't much of a pushover either. Naran tends to be softhearted like us, but Rion has become a definite force to be reckoned with. No, all in all I think our projects are safe."

Jovvi would have preferred to be in the city to be sure of that, but the conclusion couldn't be argued. The new projects were safe, but when it came to that army the same couldn't be said of the city. And it was *their* job to take care of the army, even with other Blendings available . . .

"I have a feeling we've been betrayed by one of our own," Lorand muttered, and Jovvi looked up to see their four Blendingmates standing together in the area just in front of the entrances to the various wings. Tamma stood with her arms folded, and Vallant looked less than pleased. "It would be too much of a coincidence for everyone to be here just as we're coming back, so Naran must have Seen something."

"And told the others about it," Jovvi agreed, flinching inwardly over the waves of heavy disapproval and worry coming from the four. "We'd better tell them quickly that we weren't in any danger."

"Good idea," Lorand muttered, and then he raised his voice. "Hey, everyone, we've just been trying out something new, and we're pleased to report that it works. Let's go into one of the wings and get comfortable, and we'll tell you all about it."

"Why would we want to hear about the newest way to get killed?" Tamma countered immediately, her tone icy. "We already know about the best one, and that's going out without the rest of us or a damned strong escort. Oh, but you already know about that one, don't you?"

"Tamrissa, we weren't in any danger," Lorand assured her with a sigh. "We weren't sure about how large an area the effect would cover, and that's why we kept the excursion limited to two. Now we know that all of us could have gone—as long as we stayed really close together."

"What effect are you referring to?" Rion asked before Tamma could begin scolding again. "And why would it be necessary for all of us to stay close together?"

"The effect I'm talking about is something Jovvi thought of," Lorand answered, obviously pretending he didn't see Tamma's continuing anger. "She thought it might be possible to . . . project what amounts to invisibility, by using her talent to make people believe they weren't seeing us. She spread the belief as far as she could, and everything worked fine until someone literally ran into us. After that we made sure to get out of the way in time, and so didn't have the problem again."

"And that's why we would have to stay close," Vallant said with a nod, his mind bright with interest. "To keep from gettin' in everybody's way by spreadin' out. And you had no other trouble?"

"None at all," Jovvi confirmed, deciding it was time to support Lorand with more than her simple presence. "We went to look in on how the registration for training classes was going, and were delighted to see quite a lot of people even this early."

"And most of those who came this early were asking for the evening classes," Lorand put in, turning to look at Tamrissa. "It's a good thing you thought of offering them, Tamrissa. I'd overlooked the fact that people who work for a living can't take time off to attend a class."

"We all overlooked the point," Tamma grudged, still not very happy. "If I hadn't talked to one of the servants in my wing and offered him a place in one of the classes, we'd still probably be where we were. When he said he couldn't attend the class because he had work to do . . . Well, that rang a very loud bell."

"In case you hadn't noticed, none of the rest of us talked to our people about it," Jovvi pointed out firmly, eager to change the subject. "That makes the idea yours without contention, and the credit as well. So, are all of our people ready to leave after lunch? And have we made sure that we're taking along a really good cook?"

"Everyone's ready, and we've in fact chosen two good cooks," Rion assured her with a smile, following along as Jovvi began to walk toward the entrance to her wing. "But aside from them, only we and the other three Blendings and our various link groups will be going. Oh, yes, and ten guardsmen and ten Astindans, to handle any nobles we come across or anything in general that doesn't require our attention."

"I like the way you said 'only,' " Jovvi commented ruefully. "That's more than two hundred and fifty people, not just we six alone. Some holiday outing."

"I wish it *was* just a holiday outin'," Vallant answered in a tone as rueful as Jovvi's as he also followed along. "But it's an army we're goin' out after, so we have to do it right. But there *is* one bright spot: Startin' tomorrow, we and one of the other Blendin's will be travelin' three or four hours ahead of the other two and their people, at least until we get within reach of the army. That will make huntin' and campin' a bit easier, not to mention movin'."

"I think what does need mentioning is the visitor I had this morning," Naran put in with a quick smile of apology for Vallant. "Master Ristor Ardanis came to call, along with additional members of his Sight magic people. He explained that he'd come to replace those members of my link groups that had joined one or another of the other Blendings. Somehow he knew the exact number to bring."

Naran's words had turned very dry, and Jovvi could understand that.

"How interesting that the man showed up just at a time when the only two members of the Blending equipped to tell truth from lie weren't here," Jovvi couldn't help pointing out. "It must surely have been a coincidence."

"Oh, yes, definitely," Naran agreed, the words as dry as her previous ones. "To think that he timed his visit carefully would be to assume that the man was hiding something. And you should have heard his apology for not having provided me the teachers he said he would. He assured me that trying any training now would have been a waste of effort, with everything in a flux around us at this time. But as soon as we get back from taking care of the army, we'll get right to the training."

"Of course you will," Rion said in the same tone Naran

had used, but with a slightly sharper edge. "But if there's another delay then, we'll *all* have a little talk with Master Ristor Ardanis. I may have thought of a way to track him down."

"But that isn't possible, my love," Naran said with a small laugh as she turned to Rion. They'd reached a sitting room in Jovvi's wing, one with a tea service that Jovvi headed for. Not having tea whenever she wanted some was one of the things she would definitely miss on the road . . .

"You can't track down someone with Sight magic, Rion," Naran continued with a smile. "Master Ardanis would always know when we were coming, and would make sure to be somewhere else."

"But that, my love, is the key to finding him," Rion disagreed with a smile of his own. "If enough people are looking all at the same time, won't the possibilities get so complex and muddied that he'll have difficulty knowing the best steps to take? If we can confuse the future badly enough, we'll find him standing in one place like the donkey between two haystacks, frozen by the need to decide which way to go."

"You know, that just might work," Naran said slowly, her brows high as she considered the idea. "Something else would also have to be done, I think, something I can't see yet, but I'll try to come up with what we're missing. Even if we never use the method, it will still be handy to have it available."

"That's for certain," Lorand agreed, standing behind Jovvi as he waited for his turn at the tea. "Vallant, did you explain to Pagin Holter and his people why it wasn't them we decided to leave in Gan Garee?"

"Yes, and they agree with our thinkin'," Vallant answered from where he stood next to Tamma. "Our two Blendin's, bein' the strongest and most mature, need to explore what they can do together. We can't do much explorin' if we're miles and miles apart, and with them comin' with us we might also be able to practice on that army."

"Maybe we'll find another, easier way to take them

over," Tamma put in, no longer looking or sounding angry. "And while we're out there, let's not forget that we'll be looking around for any members of the nobility who weren't here in Gan Garee in time to be arrested. We'll be sending them back to Gan Garee with the Astindans and with the rescued army segments."

"Which will save us time and effort later," Rion said with a nod of agreement. "We'll need to send people all over the empire eventually, letting the more distant areas know about the changes and taking in any members of the former nobility. If we leave them wherever they're hiding, they're bound to make trouble sooner or later."

"And that we certainly don't need," Tamma agreed, then she turned back to Jovvi and Lorand. "Lavrit Mohr also came by this morning, to tell us that the food shipments have begun to come in as of last night. In another few days things will start getting back to normal."

"Better than normal," Lorand qualified with a smile. "People will now be running their businesses for themselves rather than as slaves to the nobility. And we're almost ready to tell anyone who's interested that they can relocate to and farm any unclaimed land they like. The one thing we don't yet have a handle on is Holdis Ayl and his renegade Guild people."

"One of the Blendings staying behind intends to look into that," Naran put in with a quick smile. "Master Ardanis told me that the group now has its own Sight magic user, and he and his people will help out as best they can. I had the impression that they weren't going to help *too* much, but only because the Blending won't need much help. All the remaining Guild members have been looked at, and the three who stayed behind as spies have been identified but not arrested. As soon as any of the three get in touch with someone, they'll follow the contact back to Ayl."

"We hope," Lorand said with a sigh, then he seemed to throw off the dark mood. "No, I'm going to believe that they'll be successful. When we get back to Gan Garee, there won't be anyone left who hates us."

"What are they puttin' in the tea in this wing?" Vallant

asked with a laugh while everyone else smiled. "If you think there won't be anyone around to hate us even with Ayl and his people gone, brother, you'd better brace yourself for a shock. There's always *someone* who hates you, if only because you have somethin' they can't get. All we can do is learn to live with it."

"There may be something else we can do," Jovvi mused, having considered the matter before. "If we can help them find something they consider better than what we have, they won't have a reason to hate any longer. Our new placement service may be one of the things we can use to accomplish that end."

"Along with other things," Naran agreed with a distant look in her eyes, surprising Jovvi. "Yes, the probabilities are definitely there, so we'll have to investigate them when we get back."

"And on that note, I think it's time we separated to make our final preparations for leaving," Tamma pronounced as she straightened where she stood. "I also want a cup of tea, but if I have it here I'll be rushed later. If anyone isn't ready when it's time to do what's necessary, we'll just have to start without them."

She gave everyone a very wide smile with teeth clearly visible, and then she turned and left. Vallant grinned and followed her out after winking at everyone else, leaving Rion and Naran to chuckle their own way out. Jovvi glanced at Lorand, but he just smiled.

"I have a feeling that one of the preparations Tamrissa wants to make involves Vallant," Lorand said with amusement. "There won't be much in the way of privacy once we leave the city, so I think she has a really good idea there."

"Yes, she does, and that does happen to be what she has in mind," Jovvi agreed with a small laugh. "Everyone seems to be getting almost as good as I am at reading people, which is a pleasant surprise. Now can you tell how *I* feel about the idea, Lorand Coll?"

"Nope, I haven't got a clue," Lorand replied as he put his teacup aside and rose from his chair to join her on the couch she'd chosen. "You probably hate the idea of making love to me as much as you always do, but you've decided to put up with it just to keep the peace. Unless, of course, you somehow know what it does to me when you call me Lorand Coll. But that's not very likely, is it?"

"No, not likely at all," Jovvi murmured as his strong arms closed tightly about her, drawing her to his chest. She raised her face to join him in a kiss, and in no time at all they were ready to move on to other things. Yes, Tamma had definitely had another good idea . . .

Rion drew his mount to a halt with the others, looking around in the early evening light at the campsite that had been chosen. They'd made good time leaving the city and on the road afterward, so their group wasn't far from the first inn on the eastern road from the city. The inn certainly wasn't large enough to house all of them for the night, but maybe it could be used for another purpose . . .

"I agree with Rion," Naran said suddenly to the rest of the Blending from where she sat her own horse near Rion's. "We may have to camp out tonight, but at least we can eat at the inn if we eat in shifts."

"That's a great idea, but when did Rion say it?" Tamrissa asked from her place only a few feet away. "I could have sworn he hasn't said a word in the last hour."

"Actually, I was only thinking it," Rion said, bending an inquiring look on Naran. "Have you learned how to read my mind, love?"

"To a certain degree," Naran answered with a blush and a laugh. "You were gazing toward the inn with a half wistful, half wishing expression, and that made me remember what you've said in the past about how good the cooking is at that inn. The step from there to my suggestion is only a small one."

"Aha, then it was logic rather than mind-reading," Lorand said with a laugh all the others shared in. "Speaking for myself, I'm rather relieved. If Naran had learned how to read minds, she might have taught Jovvi and Tamrissa, and then we would have been in real trouble, brothers. A man needs to have *some* secrets from his woman."

"I thought it was women who needed to have some secrets from men?" Jovvi put with a glint of amusement in her beautiful eyes. "Is your way really the proper one, Lorand?"

"Personally, I think that *everyone* is entitled to a secret or two," Tamrissa stated with the same kind of amusement. "When people know everything there is to know about you, they decide there's nothing left for them to learn and then they start to ignore you."

"I can't picture *anyone* ignorin' *you*," Vallant said while everyone else chuckled. "Actually, I can't picture anyone ignorin' any of you ladies, and one of you has stated a desire. I'm willin' to go along with that desire and eat at the inn, but only to be sociable. It's not like my mouth is already waterin' or anythin'."

"Of course not," Rion said with a laugh, loving the close warmth they all shared. "I'm not *really* yearning to eat there either, but if the group has its heart set on the venture then I'm also willing to go along. Just to be sociable."

"Let's all be sociable and get our link groups," Jovvi suggested during the new laughter. "And since *we* thought of this first, we should get to eat first."

None of their six disagreed with that, and neither did the other Blending and their link groups. Everyone thought that eating at the inn was a marvelous idea, since they'd have more than enough of trail food once they rode farther from the city. Those who were scheduled to eat in the second wave would also set up camp, with those who ate first doing the honors tomorrow night. The chores had to be split up somehow, and that was as good a way as any.

Rion had handed over his saddlebags and bedroll and was on his way back to his horse when a young woman stepped into his path. She was tall and slender and quite attractive, with soft auburn hair and very blue eyes. She also looked nervous for some reason, and her smile was on the tremulous side.

"I hope you don't mind my bothering you, Rion, but I've wanted to say something for quite a while now," the woman said quickly in a very soft voice, her gaze locked to his. "I'm Riltha Mayner, a member of one of Tamrissa's link groups, and I just want to say how attractive I find you. I know I'm probably speaking out of turn, but I simply had to say it. Now that I have, I won't bother you any longer."

And with that the young woman hurried away, her head down as though she'd done something very difficult and possibly dangerous. Rion simply stood there staring after her, more confused than he'd felt in quite some time. It would have been understandable if one of his sisters had said something like that, but a perfect stranger? To say she found him attractive? For what purpose?

Rion continued the rest of the way to his horse and mounted, then let his thoughts roam free while he waited for the others to be ready to leave for the inn. If the young woman had said she found him odd and laughable, Rion would not have been in the least surprised. Many young women had felt that way about him while he still lived with that woman who had called herself his mother, but now so rapid a turnaround was a bit overwhelming. First Naran, and then Tamrissa and Jovvi, and now a complete stranger . . .

The reverie wasn't so deep that Rion didn't know when the rest of the party was mounted and ready, which was a lucky thing. He would not have enjoyed discussing the incident at the moment, not until he'd done quite a bit more in the way of private thinking. Could he really have changed so much that total strangers found him attractive? If so, how should he feel about that . . . ?

NINETEEN

Lorand rode into the campsite with the others, feeling the urge to stretch out somewhere and not move for a while. They'd been on the road for six days and had made fairly good progress in reaching the area where the eastern army was soon expected to be. Now they meant to stay put until the rest of their people caught up to them, and then they would see about stopping an army.

"I'm glad it's someone else's turn to set up camp this time," Tamrissa said from where she still sat her horse, looking as tired as Lorand felt. "I'm going to stay awake just long enough to eat, and then I'm going to fall into my bedroll. Rion, you said there would be large houses in the area we reach tomorrow?"

"Quite a number of them," Rion confirmed in a weary voice with a nod to match. "The area is called Sunrise Slipping, and was rather popular with the former nobles. It took quite a lot of gold to have a house there."

"Then I'm definitely going to sleep early," Tamrissa said with her own nod. "Then, after we take care of that army, I ought to have the strength for a long, lovely bath. As soon as we find a decent bath house, of course. And if the water happens to be cold, I volunteer to warm it myself after it's filtered clean."

"I may be able to do the filterin' on my own," Vallant said, looking only a bit less tired than the rest of them. "I've been thinkin' about which pattern I would use, and I

240

believe I've found the right one. I'll just have to try it and see."

"That makes me feel a good deal better," Jovvi said as she began to dismount. "If I have a bath to look forward to, I'll find the strength somewhere to fight that army. Right now, though, even the promise of a bath would be pushing it."

"That's because *we've* been pushing it," Naran told her as she and Rion also began to dismount. "We've been moving a lot faster than we ever did before, but at least we'll have the time to rest before we have to face that army. It would have been nice, though, if we could have stopped at another inn every once in a while."

Everyone made sounds of agreement, and Lorand discovered that he was now the only one still mounted. He hadn't expected them all to be this tired, and how fast they'd moved was only a part of the reason. As he forced himself to leave the relative comfort of his saddle, Lorand decided that they would *not* work with the members of the other Blending again before they all faced the army. The other Blending might be one of the really new ones that needed as much instruction and practice as possible, but the other Blending would *not* be helped if he and his Blendingmates fell over dead.

"Here, Jovvi, let me take your horse," Lorand said when he realized that Jovvi just stood there holding her rein as if unsure of what to do next. "You go and sit down somewhere, and I'll join you in just a few minutes."

"Lorand, if I didn't already love you, that offer would have made it happen," Jovvi said with a smile that was a pale shadow of its usual radiance as she handed him her rein. "If I'm asleep when you find me, please wake me up so that I can eat. For some reason I feel extremely hollow."

Lorand nodded with his own strengthless smile as he took her horse, and then he led the two mounts to where they would be unsaddled and turned loose for the night. He had discovered that it was a simple matter to use their Blending entity to make sure the horses didn't wander off, and that had become a nightly ritual for the group setting up camp. And oddly enough, the other Blending and their link groups didn't look nearly as tired as he and the rest . . .

"Hollow is too mild a word for what *I* feel," Rion said as he joined Lorand, leading his own horse and Naran's. "If left to my own devices, I just may devour all the rest of our supplies."

"Even if they happen to be raw," Vallant agreed as he joined the group on Lorand's other side, Tamrissa's horse beside his own. "I've been thinkin' about eatin' for the last hour or more."

"And not just because our cook is really good," Lorand said, making the matter unanimous. "I haven't been *this* hungry since we first began to increase our abilities and form our Blending."

"But all we've been doin' is work with the other Blendin'," Vallant protested, turning his head to look at Lorand. "Why would such a simple thing be such a drain on our strength?"

"Working with the other Blending may not be what's draining us," Lorand said after thinking about the matter for a moment. "I can see now that I have no real idea what *is* doing it, but the work may be only a part of a larger whole we're not seeing. Every time I think about the knowledge that's been lost because of those fool nobles, I get the urge to commit murder."

"As do I," Rion put in, glancing away from watching where he stepped. "I constantly find myself thinking there ought to be a better, easier way to do something, if only I knew what that way was. But I *don't* know, because the knowledge was allowed to be lost."

"I've been wonderin' if that's really the case," Vallant said, looking first at Rion and then at Lorand. "I mean, it's one thing to keep 'commoners' from findin' out certain facts, but quite another to keep the information from yourself as well. If I'd been in charge, I would have kept a careful record of what can be done and how to do it, and I would have hidden that record in a safe place."

"How can we possibly find a place that people who are so many years dead considered safe?" Rion put, asking rather than challenging. "The information could be in the safe of a private residence that collapsed generations ago, or buried under the floor of a stables that has now become the middle of someone's wheat field. How are we to know?"

"We can't, for certain, but there are facts we need to be aware of," Vallant said, his expression thoughtful. "For instance, havin' information no one else does means takin' a number of precautions to preserve that information for your family or loved ones. If somethin' sudden happens to you, you don't want the precious information lost along with you."

"So you just might store it in a bank vault along with your gold," Lorand suggested, the idea coming faster than he'd expected it to. "Keeping the information at home could well mean losing it, to theft, or fire, or water damage, or a dozen other misadventures. A bank vault is a nice, safe, dry place."

"Especially if you have a *lot* of gold in the bank," Rion agreed just as quickly. "The bankers would know better than to tamper with anything owned by people with the power to have almost anyone killed. And the records could be hidden among ordinary papers, so that even if someone looks at them who shouldn't, they won't know there's more than gold beneath the dross."

"I wish we'd thought of this while we were still in the city," Vallant muttered, the complaint valid as far as Lorand could see. "Now we'll have to wait until we get back to examine what's bein' held beside silver, gold, and copper."

"Anything we learned would probably have come in handy when we faced that army, so of course we didn't find it," Lorand said, too tired to keep from feeling depressed. "I think there's some natural law that insists we do everything the hard way, otherwise it won't count. I just wish I knew what it's supposed to count *for*."

"There's an old sayin' that claims we gain understandin' through sufferin'," Vallant offered in a sour tone. "What *I* understand is that I don't want to suffer anymore, which is what the lesson *should* be about. Maybe we can find a way to avoid for now that 'larger picture' you were talkin' about."

"How?" Lorand challenged, feeling as though he were being accused of hiding things. "If we can't yet see the picture, how are we supposed to do anything about it in any way at all?"

"How am *I* supposed to know?" Vallant countered, his tone a near match to Lorand's. "The rest of you are the brainy ones. I'm just the sailorman hangin' on for dear life, followin' rather than leadin' and glad of it. If the rest of you think of somethin', just let me know."

And with that Vallant turned away, to lead his horses to a separate place where he might unsaddle and unbridle them.

"Ending this conversation now might indeed be the best of ideas," Rion muttered when Lorand glanced at him, avoiding Lorand's gaze. "We'll speak again, once we've all had the rest we need."

And then Rion moved off with his own mounts, leaving Lorand alone to choose a place to leave the horses. As if the previous disagreement had been all *his* fault. Lorand growled low in his throat, swallowed various words and phrases that weren't very nice, and then he did find a place. A place that was apart from those fools he was forced to associate with . . .

By the time the horses were freed of tack and turned out to graze, Lorand's anger was once again replaced with depression. He had no clear idea why he'd gotten angry at Vallant and Rion, but the fact that he had made him feel ashamed. Those men were closer to him than the brothers who shared his blood, and getting angry at them for no clear reason proved that *he* was the fool.

Apologizing wasn't something he was up to yet, so Lorand finished his chore and simply hurried away from the area. Happily, Vallant and Rion still weren't as experienced with horses as he was, so they were both still working as he left the area. If possible he would avoid them until tomorrow, and then—

"Excuse me," a soft voice interrupted Lorand's thoughts,

also bringing him to an uneven halt. "I'm Berana Foldis, a member of one of Vallant's Water magic link groups. I can see that you're tired, so I'll be really brief. I think you're one of the fairest people I've ever come across, even when being that fair is painful for you. Because of that I couldn't possibly admire you more, and I—just wanted you to know that."

The smile the girl gave him was on the embarrassed side, and then she was hurrying away. She was dark-haired and dark-eyed and very attractive, and as Lorand watched her go he knew that she hadn't told him the complete truth. Oh, she *did* seem to admire him, but there had been something more behind the words . . .

It took Lorand a long minute before he realized what that something more might be, and then *he* was the one who felt embarrassed. You don't stop someone out of the clear blue sky—and when they're alone—to tell them you admire them. The girl seemed to be attracted to him, which was very flattering. For the last few minutes before the girl appeared he hadn't been feeling very attractive, but now, knowing he had an admirer . . .

Lorand silently laughed at himself as he resumed walking, glad there was still a good deal of daylight left. If it had been dark when the girl approached him, his mood would have convinced him that she was some unattractive hag who had no one else to fix her sights on. But there had been nothing of the hag about her, and feeling flattered raised his spirits to a large degree. He was still really tired, but now he felt better about it. *She* hadn't been bothered by his tiredness, and had even been considerate of the condition.

This time Lorand almost laughed aloud at the antics of his thoughts. He sounded to himself like a youngster who had just gotten his first smile from a girl, something that hadn't happened very often when he *was* a youngster. What the girl had said didn't mean anything, of course, not with all the truly important things he had to think about, but it would hurt nothing if he enjoyed the pleasure of her words for a while. The words she'd spoken, and the ones she hadn't . . .

It would have taken too much effort to whistle as he walked along, so Lorand kept silent. But the song was there in his mind and heart, a song that made him feel only a small bit of guilt. After all, there was nothing wrong with *thinking*, was there . . . ?

Vallant stretched wide as he yawned, wishing breakfast was already set out to be eaten. He'd slept most of his tiredness away the night before, which was hardly surprising. He and his Blendingmates had eaten early yesterday afternoon and then had taken to their bedrolls, and even the arrival of the other Blendings and their people hadn't awakened him. The others seemed to have slept just as soundly, and that was good. They would be facing that army today, and needed to be in top form . . .

"Vallant, I'd like a word with you," Lorand said, coming up to stand next to him. "About the way I acted yesterday, when we were seeing to the horses. I'd like to apologize for anything I may have said or done that was offensive. I felt so beaten down that good sense wasn't even a memory."

"You're just sayin' what I decided it was up to *me* to say," Vallant answered ruefully with a shake of his head. "I was so tired I felt helpless over everythin' we don't yet know, and I've never been good at handlin' helplessness. Where's Rion? He could also use some apologizin' to."

"Right here," Rion answered for himself as he joined them from Vallant's left. "But where apologies are concerned, it would be more appropriate for me to give rather than get. Instead of disassociating myself from the . . . discussion you two were having, I should have done something to help smooth things over. We were *all* too tired to be rational, and if I'd pointed that out—"

"The both of us would probably have turned on *you*," Lorand interrupted, finishing Rion's sentence the way Vallant would have. "Bickering seems to hate a peacemaker, but at least we were spared *that*."

"Which means we're now free to go and get somethin' to eat," Vallant put in, seeing the way the venison from the night before was being taken off the warming fire. "I'd be happier if there were eggs and pancakes and such, but you won't find me turnin' down rewarmed venison."

"Yes, a normal breakfast would be nice, but I don't require it either," Rion agreed as all three of them immediately headed for the food line. "I ate quite a lot last night— or late yesterday afternoon—but I feel as though I haven't eaten for days."

"So do I, and I wish I knew why that was," Lorand said, clear disturbance in his voice. "We've been really tired and hungry just the way we were when we began to use and strengthen our abilities, but we haven't been doing anything new. Or at least *I* haven't noticed anything new."

"Neither have I," Vallant answered the question in Lorand's tone, at the same time seeing Rion's headshake. "Could we be doin' somethin' new without bein' aware of it?"

"That doesn't seem very likely, but how can we know?" Lorand put, the same frustration Vallant felt clear in his brother's tone. "We'll just have to take care of this army quickly, and then get back to Gan Garee. Searching bank vaults will at least give us something to take our minds off what's happening until we find an explanation for it."

"An explanation for what?" Tamrissa's voice came, and then she and Jovvi and Naran were with them. The ladies were also clearly heading for the food line, which hadn't quite formed yet. The rest of the people in their camp were still in the process of first waking up.

"We need an explanation for why we're getting so tired and hungry all of a sudden," Lorand told her with a smile. "It feels a lot like what we went through in the beginning, but we haven't been doing anything new. Unless you girls have noticed something we missed?"

"Nothing *I* can think of," Jovvi said while Tamrissa and Naran were considering the question. "And if we were able to do something new, wouldn't it be fairly obvious?"

"Not necessarily," Naran said before any of the rest of

them could answer, her gaze unfocused the way it usually
was when she tried to See. "There's something vague and
rather far away ahead of us, and I have no idea what it can
be. There are too many other happenings in the way, most
of them with multiple possibilities. And some of *them* seem
to be . . . blocked."

"You mean Ristor Ardanis and his people are at it
again?" Tamrissa asked, the annoyance in her voice not as
heavy as Vallant would have expected. "I'd love to know
why they keep doing that to us, keeping us from knowing
about certain things. It can't be to make sure the wrong
thing doesn't happen because someone knows about it in
advance. *They* know about, so why can't we?"

"Knowing about something is meaningless if you don't
do something with the knowledge," Naran pointed out with
a sigh, her gaze no longer on distant, invisible horizons. "I
hate to admit it, but Master Ardanis and his people won't
do anything with certain knowledge, while we almost certainly would. And knowing about *some* things in advance
can mean absolute disaster rather than being a blessing."

"Will we ever reach the point of knowing when not to
act, my love?" Rion asked her, his expression filled with a
disturbance Vallant also felt. "Or is it necessary to live with
your ability available for decades or centuries before the
lesson is properly learned?"

"I don't know," Naran told him simply, her smile showing sadness rather than warmth. "That's one of the things
I still have to learn, when to speak and when to keep quiet
when more than just hurt feelings are involved. I'd also
have to stop thinking of silence as betrayal . . ."

"I think we all know you'd never betray us, Naran,"
Jovvi said, putting a hand to the girl's arm. "We also trust
your solid common sense, so if you ever have to hold back
on telling us something, we'll know you're doing it for our
benefit rather than to hurt us. Isn't that right, everyone?"

"Of course it is," Vallant said without hesitation, the others saying the same in different words. "But right now I
can see a bit of the future myself, specifically the part where
I fall over dead if I don't have somethin' to eat in the next

few minutes. If you'd rather avoid the chore of gettin' rid of my body, you'll get started with takin' some of that lovely food so it can come around to bein' *my* turn."

"Instead of being a gentleman and waiting, why don't you go first?" Tamrissa suggested with a laugh while everyone else chuckled. "I'm too happy to have my strength back to want to waste it on getting rid of a body."

"I knew there was a reason I found you so attractive," Vallant said to Tamrissa with a grin and a touch to her face as he stepped forward to start the line-forming process. "I'll go back to bein' a gentleman later or tomorrow, whenever this hunger lets up. For right now, though, I may make it necessary for our hunters to go out again sooner than they expected to."

The rest all lined up behind Vallant, and despite their teasing he wasn't the only one who took what might be considered more than an ordinary amount of food. Every rider in their party had carried an extra set of saddlebags with a certain amount of staple food like potatoes and rice and dried vegetables, so the meal consisted of more than just the venison. But their supplies were almost gone, Vallant realized as he eased the gnawing hunger in his middle. They'd have to restock in the nearest town before they headed back to Gan Garee.

But first they had an army to face. Vallant felt better with every passing minute, but that only referred to the hunger he'd been suffering from. With that consideration out of the way, he was able to tell that he wasn't feeling quite as rested as he'd thought at first. Deep inside he still felt tired, but hopefully the others weren't suffering in the same way. He knew he would hold up his part of the Blending no matter *what* it cost him, but his not being in top condition made the time uncomfortable and the coming confrontation a bit less than a sure thing.

He was just finishing the last of his meal when the guardsmen they'd sent out to scout returned to camp. They looked around as they rode, and when they spotted Vallant they headed directly for him.

"We found them, Excellence," the guardsman in charge

of the scouting party reported even before he dismounted. "They're camped just under two hours away, and once they're on the road again they'll be heading right for us."

"But we can't afford to simply wait for them," Vallant decided aloud as he put his plate aside and got to his feet. "Doin' anythin' less than makin' absolutely sure would be foolish, so that's the way we'll arrange it. Where's Holter and his Blendin'?"

Vallant looked around with the question, and a moment later spotted Pagin Holter and his people. They were sitting not far away with plates of their own, and seemed to be almost finished eating. Vallant walked over to them and Holter smiled a greeting, but it was Arinna, their Fire magic user, who spoke.

"Is it time for us to leave, Vallant?" Arinna asked with her own smile. "I'm assuming that those guardsmen are the scouts you sent out, and they've come to report back."

"You're right on all counts, Arinna," Vallant answered with a smile that wasn't quite as good as theirs had been. "The army is camped less than two hours away, and you'll have to circle around to get behind them without bein' detected. You're sure that none of you minds bein' the ones who do the extra travelin'? We're all feelin' better than we did yesterday—"

"An' we wanna keep ya like thet," Holter put in before Vallant could finish his halfhearted offer, the man's tone showing nothing of resentment or hesitation. "Our Blendin' entity'll let ya know whin we're in place, an' then ya c'n start th' show."

"As long as you're all sure," Vallant said with an inner sigh of relief, seeing that they *were* all in agreement. "You'll have to get started as soon as you're all through eatin'."

"Which will be in about one minute," Arinna assured him before finishing up the last of the food on her plate and putting it aside. "Our horses are already saddled and ready for us and our link groups are also just about through eating, so we'll be in touch shortly."

"We'll be waitin,' " Vallant answered, as most of the

group and their link people got to their feet. "Be really careful, even if it means takin' a little extra time."

"Yes, Momma," Arinna said with a laugh, coming over to pat his arm to remove the sting from the comment. "Don't worry, everything will work out just fine."

And then she and the others were moving away, heading for the horses that had been saddled for them while they ate. It didn't take more than five minutes before they were riding out of camp, proving that they were even more well-organized than Vallant had thought. Well, it was about time that *something* worked right for them . . .

Vallant took a deep breath to steady himself, then he turned back to see where the rest of his Blending was. The place where they'd been sitting and eating was now occupied by the newly awakened, and his people had relocated back toward where their bedrolls had been left. He headed toward his Blendingmates, deciding to wait a few minutes more before he began to hurry the latecomers into finishing their meals.

Holter and his Blending should be in position in significantly less time than the two hours they'd talked about, so their own force would have to break camp and move in closer to the army that would already be advancing toward them. The closer they were the less their Blending entity would have to strain, but they couldn't get *too* close or they would be detected by the army's scouts. It wasn't likely there would *be* no scouts, not when the army was moving through what had to be considered captured territory—

"Excuse me, Vallant," a soft voice said, bringing Vallant back to the world around him. A girl had stepped into his path, a small, pretty girl he couldn't remember having seen before. She had long blond hair and lovely blue eyes, and the shy smile she showed made her look like an innocent lamb.

"I'm Silni Fael, a member of one of Jovvi's link groups," the girl went on in an almost breathless way. "I—I don't believe I'm actually speaking to you, and I hope you'll forgive me for being so brazen, but I just had to tell you how I feel. I *know* you're a man who can always be counted on, and I—just wish I'd met you sooner. I'm sorry."

And with that she hurried away, leaving Vallant to gaze after her with what must have been a bemused expression on his face. The girl was sweet and precious, someone he might have once tried to get to know better, but he didn't have the interest for that sort of thing now. If he *had* met her sooner . . .

But thinking about that was a waste of time he didn't really have. Vallant resumed his stride in the direction of where everyone waited for him, more convinced than ever that there must have been some natural law that caused the best things to happen at the worst possible times. If anyone ever found a way around that law, they'd be able to sell the process for more gold than they'd be able to spend in ten lifetimes . . .

TWENTY

It didn't take us long to clear our campsite, not when we knew when we got there that we would have to remove all traces of our presence when we left. When you're aware of something like that, you don't spread out and make yourself comfortable or generate a lot of litter. You use as small an amount of living space as possible, so there's less to clean up later.

Once we were mounted we sent out scouts again, then spread out and began to move through the woods. It wasn't very fast or easy going for us, but it didn't have to be. We were, in effect, waiting for that army to get to *us*, that and for Pagin Holter and his people to be in position behind them.

Once we were on the move, I had the leisure to glance over at Vallant. He was busy coordinating everyone's movements, looking for all the world as though he had nothing else on his mind. The only thing was, I'd happened to witness a strange little occurrence, and didn't know what to make of it.

Vallant had gotten Pagin Holter and his people on their way, and then had started back to join the rest of us. He'd almost reached us when a girl stopped him, spoke to him for a moment, and then hurried off. The incident hadn't looked like much, except for the one part of it that insisted on standing out in my memory. Vallant had watched the girl hurry off, and the expression on his face had been an odd mixture of interest and regret.

So . . . What did his interest in the girl consist of, and why the regret? Had he been interested in whatever she'd said, and regretted his inability to do something about it— or had he been interested in *her*, and regretted that he couldn't immediately show that interest? I'd spent a long part of my intermittent relationship with Vallant jumping to various conclusions, a good many of them wrong. I didn't want to do the same again, but . . .

But I also didn't want to stay involved with a man who felt regret over not being able to get to know the various women he met. There's nothing wrong with a man getting to know—and even admiring—other women, but unless he considers them of less interest than the woman he's involved with, he's wasting his own time and hers by *staying* involved. Not to mention the pain and uncertainty his attitude brings . . .

I took a deep breath to banish the depression that tried to fill me, refusing to let it get a foothold in my emotions until I knew for certain that there was a good reason for its presence. In spite of all the sleep I'd had I still felt a bit weary, and I didn't need distractions when the time came for us to face that army. We shouldn't have any more trouble freeing the segments than we'd had in the past, but you can't cope with trouble when it comes if you haven't allowed for the possibility of it. If trouble came I meant to be ready, so it was time to think about something else.

The woods around us was filled with early morning cool, and my horse felt well-rested and ready to take on almost anything. My horse and I both would have enjoyed a brisk trot or even an easy lope, but the trees and bushes and other growths in the woods forced us to keep to a walk. It's much easier riding a road, but that would have put us face-to-face with the advancing army. Sneaking up on them was a better idea than facing them, better for them and definitely better for us.

Two Spirit magic link groups had been put to either side of the road before we started, and the two parts of our group had used them to judge just how far into the woods we had to go. When they were no longer able to detect us we knew we were far enough away from the road, so we went just a little farther and then turned to parallel the road. We'd given ourselves enough room to allow for inadvertent drift, and still ought to be outside the army's range of detection.

We moved on for quite a while, the air warming around us as the sun rose higher above the trees, and then the scouts we'd sent out reappeared ahead. Vallant called an immediate halt by holding up one arm, and a moment later the scouts were with us.

"They're not far ahead now, Excellence," the chief scout reported to Vallant softly. "As soon as we detected the head of the column, we came straight back as ordered."

"Good," Vallant told him with a distracted smile and a nod. "Now you can rejoin the other guardsmen at the rear of the group. Remember that all of you are to stay back until the encounter is over. You and these others linked while you were scoutin', and you got away with it because the army segments *weren't* linked. If somethin' goes wrong they *will* link, and they're all a lot stronger than you and the others. Facin' them would be suicide for you, so make sure you stay well back."

"Thank you, Excellence, we'll remember," the guardsman scout responded with a very faint smile, and then he turned and gestured to his companions. They all rode off to the position they'd been ordered to, but not before glancing at us with odd expressions.

I had a feeling that those expressions were indications of almost-disbelieving gratitude, stemming from the fact that they'd been ordered out of harm's way. Our predecessors and the rest of the nobility tended to throw away the lives of their guardsmen without a second thought, and many people obviously believed that we would be no different. But we *were* different, and the only way to prove that is to do rather than boast.

Everyone else was dismounting, so I did the same and then tied my horse to a small tree where he could graze. It was almost time for us to get to work, and for that we wanted to be sitting down.

"There's something odd just ahead of us," Naran said as we gathered together, her expression disturbed. "I've been trying to see the details for the last hour, but they refuse to come clear."

"Are you bein' blocked?" Vallant asked her as we all formed a loose circle. "Do you think it's Ardanis or some of his people?"

"I can't tell that either," Naran answered, her sigh tinged with annoyance. "It doesn't *feel* as if I'm being deliberately blocked, so maybe that 'flux' Master Ardanis mentioned is real. If it isn't, I still obviously have a lot to learn."

"Maybe the details will come clear once we've Blended," Jovvi suggested, clearly hoping to soothe Naran. "Let's try it and see."

That seemed the most sensible course of action, so we each found a place to sit down. Our link groups were arranged in wider circles all around us through the trees, and once everyone was settled Jovvi initiated the Blending.

The Blending entity came into being at once, and as was becoming usual it was the Tamrissa entity. But this time it seemed to be more Tamrissa than entity, something that pleased and amused me. I was the entity with more say than usual, but not the ordinary "I." This Tamrissa was very much the entity, and there was clearly work to be done.

It felt marvelous to float quickly through the trees until I reached the road. I was aware of the condition of every tree I passed and knew the location of every animal in the woods. I knew the content and texture of every volume of the air around me, and was also aware of its moisture content and how close the nearest body of water was. I could feel the emotions and mental conditions of everyone within my reach, and was also firmly connected to the various possible futures surrounding this time period. The only awareness that wasn't new was the ability to control fire, and even that ability seemed broader and deeper than usual.

When I reached the road I began to float along it, looking for the group of flesh forms we had come to rescue. It disturbed me that our strongest lesser entity hadn't yet contacted us, and that disturbance suddenly became entwined with the warning given so recently by the Naran flesh form. If *we* had made contact with the flesh forms called army, our lesser entity should have done the same.

It was then that I became aware of what occurred on the road ahead of me. Rather than continuing along the road in the proper direction, the flesh forms called army had stopped and were standing in place. There was a disturbance somewhere to the rear of the formation, but those flesh forms I was able to see showed nothing in the way of interest or curiosity. That must have been because they had been given no orders to do otherwise, I realized, but they were hardly my primary concern. The disturbance drew me with a sense of urgency, and I increased the speed with which I floated in that direction.

When I arrived at the center of the disturbance, the situation became immediately clear. Our lesser entity had not contacted us because it had not had an opportunity to form, not with the large number of army flesh forms currently attacking *its* flesh forms. In some way the approach of its flesh forms to the column had been detected, and now they and their link groups were engaged in defending themselves.

And defense was clearly all they attempted. Had they wished to destroy their attackers, the matter would not have been difficult for them and their tandem link groups. The army flesh forms, however, were being ordered to the attack by those flesh forms called nobles, and were therefore not to blame. To destroy them would negate much of the purpose we had had in coming to that place.

The flesh forms of our lesser entity and their link groups were holding their own, but the situation was not likely to remain so for long. Probability indicated that those flesh forms called nobles would soon lose patience and order a greater number of their enslaved flesh forms to join the attack. And, even if that possibility failed to come to be, a second possibility was that the flesh forms of our lesser entity and their link groups would grow weary and lose strength. Then they would truly be in danger; therefore was it necessary that I act now to rescue them as well as the army flesh forms.

While I assessed the situation, I had become aware of the presence of the two newest Blending entities of our group. They had approached the road and the disturbance from the positions of their flesh forms, to the right and left of the road, but had not come close. That hesitance was in accordance with the instructions previously given them, but now those instructions must change.

I quickly gathered the entities to me and caused them to understand my desires. They made no demurral, of course, but instead floated away to the positions I had assigned them. I, in turn, returned to the head of the column and took up my own position there. My own flesh forms were growing weary, I knew, and although the weariness was not unexpected under the circumstances, it cut shorter still the amount of time available to act decisively.

As rapidly as possible, then, I began to radiate the message "I am in command" toward the foot of the column and the area of disturbance. There, at the site of the attack, the two newest entities received the radiating message. In accordance with their instructions they increased the message's intensity and sent it back, spreading it through the entire group of enslaved flesh forms. When I received the intensified message I returned it, and in a short while the attack faltered and then stopped altogether.

Those enslaved flesh forms nearest my position stood at attention as though awaiting orders, which was the most that could be done at the moment. The rest would have to be done by others lacking my weariness, but one further act was necessary.

Those flesh forms called nobles stood shouting at the formerly enslaved flesh forms nearest them, demanding that their commands be obeyed. I touched the ones who shouted, ensuring that they would continue to shout but do nothing else, and then the entity was gone and I was alone again.

"Whew!" Jovvi said, sitting just a little straighter in her place. "If the entity hadn't drawn strength for us from our link groups before dissolving, I'd be flat on the ground right now."

"You and me both," Lorand agreed as he stretched wide. "At least the entity understood that we can't curl up and sleep right now. We still have too much to do."

"Like gettin' all those people released completely," Vallant said as he began to get to his feet after taking a deep breath. "Holter and his group will have to do that, along with calmin' down the people they release. We don't want them tearin' the nobles apart before we get a chance to question them."

"We'll also have to acquire food for them, and clothing," Rion put in. "Did you see how poorly they were dressed? Some are in worse case than the other segments we freed."

"And if we don't move quickly we'll lose some of them," Naran warned, letting Rion help her to her feet. "I could feel that some of those poor people are hurt so badly that their life threads are almost severed."

That statement touched me even more deeply than it did the others. It wasn't so long ago that my own life thread had nearly snapped, and I felt a shudder run through me as I stood. Vallant had given me a hand up, and as soon as we were all erect we went to the horses. Our link groups were already mounted, so we all hurried toward the waiting column.

When we reached the place where the nobles had been shouting orders at the segments, we found those nobles surrounded by the bullies called prods as they continued to try giving their former slaves orders. Actually, only one man was doing most of the shouting; the rest simply echoed whatever he said. We dismounted and left our horses with our link groups, and walked closer to the defensive group.

"All right, that's enough noise for now," Jovvi told the men inside the circle of prods, and then she seemed to address the thin air. "Yes, we *would* like you and the others to see to the captives. But you'll have to calm them as you free them, and they'll need to be examined. Naran tells us that some of them need immediate medical attention. Also please take these prods away and sit them down somewhere or use them to do something necessary. We want to question the nobles now, and would prefer that the prods don't get in the way . . . Thank you."

Jovvi had been talking to Pagin Holter's group's entity, of course, but the nobles stared at her as if she were insane. It amused me to remember that the only orders I'd given the nobles had been to stay put and continue shouting, which meant they were only loosely under control. That let them show all the outraged indignation they seemed to feel, and the apparent leader bristled up at once.

"Who in the name of Chaos *are* you peasants, and how dare you interfere with me?" he demanded, and then his complexion went even darker as the prods began to move away from him and the others. "You men get back here at once, do you hear, at once! You take your orders from *me*, not some worthless rabble!"

"No one will be takin' orders from you again, so you'd better get used to it," Vallant told the man dryly with a very hard edge to the words. "Just stand where you are, and we'll be gettin' around to you as soon as more important matters are attended to."

The noble growled deep in his throat as Vallant turned away from him to watch what the other Blending entities were doing with the former segments, and then I felt the man reach for the power. When it became clear that he had Fire magic, I took a small step toward him.

"If you feel you have to do that, it's *me* you'll be facing," I told him mildly as he fought to keep his eyes from widening. "I can tell you that you're not even as strong as the late and unlamented Seated Middle in Fire magic, so you'd better rethink your position. As I'm sure you can tell, I *am* a High rather than just being called one."

"You're a peasant is what you are, and I am not," he blustered, obviously trying to get the upper hand by using something other than talent. "You may curtsey to me and acknowledge my authority over you, and then you will come and stand before me in defense."

"I would dearly love to tell you what *you* may do, but I was raised not to say things like that," I drawled, all but laughing in his face. "Instead I'll tell you that there's a big difference between *saying* you have authority and actually being able to prove it. We've already proven our authority, so stop making a fool of yourself and just keep quiet."

One of the younger men behind the one who had spoken had been getting more and more outraged, and when he heard me virtually call the older man a fool he lost all control of himself. He screamed out his fury and then launched himself in attack against me.

Our short time of Blending had depleted the strength I'd regained, and only a small part of it had been replaced with what my entity-self had drawn from our link groups. But our link groups still had a lot of strength left, and somehow I found myself tapping that strength as I took one step back and defended myself automatically.

The younger man closed the distance between us very fast, and then he reached for my throat. He seemed to be trying to distract me from defense, but I hadn't had to stop and focus my talent for quite a while. The man's tactics might have been sound, but they depended on his actually strangling me.

Which he wasn't quite able to do. Instead of closing his hands around my throat, the man screamed and cradled his hands against his chest. The fires he'd touched instead of my throat had been very hot, and then he staggered and flailed backward into the small group he'd come from as though someone had hit him.

"And stay there, all of you," Rion ordered as he stepped up beside me. "We'll have someone see to those hands eventually, but you'll have to wait until those with real value—and those who have been hurt through no fault of their own—have been tended. Until then just stand there and keep quiet."

The man I'd burned kept silent and just looked ill, but one of the others whimpered and edged himself behind the man who'd done all the talking. That one, the obvious head of this former army, stood tight-lipped with fury with his hands turned to fists at his sides. But he also kept silent, so I joined Rion in turning away from them.

"I've put a wall around them now, and I apologize for not having done it sooner," Rion murmured to me, clear upset in his pretty eyes. "If I weren't so tired . . . Are you certain you're all right, Tamrissa?"

"I'm fine, Rion, so don't let it bother you," I soothed, reaching across to pat his arm. "I didn't have the least trouble defending myself, and you'll never guess why. I drew strength from my link groups."

"But—I didn't realize they were still linked," Rion protested, stopping to look down at me. "There would have been no *reason* for them to continue to be linked."

"Yes, I know," I agreed, giving him the sickly smile that was all I could produce right now. "But the strength was there, because I tapped into it. Would you like to venture a guess as to how and why it was there?"

"You must be joking," Rion came back with a sound of ridicule. "Even if I were well-rested and in top form I would hesitate to venture an opinion. At the moment . . . No, I think I'll wait to hear what the others have to say. If they're *able* to find what to say."

"I'm going to talk to the members of my link groups," I decided aloud, finally understanding that that might be a good idea. "If you see me sitting on the ground hiding my head, you'll know they had no idea what I was talking about."

"Could this be part of whatever new thing we seem to be working on?" Rion asked, confusion struggling with wonder in his expression. "Our continuing weariness seems to indicate that we're learning to do *something* new, and this might very well be it."

"Along with having more awareness and control when we Blend," I said, seeing at once that he might be right. "The two together would be— Why are you looking at me like that?"

"Your comment has suddenly made me wonder whether *I'm* far too tired or you are," he answered, his expression still peculiar. "When we Blended the entity used my perceptions again, but I remember nothing of more awareness and control. I take it that you do remember such a thing."

"I think I do," I responded, suddenly uncertain. "But you said that the entity used *your* perceptions. How could it have used yours and mine both at the same time?"

"I believe I've already said I have no opinions I'd care to venture," Rion returned with a groan as he briefly closed his eyes. "Obviously the Highest Aspect doesn't care for that stance, but unfortunately there's no other I'm able to take. I think we'd best mention this to our sisters and brothers as quickly as possible."

"Before I forget about it again," I agreed with a nod. "I meant to say something about it as soon as Jovvi dissolved the Blending, but it went right out of my head. Is your wall strong enough to protect those nobles as well as keep them from wandering off?"

"Protect them from the wrath of these poor people as soon as they're fully back to themselves, you mean," Rion said with a gesture of one hand. "Yes, the wall is strong enough for both purposes, so let's search out the others."

The decision was easily made, but not as easily seen to. It looked like most of the former army segments had been freed from the control they'd been living under, but not many of them looked ready to dance with pleasure or to turn on their former tormentors. Most sat slumped over or lay on the road where they'd formerly been standing, and it was easier to see now what poor condition they'd been kept in. The link groups of our various Blendings had left their horses to move among the newly freed, probably to see which of them most needed medical attention.

"I see the members of my link groups over there," I told Rion, and pointed in the proper direction. "If you'll try to locate our Blendingmates, I'll try to find out whether I was dreaming."

"Or simply imagining things," Rion agreed with a nod and an odd expression. "Now I have to decide whether I want these things to be real or imaginary. Possibly if I lie down for a nap, all these dilemmas will be gone when I awake."

And with that he walked off. I knew exactly what he meant, and felt more than a little tempted to take my own nap. If I'd had a guarantee that a nap would work I'd probably have tried it, but the sudden excitement my link group members showed when they saw me promised something else entirely.

"Tamrissa, what happened?" Deegro Lapas, one of the members of the groups, asked as soon as I got close enough. "We've never experienced anything like that before."

"That's basically what I came to ask *you*," I told Deegro and the others, letting them see my confusion. "From my end I suddenly had tandem link groups to draw strength from, even though the members of those groups shouldn't have been linked. What was it like for the rest of you?"

"We suddenly found ourselves linked for no apparent reason," Deegro answered, still speaking for the groups, a disturbance clear in his eyes. "Then we felt you drawing on our strength, and a moment later the need for linking seemed to be gone. You have no idea what made it happen?"

"At the moment, no," I conceded with a sigh. "I even thought I might have been imagining things, but obviously I wasn't. I'm going to talk this over with my Blendingmates, and if we come up with any explanations I'll be sure to let you know what they are."

"You sound as if you don't expect to find those explanations," Deegro observed, eyeing me with what looked like real sympathy. "Aren't you bound to figure something out sooner or later?"

"Tripping over a reason for something as you move through life isn't really figuring things out," I told him with another sigh. "For all we know this was a perfectly logical, natural happening, something that's really no big deal. But that's the whole problem: we don't *know* what's supposed to be logical and natural, and what should be considered a big deal. I'd love to do something really horrible to the fools who first decided to keep knowledge about Blending a privately held secret."

"If those fools were still alive, we'd all insist on joining you in that venture," Deegro said, causing most of the others to nod their agreement. "Please don't forget to let us know what the bunch of you come up with."

I promised not to forget and then left them to their tending of former captives. Rion stood a short distance off beckoning to me, which must have meant he'd found the others. As I walked toward him I realized that I was almost afraid to discuss the occurrences with everyone else. What if it turned out that no one could do what I'd done, and that I was really, really different? I didn't want to be all alone again, especially not in *this* way. But if I were, what could I possibly do about it?

TWENTY-ONE

Jovvi found herself quickly distracted from the nobles as soon as the captives were completely freed. The roiling sea of emotions was so strong that she had to shield herself from it. But she did project all the comfort and soothing she could in as wide an area as possible, trying to steady the poor victims until they could be helped physically by others.

"I don't believe this," Lorand muttered as he looked around, a faint trembling in his voice. "How could those fools have treated these people so badly and still expected to get anything out of them? By the time this column reached Gan Garee, half the people in it could well have been dead."

"Nobles weren't raised to worry about the tools they put to their use," Jovvi pointed out with an even greater weariness than she'd felt earlier. "If a tool you want to use happens to break, you simply replace it. It takes a certain amount of intelligence to understand when replacement isn't practical or possible."

"You also need to be in touch with the real world, which the fools leading this army obviously aren't," Lorand said bitterly. "A number of our people are breaking into the army's food supplies and making enough of a meal to bring some life back to these people. I'm just not sure how many of them will be able to eat well enough for the meal to do them any good. I'll be right back."

Jovvi nodded silently and watched him walk away,

knowing what he intended. At least one of their associate Blendings would have to be available to do what it could for those who were worst off, and Lorand was on his way to arrange that. The members of his link groups were already moving among the captives at Naran's direction, trying to keep from losing anyone now that freedom was within their grasp. Many people considered it a benefit to die free, but living free was Jovvi's idea of a much better choice.

When Jovvi noticed that her own link group members and those from most of the other Blendings were walking around among the newly freed and easing them as much as possible, she felt considerably better. She hated being so tired that using her talent was a chore, but it didn't seem anything could be done about that. Hopefully, it would last only a little while longer . . .

"This can't really be happening," a male voice muttered not far from Jovvi, drawing her attention. "This has to be nothing more than another dream, and I'll just wake up to find that nothing's changed. I've got to remember that, or I'll never last long enough to get even if I ever can . . ."

The muttering man sat on the ground about four feet away, his arms wrapped around his drawn-up knees, his face expressionless. What was left of his clothing was filthy and more than worn, his beard as long as his hair and just as dirty and matted. At first Jovvi thought the man might be joking, but checking him with her talent proved that he was all too serious.

"This *isn't* a dream, but I'm not asking you to believe me right now," Jovvi said to the man after stepping a bit closer to him. "You need to protect your inner self, but you also have to be prepared to accept the truth when it's proven beyond doubt. Will you do me the favor of at least suspending judgment for a while?"

"You've never been in my dreams before, so maybe I *will* do you that favor," the man responded after a long moment of silence while he studied Jovvi's face. "But how am I supposed to know when things stop being a dream and start to be real?"

"You'll know by how long everything takes," Jovvi said with a smile of support rather than amusement. The man wasn't joking, and that realization gave Jovvi a chill. "As soon as the food is prepared you'll get to eat, and at some time either before or after the meal one of our Earth magic healers will check you over. After that you'll be allowed to sleep undisturbed, and when you wake up you'll be fed again. By then we'll hopefully have found a place nearby to take you to, a place where you can bathe and cut your hair and beard. If we haven't also found clean clothing for you, the rest of us will share what we brought along for ourselves."

"What you brought along for yourselves," the man echoed, his tone saying nothing about how he considered that statement. He had very dark eyes, and he stared at Jovvi. "Assuming this *isn't* a dream, where are all of you supposed to have come from? Unless you just happened by . . ."

"No, we did *not* just happen by," Jovvi told him firmly, understanding that he was about to float away from reality again. "We come from Gan Garee, where the nobles aren't in charge any longer. *We're* in charge, and we've already freed most of the people in the armies sent west to Astinda. Now we're here to do the same for you and these others, and it's already begun. Just be patient, and by tomorrow you ought to know that you're not just dreaming."

"By tomorrow," he echoed again, the words horribly even. "All right, I'll wait until tomorrow. But what if it all *does* prove to be a dream? How will I stand it?"

"That's something I'm delighted to say you won't have to worry about ever again," Jovvi assured him, fighting not to break down and cry. "But there's something you *will* have to do, and that's help these others to understand the same truth. When the time comes, will you help with that?"

"I suppose I can do that," the man allowed, his gaze losing focus even as he spoke. "If I find out that this is real, I'll help you make the rest of them understand."

"Thank you," Jovvi said, putting a very gentle hand to his terribly thin shoulder. "It's sometimes hard for people to accept that the nightmare they've been living through is over, but it's necessary to remember that even the worst of nightmares ends at some time. I only wish that the ending could have come sooner for all of you."

The thin man didn't say anything else, and might not have even heard the last of what she'd told him. Jovvi straightened with a sigh and walked away, knowing she and the other Spirit magic users had their work cut out for them. Too many of these people would be terribly damaged in their minds, and without help they would never be right again . . .

"Jovvi, may I have a word with you?" she heard then, and turned to see Rion coming up. "Tamrissa has something that needs to be told to everyone, and that as soon as possible."

" 'As soon as possible' may take a while, Rion," Jovvi replied with a sigh. "Lorand and Naran are busy helping to take care of these people, and Vallant is coordinating all of our other efforts. And someone should pay attention to those nobles to make sure they don't do something we won't like."

"Tamrissa and I have already seen to the nobles," Rion said with a dismissive gesture, and only then did Jovvi notice his disturbance. "If the others are unavailable, are *you* free to listen? These newest matters should be thought about, and I'm sadly lacking the ability to make any sense of them."

"If it's that important to you, of course I'll listen," Jovvi agreed at once, somewhat curious but even more apprehensive. There could be few worse times for the appearance of something new and possibly serious . . .

"Good," Rion said, seeming relieved. "I'll locate Tamrissa and bring her here. She stopped to speak to her link groups first, and hopefully learned something."

Learned something? Jovvi watched Rion move off, her brows high as her curiosity grew. The new "matter" had something to do with the power? What in the world could it be? Jovvi would have had difficulty waiting very long to find out, but Rion returned in a moment accompanied by Tamma.

"Rion tells me something has happened," Jovvi said to Tamma, who looked even more disturbed than Rion had. "Is it a bad something or a good something?"

"It's two somethings, and I'd call them more disconcerting than bad," Tamma answered, trying to smile. "But you look even more tired than I feel, so why don't we sit down before I explain. There seems to be a relatively quiet spot over there."

Tamma pointed to a place farther away from the road among the trees, a spot that had neither horses tied nor people standing. Once they were settled, Tamma showed that odd smile again.

"I think I ought to start with the second happening," Tamma said. "While I was keeping an eye on the nobles, one of them tried to strangle me. I had no trouble making him sorry he tried, but only because I . . . somehow . . . drew strength from my link groups. I spoke to the people in the link groups before coming over here, and they know as little about it as I do. They suddenly found themselves linked and having strength drawn from them, but how and why we have no idea."

"Oh, dear," Jovvi said. "I see what you meant about it being disconcerting. If it's a new ability it's definitely worth having, but it would be nice to know how it happened. Why it happened is easy to understand."

"Yes, it happened because I needed it to happen," Tamma agreed with a touch of impatience. "But that's only one part of the why, and says nothing about how far the rest of it goes. Another aspect is why did it happen now rather than sooner? Will it only happen when the need is strong enough, or can I learn to control it? Will the rest of you find you can do the same thing? And let's certainly not forget the one about how far away from my link groups do I have to be before the trick doesn't work any longer."

"This probably happened to you first because you've been touching the power continuously longer than the rest of us," Jovvi said, automatically reaching out to sooth

Tamma's worry. "That doesn't make things easier for *you*, but the rest of us will be grateful for the warning. Now tell me about the other thing that happened."

"The other thing is almost stranger," Tamma said after taking a moderate breath, looking more relieved than Jovvi's efforts at soothing could account for. "When we Blended this last time, Rion tells me that the entity had *his* point of view."

"That *is* strange," Jovvi said at once, startled into speaking as she looked over at Rion. "Are you absolutely certain, Rion? I could swear that the entity had *my* point of view."

"I was afraid you were going to say that," Tamma muttered while Rion closed his eyes and shook his head. "It makes everything much more complicated, so of course it was to be expected . . . Jovvi, the entity had *my* point of view, and even beyond that it was more than just point of view. For the first time I had more awareness of self during the Blending, and even had more control of what the entity did. Can you tell me how that was possible when you and Rion both saw events through your own eyes?"

"This time I have no interest in saying 'Oh, dear,' " Jovvi stated. "I'd much rather use a phrase I learned during my time on the streets. Saying it won't help the situation much, but it would certainly make *me* feel better . . . Tamma, are you absolutely sure about what happened? Is it at all possible that you imagined the whole thing?"

"Of course it's possible," Tamma answered with a mirthless laugh. "As tired as I am, anything is possible. I just have a feeling that it isn't true, and it all really did happen. If you can convince me that I suffered from a touch of limited insanity, I'll probably love you even more than I do right now."

"Groping around blind will probably drive us all insane," Jovvi muttered, putting her hands to her face for a moment and rubbing. "We've been wondering why we're so tired, and this is probably the answer. Changes are now coming in multiples rather than one at a time, and that bothers me most right now. How many other surprises are in store, and what can we do to prepare for them? Do we have any choice other than stumbling into them by accident?"

"Maybe we can hang back and let Pagin Holter's Blending go through it first," Tamma suggested wryly, and Jovvi had the impression that Tamma was only half joking. "They're almost as strong as we are, and have been Blending just about as long."

"But he and his Blendingmates haven't been touching the power continuously as long as we have," Jovvi pointed out, then looked between Tamma and Rion. "But even so, we ought to speak to them and find out what point they're up to. Assuming they're going through the same things we did . . ."

"Let's wait until tomorrow to talk to them," Tamma said, and once again she didn't seem to be joking. "If they tell us they're going through something else entirely—or absolutely nothing—I don't think I could stand it."

Rion's expression said he agreed with that idea completely, so Jovvi nodded. She saw a parallel between what *they* were experiencing and what that man was, the one who wasn't allowing himself to believe that the rescue was real. Nightmare came in many different forms, and the ones experienced when awake were the worst of the lot . . .

Naran accepted her breakfast with a smile, then carried it over to where the rest of the Blending were sitting and eating. She'd awakened that morning a little later than everyone else, probably because she'd done so much with the captives yesterday. She'd pushed herself to the limit to find the captives in the worst condition and closest to dying, and happily everyone had been saved—for the moment. What happened during the coming days was another matter entirely, but she'd have to think about that some other time. She'd been so tired the night before that she remembered nothing beyond falling into her bedroll . . .

"Good morning, Naran," Jovvi greeted her when she took her place next to Rion. "That tiny bit of extra sleep you got seems to have done you a lot of good. If looks count for anything, you're not as tired as you were."

"No, actually, I'm not," Naran discovered aloud, realizing what she hadn't noticed earlier. "I feel well-rested, and the rest of you look the same. Have we finally worked our way through that persistent weariness?"

"I certainly hope so," Tamrissa almost growled, then sipped at her tea. "If the tiredness goes away, maybe there won't be any other surprises for a while."

"Have we had surprises?" Naran asked. "I've been so busy I'm afraid I must have missed—"

"No, love, you haven't missed anything, you just haven't been told yet," Rion interrupted to assure her, his hand patting her back. "What you were doing was too important to be interrupted, but we have the time now. The last time we Blended . . . Were you submerged in the entity, or did something else happen?"

"Why . . . now that you mention it, the entity used *my* point of view," Naran answered. "Does that mean something?"

"It means that the count is now unanimous," Jovvi told her with another smile. "You go ahead and eat, and we'll fill you in about what Tamma experienced yesterday."

The rest of them had already finished, so Naran did indeed work on her breakfast while she listened. The story wasn't very long, but it was certainly surprising.

"So . . . we may all have another ability now," Naran summed up after swallowing. "Or possibly we've just been *prepared* to have another ability, once we reach Tamrissa's level of power. But what about the other part—where she felt more in control? Will we eventually experience that as well?"

"That particular question is a bit more involved than it seems," Jovvi said with a sigh. "We were discussing it before you joined us, but we haven't gotten very far. The place we started was: How is it possible that each of us thinks that the entity used *our* personal view? It would also be nice to know why none of us seems to have *noticed* the multiple view."

"Is it possible we were too tired to notice?" Naran ventured, the only idea that came to mind. "Maybe the next time we Blend we *will* notice something."

"That's possible, but we don't have time for experiments right now," Lorand put in, his expression serious. "One of the other Blendings found a nice, big house not far from here, and as soon as everyone is finished eating we'll be taking the former captives there so they can rest. We have the army's three supply wagons to move the people who can't make it on their own, since we used up most of the supplies they held last night and this morning."

"That's something I meant to ask earlier," Tamrissa put in, speaking to Lorand. "Before we got here, everyone was managing to move on their own. Now, after they were freed, we have a large number who need to be helped. Why is that?"

"The orders they were given under the puredan forced them to keep going," Lorand answered everyone's obvious curiosity. "Once we took that prop away, everyone who was near to the end simply collapsed. If we hadn't gotten here when we did, those fool nobles would have started finding a lot of dead bodies on the road."

"They probably would have tried to *order* the rest not to die when they did find the bodies," Tamrissa said with a sound of scorn, her expression savage. "Let's make sure that nothing damaging happens to those people. If anyone has earned being handed over to the Astindans, they're the ones."

"Somehow I think that everybody forgot about feedin' that group yesterday and this mornin'," Vallant put in looking pleased rather than disturbed. "That's not really damagin' them, is it?"

"Not as far as I can see," Tamrissa agreed with amusement. "You can go for quite a long time without eating before you die, and we'll make sure to feed them before they reach that point. By the time we release them in the care of the Astindans, they may actually be relieved."

"At least until they discover what's in store for them," Lorand agreed with a smile before getting to his feet. "I'm going to supervise moving the people in the worst condition, so I'll see you later."

"Most of us will be helping with the others," Jovvi told

him as she also stood. "We've decided to let them use the horses while we walk, so there's a good chance we'll get to that house before you do."

"And Rion and I will take care of moving those nobles," Tamrissa put in, her tone harder. "We'll keep Naran company while she finishes eating, and then we'll get right to it."

"I'll be helpin' with movin' people until we reach that house," Vallant said, finishing his tea before joining the others who had already stood. "After that I want to set up perimeter guards and get everyone sorted out. Once that's done and we're together again, we can talk to our prisoners."

Everyone nodded their agreement, so Jovvi, Lorand, and Vallant walked away in different directions. Naran began to eat faster then, but Tamrissa laughed and reached over to touch her arm.

"You don't have to swallow it whole, not when a lot of the captives aren't finished yet either," Tamrissa told her kindly. "With everything you did yesterday, you deserve at least to be able to eat in peace."

"I don't have that much left, and I'm *glad* for the excuse to swallow it down fast," Naran told her honestly with a smile. "The venison may be fresh and tasty, but I can't help dreaming about eggs and fried potatoes and I miss them. Maybe we'll find some at that house."

"If we don't, I'm thinking about going on strike," Tamrissa agreed, still amused. "What about you, Rion?"

"I've enjoyed having things be different until now, but having venison for breakfast is a bit more different than I care for," Rion answered with his own amusement. "If a strike will produce eggs for us, I'll most likely join you in it—whatever a strike might be."

"A strike is something one of the Astindans told me about," Tamrissa answered after sipping at her tea. "The workers in Astinda aren't owned the way our own people were, and at one point a group of them decided to stop working until they were paid more by the people they worked for. They called the action a strike, but it didn't do as well as the strikers obviously hoped it would. The people they worked for simply hired other workers, and that was the end of the effort."

"They should have foreseen that even *without* Sight magic," Naran put in after swallowing the last of her food. "It makes no sense to pay people more for doing the same work others will do at the original pay. Without getting everyone alive to agree not to work for that original amount, they were wasting their time."

"Or without finding a way to keep those who would work more cheaply from taking the jobs," Tamrissa agreed as she stood. Naran was already on her feet, and when she finished the last of her tea Rion took her plate and cup.

"We'll be passing right by the place where these have to be returned," he told her before leaning forward to give her a brief kiss. "I'll see you later at that house."

"Yes, later," Naran agreed, sharing the brief kiss with him before watching him walk away with Tamrissa. Naran stood where she was for another moment, then she took a deep breath and went to saddle her horse. She was more in the mood to walk than ride this morning, so lending her horse would not be a sacrifice.

It was something of a surprise to find her horse already saddled, but looking around told Naran who had saved her some work. Those army members called prods had apparently been volunteered for most of the hard and dirty jobs around the camp, freeing everyone else to look after the former captives. The prods didn't seem too happy about their lot, but whichever Blending had put them to work had made sure that their opinion counted as little as the captives' had.

Naran also had no trouble finding someone who needed to ride. In point of fact there were two someones, a man and a woman. Naran's talent told her that the man would collapse if he didn't ride, but it also told her that he would most likely refuse to do so. His pride had obviously been badly battered by his time with the army, and he needed to do something positive to restore it even if that something hurt him. But with the woman also there, Naran believed she saw the way to salvage the situation.

"Excuse me," Naran said to the man as she led her horse up to him. "I wonder if I might ask you to do me a favor."

"I'd be pleased to do so lovely a lady any favor I'm able to," the man answered after a very slight hesitation, giving her a shaky smile. In truth all of him was shaky, not to mention gaunt, ragged, and hairy. "Are you in need of help in mounting?"

"Actually, I'm in need of help in getting *that* woman mounted and safe," Naran murmured, nodding toward the woman, who currently sat slumped on the ground. "She's in no condition to walk to the house we've found, but if I put her on my horse she could well fall off. I'd ride with her and hold her up, but I'm afraid I'm not strong enough to hold her if she starts to fall. A man holding her up would make her much safer, so I'd like to impose on *you* to be that man."

"Me," the man echoed, obviously not knowing what else to say for the moment. He seemed to be wondering if *he* would be stronger than a woman in full health, but it had also come to him that he'd been offered a way to ride without sacrificing any more of his dignity. When he squared his shoulders, Naran could almost see him thinking that he *would* be strong enough to help the woman no matter what it cost him, and then he smiled again.

"Lovely lady, you've found yourself an assistant," he told Naran, the words coming as no surprise to her. "Shall we get the woman onto your horse together?"

"I'd be grateful for your help with that as well," Naran replied with her own smile. "Let's see if we can get her on her feet first."

They walked over to the woman and explained what they had in mind, and the woman took a deep breath before nodding her agreement. She seemed to be someone who was normally strong and capable, and although she hated being so weak, she seemed to realize that the more she cooperated the sooner she would be fit again.

Naran did most of the helping when it came to getting

the woman mounted, but she made no effort to help the man mount. It was a considerable struggle for him, but once he sat behind the woman his obvious pleasure and pride let Naran know she'd done the right thing. After all, she *was* there to help in whatever way she could . . .

Once the two people were settled, Naran began to lead her horse to the part of the road that wasn't cluttered with people and wagons. She passed a short distance from where Rion and Tamrissa were seeing to the nobles, but neither one looked around to see *her.*

Just as well, Naran thought as she simply kept going. Seeming unconcerned during breakfast had been hard for her, and there was no need to go looking for more hardship. Rion had said he would see her at the house, and that would be soon enough to put her mask back on. A mask she hated to have to wear, in spite of its being so necessary . . .

Naran would have enjoyed being alone somewhere so that she might cry in peace. Her talent had told her it was a virtual certainty that Rion would meet another woman, one he found attractive in some way. Naran knew when that meeting took place, and she'd prayed that Rion would speak to her about it. That would have meant the contact was less important to him than she was, but he *hadn't* mentioned it.

And that meant Rion was seriously considering another woman. Naran bit her lip, wishing there was something she could do to affect the situation, but she knew better than to even try. Everything she Saw told her that any interference on her part would make things worse rather than better, but keeping silent was so *hard*!

Rion was her life, but what if he decided he no longer loved her? What in the world would she do *then*?

TWENTY-TWO

Vallant walked into the small sitting room of the very large house to find that the others were already there. Getting all the former captives to the house and settled in had been a bit of a nightmare, but it was now midafternoon and it was done. Most of the poor souls they'd rescued were sleeping again, so he'd made arrangements that they be fed whenever they woke up.

"I still don't understand how they could have been kept in such poor condition," Tamrissa was saying as Vallant took himself over to the tea service. "Very few of the other captives we freed were as bad off as most of these people, probably because they were being used to do the fighting. Since the fool in charge used *these* people for the same purpose, how could he take the chance of losing them just when he needed them the most?"

"I think that's one of the questions we need to ask those nobles," Jovvi said, sounding stronger than she had the day before. Vallant also felt more like his old self in spite of all the work he'd done. "Vallant, did you want to discuss something with us before we get to questioning the nobles?"

"I was just thinkin' that we ought to choose our stalls in the stables before they're all gone," Vallant answered as he turned away from the tea service with a nicely filled cup. "All the bedchambers and studies and spare rooms—and empty corners—in this house have been given to the former captives, so we've had to put the horses out to graze again in order to have someplace for the rest of us to sleep. If any of you have a preference in stalls, you'd better say somethin' now."

"As long as there are walls around me and straw under me, I don't care which stall I get," Tamrissa answered with a smile. "And in case you were wondering why I'm in such a mellow mood, the bath house is all ready for use. We used the prods—and the nobles—to clean the bath, and then some of your people filled the bath again. After that I heated the water, and now some of *my* people are maintaining the heat. We're letting the others bathe first, and then *we* get to soak awhile."

"That sounds heavenly, but first we do have to speak to those nobles," Jovvi said with a sigh as Vallant took a seat near Tamrissa. "Is there anything else that needs to be done before that?"

"Not anymore," Vallant answered when no one else did. "The other Blendin's will take turns keepin' an eye out for anyone tryin' to sneak up on us, the Earth magic users will be monitorin' the former captives who are in the worst shape, and some of our link group Highs have gone to a nearby town for more supplies—and whatever's ready of the simple clothin' the first Highs goin' to the town ordered. There was a tailorin' shop that also had seamstresses, so they took advantage of havin' enough gold to pay for what's needed."

"Until the new clothes are ready, the people can use the clothing we found in this house," Naran put in. "There's an awful lot of it and some of the gowns are too fancy for everyday use, but they'll do until the skirts and blouses—and trousers and shirts—are finished."

"I was prepared to share my own things, but I'm glad I don't have to now," Tamrissa said with a pleased smile for Naran. "And I'm also glad that we're up to questioning those nobles. Putting them to work around here should have softened them up a bit."

"Well, we'll certainly find out," Jovvi said, then turned to Rion. "Rion, will you please go and get them?"

"Going anywhere is unnecessary, Jovvi," Rion answered with his own pleased expression. "I checked a short while ago, and discovered that I can reach the wall I put around them from here. I thought that simply maintaining the wall was all I was capable of at this distance, but that isn't so. I can move the wall, and therefore I can move what the wall contains as well."

"And they're all the way out behind the kitchens, aren't they?" Lorand asked as he leaned forward, clearly as interested as Vallant himself was. "I wonder if the range of my own perceptions has increased."

"I was just thinkin' that very thing, but about me," Vallant agreed thoughtfully. "And if *all* of us have grown in the same way, will our Blendin' be comparatively stronger as well?"

"I don't see how it can't be," Jovvi said, her brows high with a pleased expression on her face, but then the expression disappeared. "But I also can't quite see where all of this is leading. Will we still be the same people we were when it's all over?"

"We stopped being our old selves a long time ago, when all this first started," Tamrissa pointed out with none of the qualms Jovvi clearly felt. "I, for one, happen to like the difference, but if that changes I promise to say so at once. As long as we continue to tell each other the truth—and don't start to walk all over our associates—we should be fine. And here come our . . . guests."

Vallant looked up to see that Rion had brought the nobles to them with the hardened wall of air that had kept them penned in place. The four men stumbled hurriedly along, the oldest and biggest of them looking furiously murderous, but all looking a mess. Their previously bright and pretty uniforms were now filthy and even torn in places, and the two youngest men were apparently close to exhaustion.

"No, don't even think about sittin' in a chair," Vallant told them when the two younger ones began to glance around and the oldest seemed to be headed in that direction as well. "If you can't stay on your feet, then you can sit on the carpetin'. We can have it cleaned once you're back in your proper place."

"We'll stand in the presence of rabble, just as nobles and gentlemen should!" the oldest barked, freezing the two younger ones as they began to sit down. "How long do you expect to be able to keep us prisoner like this? I warn you that every indignity offered us now will be repaid with interest when you and your rabble masters are brought down!"

"We're not offering you indignity, we're treating you like the useless dregs you actually are," Rion told the man haughtily before Vallant could speak. "And if you've gotten the notion into your head that we're not in charge both here and in the city, I suggest you rethink your position. You now stand in the presence of your lawful rulers, those who were Seated as leaders of this empire."

"But that means they're the Seated Blending!" one of the younger men, the one with red hair, blurted. "They told us the Seated Blending would never come out after us, so they lied!"

"Keep silent!" the oldest man snapped over his shoulder, then returned his glare to his captors. "If you expect us to betray our supporters, you have a long wait ahead of you. Those with proper breeding are well able to hold out against anything rabble can bring to bear against them. We may be forced to dirty our hands, but you'll never find it possible to make us betray our own."

"That little speech simply shows how foolish you are," Jovvi told the man with a shake of her head. "You and your helpers needed drugs and bullies to make people do as you wished, but we need neither thing. Tell us about your 'supporters,' the ones who led you to believe that we would stay in Gan Garee rather than come out after you."

"I was able to positively recognize only one of them, but from that found it possible to infer the identity of one of the others," the former noble said at once. "The third man seemed familiar, but I can only guess at who he might be."

"Father!" the younger man with a bandaged hand exclaimed, shock riding his features. "You ordered us to tell them nothing, and now here you are—"

"I'm not *telling* them anything, you fool boy, I'm being forced to speak the truth," the older man growled at the younger one, not even bothering to glance at him. "They're doing something to me, and I'm helpless to stop it."

"Just as helpless as your slaves were," Tamrissa confirmed with a smile that had no amusement in it. "Tell us who you think those supporters are, but first when you met them."

"I met them in a house not far from here, less than a day's travel back east," the man replied without further oration. "They had sent a messenger to me before we reached their neighborhood, inviting me and my officers to lunch. We went and spoke to them and ate, and then we returned to my command."

"Which one of them did the house belong to?" Tamrissa interrupted to ask. "Were you able to tell?"

"As far as I could tell, the house belonged to none of them," the man answered, a flash of annoyance showing in his eyes for no more than an instant. "The place had obviously been cleaned for the occasion, but it was hardly spotless and there weren't enough servants about. The house wasn't very large, but even so would have required a larger staff to see to it on a regular basis."

"The way you said you were able to recognize one of them sounded strange," Jovvi put in thoughtfully. "Was there something that was supposed to have kept you from recognizing them? And what's your own name, by the way?"

"I'm Lord Henich Rengan, and my hosts wore masks," the noble replied, again looking annoyed that he'd been interrupted. "Even so, I was able to recognize High Lord Embisson Ruhl, a man of considerable power in the empire. One of the other two must have been his son Edmin, as father and son often act in concert. The third man could have been Lord Sembrin Noll, brother to Lord Ephaim Noll, who is another considerable power. I met the younger Noll a time or three in Gan Garee, usually in his brother's company."

"And what was their purpose in invitin' you to lunch?" Vallant asked, curious about the point. "Were they simply welcomin' you back to the empire after your tour of Gracely?"

"They wanted me warned about what had been happening," Rengan replied with a grimace. "They claimed they would be in Gan Garee before my force, and would do what was possible to help me defeat any opposition. They also claimed that the new Seated Blending would be in the city rather than come out here, and suggested I might even be able to take back the surviving segments from the Astindan armies that you commoners somehow took control of. The rest of the Astindan armies, I was told, are dead."

"So they lied to you about more than whether we would be here," Tamrissa said with a good deal of satisfaction. "Too many people in the Astindan armies did die, but not nearly all of them and we didn't 'somehow' get control of them. We freed every contingent we came across, and now most of those people are working and riding with *us*. We did it just the way we freed *your* slaves, with ability you don't even come close to having. How do you feel about having been lied to by those you consider your own?"

"I think that Ruhl was a damned fool for not telling me the complete truth," Rengan answered in a blunt, flat way. "If I'd known what to be on guard against I would have made a much better showing when you attacked, but what can you expect from a politician who isn't a military man? If the fool was as good as he thinks he is, he would be back in the city in his usual place, not hiding out in his country house."

"Do you happen to know where that country house is located?" Vallant asked at once. "Assumin', that is, that they're still there and not really on their way to Gan Garee."

"I have no idea whether or not they're still there, but Ruhl's country place, called Bastions, is in the same neighborhood that I recently mentioned." This time Rengan showed a grim satisfaction in passing on the information, probably his idea of getting even with a fool. "It's even larger than *this* place, about the same size as my own country house."

"Your *former* country house," Vallant corrected with his

own satisfaction, finding the man extremely obnoxious even as a helpless prisoner. "Members of the former nobility don't own things any longer, not even the clothes on their backs. But you'll be findin' out all about that as soon as you get back to the city. Right now I want to know what you and these others did in Gracely."

"We devastated the entire countryside," Rengan answered even more quickly, the words now an emotionless statement rather than a boast or confession. "They had no chance against us, and we wiped out everyone in our path."

"Now, that's strange," Jovvi said suddenly, staring at the man. "His mind went . . . odd for a moment, just when you asked that question. I wonder . . . Tell us again what you did in Gracely, please, and add a few details."

"We devastated the entire countryside," Rengan said in the exact tone he'd used the first time, showing the same lack of expression. "They had no chance against us, and we wiped out everyone in our path."

"That's supposed to be with details added?" Vallant observed as most of the others gave low exclamations of surprise. "It's word for word what he said the first time, so he's disobeyin' you, Jovvi."

"No, actually, he's not," Jovvi murmured, staring at the man with her own odd expression, then she turned her attention to one of the others. "You with the bandaged hand. What's your name?"

"I'm Lord Vodan Rengan, my father's first officer," the second man answered, hatred and outrage clear in his tone. "You peasants have no right to do this to us, no right at all! Your supposed Seating means nothing, not when it wasn't the proper authorities who Seated you."

"By the proper authorities you mean the nobility, who took their duty so seriously that they cheated to let their own Blending win the last challenge," Tamrissa immediately put in, taking up the gauntlet. "They paid for that stupidity by losing everything they had when their puppets went down, when they could have kept everything by handling the matter honestly. Those are the people you think should still be in charge?"

"As they're members of the nobility, yes," Vodan Rengan stated between clenched teeth. "They're entitled to do anything they please, and peasants have the right to do nothing but obey them. If you and your lot hadn't interfered, they would have worked things out in their own way."

"And then died with everyone else when the Astindans reached Gan Garee," Vallant added dryly. "If you were able to think instead of just repeatin' what you've been told, we could continue this conversation. Since you never learned how to think, though, tell me what your lot did in Gracely."

"We devastated the entire countryside," the younger Rengan answered just as quickly as his father had, his expression immediately blanking in the same way. "They had no chance against us, and we wiped out everyone in our path."

Vallant exchanged a glance with Jovvi, who nodded to show that the same thing had happened to the younger Rengan's mind as well.

"They've both used the same words and are wearing the same expression," Lorand observed aloud, looking disturbed. "That can't possibly be natural, but who could have manipulated them? We're the only ones of our people to come close to them."

"Let's see if the opinion is unanimous," Jovvi said, shifting her attention to the remaining members of the group. "You with the red hair. Tell me your name, and then tell me what was done by you in Gracely."

"I'm Lord Lesshan Rengan," the man replied, his expression one of bored disinterest, but then it quickly shifted to a familiar neutrality. "In Gracely we devastated the entire countryside. They had no chance against us, and we wiped out everyone in our path."

"And you?" Jovvi said to the last of the four, the one who looked most miserable and frightened. "Tell me your name, and then tell me what was done in Gracely."

"I—I'm Lord Dalbo Rengan," the man began with a tremor in his voice, sounding and looking terrified. But then he, too, changed. "In Gracely we devastated the entire countryside. They had no chance against us, and we wiped out everyone in our path."

"Well, that makes all four of them," Naran commented with a sigh. "But now that we have them beyond complaining, how do we bring them back?"

"Like this," Jovvi answered with a faint smile. "Are all of you absolutely positive about what you just said?"

"Of course I'm positive," Henich Rengan snarled, suddenly alive again—just as his sons were. "How dare you question my word?"

"So who could have gotten to them?" Tamrissa asked Jovvi, the very question Vallant had meant to put. "*They* obviously have no idea they were reached, but this could never have happened naturally. But whoever did it has to have strength, so why don't we know about them?"

"Maybe it's because they're not from our empire," Jovvi suggested with a small headshake. "Naran, do you see anything at all to confirm or deny my guess?"

"About it being someone in Gracely who influenced them?" Naran said rather than asked as her gaze went distant. "That's the past rather than the future, so I can't use my ability to tell. What I *can* See, though, is the strengthening possibility that we'll have to visit Gracely to find out for ourselves, *before* we're faced with another horde looking for vengeance."

"We're to go all the way to Gracely, a place that may well be gathering its forces against us?" Rion asked with surprise. "Would it be wise to do such a thing?"

"I doubt if it's wise, but it will probably turn out to be necessary," Vallant answered Rion with a sigh. "If those people have a grudge against us, we need to know it before the fire starts fallin' on our heads. And we'll have to get our people out of harm's way, just as we did near the border to Astinda."

"And if there *isn't* any devastation in Gracely, we need to know that as well," Jovvi pointed out. "Someone made our people believe that they were destroying the countryside the way they'd been ordered to do. I can't fault them for not wanting to be destroyed or getting into a war to stop the destruction, but the course they chose bothers me. They could have put the nobles under control and kept them somewhere out of the way after freeing the bound members of the army, but the manipulators didn't do that. They left innocent people as slaves, and simply convinced the nobles that they were victors. I'd like to know why that was done."

"And if we don't like their answers, we can talk it over with them," Tamrissa said with a smile that was on the grim side. "But there's something else we have to do before we continue on to Gracely. We have to check out that Bastions place Rengan mentioned, to see if his loyal supporters are still there. Whether or not they are, we ought to check out the rest of the neighborhood for those missing nobles. Remember, the more of them we leave running around loose, the more of a headache we'll be making for ourselves."

"Yes, that truth hasn't changed," Jovvi agreed with a sigh. "The authority they represent is no longer real, but troublemakers can rally around their symbol and force us to counter them. But if we can find enough of them, they can be the ones to help the former captives get back to the city under the guidance of the Astindans. Our own people can continue on with us."

"And our gatherin' up those loose ends will give the people here some extra time to recover before they have to get back on the road," Vallant pointed out, mostly to a disturbed Lorand. "We'll also collect all the horses, coaches, and carriages we can along with wagons and supplies, so most if not all of them will actually get to the city alive. After that the Astindans can send the nobles on their way."

"So you *have* allied yourselves with our enemies," Henich Rengan said suddenly in disgust, reminding them that he was still there. "Obviously the foolish Ruhl didn't lie about everything, but I wish he had. Even peasant rabble should know something about loyalty."

"Loyalty to what?" Vallant demanded, this time beating Tamrissa to the commenting. "To the useless fools who started the war with Astinda, causin' more death and horror

than I ever want to see again? It's those useless fools who
are now makin' up for what they did, and the Astindans·
are our allies, just as they should have been all along. You
still think you can do anythin' you damn well please because of an accident of birth, but you'll surely learn better.
Rion, get them out of here, please."

"With pleasure," Rion answered, and then the four former nobles stumbled out in the same way they'd arrived.
Rengan's eyes had narrowed with disturbance and his son
Vodan appeared shaken, but the other two simply continued
to look miserable. Those last two were the ones who bothered Vallant the most, but at least the Astindans would treat
them fairly. Which was probably more than their own father
would have done for them . . .

"It looks like we'll be traveling again tomorrow," Lorand
said as he stood and stretched, clearly trying to appear casual instead of disturbed. "I think I'll see about getting
something to eat, pay a visit afterward to the bath house,
and then go to bed early. Anyone interested in joining me?"

Jovvi was the first to accept his offer, but the rest of
them weren't far behind. And Jovvi was the best one to
soothe Lorand's mind about the necessity for gathering up
whatever nobles were still running around loose. Vallant
knew the odds were good that the innocent would be caught
along with the guilty, but as he followed the others out of
the room he also knew that that consideration couldn't keep
them from doing the rounding up. The pendulum was now
swinging back, and those who had been privileged would
now find out what the other side of life was like.

But a small part of Vallant wished that he and his Blendingmates weren't the only ones who could make that happen. Switching off with someone else would have made it
all so much easier . . .

TWENTY-THREE

Lorand noticed that it was not yet noon when he and the others reached the area where the hidden nobles were supposed to be. There were quite a few houses in the area, so their "haul" ought to be respectable. He still felt uncomfortable with the idea of hunting people down, and had spoken to Jovvi about it for quite a while the night before. But it was talking to Vallant that had eased his mind to some extent, since Vallant felt much the same way *he* did about gathering up escaped nobles. Jovvi looked at the matter more the way Tamrissa did, but since they were both women that was perfectly understandable . . .

"That noble's idea of a day's march is almost half a day's ride," Rion observed to everyone in general. "No wonder those people were ready to fall over."

"Most of the houses we passed had people in them," Tamrissa said, also offering an observation. "How are we going to find the house we want first, the one with Rengan's 'associates'?"

"The house called Bastions should be the one over there," Vallant answered her, pointing toward a mansion sitting on a gentle knoll in the near distance. "I had Jovvi question Rengan again, and he knew more about the location of the place than he admitted at first. He had to answer any question put to him, but holdin' back on what we needed to know but didn't ask about wasn't disallowed."

"It is now," Jovvi put in, annoyance flashing in her eyes. "I should have known better than to allow him that loop-

289

hole, but you all know how I hate to control people. From now on I'll pay closer attention."

"I've been paying closer attention myself, but to the weather," Lorand put in as he glanced at the sky again. "It's going to be raining in a couple of hours, so let's not waste any time getting to that house and looking around. As it is, some of the rest of our people might not make it before those clouds open up."

"They're ridin' in groups of ten, but not all strung out," Vallant supplied. "Just because we didn't want to make noticin' us easy doesn't mean some of them are an hour behind us. They're mostly only a few minutes away, so they ought to get to shelter in plenty of time."

Lorand nodded to acknowledge the information, even though he'd known it well enough even before Vallant had spoken. The ride had been a pleasant one in spite of the threatening rain, but there was something disturbing Lorand that he just couldn't put his finger on. The closer they got to that house, the more the disturbance seemed to grow . . .

Vallant had begun to lead them forward again, and Lorand simply rode with the others as he tried to figure out what could be bothering him. The area was lovely, the temperature was comfortable, the humidity wasn't excessive even with the coming rain, the birds—

"Stop!" Lorand called, not realizing that he hadn't been the only one to speak until after the word was out. Both Jovvi and Naran had said the same thing at the same time, and that made the others pull their mounts to a halt.

"What's wrong?" Tamrissa asked, looking from one to the other of them with concern. "Have you discovered that we're going the wrong way?"

"Something's going to happen," Naran said, her expression disturbed as her inner sight examined images invisible to the rest of them. "There's a lot of . . . roiling and I can't quite make out the details, but something is definitely about to happen."

"Possibly that something will happen because we aren't alone out here," Jovvi added, her own gaze on the woods to the left. "We seem to have quite a lot of company."

"I noticed that, too, right after I noticed that the birds were too quiet," Lorand put in as he stared in the same direction Jovvi did. "There's a large number of people in the trees over there, and I don't think they're looking for berries and nuts."

Vallant seemed about to say something, but that was when the people in the woods chose to show themselves. The first of them stepped out from behind trees with the rest following, and Lorand felt immediate shock. Those who had lurked in the woods came out in pairs and groups of pairs, with a man behind holding someone in front of him by his arm around the front person's neck. The one behind also held a knife, and a large number of those being held were women.

"Now you've got a problem, don't you?" one of the men holding a hostage called, heavy amusement in his voice. "If you don't give yourselves up to us we'll kill these people and then disappear, and their deaths will be *your* fault. Are you going to let innocent people die in your place?"

"I'll bet you believed those nobles when they told you how easy it would be to capture us," Tamrissa called back, saying just what Lorand had been thinking. "They dangled silver or gold in front of you, and the sight of it turned their every word true. Well, just remember that when you don't have hostages any longer, because as soon as you release them they're going to run away as fast as they can."

"The only way they'll be released is when they're dead," the same man countered, still highly amused. "You're not very good at bluffing, girl, so why don't you just keep silent and let men discuss what has to be— Yow!"

The man's shout of pain was echoed and accompanied by the same from every man holding a hostage. Also at the same time all the hostages were released, which told Lorand that Tamrissa had used Fire magic to free them. The former hostages did indeed start to run at once, and were quickly out of the easy reach of their captors.

"Maybe I'm not very good at bluffing because I wasn't bluffing," Tamrissa told the man who was no longer amused. "And now that I've . . . said my piece, you can have the next conversation with a man."

"Me, for instance," Rion took over, smiling as those who tried to chase after their captives ran into an invisible wall. "I don't speak quite as forcefully as Tamrissa does, but my efforts are usually adequate."

"And so are mine," Lorand put in, reaching to all the men but the one who had spoken. There was a total of twenty-five in the group, and twenty-four of the men suddenly became very sleepy. Lorand hadn't been sure he had the strength to affect twenty-four people at once, but the attempt became effortless as additional strength suddenly flowed into him. He knew at once where the strength came from, of course, and finally understood why Tamrissa had been upset by the experience.

"But *my* efforts are a good deal more gentle," Jovvi said as the men Lorand had touched folded silently to the ground. "I'd like you to tell us who you are and what you hoped to accomplish. Surely you didn't really think we could be taken *that* easily?"

"I'm Isbirn Gelin, leader of this group," the only man left standing replied at once, still rubbing his arm as he glanced around. "The life of an outlaw is usually a good one in this empire, as long as you know enough to stay away from the nobility. What we were trying to do was earn some extra silver the easy way, by seeing to a chore for one of the nobles. And why *shouldn't* you have been that easy to take? If your bosses sent you way out here, you can't be very important."

"You still haven't told me what that chore you agreed to do is all about," Jovvi said, and some of the gentleness was gone from her voice. "That means you were supposed to kill us, doesn't it?"

"No, we were only supposed to kill you as a last resort," the husky Gelin replied, gesturing with one hand. "The noble told us that you'd probably be stupid enough to trade yourselves for our hostages, especially if they were mostly women. Once we made you our prisoners we were supposed to kill the hostages anyway, and then take you to

Gan Garee. By the time we got there, the noble expected to be in a position to do some bargaining."

"I'm still havin' trouble followin' this," Vallant put in with a frown. "I could tell that you were no more than a Low talent when you tried to use your Water magic, so chances are good that your men aren't much better in their own aspects. With that bein' so, can you explain how you expected to capture six High talents with another sixty of the same not far behind them?"

"But . . . you can't be High talents," Gelin protested, his skin going pale enough to notice. "The noble said you would be nothings, out here doing the dirty work your higher-ups didn't want to bother with. Who would send High talents all the way out here to check on which houses have been recently used?"

"So that's what he told you we were out here for," Tamrissa said with a very unladylike snort. "And you believed *that* right along with the rest. Didn't it once occur to you to wonder why a noble would want us if we were that unimportant? If he was going to use us in his bargaining, we had to have *some* value."

"Maybe to the people who sent you, but not necessarily to anyone else," Gelin replied with a shrug. "The noble said that the new Seated Blending peasants were soft-headed instead of being practical, so he probably could have done a good trade. But that doesn't explain how he expected us to be able to capture High talents, does it?"

"That little mystery might explain something else, though," Naran put in thoughtfully. "The noble might have been high in the old government the way that army man Rengan said, but that doesn't have to mean he knows more about High talents and Blendings than anyone else. Rengan actually worked with Highs, but still knew almost nothing about them."

"That's an excellent point," Rion agreed at once. "We also must remember that our predecessors used Lows and ordinary Middles to do things for them, so that noble may have assumed we would do likewise. *He* considers Highs too dangerous to be involved with, and so might naturally assume that we would also avoid them whenever possible."

"Actually, that makes excellent sense," Vallant agreed with his own thoughtful expression. "It's stupid to keep throwin' away tools like the army and this bunch here, but less so if you realize that the man doesn't know what he's doin' for lack of complete information."

"Which makes *me,* at least, feel a good deal better," Jovvi said with a smile. "If given my choice, I'd rather have a confused enemy than a clear-headed one. Shall we gather up this bunch and send them back to Gan Garee along with any nobles we find?"

"Let's do that and something else as well," Lorand suggested, the idea fairly obvious at least to him. "I've been waiting for someone to realize that these men know the area and who can be found where, so we ought to use them first as guides. Or isn't that a good idea for a reason I'm not seeing?"

"Why, Lorand, that's a marvelous idea," Jovvi said at once, but her expression seemed odd. "But I wouldn't have expected something like that to come from *you.* I do know how you feel about the way we're going after the nobles, so I'm curious as to why you made the suggestion."

"I think that part about using hostages—and then killing them—has made me change my mind," Lorand said after a short hesitation, aware that the others were also listening closely. "I still don't like the idea of hunting people down, but hearing what that outlaw said reminded me of other things the nobility has done without a second thought or a regret. If we give them a chance to regain their standing in the empire, thousands of people will suffer through no fault of their own."

"It's about time you understood that, my friend," Tamrissa said, her words on the dry side. "Men always have trouble seeing the obvious for some reason, which makes it a good thing we women are around. You all like to pretend that you're so hard and stern, but when it comes to the necessities, it's usually women who have to do them."

"Which is why we men consider ourselves lucky to have you women around," Lorand said while everyone else chuckled. "I may be foolish in *some* things, but if you think I'll ever get into an argument with *you* then you're the foolish one. Let's get these people properly taken care of, and then we can have a look at that house."

This time there was laughter, but that didn't stop them from Blending briefly to put all twenty-five men under their control. The Lorand entity first woke up the ones that had been put to sleep, and then the entire group was neutralized as a danger before being made into reluctant allies. The Lorand entity allowed them their reluctance, but not refusal.

When the entity was dissolved, the former outlaws were sent to get their horses. While Lorand and the others waited, Jovvi turned to Tamrissa.

"This is the first time we've Blended since you had that odd experience," Jovvi said, mentioning something Lorand had also been thinking about. "Did it by any chance happen again?"

"It certainly did," Tamrissa confirmed, frowning. "But this time it felt even more natural, as though it should have been happening all along. What about the rest of you?"

"Once again the entity seemed to have *my* point of view, and I felt nothing unusual," Jovvi said, looking around to see if the others had experienced the same. When she'd gotten nods from everyone including Lorand, she heaved a moderate sigh. "So nothing has changed for anyone but Tamma. All right, we'll obviously have to wait until something does change. If and when it does, please let the rest of us know immediately."

Lorand again joined the others in agreeing to the request, and then the outlaws were back with them. Vallant had the outlaws fall in behind their Blending members, and then the enlarged procession moved off toward the mansion on the knoll. It took only a short while to get there, and the outlaws were left mounted while their six walked up to the door and knocked.

"We're here to see the man named Ruhl," Vallant told the servant who opened the door. "Please take us to him immediately."

"*High Lord* Embisson Ruhl is not at home," the servant

corrected with a frown of disapproval and a very superior attitude. "Please return at another time after making an appointment."

"We already have an appointment," Tamrissa told the man dryly while Vallant kept the door from being closed in their faces. "It was made the day we were Seated as the empire's newest ruling Blending. And for your information, the man Ruhl is no longer any kind of lord, high or low. We're coming in now, so you'd better get used to the idea."

The servant seemed to be pushed back from the door more or less gently, which meant that Rion was also helping. They all walked into the very large entrance area, and Lorand couldn't help feeling impressed. The house's entrance area alone was almost the size of the entire house Lorand had grown up in, which made him want to see the rest of the place.

"This is an illegal invasion of private property," the servant blustered, his expression showing his indignation. "How dare you force your way in here, pretending to be what you're not—"

"You sound awfully certain that we're lying," Jovvi interrupted, her tone gentle. "Can you tell me why that's so?"

"High Lord Embisson told the entire staff the truth before he left," the man replied stiffly with a look of faint surprise in his eyes. "We were warned not to believe anything you told us if you came here, which might happen even though the house is being guarded. You shouldn't really be here at all . . ."

"Yes, that's right, we've already seen to those . . . guards," Tamrissa put in as the servant hesitated. "But they weren't guards they were outlaws, ready to kill the people they'd taken as hostages. That doesn't bother you even a little?"

"That can't be true!" the man blurted, but this time he seemed more upset than doubting. "The High Lord explained that the people used as supposed hostages would be perfectly all right, and would be released as soon as the intruders were captured. That's why I agreed to let my daughter be one of them . . ."

"She would have died with the others if we hadn't stopped those marvelous 'guards' of yours," Tamrissa told the man with a bluntness that Lorand never would have used under the circumstances. "The outlaws are just outside right now, and if you don't believe *us* you can feel free to ask *them*. But right now we need to see every person in this household."

The servant had become too disturbed to be of much help, so they used their Blending instead. And this time Lorand noticed something odd. The entity was much more him than a simple combination with his point of view. Lorand knew he could guide the entity rather than just going along while *it* controlled all actions, and that felt good. There were things that had to be done, and he was more than prepared to do them.

One by one he put all the servants under control, and once it was done he noticed that the cooks immediately began to throw away the food they'd been preparing. Obviously the food had been tampered with, a prearranged backup plan in case the trap with the outlaws didn't work . . .

"And that's that," Jovvi said once she'd dissolved the Blending again. "I'm glad that the cooks are starting to make something for lunch that will be safe to eat. I'm beginning to get hungry, and it won't be long before all the others and their own appetites get here. Is there anything else we have to do?"

"I think what you need to do is hear the latest," Lorand said, interrupting everyone else's headshake or denial. "Tamrissa's newest condition seems to be spreading, because now *I* have it. And she was right about it feeling completely natural. It seems so unremarkable, in fact, that I came close to forgetting about mentioning it. Only the way Jovvi made a deliberate point about discussing the matter has made me remember."

"Two of you now," Jovvi exclaimed, more excited than disturbed. "But what about you, Tamma? Did you go back to feeling that you were just a point of view of the entity?"

"No, not at all," Tamrissa replied, her brows high. "It

continued to feel as though I were the only one there in complete charge. But what about the other thing, Lorand, about reaching your link groups without warning them first? Or wasn't there a time when you had to?"

"Oops," Lorand said, definitely shamefaced. "I meant to tell everyone about that, but we were still dealing with the outlaws and then I forgot. Why are these new things so easy to forget?"

"Possibly because of what both of you have said," Rion offered when no one else seemed to have a ready answer. "If something is natural and normal, you don't remark on it in ordinary conversation. It would be like mentioning that we walked in here, are now standing here, or that we're all breathing in and out."

"That could very well be," Jovvi agreed with a thoughtful nod. "All right, then we'll have to work harder at remembering, and possibly even make a habit of mentioning that we're breathing in and out. But Vallant, what about the noble who lived here? He's obviously gone, and probably on his way to Gan Garee."

"There's nothin' we can do about that right now," Vallant answered with a headshake. "I'd love to take our people and go after him and whatever friends have gone with him, but we can't afford the time. We still have to round up the nobles in this area, and then we have to head for Gracely. We can send word to Gan Garee by pigeon, but we ourselves have to continue seein' to our own business."

"Which is unfortunate," Tamrissa said. "After what we've learned about this leech Ruhl, it would have given me a good deal of pleasure to catch up to him. He might have been stupid enough to try resisting us."

"Maybe he won't do anything to bring attention to himself in Gan Garee before we get back there," Lorand offered, suddenly aware of the fact that he knew *exactly* how Tamrissa felt—and shared that feeling. "After all, we just have to take a quick look at Gracely to make sure that nothing horrible has been done there. After that we'll be free to return home."

Rion and Tamrissa murmured agreement with that hope,

but Lorand noticed that Jovvi, Vallant, and Naran were eyeing him in a strange way. Lorand didn't know why that was, but it didn't really matter. What he wanted most right now was a good meal and a hot bath, and after that a place to sleep. They'd eventually catch up to that so-called noble, and when they did . . .

High Lord Embisson Ruhl stood in the middle of the inn's private dining room and stretched wide. Traveling by coach all day was extremely tiring, and they still had quite a few days' travel left ahead of them. The others were also standing and walking about rather than sitting, and Embisson considered them without looking directly at any of them.

Edmin was there, of course, and he and Sembrin Noll were chatting about inconsequentials. Noll's wife Bensia stood sipping from the cup of tea she'd insisted on having brought immediately, a slight smile on her face as her thoughts clearly ranged elsewhere. She was an attractive and graceful lady of obvious station, and never intruded when men talked business.

But there seemed to be something about her that Edmin wasn't comfortable with. Embisson knew his son a good deal more than passing well, and although Edmin was never anything but gallant and gentlemanly toward the woman, Embisson was certain Edmin didn't like or trust her. In an effort to keep peace Embisson had tried to subtly reassure Edmin that Lady Bensia was nothing but a woman, but the words hadn't seemed to register with Edmin. It was probably just that Edmin had no woman of his own, but that matter could be seen to once they reached the city.

The last of their inner group had also stood for a time, but now he sat in a chair with a brooding air about him. Lord Rimen Howser, who had had his hopes dashed of ever becoming a High Lord as long as the peasants stayed in power, was more than simply an unhappy man. Howser's dislike of peasants had grown well beyond obsession, and Embisson had the feeling that nothing but Howser's current lack of physical well-being kept him from going out and slaughtering those he hated so deeply.

But Howser was on the mend, and by the time they reached the city he would be closer to physical fitness than he'd been since the beating. The terrible beating given him by those he referred to as animals. The man must have a large number of deep insecurities for him to always refer to peasants in that way, not to mention having the mother he did. The woman was considered a snob even by her former peers, and she must have demanded that Howser live up to his heritage or some such nonsense . . .

All of which meant that Howser had to be carefully watched once they reached the city. They would be able to make good use of him, but only if they managed to keep the madman from going off on his own. He could well expose all of them if he allowed his madness free rein at the wrong time, and that disaster Embisson would not allow to occur . . .

A knock came at the door, and Embisson turned with the others to see one of his servants look in. It would have been nice if their food was being brought sooner than expected, but that wasn't the case.

"My lord, that man you directed me to watch for has just ridden in," the servant announced. "Would you like me to guide him here once his horse is taken care of?"

"Yes, do, Rachers," Embisson replied, and the man nodded, quickly stepped back, and closed the door. Rachers was only one of the servants Embisson had brought back with him, and the entire group would have to be confined to the house when they reached the city. The madness that affected the other servants in the city couldn't be caught by those he brought back with him if all contact was disallowed.

"I certainly hope that my man is bringing good news," Noll remarked from where he still stood beside Edmin. "We should be well past the last of those peasants sent against the army, but I'd still like to hear that the army has taken care of them. Not to mention finding out about our other arrangements if by some chance the army *wasn't* successful."

"There's very little chance that Lord Rengan *won't* be successful," Embisson remarked, too weary to work up much enthusiasm. "He has High talents at his disposal, after all, and the peasants won't be more than Middles or Lows. Sending a stronger force against Rengan's host would be too dangerous for the Seated peasants. A stronger force could well decide to use the army themselves, taking it back to the city to wrest the throne away from those now Seated on it. No, Rengan won't have any—"

Embisson's comments were interrupted by a knock on the door, and then the door was opened to allow Noll's agent entrance. The slender man was filthy with road dust and looked as though he hadn't slept in some time. Embisson was about to remonstrate with him for not making himself more presentable before reporting when the man spoke first.

"My lords and lady, bad news," the man gasped out after offering only the slightest of bows. "Lord Rengan's army won't be following you to Gan Garee, at least not with Lord Rengan leading it."

"You can't mean that something has happened to Lord Rengan," Embisson blurted, shocked that a tool he'd hoped to put to good use was no longer available. "Was it an accident? Did he capture or kill all those peasants first, or did some of them get away?"

"My lord, it was Lord Rengan and his officers who were captured," the man said, clearly fighting to catch his breath. "And from where I watched, there was nothing accidental about it. May I have a glass of water?"

Embisson was about to snap out a refusal and demand that the man get on with telling his story, but Noll moved to interfere. Noll took up the goblet his wife hadn't used and filled it from the pitcher on the table, then walked over to give it to his man. The scout took the goblet with a better bow of thanks, drained it quickly, then looked bleakly at Noll.

"My lord, that army never stood a chance against those

people," the man stated. "They were spread out all over the place, encircling the army, and then the contingent at the rear was discovered. Lord Rengan attacked them with a large part of his force, but the attack did no damage at all. Then the others came to the rescue of the ones under attack, and in no time at all that attack was over. I felt some of the force being used, and I have to say that I've never experienced such strength before in my life. Lord Rengan and his officers were penned up behind what had to be a wall of air, and then the victors began to tend the people who were no longer an army."

"They 'tended' them?" Noll said while Embisson found himself even more deeply shocked. "Why did the members of the army need to be tended? Were they hurt when the others broke up the attack against one part of their force?"

"No, my lord, they weren't hurt," the man replied, and the idea seemed to disturb the man as deeply as it disturbed Embisson. "One minute they were just standing there quietly, and the next they were collapsing to the ground with groans and whimpering and crying. They didn't look to be in very good shape to begin with, but suddenly they were acting as bad as they looked."

"The defending force released them," Edmin said quietly, the words tinged with disbelief. "While they were under control they could only do as they were ordered to, but once they were released they were free to— Why in the world would those people release the members of an already organized army? I refuse to believe that they had no use for such a powerful tool."

"If they were so bad off that they weren't even able to stand when released, they couldn't have been that powerful a tool," Noll pointed out. "But what *I'd* like to know is what happened after that."

"You mean with the baited trap," the scout said with a nod that was more than weary. "Instead of going to the house where the meeting with Lord Rengan was held, they went in groups to High Lord Embisson's house. I know that Lord Rengan was questioned, and somehow he must have recognized High Lord Embisson. He also must have known where the High Lord's house is."

"So much for having worn those masks," Noll remarked dryly. "I'm afraid that there *is* such a thing as being too well known, at least in these times. So they missed the outlaw trap entirely?"

"No, my lord, they didn't," the man disagreed with a small headshake. "Isbirn Gelin had a couple of his men watching those people, and when his men realized where the groups were heading they rode to tell Gelin. Gelin got his men relocated to the woods around the High Lord's house, and that's where they caught the first group of those people."

"*Caught* them!" Embisson echoed with sudden relief and satisfaction. "So they didn't get away with it after all."

"I'm sorry, my lord," the man interrupted, ruining the good feelings Embisson had begun to experience. "Obviously I used the wrong phrase. I should have said that that's where Gelin and his men caught *up* to the first group. There were only six of them and Gelin had twenty-four and himself, but that seemed to make no difference. First the hostages were lost, and the men weren't able to retrieve them. Then all the men sort of folded to the ground as though they'd fallen asleep on their feet, and only Gelin was left awake. I expected Gelin to do something violent like attack them alone, but all he did was stand there and talk to them. I was too far away to hear what was said, and rather than take the chance of getting closer I simply turned and rode after your party."

"It's a good thing you did," Noll told the man while Embisson felt yet another shock. "Those couldn't possibly have been just any six people, they must have been a Blending. And unless I'm completely mistaken, they were the Seated Blending."

"How can they possibly feel secure enough *this* soon to leave the city?" Embisson demanded, close to outrage over the idea. "Don't they know that there's probably a power struggle going on right now, one that started as soon as they were out of sight? What can they possibly be thinking?"

"That's something we can't know, but I know what *I'm* thinking," Edmin said slowly. "If those peasants have left the city in a turmoil, then we should have no trouble riding in and getting started on our plans. They may have stopped the army but they can't *use* the army, and we have more than three hundred newly hired guardsmen following us. When they finally get back to the city, they'll find it already in our hands. Assuming they live long enough to *get* back."

"Why wouldn't they live?" Noll asked Edmin, his curiosity sounding young and innocent. "They stopped an army and defeated attackers who were twenty-five to their six. What could possibly harm them?"

"Any meal they take at my father's house," Edmin answered with a faint smile. "There was always the possibility that they would win through and try to move in, so I convinced the kitchen staff to . . . add to any meals they made for the peasants. Unless the peasants were incredibly alert, they didn't live past the first meal."

"I sincerely hope they didn't, but we can't count on that," Embisson said, already in the process of pulling himself together. "And you're right about this being an excellent chance for us. If we have just a *few* days in the city before those peasants get back, they'll find themselves arrested as they ride up to the palace."

"And then, as Rengan suggested, we can have a group hanging," Noll said with a smile of approval before he turned to the scout again. "You did well, and the gold you were promised will be given you in the morning. For tonight get a meal, a room, and a good night's sleep, and you can continue on with us tomorrow."

"Thank you, my lord," the scout said with a bow, and a minute later the man was gone—just in time for their food to be brought by the inn servants. Embisson joined the others in going to table, profoundly glad that his appetite was no longer ruined. They *would* take control of the city back, there was no doubt in his mind. And when those six peasants did get back, the amusing times would really begin . . .

TWENTY-FOUR

Sembrin Noll followed his wife Bensia into their room at the inn and paused to close and lock the door. When he turned back he saw that Bensia had brightened the lamp and was now in the process of removing her clothing.

"I'm afraid you'll have to unlock that door again, my dear," Bensia said with a smile. "I mean to have a bath before I retire, otherwise I won't sleep a wink. Being covered in road dust is quite unappealing."

"Then I'll certainly do the same," Sembrin said at once, knowing full well that she would withhold her favors if she found him . . . unappealing. "Once we reach the city, we'll no longer have to worry about road dust."

"But that's not to say we'll have nothing to worry about," Bensia returned, giving most of her attention to undressing. "I do wish I'd brought my maid with me . . . But when we consider things to worry about, our illustrious High Lord must head the list."

"Yes, I also noticed his reactions when he learned about what had happened to the army and his outlaws." Sembrin's agreement was accompanied by a frown as he also began to undress. "It's one thing to be self-assured, quite another to believe that life will conform to your own opinions of how it *should* go. I tried to warn him that the new Seated Blending could well show up to face the army, but he persisted in believing that they would behave as *he* thought fit."

"Yes, and worse than that he had trouble accepting what

305

the Seated Blending seems capable of doing," Bensia said, pausing to grimace. "At one time I'm sure he would have simply accepted what he heard and then revised his plans to suit the new situation, but this time was different. It took him a number of minutes to regain control of himself, and rather than accept the changed conditions I think he dismissed them. We may have chosen a tool for ourselves that has aged beyond the point of true usefulness."

"At this point, what choice do we have about using that tool?" Sembrin asked with a sigh. "I agree that Ruhl may be losing the sharpness of mind that made him one of the most feared men in the empire, but what can we do other than continue to use him?"

"We can give thanks that the children are following so closely behind us," Bensia said, her smile a thing of beauty once more. "Ruhl won't know them even if he happens to see them here, so he won't understand that we meant to use their talents once we reached Gan Garee. Now, however, we have a more pressing need of their talents."

"What do you mean for them to do?" Noll asked, feeling the least bit of anxiety. "You told me that Edmin also has Spirit magic talent, and if the children manipulate his father he's bound to notice."

"But he *shouldn't* notice if the children manipulate the leaders of our very large escort," Bensia countered, her smile now downright gleeful. "Ruhl has paid those more than three hundred men with his own gold and what he collected from the others. After your bath you'll take the children to visit each of those leaders in the woods where they now camp with their men, and after the visit the loyalty of those more than three hundred men will be ours. Isn't that a delicious idea?"

"More than delicious," Sembrin agreed with a small laugh and a great deal of amusement. "I've become convinced that Ruhl would have thrown away those men in some useless effort to reestablish himself, but we can be much more subtle in their use. If we strike at the enemy where they aren't expecting to be hit, we can cause a lot of serious damage."

"And when the pandemonium is at its height, then *we* can take over," Bensia said, walking over to him in the nude to reach up and stroke his face. "We'll have it all, but I'm afraid that High Lord Embisson and his son can't be allowed to share it. They'll be outraged over having been manipulated and outthought, and Edmin could well come up with something to discomfit us. We'll eliminate them quickly, and then choose others to be part of our court."

"Others who are more easily managed," Sembrin murmured, his hands already stroking Bensia's body. "Are you certain that your desire for a bath is all that immediate? You'll be going to bed afterward, but I won't be. If we take a few minutes now . . ."

"I'll wait up for you," Bensia murmured back, then gracefully moved away from him and the motion of his hands. She walked three steps toward the wrap that was laid out waiting for her, then paused to look back at him over her shoulder with a smile. "If you know I'm waiting up, you'll surely waste no time seeing to your task."

"No, I surely won't," Sembrin muttered, taking a deep breath to help him regain control. When it came to serious matters, Bensia was all business. If she weren't so eager at almost all other times, Sembrin might have considered feeling resentment. But she *was* that eager at other times, and when she promised to wait up for him she always kept her word . . .

Rather than waste any more time, Sembrin finished undressing and went for his own wrap. The sooner he finished bathing and seeing to his chore, the sooner he could get back to what would be waiting for him. And possibly, once the empire was theirs, Bensia would find herself in a position other than the one she now envisioned. If her place was in his bed rather than on the throne beside him . . .

Sembrin stopped for a moment, feeling as though he were about to drift off to sleep while still standing up. His thoughts blurred for no more than an instant, and when they cleared he immediately realized how wrong his previous attitude had been. Bensia was the most marvelous woman in the entire universe, and if she wanted to rule the empire

then that was what she deserved to do. It was *his* privilege
to make it happen, an honor that brought him more happiness than he'd ever before had in life.

Except for the times that he made love to Bensia. Sembrin smiled at his wife where she stood by the door waiting
for him, and her answering smile was, as usual, the most
marvelous sight he could imagine. He walked over to her
and kissed her cheek, then escorted her out of the room.
As soon as he finished seeing to his task in the most efficient and effective way possible, he would then be able to
return to *her*.

As Sembrin closed the door behind the two of them, he
knew without doubt that he was the luckiest man alive . . .

Kail Engreath strode along behind the wagon, finding it
hard to believe his eyes. The Astindans in charge of them
had warned them that morning that the trip would soon be
less pleasant than it had been. Kail had snorted his opinion
of how pleasant the trip had been to begin with, but now . . .

"I don't believe this," Renton Frosh said unsteadily from
where he walked to Kail's right, taking the words from
between Kail's mental teeth. "Who would do such a terrible
thing, and for what purpose?"

"I have an awful feeling that *we* did this terrible thing,
or at least some of us did," Kail answered, staring at the
devastation all around them. "They said yesterday that we
were crossing over into Astinda, and we're now at a point
where this countryside can't be seen from the empire side.
Our marvelous conquering armies did this."

"That's not possible!" another voice protested before
Renton could speak. "What point is there in conquering a
land if you destroy it as you go?"

Kail turned to see that the speaker was the man named
Belvis Drean, who walked a short distance behind him.
Drean had once been a moderately high noble in the government, or so Renton said, and at first it hadn't been clear
whether the small man would survive the march. But Drean
had surprised everyone by trimming down and hardening

up, and now he looked around with the same horror Kail felt.

"If you destroy the land, then you drive its true owners off it," Kail pointed out with less superiority than he once would have used. "After those true owners are gone you can claim the land, and use your own supply of slaves to make the land livable again. Can you deny the fact that most of us thought of the peasants as possessions to do with as we pleased?"

"But they *were* peasants," Drean protested again, apparently unable to take his gaze from the horror they walked through. "It was our place to run things, and theirs to obey orders from their superiors. That was the natural order of things, a natural order that lasted for centuries. How could it have been wrong? And what does that have to do with what was done here?"

"It's really quite simple, my friend," Renton told the bewildered man gently. "When you consider yourself beyond any sort of condemnation, you do as you damned well please and never even think about possible consequences. Killing miles and miles of once living land is meaningless, because you won't be the one who has to work until you drop in order to restore it. When people aren't held responsible for what they do, they stop *being* responsible in every sense of the words."

"And I once read somewhere that the wise man refuses to allow slavery of any sort," Kail added, wondering if Drean actually heard what they were saying. "Just because you aren't the one being enslaved today doesn't mean that you won't be chosen tomorrow. The only way you yourself can be safe from slavery is to make sure that *no* one can be enslaved."

"And I believe I can also answer your other question," Renton said to Drean, apparently ignoring the small man's distraction. "You wanted to know what that 'natural order' of yours had to do with what we see around us. I suspect that that natural order is more political than natural, and that the pendulum is now in the midst of swinging to the opposite side of the political spectrum. Those who were lords have now become slaves instead, and will personally reap what they've sown. We're being held responsible for what was done, and we'll be the ones to clean up our own mess."

"But I didn't do this," Drean whispered, still looking at nothing but what they walked through. "I didn't even know this was being done, so how can I be held responsible? It isn't fair!"

Renton said nothing to that, and Kail was too busy with his sudden thoughts to respond. That protest of "It isn't fair!" sounded very familiar, and Kail could almost hear *himself* saying the words. But the disturbing thought had just come to him that it *was* fair, possibly the fairest outcome among everything possible. He hadn't been directly responsible for that devastation any more than Drean had been, nor would he have approved causing the destruction if asked.

But the truth of the matter was that he hadn't *wanted* to know, and he hadn't lifted a single finger to find out what was being done in his name. When his father had arranged for him to have a place in the government, he'd hated the idea. If he'd been given the choice, he would have stayed with his friends and played with magic instead of doing something productive. But that should have been something *really* productive, not his father's definition of it. Like finding out what the fools running the empire were up to . . .

The devastated countryside encouraged brooding, and Kail realized that he wasn't the only one engaged in the activity when the wagon began to slow down. Everyone seemed to be coming out of deep introspection, including Renton.

"I wonder why we're stopping?" Renton said as he looked around. "It isn't quite noon yet, and they've never varied from the schedule before."

"It can't be because this is the perfect place to stop," Kail agreed, also looking around. "There isn't even any grazing for the horses—"

Kail's words broke off at Drean's exclamation of horror,

and a glance back showed Drean staring ahead with a face gone pale. Kail, wondering what had so disturbed the small man, leaned a bit out of line to get a better look, and immediately wished he hadn't.

"What is it?" Renton asked, clearly bothered by the way Drean now leaned over and emptied himself of what seemed to be everything he'd eaten in the last month. "Kail, what is it? You're almost as pale as *that* poor fellow."

"There . . . was once a house a short way ahead," Kail got out, staring down at the road to keep himself under control. "There's very little left of the house, but the people who once lived in it are still here. Hanging in front of the house."

"I'm sorry I asked," Renton muttered as he, too, paled. "No wonder poor Drean there couldn't control himself."

"No, you don't understand," Drean himself said after wiping at his mouth with a filthy shirtsleeve, his eyes looking haunted. "I . . . have Earth magic, and I'm not too weak a Middle talent. Those people, including the children, they . . . weren't dead when they were left there. To treat anyone, even peasants, like that . . ."

Drean shakily lowered himself to the road as far as possible from the small, vile pool he'd made, and then buried his face in his hands. Kail watched the man for a moment with a sense of great distance, taking that long to realize how shocked he was. Renton seemed almost ready to empty his own insides, and sounds of protest were coming from most of the people who had heard Drean.

But Kail himself was suddenly furiously angry rather than ill. There was a difference between irresponsible and bestial, and the so-called people who had come through here had too obviously crossed the line. No wonder the Astindans had come to level Gan Garee; the true wonder was that they treated their prisoners as well as they did.

"Does anyone here still feel the least pride in having been one of the empire's leaders?" Kail demanded of those around him, his hands closed to fists at his sides. "It doesn't *matter* that most of us didn't know about things like this. We *should* have known!"

"Your juvenile reaction proves the exact opposite," a female voice stated coldly, and Kail turned to see who spoke. The woman was apparently in her early forties, and was tall and thin. Her gown had once been very expensive and stylish, and her narrow face retained a look of pure haughtiness. She stood straight with hands folded firmly before her, and her expression was full of disdain.

"So you think my reaction is juvenile," Kail said flatly, his anger growing. "You also sound as if you *did* know what was going on."

"Those of us mature enough to handle the information did indeed know," the woman answered, all but sneering. "We understood that these peasants meant nothing, and that there were enough of them that throwing some away as an object lesson for the others was nothing more than common sense. You and these others are weaklings, and if you'd been told what your superiors were up to you never would have had the stomach to support the actions. That's why you weren't told."

"And it means nothing to you that now you're one of those who will be made to undo those marvelous actions?" Kail's demand contained growing outrage along with anger as a number of the people around them muttered with anger of their own. "That what you did put *our* necks in the bind right along with yours is incidental and unimportant?"

"It's *all* incidental and unimportant," the woman retorted. "It's necessary that I put up with this outrage for the moment, but a moment doesn't last forever. When I'm freed from the capture of these barbarians, I'll then take very great pleasure in watching them die very slowly and in very great pain. And *you* people who worry so greatly over what's done to and with peasants will be allowed to become peasants yourselves. You'll certainly never again be fit to be called a peer of *mine*."

"A fact for which I thank the Highest Aspect most solemnly," Drean growled from where he sat, startling Kail and apparently just about everyone else as well. "I've been walking along considering myself completely blameless for whatever was done, but I can see now that I was wrong.

My blame lies in considering people like *you* superior, and in supporting you with my silence. You can be certain you'll never have that silence again."

By then Drean was back on his feet, standing tall and proud despite his small stature. The woman sniffed and dismissed him and what he'd said by pretending he'd become invisible, but most of the people around her seemed to disagree. Those people withdrew as far as possible from where the woman stood, and nodded to show Drean that they agreed with him. A few others withdrew into themselves without voicing an opinion, but Kail realized that that was to be expected. Some people couldn't make up their minds which way to jump even if their lives depended on the decision.

"Well, it seems that the former Lady Froma only has one supporter in the area," Renton commented as he eyed the sole man whose expression said he agreed with the woman completely. "At this rate, we could be surrounded by all sensible people in no time."

Kail was about to add his own additional comment when one of the Astindans appeared. They all seemed to be rather serious people, but so far none of the captives had been abused in any deliberate way. The one who approached them was a plain woman in trousers and a shirt like a man, and everyone stopped speaking when they saw her. It was part of the captives' buried orders to fall silent in the presence of an Astindan, Kail knew, and this time was no different from any other.

"As you can see, a burial detail is required," the woman told all of them quietly. "For this one time, I'm asking for volunteers rather than ordering the chore done. Would any of you care to volunteer?"

"I would," Kail said immediately as he stepped forward, knowing without a doubt that the decision was his rather than forced on him by something the Astindan had said. "It's a decency that should have been done a long time ago, not to mention being something that shouldn't have been necessary in the first place."

"I would also like to volunteer," Renton said, moving

forward as the woman nodded soberly at Kail. "I've never done anything like this before, but if someone tells me what's necessary I'll make sure that it's done properly."

The woman also nodded at Renton, then seemed surprised when Drean and three other people stepped forward to volunteer as well. Drean and the last three people said not a single word, but when the woman gestured that they all follow, none of them hesitated.

It became clear that the Astindans had asked for volunteers at each of the wagons. The six people from Kail's wagon were joined by captives from the other wagons, but no more than two or three from each of the others. At another time Kail would have felt ashamed to be part of a group that had so small a sense of what was proper, but at the moment the lack of willing cooperation was unsurprising.

"Give me your attention, please," a male Astindan said when the last of the volunteers had joined the group. The man was slightly older than the other Astindans, and just a touch on the heavy side. "There are six bodies that need to be cut down, so you'll form into groups of three. Two of the three will hold the body while the third cuts the rope, and then the bodies are to be lined up on the ground near what's left of that tree."

Everyone nodded their understanding, and when Kail and Renton moved together, Drean joined them to make a third. A brief moment later all the groups were formed, and then another Astindan came over with six knives. This Astindan made no effort to speak to anyone, instead simply giving a knife to one member of each group of three.

Renton was the one given the knife in their group, and he stared at it in his hand as though he'd never seen anything like it in his entire life. Kail watched his friend weigh the weapon on his palm until they were called forward, and then Renton closed his fist about the knife as though he thought it might try to escape. Thinking about Renton and the knife he held was easier for Kail than thinking about what they had ahead of them. With Renton holding the knife, Kail and Drean would be the ones handling the body.

But handling a long-dead body wasn't the worst of it. It turned out that Kail, Renton, and Drean were stopped near the body of a child, one that couldn't have been more than twelve years of age. Kail thought it likely that he would be sick once he touched the body, but there was no smell to trigger the reflex. He and Drean got a good grip on the body, and then Renton reached up high to cut the rope.

But that wasn't all Renton did. He also began to cry as he reached to the rope, and by the time the body was cut down Kail and Drean were also crying. This body they held had once been an innocent child, someone who was now dead only because his family had had something the beasts of the empire wanted. Those beasts were no longer in control of the empire, but that didn't stop the child from being dead. Nothing would stop the child from being dead, and the tragedy of that tore at Kail's heart as he and Drean looked at the body they held.

By the time they were done, all of the volunteers were sobbing. Three of the six bodies were those of children, and the other two had been younger than the one handled by Kail and his group. Two of the three adults were women, and that was almost as bad for Kail—and many of the others, apparently—as the children. All six bodies were carefully and gently laid out near the tree that had died because of the poisoned ground, and then the volunteers stepped back.

"Thank you," the older Astindan man said to them quietly from his place in front of the dozen or so Astindans who had gathered to watch the efforts. "You grieve for our dead almost as deeply as we do, and for that tribute to their memory we thank you. You may stay where you are until graves are dug for the bodies, and then you will be permitted to place the bodies in those graves."

The spokesman and the others then turned away to go back to the wagons, and Kail exchanged a surprised glance with Renton and Drean. From their expressions they'd believed, as Kail had, that the volunteers would also dig the graves. Kail had been fully prepared to do that backbreaking job, but instead he and the others just stood there and watched those who hadn't volunteered being ordered to the chore.

It took quite a while for the six graves to be dug. No one was allowed to use talent in the effort, just the spades that were handed out. Two people dug each grave at a time, and after a few minutes, when the diggers' backs and hands gave out, two more people were put in to replace them. Almost everyone from every wagon was given a turn—including that haughty woman Lady Froma—and then the job was finally done.

When Kail and the others were gestured forward, they lifted the bodies carefully and carried them to the graves. Two lengths of rope had been placed across each of the openings in the ground, and various Astindans came to hold the ends of the ropes as the bodies were placed in the middle. The three children and the smaller of the two women were put in the inner graves, the man and larger woman in the outer ones. The Astindans lowered each body slowly into its final resting place, everyone around the graves stood in silence for a few moments, and then the diggers were called back. They replaced the dirt in the graves in the same order that they'd used when digging.

When all of the graves had finally been closed, Kail and the other volunteers were surprised by not being sent back to their various wagons. They were kept together, and assigned a wagon of their own instead. As they sat down on the side of the road near their new wagon to wait for the bread and cheese of their lunch, Kail felt relieved that they were being kept separate from the others. All the others had been forced to dig, and most of them wept as they cradled aching hands. The rest glared at Kail's group, as though it had been *their* decision not to dig . . .

But being separated from the others *was* odd. Kail spent some time wondering why it had been done, but then lunch was brought and his thoughts turned elsewhere . . .

TWENTY-FIVE

Honrita Grohl was certain that she glowed as she walked
along the street. Two days ago she'd completed the first
week of her training, and even then had felt as though she'd
been at it for years. The experience was marvelous, delightful, electrifying, every positive description it was possible
to lay tongue to, and tonight they would be starting the
second week of training.

"Dama Grohl, please wait," Honrita heard, and she
stopped and turned to see that girl from her class whose
name she couldn't remember hurrying up. The girl looked
at her with such awe that Honrita couldn't keep from smiling.

"What is it, child?" Honrita asked, only a hint of her
impatience in tone and mind. "I'd like to get a cup of tea
before we start the new training."

"I just wanted to say how wonderful I think you are,"
the girl burbled, following as Honrita resumed walking.
"You're the best in our class, and the strength you've developed is an inspiration to us all."

"I suppose that's as it should be," Honrita allowed with
a smile and a small inner laugh. She *was* the strongest in
their class, and because of that was given the kind of respect she'd never before been accorded. She'd also taken
to . . . practicing at work, and because of that effort was
given praise and had gotten an increase in her wages. Her
income was now no longer minimal, and once her training
was done she would improve her lot even more.

317

"I can't wait to meet the new instructor," the girl burbled on as they walked. "Our original instructor was nice and he was really impressed with your progress, but he seemed kind of limited. Maybe the new instructor will have more to teach, and then you can impress him or her as well."

This time Honrita laughed aloud, too pleased to keep the feeling inside—even if it would have done any good. The girl had the same Spirit magic Honrita did, and although she wasn't as strong as the woman she admired, she'd still learned to handle her ability with more certainty. The girl knew her words were giving Honrita pleasure, and that was what the girl intended to do. Her own standing would rise when she walked into class with Honrita, an honor there was no reason to deny the poor little thing.

It had already grown dark out, but Honrita and the girl were unafraid as they walked the streets to where the class was being held. There were a fair number of people out and walking around, and some of them were undoubtedly patrol members. The various patrols helped the guard, the members of those patrols having learned to link to certain guardsmen and each other. Any trouble would quickly have guardsmen on the scene, and those who were prone to starting trouble were quickly learning that lesson.

Honrita and her supporter reached the training building and walked inside. Some of the rooms in the building were lined with resin, and the class had been told that they'd practice certain things within the resin when they were ready. Honrita felt that she *was* ready, and would have said so to their instructor if he'd returned. She was prepared to say the same to the new instructor, and would do so if the new person didn't quickly see the truth of her position.

It was nearly time for the class to begin, so Honrita and the girl walked into the open practice room to find that most of the class had already arrived. Everyone looked up quickly when the two women entered, but then those already seated looked away again with a definite air of disappointment. Honrita was prepared to feel injured and insulted over such a reception, but then she realized that the new instructor hadn't yet arrived. So *that* was the reason for the disappointment . . .

"Let's get our tea and sit down," the girl whispered to Honrita. "The new instructor should be here at any moment."

Being told what to do annoyed Honrita, but the girl was already on her way to the tea service so Honrita followed with an odd anger building inside her. For years she had been forced to obey everyone else as well as bow and scrape, but it had come to her the day before how unjust that was. *She* was the one with the talent, so why did it have to be her place to make everyone else feel good or important? Now that she knew just how strong a talent she had it was time that *she* gave the orders. And had others bow and scrape to *her*. It felt marvelous to make the decisions rather than have the decisions made *for* her, and Honrita had no intention of returning to the way things had been.

So the foolish little girl needed to be taught a lesson about the proper way to associate with someone like her. The girl was already at the tea service, holding a cup beneath the spigot, and the hot tea poured briskly into the cup. It was an action repeated so often that the girl paid very little attention to what she did—until her hand wavered and the hot tea splashed onto her skin.

The girl cried out and dropped the cup as the hot tea burned her nicely, and Honrita joined some of the others in hurrying over to soothe the poor little thing. It was Honrita who had caused the girl to momentarily lose her sense of balance and that loss had caused the "accident," but happily no one in the room seemed to have noticed.

One of the other women wrapped the girl's hand in a cloth and began to lead the girl out to find a healer. Burns could be nasty things if not treated quickly and carefully, and Honrita smiled sweetly as she offered her hope that the girl would soon be able to return to the class. Then Honrita turned to watch the two women leave—and abruptly found herself meeting the gaze of a woman she'd never seen before.

"There's a class of Earth magic users three doors down," the strange woman told the whimpering girl and the woman who helped her. "Go in there and speak to the instructor. I'm sure he'll be able to treat the burn at once."

The girl—who was no longer whimpering—smiled her thanks at the unknown woman, and then she and the woman helping her disappeared up the hall. The newcomer entered the room and walked toward the desk, proving that she was the new instructor. Honrita felt decidedly uncomfortable, a state she detested with her entire being. She'd spent most of her life feeling uncomfortable and worse, but now she didn't have to suffer like that. She had *talent*, and there was no reason not to use it.

Until now Honrita had kept her mind away from the strange woman, in part because she'd gotten the impression that the woman knew what she had done to cause the accident. Now Honrita smoothed down the skirt of her new dress as she watched the newcomer reach the desk and turn—and without warning Honrita sent her talent toward the woman's mind. The woman would find that she suddenly liked Honrita better than any other person in the class, and for that reason would help her as much as necessary.

Only things didn't work out like that. Honrita gasped as her mind met that of the new instructor, a mind that was so much stronger than hers that it didn't seem possible.

"Yes, I can see that my predecessor was right and you *are* a really strong Middle talent," the new instructor said to a shaken Honrita. "He was also a Middle talent, but as you've just learned, I'm not. I'm a High, and you, Dama, are no longer part of this class. Please go next door to the empty room, have a seat, and wait for me. We need to talk, which we'll do as soon as this class is over."

Honrita was mortified as well as shaken, and if she'd had the choice she would have left the building and run home. But she hadn't been allowed the choice, and despite the humiliation of being stared at by the rest of the class Honrita did as she'd been told. She entered the empty room next door, sat down, and then waited. She also suddenly remembered the day she'd registered for the class, and the two people who had been so much stronger than she. Until now the memory had gone completely out of her head, and it made her furious. No one should be that much stronger than she, *no one*. Then the fury died along with the rest of what she'd felt, and calm took its place.

The wait was long enough that Honrita should have been feeling something other than calm patience, and the lack of other emotions confused her. The fury and humiliation and mortification had completely disappeared as though they'd never been, but before she could understand what was happening, the door opened and the new instructor walked in.

"Dama Grohl," the woman said as she came to a chair near Honrita's and sat. "I'm Cadria Norl, and now we have time to talk. Tell me why you made that girl burn herself with the tea."

"Why, it was because she tried to tell me what to do," Honrita answered, distantly surprised at her lack of hesitation. "I spent my life being forced to listen to others, but now I no longer have to let *anyone* tell me what to do."

"I see," Cadria Norl said quietly, an odd frown creasing her brow. "You're making up for a lifetime of not asserting yourself, but you don't view the matter in that light. Give me the exact words the girl used when she 'told you what to do.' "

"She said, 'Let's get our tea and sit down,' " Honrita answered promptly, pleased that she could prove she wasn't simply imagining things. "The girl had no right to tell me what to do."

"The girl wasn't telling you what to do," Cadria replied calmly and soothingly, leaning a bit forward in her chair. "Her words were a suggestion, not an order, and if you think about it for a moment or two you might see that. Try thinking about it."

Honrita did as she was told, but after the moment or two she shook her head.

"The girl tried to tell me what to do," Honrita repeated. "She had no right to give me orders."

"I was afraid you'd say that," Cadria muttered as she

leaned back again. "You're not the first to show this problem, and it wasn't one we were expecting as a result of the training. Do you have a family, Dama Grohl?"

"I've been living alone ever since my father died," Honrita answered. "Why do you ask?"

"I ask because there's a very special class you'll soon be a part of," Cadria replied with a smile that made Honrita feel really good. "You'll do much better if you live with that group while you're working with it, and it makes things easier that you have no family to cope with your absence. Come with me."

Honrita rose as Cadria did and followed her out of the room. In the hallway there were three men standing together, and Cadria gestured one of the three over.

"Dama Grohl here will need to get some clothing and essentials, and then she's to be taken to the special group," Cadria told the man who had joined them. "Please tell whoever you turn her over to that her talent is Spirit magic."

"Yes, Dama Norl," the man agreed politely, and then he gestured to Honrita. She joined the man gladly, and let him conduct her out of the building while she reveled in delight. A special class! She'd been assigned to a special class, and soon everyone would know just how good she was. It looked like she was leaving that boring job of hers even sooner than she'd expected, and good riddance to it. She was meant for much better things, and this was definitely the start of them . . .

Cadria Norl watched the guardsman conduct Honrita Grohl out of the building, depression touching her even after the two had disappeared. The scene she'd been a part of had gotten much too familiar in too short a time, and this was only the beginning of it . . .

"I take it you've just dispatched another one," a male voice said from behind her, making her turn. "Did it have anything to do with that burn I treated?"

Rebid Tantas, High talent in Earth magic, wore an expression of sympathy that Cadria could feel echoed in his mind.

"Yes, it certainly did have something to do with the burn you treated," Cadria answered with a sigh. "The woman made the burn happen because she 'didn't want to be told what to do.' The girl she burned had said, 'Let's get some tea and sit down.' Did *you* have any idea that these training classes would produce so many problems?"

"To be honest, no," Rebid admitted with his own sigh. "I expected accidents from horsing around or carelessness or even someone trying to do too much, but these more extreme reactions? How could *anyone* anticipate them?"

"I can't help feeling that we should have seen at least a part of the problem," Cadria grumbled, knowing that Rebid would understand her mood. "Under the rule of the nobility, no one was allowed to exercise a talent. Now we're not only allowing that exercise, we're encouraging it and training talent. We should have expected that some of those we trained would lose their heads to their newfound power."

"Well, if we didn't know about it before, we certainly do now," Rebid said ruefully. "What are they going to do with the ones we collect?"

"They're going to try to restore balance to their minds with Spirit and Earth magic," Cadria answered, back to sighing. "We don't know if that's possible, but we're certainly going to make the attempt. What bothers me most is what's going to happen if the balance *can't* be restored."

"Damn, I never thought of that," Rebid responded, his mind filled with a shocked awareness. "The woman *I* had to send is a fairly strong Middle talent in Earth magic. She can't be allowed to run around free the way she is, or a lot of innocent people could be hurt. If she can't be brought back to balance, she'll either have to be put under permanent control or she'll have to be put down. I don't like either option, but which one do you think they'll choose?"

"The choice won't be made by 'them,' it will be made by *us*," Cadria pointed out gently. "Our various Blendings have been left in charge, so we'll have to have a recommendation ready for Jovvi and the others when they get back. They're the ones who will have to give the final word of approval, but *we'll* have to make the decision for them.

You can say it's part of the job we've been asked to do."

"And since we didn't refuse to begin with, we're now stuck with it," Rebid said, his tone having grown morose. "I'm suddenly finding the idea of running away from home more attractive than it's ever been."

"Let me know if you decide to do it," Cadria told him with something of a smile. "I may let you come with *me*."

Rebid returned the weak smile, but Cadria knew he was no more amused than she was. Running away would have felt awfully good, but unfortunately that wasn't one of the options available to them . . .

Driffin Codsent entered his private bedchamber in the warehouse and stopped short in surprise. Idresia was not only out of bed, but she'd obviously been doing quite a bit of cleaning. Dirty clothing no longer lay in piles, the bed was neatly made with what looked like clean linen, and a lamp brightened the room's previous dimness. Idresia herself sat in a chair near the lamp with a book, and when she looked up and saw him she smiled.

"I'm glad you're back, Driff," she said, putting the book aside before standing and walking toward him. "How did the new class go?"

"Obviously not as well as my out-of-class work," Driffin said with a laugh of delight, opening his arms to gather her up. "Are you sure you're strong enough to be doing this much this soon?"

"I did very little," Idresia assured him, looking up into his face with the same expression Driffin knew *he* wore. "It's only because of you that I'm not bedridden any longer, so I thought I'd give you a small part of the reward you've earned. Tonight I'll give you another part, but right now I'd like to hear how things went. We'll do that while we get you something to eat."

Idresia had spoken so firmly that Driffin simply laughed again and agreed. His lady was a woman of Fire magic, and arguing with her was usually a waste of time. Now that she was beginning to get her strength back, it would be harder still to avoid doing what she considered necessary.

Not that Driffin *wanted* to argue. The hollowness inside him said that it was more than time he had a meal . . .

"Before you tell me about *your* day, I have some good news," Idresia said as they left the bedchamber holding hands and headed toward the kitchen area. "Affli Domore has been hired by a merchant to design and Encourage a garden at the back of his house. The man made her the offer today at the end of Affli's school training class."

"That's what you consider *good* news?" Driffin asked, eyeing Idresia as they walked. "Affli is really talented in Earth magic, but she's still too young to leave school. And anyone who hires a schoolgirl instead of a mature practitioner is trying to get a job done without having to pay what the job is really worth."

"Normally I would agree with you, but there are a few points you don't yet know about," Idresia told him with an impish smile. "The merchant won't hear of Affli's leaving school, and will only hire her if she continues to go to class. She'll be permitted to work only *after* school, and she'll be paid two-thirds of what a mature practitioner would charge for the same job. She'll gain experience—and earn silver—while still in school, and the merchant will have the job done at a lesser cost. Also, his wife and daughters will be there whenever Affli is, so we won't have to worry that the man wants something other than a garden."

For the second time that day—and the hundredth time in the last week or so—Driffin felt confused and almost completely at a loss. He'd made a lot of plans when he'd first found out about the training classes, but for some reason his plans weren't working out as well as they usually did.

"Something's bothering you," Idresia observed after a moment or two of his silence, her hand tightening around his. "Why don't you tell me what it is."

"Your talent should be Spirit magic rather than Fire magic," Driffin informed her ruefully. "You always seem to know when I'm bothered by something, but this time I don't think you can help. It looks like I've started to lose my edge."

"What makes you say that?" she asked, tilting her head

a bit to one side to study him. "To me, it looks like you're more alert and ready than ever."

"That's only what it *looks* like," Driffin disagreed with a distracted shake of his head. "On the inside I'm so confused I can barely stand it, and I'm beginning to think that someone has put me into another world while I wasn't watching. Worst of all, though, I can't decide whether or not I like this alien world."

"Unexpected things have been happening to you," Idresia interpreted, leading him into the kitchen area. "Why don't you tell me about them while I make you something to eat. It will only take a minute or two."

"You'd better know that I'm monitoring your body readings," Driffin warned her as she left him to go to the stove. "If I catch you starting to overdo, you'll go straight back to bed."

"I wish you had more faith in how strong a talent you have," Idresia said with a glance over her shoulder as she bent to see if there was wood in the stove. "Overdoing gets harder every day, a development that's been delighting me. Sit down and start to talk to me."

"When I first found out about the training classes, I made some plans," Driffin said after a very brief hesitation, seating himself at the large kitchen table. "The new system was full of holes that were meant to be used by those who were smart enough, and I was prepared to start that using as soon as possible. Now . . ."

Driffin's words trailed off, and he barely saw Idresia light the wood in the stove with her talent before she reached for a pan and some eggs and cheese. Trying to put his feelings into coherent sentences was difficult.

"Now you obviously feel differently," Idresia said, apparently paying less attention to the cooking than to the conversation. "What made you change your mind?"

"As I look back, I think my mind began to change on the very first day of training," Driffin answered, his own attention returning to the day he spoke of. "I walked into the class expecting to find oh-so-superior instructors who taught very little but expected to be bowed down to for that little. Instead, our instructor was this shy little woman with a big talent who quietly encouraged everyone in the class no matter how strong or weak they were."

"And the people in the class made every effort to learn rather than to curry favor by boot-licking," Idresia added as she broke open the eggs. "I remember you telling me that when you got home."

"Yes, there were no teacher's pets except, possibly, for me," Driffin agreed with a wry smile. "I tried to stay back out of things and simply learn as much as possible before they decided I didn't fit in, but they never decided that. When they discovered I was the strongest in the class they gave me special encouragement, and just before week's end they . . . approached me. That I didn't tell you about."

"No, you didn't," Idresia said with raised brows. "What did they approach you *about*? Did they want you to join whatever scam they're running?"

"That's one of the things that's making me think I'm losing my edge," Driffin replied. "I was convinced that there *was* a scam somewhere, but I just couldn't see it. They told me that they expected me to qualify as an instructor when I finished my own training, and wanted me to take over some of the beginners' classes. When they told me how much I would be paid I almost told them they had to be lying, and then they added to my shock."

Driffin paused a moment, still finding discussing the matter difficult, and Idresia helped by remaining silent.

"They . . . know about the healing I've been doing on the side," Driffin said at last, his gaze on his hands where they lay on the table. "I would have sworn *no* one knew about that, but somehow they got around all the precautions I took. They also knew I wasn't charging for the healing, and the only thing disturbing them about the whole situation is that they believe I *should* be paid. So they asked if I would be willing to open a free care shop for those who can't afford to pay, and the silver and gold would be provided by the new government."

"Why, Driff, that's marvelous!" Idresia exclaimed, now keeping only one eye on the cooking eggs and cheese.

"People have finally noticed how good you are, and rather than trying to push you back down they're offering you a hand up. I don't understand why that upsets you."

"It's upsetting me because that's not how the world was," Driffin all but wailed, the turmoil in his mind increasing. "Just a little while ago it was every man for himself, chaos take anyone who got in their way. Now people are actually helping each other, and those who won't—or can't— change are slowly being weeded out. People who want to work are being encouraged instead of shoved back down, and anyone looking for a free ride is being tossed off the wagon of general effort. But I know that things never really change, so how can I believe that all these new ways are really real?"

"Why is that such a terrible problem?" Idresia asked quietly, bringing over the plate she'd just filled. After putting the food in front of him, she sat down to circle him with one arm. "If believing completely in these new ways is impossible for you right now, that's all right as long as you don't show your disbelief. Just tell yourself that you're pretending to go along, and make the best plans you can to protect us all if there does happen to be a scam going on. And if it turns out there *is* no scam, you'll still be in a position to add your effort to the new practices."

"And doing it that way will protect us no matter *what* happens," Driffin exclaimed, suddenly wide-eyed. "Now, why didn't *I* think of that?"

"You didn't think of it because you're hoping too hard that everything *is* real," Idresia told him with a fondly amused smile. "You've never been as hard and practical as you considered yourself, not when you're basically a dreamer. You've always done what was necessary, but you also always wished you didn't have to. Don't you think I know all that?"

Driffin stared at her, briefly wondering how *she* knew something he never had. He *had* always considered himself tough and able to handle whatever came, and the tiny part inside himself wishing things could be different had never really mattered . . .

"All right, so you know me better than I know myself," Driffin admitted with a small rueful laugh. "And I really do want this new arrangement to work. They've even opened houses for street children, a place where the children can eat and sleep and be part of a family of sorts. For myself, I've been . . . thinking about recruiting help for the healing shop from the night-siders who don't want to steal any longer."

"You'll probably find more volunteers than you can use, or none at all," Idresia said with her darling, dimpled smile. "I heard just yesterday that the new patrols have been catching thieves by the handful now that using talent isn't against the law any longer. Those thieves that haven't been caught are hiding out, and before very long they'll have to find something else to do or starve."

"Then I ought to get started with opening the shop," Driffin said, reaching for the fork that Idresia had put on the plate of food. "And it's just come to me that I need to list all the people who like this new way of doing things as well as I do. If those government people suddenly decide to change their minds, the rest of us can work to put things back the way they belong."

"Now, that's a good idea," Idresia said as she rose again to return to the stove. "I'll have a cup of tea for you in just a moment. And I've been wondering . . . What's being done to guard against trouble coming from someone other than the government people? I mean, there's bound to be some fools who want things to go back to the way they were. What's being done to protect the new ways against *them*?"

"You know, I think I'll step aside and let *you* be in charge around here," Driffin stated after a moment of sitting with the fork poised three inches from his mouth. "Damned if that question occurred to me, and it certainly should have. I don't know what the government people are doing about the possibility, but we obviously need a line of protection at the people level. I'll have to set something up as soon as possible."

"I'd like to help," Idresia said. "This new way of doing

things has given me my life back, and I'd like to help protect it."

"I was about to say I'll put you in charge of whatever I arrange, but I've suddenly changed my mind," Driffin told her, his mind finally working at the speed it used to. "An extra layer of protection inside the line of protection won't hurt anything, and can even do a lot of good if the arrangement is somehow compromised. In other words, how would you like to be my spy?"

"Oh, I'll love it!" Idresia burbled, those dimples showing again. "A secret power hidden inside the meek and mild woman worker. No one will have the least idea."

Driffin was about to laugh at the idea of Idresia being meek and mild, but chose the smarter course and closed his mouth with food. The woman he loved would be perfect to keep an eye on whatever he arranged, and if *she* couldn't be trusted then no one could be. He'd be able to pay attention to his own efforts with a clear mind, knowing that his side project was in good hands.

And as Idresia brought him a cup of tea and some bread, Driffin noticed that her body showed no signs of strain at all. Maybe tonight would be a time of mutual reward after all . . .

TWENTY-SIX

Frode Mismin followed the servant to the garden where Antrie Lorimon sat drinking tea with Cleemor Gardan. Mismin, as head of the special investigations branch, usually reported to the entire assembly. These days, though, that meant Antrie Lorimon and her closest associates.

"Good morning, Frode," Antrie greeted him with a warm, true smile. "Please sit down and join us in having tea."

"As long as tea is all I need to swallow, I'll be pleased to join you, Exalted One," Frode answered with a bow after stopping in front of a chair. "I'm afraid I've lost my appetite for actual food."

"You have bad news, then," Gardan said heavily as Frode sat down. "And please, feel free to use our names. I always feel pretentious when I'm called 'Exalted One' in private."

"As you like," Frode agreed, accepting a cup of tea from a servant. As soon as the servant was gone, Frode was free to continue with, "I have word about the Gandistran army."

"Then things went badly rather than well for us," Antrie said with a sigh. "Somehow I knew our luck would run out in that particular area."

"I think it would be more accurate to say that the luck ran out with a vengeance," Frode told her after sipping at his tea. "It was the new Seated Blending themselves who questioned the officers of the army, and there was no getting the impressed statements past *them*. For a time there was still the possibility that the Seated Blending would return to Gan Garee after sending some of their followers to see what was going on. At the moment, however, that possibility is no longer viable."

"So they're coming here themselves," Gardan said, exchanging a glance with Antrie. "A visit from them was always a strong possibility, but I wonder just how prepared for that visit we really are."

"We're as prepared as we can be," Antrie replied, knowing the question had been put to her. "Our investigation will have proven that Ebro Syant was responsible for what was done to the army officers. Syant is no longer a member of our assembly, something we can prove when we apologize to those people for what was done to the officers of the army."

"My advice would be to apologize for the intrusion, but

not for the action," Frode said, gaining Antrie's immediate attention. "It was necessary to keep our countryside from being destroyed, but we might have found a less invasive way of doing it if we'd looked. We should regret nothing but not having looked for that other way."

"Are the members of the new Seated Blending really that reasonable?" Antrie asked, her brows high. "Members of the old nobility would have had not the least interest in hearing of reasons why we thought we were justified in defending ourselves. These new people might listen?"

"My agents tell me that they spent quite a lot of time and effort healing and caring for the members of the army," Frode responded. "There was really no one around to impress, so the effort wasn't just for show. The officers in charge of the army were fools, and kept their people in such bad shape that they would have lost at least half their fighters before they reached Gan Garee . . ."

"Are you thinking what I suddenly am?" Antrie asked when Frode's voice just trailed off. "No matter how important you think you are, if you want to stay the leader of an army you take reasonable care of that army. Why did those officers do just the opposite?"

"I don't want to think that killing their fighters with neglect was part of the ideas the officers were impressed with," Frode said slowly. "Zirdon Tal was in charge of taking care of the beliefs of the officers, and I don't feel very comfortable speaking against a member of the assembly."

"Then let *me* do it for you," Gardan put in with a growl. "Tal is a fool and always has been, and I would *not* put it past him to . . . embroider a straightforward idea of defense into something no normal person could live with. He would consider it 'simply making sure.' "

"With not a thought to the consequences if his actions were ever discovered," Antrie agreed with her own near-growl. "If we hadn't realized what was done, we'd have been completely unprepared to cope with the accidental discovery of the matter. But to tell the truth, I don't know how we *will* cope. If those Gandistrans are as caring as Frode believes, this is the part they'll have the most trouble for-giving."

"Can we simply pretend we know nothing about it?" Gardan asked, looking back and forth between Frode and Antrie. "That way if the truth comes out, we can act as shocked as our guests will be."

"We're members of the assembly, and the assembly is supposed to be in charge, Cleemor," Antrie pointed out wearily. "If we pretend to know nothing about what was done, we'll not only look like fools, but also like liars. Any chance we had of concluding a treaty with Gandistra will go straight out the window."

"Then what can we do?" Gardan demanded, his anger clearly for the situation rather than for Antrie. "If we get into a war with Gandistra now, we won't stand a chance of defeating them. And a war with Gandistra could con-ceivably mean a war with Astinda as well."

"We would probably have Astinda to worry about only if we did defeat Gandistra," Frode put in quietly. "The As-tindans have a large part of their country to rebuild, so they might well stay out of any conflict that doesn't threaten them directly."

"Or they might decide that Gandistra's defeat *would* be a threat to them," Antrie said with a shrug and a headshake. "There's no true way for us to know beforehand, and af-terward will be too late. Our wisest course of action is to avoid war altogether."

"If we're given the choice, you mean," Gardan grumbled before he rose to his feet. "All right, we have to think of a way to avoid that war, so I'm going home. I usually do my best thinking when I speak my thoughts to Tenia. For a woman, she's unusually sharp."

"She certainly is, if she lets you believe that all the good ideas are yours," Antrie teased. "Please remember to give her my best."

"I always do," Gardan returned with his own smile and a bow for Antrie. "I'll let you know if I think of anything."

Antrie smiled again, and after nodding to Frode, Gardan took himself off. Frode had risen to his feet, of course, then he hovered with indecision he certainly wasn't used to. There was more that needed to be said to Antrie, but Frode wasn't sure he had the courage . . .

"Please do sit down and stay awhile," Antrie offered as Frode continued to stand in front of his chair. "Unless you happen to be pressed for time, I would enjoy your company. We never get to talk unofficially to each other."

"There's . . . something else that needs mentioning," Frode said as he sat again, taking the coward's way out. "I tried to have some of my people keep track of Ebro Syant just to see where he would finally settle, but they somehow managed to lose him. I don't know if his disappearance is a problem, not when he no longer has any ability in magic, but I thought that someone in the assembly ought to know."

"I'm glad you mentioned the matter," Antrie said, a faint shadow creasing her brow. "I'm tempted to dismiss Syant as neutralized, but it was only his talent that we took. In order to do what he did he had to have intelligence as well, and that he still has. Can your people keep looking until they find him?"

"It so happens I've already given those orders," Frode admitted, privately wondering why the previously comfortable chair seemed to have changed. "Since we can soon have important visitors, I thought it best to keep an eye on anyone who might cause trouble."

"You do have a definite talent for anticipating what the right move is," Antrie said, and her smile and clear approval made Frode's discomfort extreme. "I commend you for your excellent efforts, and would like to ask a favor. Won't you please get to what you really came here to say?"

The abrupt question shocked Frode, since Antrie's talent was Air magic, not Spirit magic. How, then, could she possibly have known . . . ?

"I can tell that there's something on your mind from the way you're acting," Antrie said, startling him again by reading his thoughts. "I've never seen you so nervous, so whatever you want to talk about must be important. If you tell me what it is, I promise not to scream and faint."

"You may not be able to keep that promise," Frode countered, forced to smile in spite of himself. "I've . . . been steeling myself to speak to you for some time now, but the proper opportunity never presented itself. If this doesn't happen to be the right time either, I'd be happy to come back at—"

"No, this is the perfect time," Antrie interrupted firmly, obviously determined not to let him talk himself out of speaking up. "Please go ahead with what you want to say."

"All right, I will," Frode decided aloud, tired of playing the coward. "If you don't like what you hear, you only have to say so and I'll stop and never raise the subject again. I don't want to make a hairy nuisance of myself, but I can't seem to get the idea out of my head. I know I'm nothing to look at, so this is really the first time I've done this sort of thing. As I said, if you don't like the idea—"

"Frode, please," Antrie interrupted, her expression odd. "Are you saying you'd like to come courting?"

"Well, yes," Frode agreed, confusion threatening to enfold him. "Haven't I been saying just that?"

"No, you've been saying everything *but* that," Antrie countered, and Frode noticed with relief that she didn't seem to be insulted or disturbed. In fact, she smiled as she continued, "I find it amusing that the strongest and most capable of men seem to fall apart when the time comes to speak their heart rather than their mind. But if my cruelty hasn't put you off, I think I would very much like having you come courting."

"You mean that," Frode said in surprise, his Spirit magic confirming the fact. "I expected you to be kind to the ugly man who had decided to overstep himself, but you aren't refusing to even consider the idea. You're actually accepting."

"I always knew you were a brave man, but never before knew just *how* brave," Antrie said with the warmest, most marvelous smile. "You expected nothing but rejection, but went ahead and spoke up anyway. Don't you know, my dear, that it's men who most prefer to judge on looks? Women tend to be more practical and try to consider a man's insides as well as his outsides. On that basis, you're a very handsome man indeed."

"For the first time in a very long while, I find I don't know what to say," Frode admitted, feeling an unbelievably foolish smile crease his features. "Except for voicing my thanks for your agreement, that is. I'll try not to make you regret the decision."

"I'll be very surprised if I do regret the decision," Antrie returned, and then she stirred and got to her feet. "But I'll definitely have regrets if I don't tell my cook right now that there will be a guest for dinner. You *can* stay, I hope?"

"Dear lady, I'm at your disposal," Frode responded at once as he stood and bowed. "If you don't mind, we can use the intervening time to get to know one another. You, in particular, must have many questions that need to be answered."

"And you, my dear, must learn that there's more to a woman than her appearance," Antrie countered with amusement shining in her beautiful eyes. "I'll be back in a moment and then we can begin."

Frode bowed again, then watched Antrie walk away toward the house. For a moment he felt as though he stood in a dream, his most fervent wish about to be fulfilled. But he knew well enough that this was no dream, it was a reality that could be ruined beyond repair by doing the wrong thing. He'd planned to show only the best side of him if he were given the opportunity to do anything at all, but he'd suddenly changed his mind.

"No, Antrie Lorimon deserves to have nothing but the truth," he murmured to himself, staring at the door she'd disappeared through. "If something comes of this, I want it based on what really is, not on pretense and artificiality. Then, if she accepts me, it will be *me* she's accepting and not some false picture drawn to deceive her."

But, on the other hand, if she rejected him, it would be *him* she refused, not a convenient fiction. Frode took a deep breath before sitting down again, distantly wondering if cowardice was really all *that* bad . . .

* * *

Ebro Syant huddled into his rags in the corner of the old building, crouched down so that he would be harder to notice. His previous wealth *had* been put out of his reach, and the only place he'd been able to find where he could live was this oversized public assistance shack. He'd been assigned a pallet and a thin blanket, and was allowed to join everyone else when the free meals were served.

But the portions served were much too small to satisfy him, and for days he'd walked around with his insides growling. He'd also had most of his few personal possessions stolen while he slept, and he constantly felt filthy—which he was. No one was interested in knowing him, just as they were uninterested in knowing each other. It was against the rules of the place to form small private groups, and no one wanted to be thrown out for breaking a rule.

"But it's the best possible hiding place for me," Ebro whispered to himself, just as he'd done so often during the past days. "I'm free to make my plans without interruption, and none of my enemies knows my location. And I just have to put up with this for a short while. Once my plans have started to work, I'll be able to live like a human being again."

Ebro believed that fervently, and it was the only thing keeping him sane. The large building stank with an odor that the slap-dash cleaning of its inhabitants never got rid of. Some of the human trash living in the building were bullies, and would waylay those smaller than them and take whatever coppers those smaller people had managed to beg during the day. Ebro refused to beg, so at least he was spared *that* . . .

A growling came to Ebro's thoughts when the subject of begging arose. Before coming to that public shelter he'd gone to his parents, knowing that once he was part of their household again he'd be dismissed by his enemies as being out of the game entirely. He could have lived like a human being *there* while he planned, but his parents had chosen to lie rather than help.

"I'm sorry, Ebro, but I just can't afford to support you as well as myself and your mother," his father had said stiffly once he understood why Ebro had come. "Life has been really hard for us, and we're only just managing to make ends meet. Besides, everyone knows about what you did. If we took you in they would all turn their backs on us, and I would never rebuild my business. No, don't beg. That won't make me change my mind."

And then the fool had simply closed the door in his face, giving him no time to point out that he'd been about to mention the help *he'd* supplied. Begging had never even entered Ebro's thoughts, but now he had to live with the humiliation suggested by an old fool he should have destroyed completely rather than toyed with. He'd left his family alive on the faint chance that he might need them again at some time. Fat lot of good they'd done when he *had* needed them . . .

Ebro stirred where he crouched, then rose stiffly to his feet. Everyone who had returned for the midday meal had now left again, so it was time for *him* to go as well. He wanted to pay his tool a visit, and get the first of his plans set in motion. He would have preferred to visit Tal at night, using darkness to cover his presence, but the shelter had a curfew. Anyone who wasn't in by the curfew was refused admittance the next time they showed up. That was to keep the shelter from housing burglars, supposedly, but Ebro knew in his heart that they were just trying to make things harder for *him*.

As if *they* could keep him from exacting revenge. Ebro snorted his disdain as he made his quiet way out of the shelter, knowing *no one* could stop him. He would see Cleemor Gardan and Antrie Lorimon crushed, he would make Zirdon Tal his puppet, and then he would turn his attention to everyone else in the empire of Gracely. They would know the same misery *he* had been forced to endure, and he would make them live with it.

But the same wouldn't be done to his parents, oh, no. Ebro smiled as he thought of his plans for his parents, plans that would bring him much more pleasure than simply destroying them. He would see to it that his father's business grew and prospered, even while his parents' neighbors began to have less and less. Those friends and neighbors his father had been so concerned about would grow to hate his father for having what they didn't, and then his father's business would falter for lack of patronage . . .

Enjoyable thoughts occupied Ebro as he made his way on foot to Tal's house. He would have preferred going in a coach or carriage, but he'd decided that he wouldn't have used a conveyance even if he'd had the silver to pay for it. Tal was his secret weapon, and one took pains to keep a secret weapon secret.

When Ebro reached Tal's house, he nearly went to the front door. His sense of dignity *wanted* him to use the front door, but his sense of caution knew better. So he made his way around to the servants' entrance instead, and when a servant appeared, Ebro's dignity was served very well indeed. The servant bowed nervously when he learned who was calling, and quickly ushered Ebro inside.

There was a very short delay during which time Ebro was offered a cup of tea and some sweet bread, an offer he quickly accepted. The delay lasted only until Ebro finished the refreshments, and then he was led to the door of Tal's lounge. An answering bell-ring brought Ebro into Tal's presence, and the bigger man smiled when he saw who had come calling. Ebro wasn't surprised to see that Tal had obviously reconciled himself to the situation; Tal was an idiot, and idiots had the ability to talk themselves into accepting just about anything.

"You may leave us," Tal said to his servants, who bowed with respect and departed at once. When they were gone, Tal smiled at Ebro again. "I've been looking forward to this visit from you. Your plans are all formulated?"

"Indeed they are," Ebro agreed, walking to a chair and sitting. The chair was marvelously comfortable, and he wallowed in the memory of what it was like to live normally.

"So what are we going to do first?" Tal asked, clearly eager to begin. "Will there be terrible accidents to befall Gardan and Lorimon, I hope?"

"You really must learn the proper way of doing things," Ebro told the fool with a sigh. "Simply killing your enemies puts them out of their misery much too quickly. What you want to do is make them suffer for as long as possible before you rid yourself of their presence. Gardan and Lorimon have made themselves leaders of the assembly. That position is just fine as long as there isn't any trouble to disturb people. If there *is* trouble and the assembly leaders don't do anything to stop it, their position becomes a good deal less enviable."

"Why won't they do anything to stop it?" Tal asked, the interest in his eyes having grown. "They aren't fools, after all, so keeping things peaceful should be their first concern."

"There are two reasons why they might fail to stop trouble," Ebro answered, distantly surprised at the patience he showed. "One reason is, of course, that they aren't *able* to stop it. Under those circumstances, their inability would be publicized and stressed."

"And the second reason?" Tal said, leaning forward in his chair as though taking mental notes.

"The second reason for their failure would be that success isn't in their best interests," Ebro supplied. "If stopping the trouble would cause even greater trouble, they would have to look for another way out of the problem. Under *those* circumstances, the greater trouble would be played down or completely ignored when their lack of action was brought in front of the people."

"But what if they countered with an explanation of what could happen?" Tal put next. "That would make the one accusing them look like he didn't care about what happened to everyone."

"Not if the accuser claimed they were just making excuses for their lack of ability to handle the problem," Ebro pointed out. "People don't want to hear excuses from their leaders, they want definite action. And if the one accusing them then came up with a plan of action that took care of the problem, how much of a following would the former leaders have left?"

"Very little if any at all," Tal agreed with evident satisfaction. "Yes, I definitely like the way you think, Syant. So what do we do first?"

"First you put together a large amount of gold," Ebro instructed, ticking things off on his mental list. "Then you find someone to act as your intermediary, and use your Blending to put him under control. That way you won't have to worry about his betraying you no matter what happens. Your Blending members *will* support you in that, won't they? Do they have enough ambition to want to join you as leaders of the empire?"

"Yes, they certainly do have the proper ambition," Tal all but purred, his enjoyment almost palpable. "If I become supreme leader of the empire, they'll join me in that position. So what do I have the intermediary do?"

"You have him do all the dirty work," Ebro said, distantly wishing he had another cup of tea. "He hires the thugs who will cause the trouble, he gives them their instructions, and he sees to getting rid of them when their usefulness is over. Your own hands are completely clean, and no one should be able to even suspect a connection, let alone prove one."

"I do like the sound of that," Tal said, leaning back and sipping from his own teacup. "But what kind of trouble can we make that will cause the most difficulty for Gardan and Lorimon?"

"We can have the honored guests Gardan and Lorimon expect attacked and killed," Ebro answered, the pleasure of the thought suffusing him. "That Seated Blending from Gandistra will be here soon, and our enemies want to make peace with those people. Our great leaders are fools who don't understand that getting rid of their new Seated Blending will throw Gandistra into a turmoil. We can take their empire over while confusion reigns, and then we'll never have to worry about those people again."

"But where does causing trouble for Gardan and Lorimon come in?" Tal asked, now looking confused. "I don't understand how the attack you mentioned will reflect badly on *them*."

"Once the visitors have been killed, you'll accuse Gardan

and Lorimon of carelessly letting it happen," Ebro said, again distantly surprised at his patience. "You'll point out that those two were in charge, and their carelessness has put us all in very great danger. You'll tell everyone that the only thing we can do is attack Gandistra at once before their armies come to take revenge. Gardan and Lorimon still won't want to start the war, their sort never changes a stance like that. That's when you'll accuse them of working against the interests of Gracely, and the common fool in the street will be too frightened at the thought of being attacked to doubt the accusation. Everyone will back *your* demand for our empire to attack first, and our enemies will be out in the cold."

"You know, I would never have been able to think of something like that," Tal said, his expression having changed to one of admiration. "You do have an incredibly complex mind, and I'm delighted that we're working together. I'll get started at once with finding that intermediary, and I want you to tell my chief servant where you can be reached. You'll be the one to deal with the intermediary, and I'll want to consult with you about my various moves before I make them. For the moment, though, you may go."

"Certainly," Ebro agreed, getting out of the chair to go immediately to the door. A servant waited just outside, and after Ebro told the man where he could be reached, the servant led him to the same side door he'd used to enter the house.

Ebro was halfway back to the shelter before he remembered that he'd meant to have Tal feed him a proper meal. He didn't know how he could have forgotten something he'd so looked forward to, but for some reason it no longer seemed to matter. His only interest now was in giving Tal all the information he needed to make the plan work . . .

It was still fairly early in the afternoon, but Ebro didn't notice the pretty weather of the day. His mind insisted on wondering why he hadn't mentioned to Tal the fact that war with Gandistra would be no easy win for Gracely. Ebro wanted the people of Gracely to suffer, and so he'd made his plans with that end in mind.

"Maybe I didn't tell him because he didn't ask," Ebro muttered to himself as he walked, an answer that seemed to quiet the wondering. "Yes, that has to be it."

Figuring that out pleased Ebro, and he was able to return to the shelter with newfound peace of mind. Everything was working out perfectly, and soon Tal would be supreme leader of the empire of Gracely. Of course, there would be very little of Gracely left for Tal to be supreme leader *of*, but that didn't matter. Tal liked his plans, and that was all that really mattered to Ebro . . .

As soon as the fat little slug was gone, Zirdon Tal called in his servants and had them take out and clean the chair Syant had used. The slug was no longer as fat as he'd been but now he was filthy, which Zirdon considered to be a good deal worse.

"But the fool's mind is as brilliant as ever," Zirdon murmured to himself, smiling as he remembered the plans he'd been given. "I may not be brilliant in the same way, but I do have my own strengths."

And one of those strengths was in knowing how to use people. Zirdon had left orders to be told at once when Syant appeared, and then the man was to be delayed for a short while. During that short while Zirdon had used his Blending to put Syant under his control, and now the little slug was his, body and brilliance. Syant would also find it impossible to tell anyone about what Zirdon had done with Sheedra Kam, solving the problem without having to give up Syant's tactical ability.

"And the best part of all this is that my Blending members are completely behind me," Zirdon murmured again with pleasure. "They're just as ambitious as I am, and together we'll rule this empire for as long as we live."

Zirdon thrilled to that idea again, and then rang for one of his servants. He would celebrate with the best wine in his cellars, shared happily with his Blendingmates. The plan Syant had given him would work perfectly, and as soon as the celebration was over he would start to implement it. The first step, so to speak, on the way to meeting his destiny.

Zirdon actually hummed as he waited for the wine.

TWENTY-SEVEN

It took quite a long time for us to get started on our way to Gracely. Using our own Blending along with the others, we combed the area to locate the hiding members of the former nobility. Of course *they* didn't consider themselves *former* nobles, so when we began to round them up we were almost deafened by demands and complaints.

For the most part the servants were delighted to hear about the changed circumstances in Gan Garee. Some, however—usually those with privileges above the other servants—were almost as outraged as the former nobles. They also tried to argue, but not for long. Most of those upper class servants met with . . . accidents, courtesy of the people they'd been pushing around for so long.

The former members of the army spent their time healing and growing stronger while we were ingathering. When we were ready to send everyone back to Gan Garee, a large number of the former army slaves volunteered to help herd the former nobles along. All that talk of former this and former that was confusing at times, but once they were all on their way—with the Astindans to help—the confusion was behind us.

When we finally took to the road we split up into two groups again, which made moving, camping, and hunting much easier. The days passed quietly and uneventfully for the most part, except for the time we found that a group of outlaws had taken over a small town. We Blended and took control of the outlaws, then rode in and let the townspeople

344

know that they were free again. Right after that we left the town, to spare ourselves the sight of what the people did to the outlaws.

"You look preoccupied, Tamma," Jovvi said as she moved her mount up beside mine once the town was behind us. "Are you thinking about what's being done to those outlaws right now?"

"Not really," I answered with a sigh as I withdrew from my thoughts. "Those outlaws did a lot of ugly things to those people in the town, making no effort to control themselves because they thought they could get away with it all. Now they're learning better, just the way the nobles are learning the same lesson. If you do it, you'd better be prepared to pay for it. What I was really thinking about was how soon our message will reach our people in Gan Garee."

"The two guardsmen carrying the message will move as fast as they can without killing their horses," Jovvi assured me, but she sounded more assured than she looked. "If you're wishing that *we* could be there to handle whatever that Ruhl man intends to do, I can only say I share that wish. I know the people we left behind are good, but I still wish we could be there to help."

"I don't exactly have a bad feeling about what will happen, but it isn't a good feeling either," I confessed, wondering if she felt the same. "I'd love to think that we're wasting our time going to Gracely and start to agitate for turning back, but for some reason I can't. It's another feeling I can't explain, and I'm getting very tired of wrestling with it all."

"For the second time, I know exactly how you feel," Jovvi said with a small, humorless laugh. "I've been getting those same impressions ever since we Blended near that town, when— Oh, rot!"

"Do I take that comment to mean that you experienced what Lorand and I have, but also forgot to mention it?" I asked dryly, enjoying her expression of frustration. "Now there are three things we can feel the same about."

"I don't understand how I could have forgotten to mention something that important," Jovvi grumbled, her annoyançe directed at herself. "I thought you and Lorand were just distracted when it happened to *you*, but this isn't simple distraction. It *is* like forgetting to mention that you're breathing in and out, an action so natural that you take it for granted. But when you stop to think about it, what happened is amazing."

"Yes, actually becoming the entity with your own awareness is incredible," I agreed, but then had to shake my head. "What I still can't understand, though, is how Lorand—and now you—can have the same experience at the same time that I do. How can the entity have your awareness or Lorand's when it has mine?"

"I wish I knew the answer to that," Jovvi said, still grumbling and annoyed. "Since this is happening to us one at a time it's most likely part of a natural process, but we have no idea about what happens next—or what we're supposed to do with this new awareness. And I think we'd better make a practice of checking with the others to find out if they've reached the same point. We can't count on having them announce it when it happens."

"We should have started to do that after every time we Blended," I pointed out, now sharing her self-annoyance as well. "Maybe part of the process is to make us colossally stupid."

"You won't find *me* arguing against that possibility," Jovvi agreed, but a bit of her usual good humor seemed to be returning. "Let's start our questioning with Naran. She's been acting distracted lately, and it might be because of the new process."

I smiled to myself as I urged my horse to follow Jovvi's, both of us heading for where Naran rode. Someone else with Jovvi's ability might have used her talent to find out what Naran's distraction was about, but Jovvi was still playing fair and respecting people's privacy. I wondered if *I* would be that good about it, then dismissed the question. Luckily, the situation would never arise.

"Naran, Tamma and I would like to ask you a question," Jovvi said as soon as we were riding to either side of our sister. "Have you by any chance experienced what she and

Lorand—and now I—have during Blending? You know, feeling that the entity has your awareness?"

"I don't really understand what that means, so I'd guess that the answer is no," she replied, looking as though pulling herself out of her thoughts had taken a tremendous effort. "But since I was the last one to join the Blending, that makes sense, doesn't it?"

"Yes, that makes a great deal of sense," Jovvi agreed in a soft and gentle voice, her expression suddenly filled with concern. "But that also means you're being distracted by something else entirely. Can we be of help in any way, even if it's only to listen?"

Naran hesitated for a very long moment, and I was about to offer to let the two of them talk alone when Naran looked up from a study of her hands.

"I'm . . . afraid I may be losing Rion," she said in a whisper, looking straight ahead rather than at Jovvi or me. "He's been approached more than once by a certain woman, and the probabilities are very strong that he'll decide to—to—"

"Rion?" I couldn't help blurting, a glance showing me that Jovvi was just as shocked. "I think the world may be coming to an end. If there was ever a man who found the woman of his soul, I would have sworn it was Rion. Has he . . . done anything with that certain woman?"

"Nothing yet beyond talking to her," Naran admitted, but I didn't miss that "yet." "She's the one who comes to *him*, but he isn't doing anything to discourage her. From a word or two I've picked up, she . . . admires him."

"Then it can't possibly be as bad as you're imagining," Jovvi said, obviously trying to sound hearty and reassuring. "A man from one of the link groups has come over to *me* more than once to say how much he admires me, and *I* haven't done anything to chase him away either. It's flattering to have someone feel that way about you, but it doesn't necessarily mean you intend to do anything about accepting their unspoken offer."

"Now, that's odd," I couldn't help commenting. "A girl from one of the link groups also approached Vallant, and from the way he looked at her I was convinced that he felt some attraction for her. But I also happened to see them when she approached him a second time, and he just about yawned in her face. That made *me* feel good, I can tell you."

"I can imagine," Jovvi said, her brows high as she obviously thought about something else. "So Rion, Vallant, and I have been approached by members of the link groups. I wonder if any of the rest of us have had the same experience."

"Well, I may have been *almost* approached," I answered slowly, not quite sure I wasn't imagining things. "It was during the time we were gathering up those fool nobles, and I was in a particularly bad mood. One of those 'highborn' fools had a strong Middle talent in Fire magic, and he set one of his servants on fire in an attempt to distract the guardsmen who were putting everyone together. I'm sure he meant to try to sneak away during the confusion, but things didn't quite work out for him."

"Yes, I remember that," Jovvi said, her smile on the grimly satisfied side. "I never knew it was possible for you to work that fast, but you protected the servant until you were able to put the fire out. Then you went after that noble and burned every bit of clothing off his body before doing the same to all his hair. No one had any trouble seeing him wet himself, and it couldn't have happened to a more deserving person."

"That's the way *I* looked at it, but the incident still put me in a bad mood," I said with a nod. "If I hadn't been paying close attention, that servant would have gone up in flames before I could do anything to help. A few minutes after everything had settled down again, a rather handsome man started to approach me. He looked vaguely familiar, but I was in no mood to be friendly with *anyone*. He started toward me with a smile, hesitated when he met my gaze, then wisely changed his mind about coming over. I probably would have jumped up and down on him even if he'd just said hello."

"What about you, Naran?" Jovvi asked next, and I joined

her in looking at a now-frowning Naran. "Has anyone made an attempt to approach *you*?"

"I've been thinking about it ever since you first brought up the point, and my answer may be the same one Tamrissa gave but under other circumstances." Naran spoke slowly now, as though choosing her words carefully. "The time was also when we were going after the nobles. I kept an almost constant check on the probabilities to make sure none of them got away, and at one point a rather handsome man seemed about to come over to me. He was only about five or six feet away when his smile faltered and he stopped short, stared at me for a moment, then turned and walked away. It was almost as though he knew what I was doing and didn't want to disturb me."

"So that makes everyone but Lorand, and *he* was probably approached as well," I said as Jovvi took her own turn at frowning for a moment. "I don't know about you two, but this makes me very suspicious. If only one or two of us was approached, it would mean nothing. With all of us involved, attraction and admiration probably have nothing to do with the matter."

"Yes, I'm inclined to agree," Jovvi said, obviously dismissing whatever had made her frown. "With all of us involved, I'd guess that someone is trying to drive a wedge between all the members of our Blending. I think we'd better have a meeting with the men, to see if we can figure out who's behind the attempt."

"That isn't going to be easy," Naran said, her previous disturbance apparently eased to a certain extent. "I've just been checking the probabilities about this, and I can't seem to find anything at all. That flux Master Ardanis mentioned keeps getting in the way."

"So we have to do it the hard way instead of the easy way," Jovvi said, all but shrugging a dismissal. "It would be nice to know for certain and have the information confirmed, but formulating a logical theory could work just as well. At least we'll be warned, and can be on the alert for any other tricks."

"You know, a possibility just occurred to me," I said

slowly as I examined the thought. "Whoever tampered with
the minds of the nobles leading the army has to be from
Gracely. The army was on its way to destroy Gracely, and
had to be stopped. Now *we're* on our way to Gracely, and
someone may consider us the same kind of threat. Having
us all end up hating each other would be one way to end
the threat."

"You're right, that's a definite possibility," Jovvi agreed
as Naran stared at me with raised brows. "I think we'll have
to find the people involved in the plot, and ask them a few
questions. And I'm also willing to bet that they won't turn
out to be members of any of the link groups either."

"They can't be if they're working for Gracely," I said
with my own brows high, realizing her guess had to be the
truth. "Our link groups are made up of people we rescued
from the Astindan armies, an unlikely place for Gracely
supporters to be found. We ought to tell the men about this
right away."

"We're probably less than an hour away from making
camp," Jovvi said after a glance at the sky. "Let's wait until
then before we call a group meeting. If we're lucky, the
Gracely people involved won't realize what's going on until we have some of them in our hands. If we cause a flap
now, they might well understand what's happening and
simply disappear."

"That's a good point, so I'll go along with it," I grudged,
hating the delay but seeing the need. "Those people won't
be happy that I have to wait, though. I hate having to wait
for things, and I intend to take my mad out on *them*."

"I hope you start with that certain woman," Naran muttered, so low I could barely hear her. "Seeing *her* fry would
be a downright—"

Naran's words broke off, but I had no trouble completing
the thought—or understanding the feelings behind it. Naran
was basically a very gentle soul, and what she hadn't quite
said aloud was a measure of her deep disturbance. I'd have
to see what I could do to make her half wish come true.

The three of us continued to ride together until our group
found a place to camp, and then we took care of our horses

and chose places to sleep. By then a fire had been built for our group meal, and while it was being prepared we casually gathered up the men and took them aside.

"I have the feelin' that we're not goin' to be talkin' about the weather," Vallant commented once we all strolled to a quiet place away from the others and sat down. "It may be my imagination, but you ladies look like you mean business of some kind."

"We do," Jovvi agreed with a smile that looked perfectly natural. "We have something to tell you men, and it would be better if you didn't react outwardly to what you hear. There's a good chance we're being watched."

"Who would be watching us?" Lorand asked, and I could almost see him struggling not to look around. "There doesn't seem to be anyone in the vicinity but our own people."

"I think if we counted heads we would discover differently," Jovvi denied with the same easy smile. "Tamma and Naran and I got to talking, and we discovered that we were approached by men who claimed to be members of the various link groups. These men said they 'admired' us, but after the first visit it was clear that they had something other than admiration in mind. We were wondering if you men were also approached."

Naran had seemed to be holding her breath, but when she heard the way Jovvi put things she slumped a bit with relief. Jovvi had been something less than completely accurate in her statement, but the men never noticed.

"I knew there was somethin' odd about that woman," Vallant said immediately, then forced himself to speak more quietly. "What I mean is, a woman also approached *me*. At first I couldn't help thinkin' how attractive she was, but then it came to me that she was bein' *deliberately* attractive, if you can understand that idea. Tamrissa and the rest of you ladies are attractive just standin' there, but that woman was really *tryin'*."

"I understand exactly what you mean," Lorand said to him, then glanced at the rest of us. "I think you know that means I was also approached, and at first I was very flat-

tered by the attention of someone who thought so highly
of me. After a short while, though, I began to wonder. All
our people know the six of us have more than a Blending
relationship in our group, so approaching me the way the
woman did was at the very least improper. If she thought
all that well of me, why did she believe I would turn away
from the woman I'd paired with for a passing stranger?"

"We probably weren't supposed to be noticin' things like
that," Vallant put in sourly with a small headshake. "That
makes five of us, so let's see if the thing is unanimous.
What about you, Rion?"

"What?" Rion said with a start, just as though he'd been
abruptly awakened from a sound sleep. Then he seemed to
regain control of himself. "Yes, I was approached as well
and in the same way. By someone who meant none of what
she said."

"That's it, then," Vallant summed up, now looking toward Jovvi. "Someone's been goin' after every one of us.
Do we have any idea who the someone is?"

"Tamma suggested that it could well be people from
Gracely who want to neutralize what they see as a threat,"
Jovvi answered. "We *are* heading for their country, after
all, right after having deposed the leaders of our own country. They may have decided that we've got conquest in
mind for Gracely as well."

"And Jovvi thinks they aren't really members of our various link groups, and could easily disappear if they think
they've been found out," I said, leaning casually forward.
"If we want to question any of them to learn the truth, we
ought to go looking for them right now."

"You mean as a Blending, I take it," Lorand said, his
nod thoughtful. "Yes, that's probably the best way. If we
try to find them as individuals, we might end up having to
destroy them in order to save our own lives."

"Exactly, so let's get started," Jovvi said, looking around
at us. "Is everyone ready?"

No one said they weren't, so an instant later I was once
again the entity. I knew exactly what my flesh forms intended, of course, and quickly went about the search. A

number of minutes passed as I examined everyone in our camp and then did the search again, but the conclusion was inescapable. Those flesh forms I sought were no longer in range of my senses.

"How could they have known?" Jovvi demanded as soon as she dissolved the Blending. "We didn't figure out what was going on until about an hour ago, but they're already out of our reach. That means they parted company with our group a lot earlier than that hour. If they hadn't, they would still be in reach of our entity's sensing."

"Maybe they *didn't* know," Vallant suggested after a moment when no one else came up with anything but grumbling. "We aren't all that far from Gracely now, and they may have ridden on ahead to warn their people that they've done just about all they could to separate us. Continuin' with the game when we might start usin' our link groups at any time would make them stand out as strangers."

"And they could be hoping that their ploy might still work," Lorand added with a nod. "Not seeing them doesn't necessarily mean not thinking about them, and it would be the thinking that caused trouble among us."

"Right now the only thing *I'm* thinking about is cold-blooded murder," I muttered, feeling more than a little annoyed. "Not only do they have the nerve to sneak into our traveling group, but they actually come right up to *us*. I think we need to do something to make sure nothing like this ever happens again."

"What we should have done was arrangin' the same thing we did in the palace," Vallant put in, looking just as annoyed. "Makin' sure that everyone knew everyone else and that they ought to be alert for the appearance of strangers. If we keep this to ourselves, we're only askin' for this mess or one like it to happen again."

"Yes, I think we'd better start by telling the other Blending," Jovvi agreed with a sigh. "Then we can all tell our link groups, and have them get started with learning the faces of people they don't yet know. We'll be across the border into Gracely soon, and it's not far to Liandia from there."

"Then let's get to it," Lorand agreed, and we all began to get to our feet. It took until we were standing before we noticed that Rion hadn't gotten up with us. Naran stood beside him, just short of hovering, staring down at the way Rion sat with his arms wrapped around his raised-up legs.

"What's wrong, Rion?" Jovvi asked, a sudden worry in her tone. "I should have paid closer attention . . . Why are you feeling so disturbed?"

"Since I'm the biggest fool among us, it's fitting that I be most disturbed," Rion answered in a distant, pain-filled voice. "Please don't concern yourself with me, I'll be along in a moment. To help tell people what a fool I've been."

"But you weren't the only one who was fooled, so why are you so upset?" Jovvi pursued, the worry in her eyes increasing. "Did you somehow miss the fact that all of us were approached?"

"Yes, we were all approached, but I was the only one dense enough to believe there was honest interest behind the contact." Rion looked at no one as he spoke, most especially not at a suffering Naran. "I was so taken by the thought that an attractive woman not of our Blending could find interest in me, that I forgot about the woman who gave me all the love in her heart from the first moment we met. I'm a complete moron and fool, and don't deserve to have the love of that most wonderful of women. Not knowing when I'll next start to look around will kill that love if it isn't dead already."

"We all make mistakes, Rion," Lorand said, empathetic pain in his own voice. "I also came close to making a fool of myself, so you mustn't think you're alone in this."

"But you only came close, Lorand," Rion countered, still without looking up. "I went the entire way, and wasn't bright enough to know I was being lied to. If my love was a true match to Naran's I would never have been tempted, but I was more than tempted. I don't deserve Naran and her love, even if I still have it. There's no knowing when I'll hurt her again, and I refuse to give her any more pain."

"I really don't understand you, Rion," I blurted, finding it impossible to hold the words back when Naran seemed to crumple into herself. "You know you have less experience with people than the rest of us, but you still insist on thinking you shouldn't have felt tempted. When even Vallant was tempted, you have no real cause to complain about what *you* did."

"What do you mean, if even I was tempted?" Vallant put in before Rion could say anything, faint annoyance in his tone. "I'm just as human as the next man, so why *wouldn't* I be tempted? Even though I wasn't, not really."

"Oh, right, you weren't tempted," I scoffed, turning to face him. "I happened to see that non-temptation, and for someone who's had more experience with women than any other man here, *you* were the one acting like a fool. Considering all the women you've known, you should have seen right away that a baited hook was being dangled in front of you."

"I did notice the hook, that's why I *wasn't* tempted," Vallant insisted, the annoyance increasing in his pretty blue eyes. "But what about when *you* were approached? Were you by any chance feelin' too flattered by the attention to understand what was goin' on? Are you accusin' *me* because *you're* the one feelin' guilty?"

"I don't have anything to feel guilty *about*," I returned, my own annoyance growing higher. "I'm not a male who has to paw the ground like a mindless stallion at sight of a pretty woman just to prove how much of a man he is. I didn't—"

"No, that's right, you *aren't* male," Vallant interrupted in a growl. "You're a female who walks around swingin' her hips in front of every man she passes, just to show him what he's missin'. If you think I haven't seen you doin' that, you're—"

"I do no such thing!" I shouted, outrage flaring so high that I felt the heat in my face. "You're lying just to cover the fact that you—"

"Tamma, Vallant, please!" Jovvi interrupted, stepping between us as Lorand took Vallant's arm and Naran took mine. "If we let ourselves fall to bickering like this, the plotting of those people will be a success. Is that what we really want, to let them win?"

"No," I grudged, feeling as though I'd come down with a case of the stupids again. "Since arguing was what they were after, I won't let them have the satisfaction. But I still know what I know."

Vallant's head came up when he heard what was nothing but the simple truth, but he didn't get the chance to comment. Naran made a sound as if she were in pain, and we all quickly turned to see what the problem was.

"He's gone," she whispered, staring at the place where Rion had been sitting. "He walked away without even trying to speak to me. I've lost him after all, not *to* that woman but because of her. What am I going to do?"

Just a minute ago I'd been filled with any number of words, but right now I couldn't think of a single one that would answer Naran's question. A glance at the others showed that they suffered from the same lack I did, and I don't know how long we stood there before Vallant and Lorand went off to find our missing sixth . . .

∞

TWENTY-EIGHT

∞

Rion rose to his feet and hurried away from the others, the misery he thought complete actually increasing. Not only had he ruined things for himself, now Tamrissa and Vallant were also bickering. And because of him, only because of him.

It was a good thing he had learned at a very early age never to let anyone see him crying, he reflected. If not for that he would have added to the mess he'd caused by embarrassing himself completely. It was just about sundown, a time of day he was usually particularly fond of, but today the coming darkness was the only thing Rion sought. It was easier to hide in the darkness, and hiding forever was the only thing left to interest him.

It took only a moment to reach the sleeping pad he'd put down near Naran's, and another moment to collect the pad and the rest of his few belongings. Once he had it all he headed into the darkening woods, intent on losing himself as thoroughly as possible. It wasn't until he was completely out of sight of the camp that he stopped, feeling even worse than when he'd been a prisoner of that woman who had stolen him from his true parents. The situation then had not been of his own making; this one definitely was.

Rion simply dropped his possessions without caring about order and then sat himself on his sleeping pad. How could he have been such a fool, to be so deeply flattered by the attentions of a strange woman? He'd ruined everything, destroyed the life that he'd fought so hard to make his own, shattered the woman who had given him *real* love—

"This isn't a very good spot you've chosen, Rion," Lorand's voice suddenly came out of the blue. "If you aren't going to pay attention to your surroundings, you need to stay in camp where others can do it for you."

Rion looked up to see that Lorand and Vallant had followed him away from camp, but then he lowered his head to his hands again.

"I appreciate the concern you're undoubtedly feeling, but I prefer to be alone right now," he muttered. "I ask the favor of being allowed the company of nothing but my own thoughts."

"If we leave, that's not the only company you'll be havin'," Vallant put in, the words sounding dry. "Lorand tells me there's a hunting cat not far from this area, and if you stay here in your current mood you'll end up bein' his supper."

"Which would make our loss almost as great as your

own," Lorand added just as dryly. "There are times when a man *should* be left alone with his thoughts, but this isn't one of them. You need to hear from those with more experience in life than you've had yourself."

"Are you going to try to prove to me that I wasn't a fool?" Rion demanded, more distraught than angry as he raised his head to look at his brothers. "I wish that were possible, but I know it isn't. I *have* learned enough about life to judge foolishness, and after the judgment comes condemnation."

"Then you might as well condemn me right along with yourself," Lorand said, walking closer before crouching down near Rion. "I didn't want to say so in front of Jovvi, but when that woman came on to me I was really tempted to find out what I might be missing. It finally came to me that what I thought I was missing was someone to simper out how wonderful she knew I was. I hadn't thought I needed that and usually I don't, but that woman caught me in a vulnerable moment. We all have vulnerable moments, Rion, even those of us who have known more women intimately than you have."

"And as Tamrissa pointed out, I've known more than my share," Vallant said, also moving closer. "It seems to be part of some men to look at an attractive woman and wonder what it might be like to bed her, but that's just a reflex. After wonderin' that about the woman who approached *me*, the next thing I realized was that it didn't matter *how* good the woman might be. Tamrissa is good for me *all* the time, and that's more important to me than just beddin'. It took havin' a lot of women to teach me that, but I tend to be slow in some things. That doesn't mean you have to be just as slow."

"But I don't understand!" Rion protested, fighting to hold onto his shredding control. "Weren't you just arguing with Tamrissa, an argument that started because of *me*? You can't just dismiss the argument as though it never happened!"

"Of course I was arguin' with Tamrissa," Vallant answered with a pleased smile rather than with distress. "If I hadn't argued, she might have started to think that what she accused me of was true. She knew I wasn't seriously considerin' that woman for more than a minute, but she still needs a lot of reassurance. That's why I accused *her*, to remind her that she wasn't the only one who was occasionally touched by jealousy. As soon as she calms down things will fall back into proper perspective, and she and I can apologize to each other."

"And speaking of apologizing, that's something a smart man learns how to do," Lorand said, taking over the lecture with a smile. "A very wise ancient once said that women have a greater capacity to forgive than men do, so it would be a crime to waste that capacity. Naran still loves you with all her heart, Rion, and thinking that she's lost you has devastated her. Apologizing will only do *you* some good. As far as I can see, Naran has already forgiven you without hearing the first word."

"How does one apologize for betraying the love of his life?" Rion asked in a whisper. "And how am I to assure her that the same will never happen again when *I'm* not certain that it won't? When one makes a great fool of oneself, one may only be setting the stage for more repetitions of the same act."

"Anyone can get caught the first time, especially when he doesn't have a lot of experience with life," Vallant said with a sigh. "If you find yourself gettin' caught a second time, then you really are a fool. Are you willin' to be caught a second time?"

"Willing, certainly not," Rion assured his brother, the very idea bringing him distant outrage. "But willing has very little to do with the matter if it simply happens again the way it did the first time. How am I to know that it won't?"

"Are you a grown man, or a little boy bein' led around by the nose?" Vallant demanded, no longer sounding quite as patient as he had. "If a man makes up his mind that somethin' won't be happenin', he doesn't let it happen. A little boy has things happenin' to him whether he wants them to or not. A grown man takes control of his life, and doesn't waste time makin' excuses. So which are you, Rion?"

"I know which I'd prefer to be," Rion muttered, a sudden thought occurring to him. Was he having so much trouble coping with what had happened because inside he *was* no more than a small boy? That was what he had been raised to be, a child who would obey his "mother" in all things and allow her to design and rule his entire life. He now had to fight that arrangement harder than he ever had, but doubt about the outcome of the battle smothered the small amount of hope he'd been able to muster.

"I know which I'd prefer to be, but I've suddenly become unsure about whether I can achieve that state," Rion said after taking a very deep breath. "Only time will show what level of maturity I've reached, which means that committing myself now to a particular outcome would be yet another act of a fool. I need to speak to Naran."

After making his decision aloud, Rion began to get to his feet. Vallant frowned and began to question him, but both question and response were overridden by Lorand's sudden actions. Lorand whirled to look out into the gloom of the night shadows, and then he held out his hand as though warding off something. And the something was indeed palpable, a tawny hunting cat that had paused in mid-leap.

It was instantly clear that Lorand had taken control of the big cat, and without the help of the Blending. The cat snarled and fought the constraint laid on it, but seemed unable to break free. Nevertheless, Rion decided to make certain of the safety of his brothers, and therefore erected a wall of hardened air between the cat and the rest of them.

And no sooner was the wall in place, than the poor cat was treated to a bath in what looked to be extremely cold water. The cat shrieked and jumped, and then it was bounding away back into the woods.

"That ought to teach it not to mess around with people," Lorand murmured with what seemed to be a sympathetic chuckle. "Having cold water dumped on you isn't very pleasant, but it's better than having all the moisture pulled out of your body, having your heart stopped, or having the air you breathe taken away. That was a nice cat, and I'm glad we didn't have to really hurt it."

"I tend to be partial to cats myself, but not ones of *that* size," Vallant returned, his words very dry. "If you're missin' not havin' a pet, Lorand, please let *us* pick one out for you."

"But a pet that size would be very useful," Lorand came back, obviously teasing Vallant. "No one would crowd me when I walked along the street, I could leave my valuables around without locking them up, and I'd have a topic to talk about with everyone I met."

"We haven't walked along a street in weeks if not months," Vallant retorted firmly. "In addition to that you don't have any valuables, and you never have trouble findin' what to talk about. With all that in mind, let's get Rion back to camp before we have another visitor with no manners."

That was a more than sound suggestion, so they all began to comply with it. Lorand and Vallant gave Rion help in gathering his possessions, but carrying them wasn't difficult so he did it alone. What *was* difficult was thought of the coming discussion he would have with Naran, but the discussion wasn't something that could be avoided. The very least he owed Naran was making the effort . . .

When they were once again in the camp proper, Rion chose a place to sleep that was more or less solitary. He left his sleeping bag and possessions there before going to look for Naran, an errand his brothers had left him to do alone. It took a few moments, but eventually Rion located the woman of his heart and walked up to her. It felt odd to find her anywhere but right beside him, an oddness he was only just noticing after the last few days.

"Rion, are you all right?" she asked at once when he came up to her, relief flooding her lovely features. "I was very worried when you disappeared like that. The flux Master Ardanis told me about seems to be ruining Sight of everything I most want to see."

"I'm as well as someone of my sort is able to be," Rion

responded unevenly, firmly refusing himself the extreme pleasure that putting his arms about her would bring. "I—went off alone to do some very necessary thinking, and I've a horrible confession to make."

Naran nodded without speaking, and Rion had the impression that she wasn't *able* to speak. Fear glinted from her lovely eyes, but Rion still found the strength to continue.

"I'd thought that I was . . . free of that noblewoman's influence, but I've discovered that there are still . . . aspects of her teaching controlling me." The admission was very painful to make, but Rion stumbled on in spite of that. "I should never have been so foolish and pliant as to look at a woman other than you, but in all truthfulness I can't be certain that I'll never do the same again. You deserve a man who really is a man, someone who has no trouble holding to the knowledge that the woman he loves is the only woman he cares to concern himself with. Until I can prove to my own satisfaction that I've become that sort of man, I won't trouble you with my presence again."

"Rion, wait!" Naran called as he turned and hurried away. "You don't understand . . ."

Rather than wait, Rion moved so fast that the rest of what she said was quickly lost. Naran was undoubtedly prepared to tell him that she didn't mind his paying attention to other women, an attitude easily expected from so marvelous a person. But the situation was unacceptable to *him*, and he would *not* return to her side until that situation was completely resolved.

If he managed to live that long without her . . .

The day was warm but dark with a promise of rain, muggy and uncomfortable and affecting everyone's mood. Jovvi rode along blocking out those various unhappy moods, but that didn't mean she wasn't aware of them. In point of fact she shared them, and knowing they would come in sight of Liandia, Gracely's capital city, at any time didn't seem to help.

Possibly it was the fact that so far Gracely had proven

to be untouched by destruction, Jovvi reflected. They had ridden through lovely countryside and peaceful woods, every now and then seeing what appeared to be a prosperous farm. The undemolished landscape proved that their suspicions were correct, and the nobles leading that army *had* been controlled by someone. Someone in Gracely . . .

Jovvi sighed as that thought led to a more important one. Almost everyone was convinced that the people who had approached her Blending were also from Gracely, the intent of those people being the loosening of bonds between the leaders of the expedition. And those bonds *had* been loosened to a certain extent, at least as far as Rion and Naran were concerned . . .

"You look as if you're ready to start talking to yourself," a voice said, startling Jovvi out of her thoughts. "If you are, then I know how you feel."

It was Naran herself who had spoken as Jovvi's horse brought her in close proximity to Naran's, and Jovvi noticed that there seemed to be something odd about the girl. Naran had been wrapped up in her own world for quite some time, but now she was apparently prepared to rejoin their common world.

"I do consider myself a good conversationalist, but I prefer to talk to others rather than myself," Jovvi answered with a smile. "Unless you're in the mood to start a fight, that is. There's too much of that going around already."

"At the risk of repeating myself, I know how they feel," Naran said, glancing around at the threatening day they rode through. "We're going to start getting wet pretty soon, and soggy isn't my favorite state of being. When we finally ride into that city ahead, we'll look like a bunch of drowned cats."

"Is that a prediction, or an uninformed guess?" Jovvi asked, suddenly concerned. "What we look like when we enter that city will influence how those people treat us. I'd hate to see us having to stage a demonstration in order for us to be given some ordinary respect."

"Don't worry, it's just a guess," Naran said with a sigh that seemed more than heartfelt. "I'm Seeing very little these days, no more than a hint here and there that makes it through the flux. No one in my link groups seems to be doing any better, and most of them are very upset. We tried to link up to break through the flux, and it didn't work more than marginally. Apparently no one expected the flux to get this bad."

"I don't enjoy having your talent blocked, but we'll find a way to cope," Jovvi assured her, leaning over to pat her hand. "How are you doing otherwise? This trip is beginning to be hard on everyone."

"It was *very* hard, until I began to do some serious thinking," Naran answered, an unexpected calm in her face and eyes. "When Rion announced that he had to prove something to himself and then marched away, I thought my life was over. But then I finally remembered what Tamrissa went through with Vallant, and what she said about Vallant's needing to prove something to *her*. If Rion ever decides he's ready to come back to me, he'll find that proving things to himself was the easy part."

"Is that why you suddenly remind me so much of Tamma?" Jovvi asked, the question more for herself than for Naran. "You seem to have adopted the same attitude, which is somewhat surprising. A good part of Tamma's attitude comes from her having Fire magic."

"You don't have to have Fire magic to lose patience with someone's foolishness," Naran pointed out with actual amusement. "I know that Rion is my other half, but that doesn't mean he's perfect. Thinking he *was* perfect was *my* mistake, a blindness I won't be guilty of again. If he can't find his way past the troubles he's created for himself I'll mourn his loss, but my life will go on. And my help will be available if he happens to ask for it, but I won't volunteer it again."

"How did you get to be so wise?" Jovvi asked with a bemused smile, teasing only a little. "Instead of being weakened by what happened, as soon as Rion pulls himself together we'll be stronger than ever. Or at least I hope we will be, and I hope the strengthening will be in time to let us cope with whatever is waiting for us in this country. You can't see anything ahead of us at all?"

"Seeing through that flux is almost impossible, but I did get a glimpse or two," Naran said with a small headshake. "I got the impression that we'll be approached by a small welcoming committee, but I'm not certain when it will happen. Sometime after we come in sight of the city, I think."

"Does that phrase 'approached by' mean greeted or attacked?" Jovvi asked, adding her frown to Naran's. "It makes a considerable difference."

"Again, I got no more than an impression, but I think we'll be greeted, at least at first," Naran replied after a brief hesitation, her expression telling Jovvi that the girl tried once again to See something clearly. "There *is* going to be trouble for us at some point, but when it will happen and whose fault it will be are two things I can't make out."

"I hope that flux clears up soon," Jovvi muttered as she considered what she'd heard. "No one is feeling very friendly toward the citizens of Gracely, and it would help to know if we're facing potential friends or potential enemies. We may have to go after the truth with our Blending."

Naran was about to add something when a stir up ahead took the attention of both of them. The head of their column, which wasn't that far away, had stopped moving, so Jovvi rode forward to see what was going on. Naran followed along behind, much of the girl's previous shyness apparently having disappeared.

"Well, there it is," Vallant said as Jovvi guided her horse to a place near Lorand's. "Do we keep goin' and just ride into the streets as if we belonged, or do we stop and make camp somewhere and wait for them to notice us?"

No one answered Vallant immediately, not when they, like Jovvi, were all busy examining what lay before them. The road they'd been following had topped a hill, and from there it was possible to see the city of Liandia, which lay about two miles away.

Or at least that was where the city walls began, a very wide gate standing open in those walls. Horse and wagon traffic moved freely both in and out of the gate, with any gate guards currently hidden from view. Occasional towers lofted above the height of the encircling walls, and what could be seen of other buildings showed a surprising amount of grace added to utility.

Jovvi had expected the land near the city to be open, just the way it was near Gan Garee. The landscape was indeed open, but not empty by any means. What looked to be a large inn stood to the left, about a mile or so from the city walls. Between the inn and the city were various small houses of some sort, and the land to the right held what appeared to be fenced pasturage next to a building surrounded by coaches and carriages. It seemed an odd place to keep coaches and carriages, but before Jovvi could say so a distraction came.

"Does anyone else think that those people comin' from the inn aren't surprised to see us?" Vallant asked, redirecting everyone's attention. "They were in a hurry to get mounted, but now they're movin' more slowly."

Jovvi looked at the three people who had ridden to the road and were now coming directly toward them. They were all male, and Jovvi's talent told her that there *was* no surprise in any of them. In fact those three had been waiting for them, and their cautious approach was perfectly understandable.

"They're moving slowly because they don't want to disconcert us," Jovvi explained with a wry smile. "And it might interest everyone to know that they're all Highs in Spirit magic. The only odd thing is, they didn't open to the power until they reached the road. If they're allowed to use their ability in this realm, why aren't they opened to the power *all* the time?"

"Maybe they're as new to the freedom as our own people," Lorand suggested, his tone containing a shrug. "Or maybe they don't know that they ought to be. You can't be in full control of your ability unless you're in very close touch with it."

"Well, if they don't know that, let's not tell them," Tamrissa put in, her own tone serious. "At least not until we know exactly who and what we're dealing with. If they turn out to be something other than friends, what they don't know can't hurt us."

"I agree," Vallant said, his gaze still on the approaching figures on horseback. "Let's start movin' again, and meet them halfway. But let's also make sure that we move just as slowly. They probably know just how many people we have with us, but knowin' and seein' that many comin' at you are two different things."

The suggestion was much too sensible to ignore, so they all began to ride down the hill. The road was a decent one, Jovvi had noticed, and had been surfaced with something dark that Lorand said was tar mixed with other things. The warm weather had softened the dark mixture, but in winter it must make a superior road surface to travel on. The Gandistran empire had nothing like it, which was another point to thank the nobles for. If they'd had more interest in trade and less in conquest, Gandistra might have had the surfacing process many years earlier.

It took some time to reach the approaching men, who eventually stopped and waited for the newcomers to get to *them*. Since Jovvi's group was headed toward the city it made sense for the men to wait, but they still looked—and felt—somewhat uncertain when Jovvi and the others rode up to them.

"Greetings," the man in the lead said with a nervous smile. "We've come to welcome you to the empire of Gracely, and to guide you to the accommodations that have been prepared. Our leaders are sure you'll all want to see the city, but it would be more prudent to have you visit in smaller groups than you're now in. We don't want our people to believe that we're being invaded."

"Most especially since they're *not* being invaded," Jovvi told the man with her best smile, finding it impossible not to notice how he and his companions seemed to want to stare at her. "We'll try to arrange something that will satisfy everyone, but at the moment we'd like to be shown to the accommodations you mentioned. I'm told that the rain is likely to start at any time."

"Yes, we've been told the same, so we'll certainly

hurry," the man responded, then couldn't seem to control himself any longer. "Please excuse our rudeness, Exalted One, but I, for one, feel completely overwhelmed. I've never met *anyone* with your strength of talent, and all I seem to want to do is stand and stare in awe. But since that would also mean standing and watching you get soaked in the rain, I'll put the staring off until later. Please follow us."

Jovvi smiled her amusement and nodded agreement, and the three men turned their horses and led off up the road at a faster pace than they'd used coming down. Vallant turned to wink at Jovvi before he followed, Lorand flashed her an amused but proud smile, and Tamrissa looked satisfied. Nothing had changed Naran's serene expression, and Rion looked as distant and distracted as he had for the last few days.

Jovvi also urged her horse forward, pleased to find that many of the people following them had relaxed the least little bit. The man's joking reference to his feelings had dissolved a bit of tension, and now everyone was more alert than worried. The man had been frank on purpose, Jovvi knew, in an effort to lessen the tension he'd also been aware of.

But that was only the first step in the initial encounter with these people. Jovvi hadn't liked the way the man had immediately found a reason to separate their group, a reasonable reason they would be hard put to get around. If they decided to get around it in the first place. They all knew that chances had to be taken here in Gracely if they were to find out what was going on. And, more importantly, what would be going on between their two empires once all initial questions had been answered.

Jovvi pushed away the worry that wanted to flow through her mind, knowing it wasn't the time to worry. That time would certainly come along, but in the interim she was very glad that their hosts seemed to know nothing of the second group following a few hours behind them. The Blendings in that second group would watch carefully to see how *they* were treated, and would intervene or come to their rescue if it turned out they needed rescue.

At a time, hopefully, that would *not* be too late . . .

TWENTY-NINE

Embisson Ruhl hated the way the entire area they rode through was filled with the quiet of emptiness. In more normal times it had been possible to *feel* the presence of noble peers in their homes as one rode past, a feeling that assured one that he was among his own. That comfort and delight was gone, and the lack turned Embisson bitter in spite of his best efforts.

"Father, I do wish you'd reconsider," Edmin said from where he sat beside Embisson on the coach seat. "Letting Noll and his wife and that madman Howser go off on their own isn't the best of ideas. I'd feel better if they were in a place where I could keep an eye on them."

"Keeping an eye on them is an extra chore we don't need," Embisson answered, trying to be gentle with Edmin. "I wasn't looking forward to spending my time holding my breath while waiting for one of them to do something to betray our presence in the city. When Noll mentioned that he and the others would be more comfortable in their own home, I jumped at the chance to agree."

"In that case, you ought to be more worried than relieved," Edmin persisted, bringing Embisson a touch of impatience. "If we aren't there to watch what they do, they'll betray themselves—and us—that much more quickly."

"They may betray themselves, but they won't be able to do the same to us," Embisson corrected, his somber mood lightening. "Our driver isn't taking us to my house here in the city, we're going somewhere else entirely. A somewhere the Nolls and Howser know nothing about."

"Then you meant to cut us off from them as soon as we reached the city," Edmin said slowly, and Embisson could feel his son's stare. "If that's so, why do our plans include Noll's agents? Noll won't be able to find us even if he and the others *aren't* caught."

"That's a minor detail," Embisson said, fighting to keep his irritation from showing. "Now that we're back you can rebuild your own sources of information, making Noll's sources irrelevant and unnecessary. We don't need those people, Edmin, and now we won't have to pretend that we mean to give them more than we actually planned to. You and I—and our three hundred guardsmen—will take care of everything ourselves."

"I see," Edmin said quietly, a capitulation Embisson found satisfying. "We'll be using my sources of information rather than Noll's. But you've never mentioned how you intend to use our guardsmen."

"You should get a chuckle out of that part of it, just as I do," Embisson replied, sounding the chuckle he'd mentioned. "It so happens that the law gives members of the nobility the right to appoint guardsmen as official peacekeepers. Once our men have made it into the city in small groups that ought to go unnoticed, we'll send them out as officials of the true government—in other words, us. They'll arrest—or finish off—every fool who tries to get in their way. The ones the Seated Blending left to watch over things will be too involved in trying to take over themselves to notice what's happening until it's too late for them. We ought to be back in power in no more than two or three days."

"I'm sorry, Father, but I'm afraid that that plan won't work at all," Edmin responded after a moment, startling Embisson into turning and looking at him. "There are too many points of objection that it doesn't take into account, so we'll have to sit down and discuss the matter as soon as we get where we're going. In fact, it might be a good idea to leave the planning for tomorrow, after we've both had a good night's sleep."

"What's wrong with you, Edmin?" Embisson barked with a frown, completely out of patience. "There's nothing to object to in my plan and you ought to know it. Have you lost your nerve, is that it? Brace up, boy, and try to act like a man anyway."

"Father, I think you've gotten confused," Edmin countered, his words and tone still even and calm. "Your plan might work if things were as they used to be, but conditions have changed drastically. For instance, we were told there are other Blendings in the city, not to mention quite a few High talents. If we bring our men out into the open with no attempt to disguise them, they can be taken over as easily as Lord Henich's army was. Not to mention the fact that there's no longer such a thing as nobility recognized in this city. How, then, can any men we send out be considered even remotely official?"

"Don't be a fool, Edmin, of course our men will be official," Embisson blustered as he tried to ignore a cold chill that formed in his innards. "Things can't possibly have changed *that* much, not after all the decades and centuries we controlled them. Once we've taken over the city again, you'll see how fast everyone reverts to acting the way they used to. And those fool judges in the courts will back us as usual, because they'll still be afraid not to. Don't you worry, everything will be just fine."

Embisson patted his son's shoulder before turning away from him again, horribly disappointed but refusing to let the emotion show. Edmin had once been his strongest supporter and aide, but now that the boy had lost his nerve it was clear to Embisson that he would have to continue on alone.

For a moment Embisson had been shaken by something Edmin had said, but reason had returned soon enough to calm all unreasonable fears. It was mindless to think things had changed so much that his carefully thought out and effective plan would fail to work. No, the only thing he could no longer count on was Edmin, but that was all right. He would take care of Edmin, and afterward no one needed to know about the lapse. After all, Edmin was the only one left to succeed him, and he would *need* a successor. He *would*!

Edmin sat back on the coach seat with an inaudible sigh, giving up the idea of forcing his father to acknowledge the true situation they were in. High Lord Embisson Ruhl had returned to live in the days of his glory, refusing to understand that those days were gone. It was still possible to regain former power, but not when one cut oneself off from reality.

Rather than ask where they were going, Edmin stayed silent and used the travel time to list in his head the names of his former employees who might still be around. If those three hundred men were used wisely to foment discord in an anonymous way, they could end up being more effective than twice or three times their number used badly. But this was the last chance any of them would get. Edmin knew that without the least doubt, and knew as well that his father would have to be kept out of things until their war from the shadows rewon what they'd lost.

By the time the coach began to slow, Edmin had pruned his list of employees down to seven names. Those seven would be loyal and discreet, and chances were excellent that he would still be able to locate the men. They would have had no reason to leave the city and every reason to stay, which meant they would know everything going on. Edmin knew he would need the details of what was happening to know where to send his men, where those men could cause the greatest amount of disruption . . .

"Ah, it seems we've finally arrived," Edmin's father said, his tone showing that he was being deliberately jolly. "Once our two coaches have reached the house, I'll send some of the servants back to brush at the tracks we're making going in. It will be best if no one knows we're here until we have control of the city again."

"As you say, Father," Edmin agreed, knowing there was no use in speaking of anything else. "We can have a meal from what we bought at that last inn, and then I'm for bed. By the way, who did this house belong to?"

"I know you've never been here, but I used to visit quite often," Embisson answered, a disturbing smugness to his tone. "This was Advisor Zolind Maylock's house, and Zolind was the most powerful man of his time. That same power will soon be in *our* hands, which makes this house the most appropriate place we can stay."

Again Edmin nodded without saying anything, as the only thing he had to say would be less than complimentary. Advisor Zolind Maylock was, according to his former sources, probably the first casualty of the Blending he had allowed to come to power. There had been more than enough witnesses to the man's "heart attack" the night he died, but the death had been too convenient for the interlopers. If Zolind had lived he would have found *some* way to bind or destroy the five people he disliked so much, but those five people had proven to be stronger than anyone had ever dreamed they could be . . .

"We'll have to have at least one lamp lit before we go inside," Embisson said, drawing Edmin's attention again. "After that I want *all* the lamps lit, as a statement of our arrival. This house is far enough out of the way that no one will notice."

"But if someone does notice, we'll have thrown away the secrecy we need so badly," Edmin countered, not about to let *this* point slide by. "Once we're successful we can light all the lamps, as a statement of victory that no one will be able to miss."

"Oh, all right," Embisson grumbled after a moment, his glance at Edmin showing disgust even in the dark of the coach interior. "If you'll feel safer having the lamps unlit, we'll keep them unlit. But you really must get over this sudden squeamishness of yours, Edmin. We won't find it possible to succeed unless we move forward with boldness."

"As you've said so often, Father, there's a difference

between boldness and foolishness," Edmin pointed out in a way he hoped would do some good. "Boldness *will* win us the day, if we make certain not to cross the line."

"Yes, yes, I know that well enough," Embisson said, still grumbling but in a lighter key. "We're almost to the house now, and I really need to stretch my legs before I find someplace comfortable to sit down."

"Then why don't you take two of the servants inside while I direct the rest in covering our trail," Edmin suggested, deliberately trying to sound casual. "That way everything will still get done and we'll also be able to eat sooner."

"That's a good idea," Embisson agreed, now sounding as though he hid extreme weariness. "And sleeping in a decent bed is another idea with appeal. Tomorrow we'll both be feeling like our old selves."

Edmin fervently hoped so, but there wasn't enough time to dwell on the hope. Their coach pulled up in front of the very large house, and once both coaches had stopped it was time to get things done.

They had brought eleven servants with them, and seven of the eleven had had to travel in the second coach. With someone sitting on the coach floor the space had been extremely crowded, but no one had seriously expected Edmin and his father to share *their* coach. The two drivers—and the one servant sitting with each on the boxes—climbed down to help everyone get out, but having Embisson stand around for too long a time wasn't wise.

For that reason Edmin took the first two female servants helped out of the coach, and told them to go inside the house with his father. He also gave them the small stable lamp he'd had the foresight to include with their luggage, and once the lamp was lit Embisson was able to lead the two women inside.

After making sure that his father was indeed gone, Edmin then gathered the remaining servants and explained that his father was suffering from the pressure of events which had upset him greatly. For that reason any orders given by Embisson that might lead to their discovery in the house were first to be cleared with Edmin. The servants seemed more relieved than surprised at the order, leading Edmin to believe that they'd noticed his father's oddness even before he had.

After that it took only a moment to send three of the men to brush out their trail, and the rest to see to hiding the coaches and horses. The other two women were sent into the house with instructions to pass on his orders to the first two women about not listening to his father once it was possible to get them alone. All the servants had been told that if Embisson and Edmin were caught, *they* would be tried and imprisoned along with their employers. The servants now believed that everyone in Gan Garee had gone crazy, and none of them cared to risk prison to find out if they'd been told the truth.

Dinner was a quick and simple affair, after which Embisson took a lamp and retired to the rooms that had been Zolind Maylock's. Dust covers had been removed from the furniture and clean linen found in storage chests, and all the necessary beds were ready to be used.

But Edmin couldn't retire yet despite what he'd said to his father in the coach. Embisson had given private instructions to the leaders of their guardsmen, which presumably meant the guardsmen would know where to find them. The entire force was supposed to be in the city well before midnight, and the leaders were supposed to report as soon as they arrived. Those leaders also needed to be told about taking orders from his father, so Edmin waited up to take care of the matter.

A book kept Edmin company—and kept him awake— for quite some time, but then sleep managed to creep over him. Edmin dozed for a time, waking up and falling back asleep, and then the sound of a footstep and the gleam of a lamp woke him all the way. He sat up to see his father entering the room, a frown on the old man's face.

"Edmin, it's four in the morning," Embisson announced with disapproval. "I got up to get a drink of water and saw the light of your lamp. Why haven't you gone to bed yet?"

"I was waiting for the leaders of our men to report,"

Edmin answered with a frown of his own. "You did tell them where we were going, didn't you, Father?"

"Of course I did," Embisson responded, annoyance quickly turning to disturbance. "They should have had no trouble getting into the city, so why haven't they arrived yet?"

"There are only three possibilities," Edmin said slowly, a nasty thought coming to him. "They could have been caught coming in and are under arrest, but that isn't very likely since they weren't all coming in at the same time or place. They could have decided to start an enterprise of their own, but that isn't very likely either. They're not so dim that they would give up the promise of wealth and position for a quick hit and run attack."

"No, they knew well enough that their best chance lay in cooperating with *us*," Embisson said, his disturbance clearly growing stronger. "So what could have happened to them?"

"The third possibility," Edmin answered in a growl as he stood, much too tired to play games of false politeness. "Noll somehow got to them, he and that wife of his. It was our gold that paid those men, so their loyalty should have been ours. I told you that woman was up to something, but you insist on thinking of women as helpless. Only a fool discounts an enemy because of gender."

"How dare you speak to me like that?" Embisson demanded, his skin darkened with outrage—and something else. "That woman is nothing any *man* has to worry about, but not having a woman of your own twists your thinking on the subject. You—"

"Wake up, old man!" Edmin interrupted harshly, glaring at the person he so used to respect. "You've messed up all the way around, you and that stupid plan you thought so much of. We've been used and now we have to get out of here. Noll and his wife won't want us running around loose while they put their own plans into effect, and as soon as the men reached them the Nolls knew where we intended to go. They won't turn us in to the city officials, but that doesn't mean we won't end up dead at the hands of the men who used to be ours. We have to leave here right now, and I just hope it isn't too late."

"Cowardice really has a hold on you, doesn't it, boy?" Embisson snarled, his face pale. "Those people won't do anything to *me*, they wouldn't dare! They know I'm a High Lord even if *you've* let yourself forget the fact. I'm not going anywhere but back to bed, and tomorrow I'll put together a new plan that doesn't include the guardsmen—or you. You'll be too busy running and hiding to give me any help anyway."

And with that Embisson turned and stalked out of the room, leaving behind an Edmin who had only one choice left. Dragging along the senile wasn't practical when one had a mission to complete—or when one had vengeance to arrange. The father Edmin had so loved and admired was gone forever, and he knew the sooner he accepted that fact and got on with life, the sooner he would accomplish what he had to.

The servants woke immediately, and once Edmin told them that they weren't safe in that house they worked fast to get the coaches ready. Edmin also took the gold they'd brought from Bastions, leaving only a small amount for the foolish old man who still thought he was important. It was all he could do for the old man, all he had time for.

This time Edmin shared his coach with three of the servants, an effort meant to deliberately remind him that they were all fugitives together. If his plans turned out to be successful he would be their superior again, but for the moment he was no better than they.

But he abhorred being common, so he had adequate reason to do his best to return himself to his former position. It would be a fight, but he'd been in fights before and he'd won. But first he had to concern himself with Noll and his wife, and Edmin suddenly realized he knew exactly the place from which to accomplish that concern . . .

High Lord Embisson Ruhl sat in the bed that had once belonged to Zolind Maylock, annoyed with himself for not being able to sleep. He'd been lost in his thoughts for quite

some time, the distraction starting when he heard the
sounds of a coach leaving. He'd hoped that Edmin would
pull out of whatever madness had taken him over, but instead Edmin had actually left. The poor fool was welcome
to the coach, especially since Embisson was well able to
afford another if he needed it.

But he *had* no need of another coach, not when he'd
already established himself in Zolind's house. This house
was a symbol of success that Embisson meant to use as a
rallying point, a familiar and reassuring symbol for all those
who would join him in his efforts. He would put the word
out, and every noble who heard about his return would
come forth to volunteer his help . . .

"But that can't be," Embisson suddenly muttered, wondering where such a foolish idea could have come from.
"There aren't *any* other nobles left in the city, everyone
knows *that*. How can I rally people who aren't here?"

It seemed to Embisson that he'd been living in a world
surrounded by mist, and now the mists were dissipating a
bit. The Nolls, the people he'd expected to use, had used
him and Edmin instead, and now he and Edmin were in the
city without the support they needed. Staying in the city
would be, at best, useless, and at worst, suicide. They had
to retreat and regroup, and decide what their best plan of
action would be.

Once Embisson realized that, he lost no time getting out
of bed despite the way confusion and rethickening mists
swirled in his head. Edmin had to be roused along with the
servants, and then, for some reason, they all had to leave.
Embisson dressed quickly in spite of the confusion, ignoring the fact that he hadn't been able to bathe, and then he
went to search out Edmin.

He'd checked the three bedchambers nearest his before
he began to wonder what he was doing. He was High Lord
Embisson Ruhl, wasn't he? Since when did a High Lord
have to run from *anything*? He could stay right where he
was and do anything he pleased, and no one would be able
to say a word or do a thing about it.

"And what I please right now is to have breakfast," Embisson decided aloud, annoyed with himself for having

doubted his power even for a moment. "Once I've eaten, I'll begin making my plans, and in two or three days things will be right back to where they were before this idiocy began."

Pleased with his decision, Embisson went to ring for a servant. He pulled the bell cord more than once, but long minutes passed and there was no response. Annoyed beyond bearing, Embisson took a lamp and started toward the servants' area, fully intending to give those lazy fools an earful. He might even dismiss some of them, which would certainly cause the others to work harder to keep their own positions. Just the way things were supposed to be . . .

Embisson hadn't gone far before he heard the sound of movement coming from the front of the house, and his mood immediately lightened. So his servants weren't lying slug-a-bed after all, but had risen early to get the house in shape for him. They hadn't expected *him* to be awake so early, and so hadn't left anyone to listen for a ring.

An expansive feeling replaced his anger, letting Embisson head for the front of the house wearing a smile of approval. That was the key to training servants, he knew, being firm when they needed firmness and giving them approval when they behaved properly. This was definitely a time for approval, and he would—

"Who in the name of chaos are *you*?" Embisson demanded, stopping short when he saw the six strange men who were crossing the large sitting room. "And more importantly, what are you doing here? This is *my* house now, and I want you out of it!"

"We were looking for *you*, Lord Embisson," one of the men said after a brief hesitation, having exchanged a glance with the others. "We thought the house was empty and were about to leave. Aren't your son and all those servants still with you?"

"What do you mean, the house is empty?" Embisson demanded again, shock hitting him hard. "Edmin ran off because of his cowardice, of course, but he couldn't have taken the servants with him! Something like that would be intolerable, and I would never stand for it."

"Of course you wouldn't," the same man soothed, coming closer to take the lamp that Embisson held. "You're an important man, and we've been given very definite orders about how we're supposed to treat you. But . . . where did you say your son went? If he isn't allowed to live *here* any longer, where would he go?"

"He probably crawled back to his own house to hide," Embisson told the man with a snort of disdain. "I used to think he was a son worthy of a man like me, but he finally showed his true colors. I don't know who you men are, but I'm hungry and would like breakfast. Tell the servants to prepare the meal immediately, and after I've eaten I'll allow you a few minutes to tell me why you've come."

"That's all right, Lord Embisson, we won't need much time to tell you why we've come," the man answered smoothly as a second man came to stand to Embisson's left. "In fact, we can take care of that little chore right now."

The man smiled at Embisson, but a sudden pain in Embisson's back kept the High Lord from rebuking the man for disagreeing with him. The pain was sharp and very unexpected, and Embisson staggered when his knees suddenly failed to hold him upright. In an eyeblink Embisson lay on the carpeting, having no idea what could have happened.

"Clean your knife and then let's get out of here," the same man said, speaking through a ringing in Embisson's ears. "The boss isn't going to be happy to hear that the other one got away—and took the servants with him."

"Yeah, they were countin' on havin' those servants to do for *them*," another voice agreed distantly as everything around Embisson began to fade. "Not to mention wantin' to hear that the second also went the way of the first. Too bad we couldn't get the old man to tell us where the other one went. Now we gotta go lookin' for him."

The first man said something else as the entire group began to leave, but Embisson was no longer able to hear the words. The ringing and fading were increasing, and then the black—

THIRTY

Sembrin Noll knocked gently on the door of the bedchamber Bensia had claimed for herself. The house was much larger than the one they'd owned here in the city before the trouble, but the paintings and expensive decorations were gone. Since the doors and windows of the house were still whole, Sembrin assumed that the decorations had been confiscated rather than looted. Which said quite a lot about the new administration . . .

"Come in, dear," Bensia called out from inside the room, and Sembrin walked in to see her sitting at the room's dressing table. "Do you have word yet from the men you sent after the Ruhls? I'd really enjoy having those servants fix a lovely breakfast."

"I'm afraid we're going to have to fix our own lovely breakfast for a while," Sembrin told her as he closed the door behind him. "The men are back, but the plan didn't go as well as we hoped it would."

"You can't mean that Ruhl didn't go to Maylock's house after all," Bensia said, turning on the bench to look directly at him with her disturbance. "The man would have had to come to his senses for that to happen, and I don't believe he was able to."

"Well, you're right about that," Sembrin allowed as he walked to a chair not far from her and sat. "The men found Embisson Ruhl right there in the house, but apparently he'd been deserted. Edmin, the servants, and the two coaches were gone, and we don't yet know where they've gone *to*.

381

The men asked Ruhl about it before they killed him, but he had no real idea about where his son might have gone."

"So now we'll have to search Edmin out," Bensia muttered with a grimace. "I was certain he would die rather than desert his father, but apparently he has more sense than to stay with a sinking ship. But Lord Embisson has definitely been taken care of?"

"I was told that the deed was done with a knife in the back," Sembrin responded with a nod. "Embisson is no longer of concern to anyone, but the same can't be said of Edmin. I have the definite feeling that he'll be very difficult to locate."

"Even so, he shouldn't be much of a problem," Bensia decided, turning back to the mirror and picking up her hairbrush. "He can't 'betray' us when he doesn't know where we are, and sending an anonymous warning to the authorities now in charge will only set *them* looking for him as well. We'll put our plan in motion just as soon as you find out where those people are most vulnerable, but we *will* have to use the men for one other purpose. I can't abide not having servants, so they'll have to kidnap some for us."

"You want the men to kidnap servants?" Sembrin echoed, not quite believing his ears. "Don't you think people will notice when we cart off their neighbors?"

"We *will* be a bit more subtle than that, my dear," Bensia replied with a small laugh of amusement. "You'll have some of the men locate suitable servants, and then the children will pay those people a visit. After the visit the people involved will cooperate with the kidnapping, after having given their neighbors an excuse for their upcoming absence. There will be no hue and cry, and we won't have to worry about eating the food they prepare."

"Well, this house *will* be more comfortable with servants to care for us," Sembrin grudged, his objections evaporating almost immediately. "Yes, that does sound like a good idea, but for the moment I've borrowed the cooks who took care of the men on the way to the city. I'm not quite sure how edible the food is, but it's hot and ready for us to taste right now."

"I think we ought to have our new servants bring an adequate supply of food with them," Bensia mused as she put her brush aside and rose. "I'll make sure that the children take silver to give them, and the men who 'kidnap' them will have to help transport those supplies. The men themselves, though, will have to go in small groups to buy their own supplies. We can't announce our presence by bringing in tons of food."

Sembrin made no mention of the fact that what she'd said was obvious; he simply rose himself and followed Bensia out of the room. Once downstairs he led the way to the smaller of the two dining rooms, which was still large enough to accommodate a dozen people or more. The instructions he'd given for putting the food out on the buffet had been followed, so he and Bensia helped themselves and then sat down to eat.

"Well, at least it's hot," Bensia pronounced after a taste of everything she'd put on her plate. "The eggs are almost adequate, but the rest is in desperate need of proper seasoning. Let's try to get those servants in here before lunchtime."

Again Sembrin simply nodded as he continued to eat, knowing he'd be given no rest until Bensia had her servants. The biggest problem was that the children were still asleep, and would probably stay asleep until someone woke them. If the men managed to locate suitable people for servants quickly enough, the children would get a good deal less sleep than they were expecting. Which would bring problems of its own due to less than pleasant moods . . .

Despite Bensia's criticism of the food, she still finished everything on her plate. Sembrin noticed that as he finished the last of the tea in his cup, but knew better than to mention the fact. He had just risen to refill his teacup when one of the men standing guard entered the dining room.

"There's someone here to see you," the man told Sembrin, using nothing of titles or names. He'd been given orders to that effect, to make sure no one slipped in the presence of outsiders, but the lack of a proper title still annoyed Sembrin.

"I take it that the someone is a man who provided one of the passwords I gave you," Sembrin said, even more annoyed that the guard hadn't supplied that information to begin with. When the man nodded, Sembrin performed his own nod. "Take the caller to that small study near the front hall, and tell him I'll be right there."

The guard nodded a second time before turning and leaving the room, and Sembrin continued on to the tea service.

"I hope your visitor has all the information we need to get started," Bensia commented from where she still sat with her own teacup. "It's only a matter of time before someone notices that we're here, but if they're distracted by other, more important problems, we won't have to worry."

"We'll still have to worry, but not as much," Sembrin commented as he refilled his teacup. "We'll have to keep alert until the very moment we take over the palace, and then we'll only have to worry about our peers. As soon as we create them, of course."

"A task I can't wait to begin on," Bensia replied with a laugh of enjoyment. "They'll be really amusing at first, and won't become dangerous until they get used to their new standing. Please let me know how quickly we can get started as soon as your visitor leaves."

"Of course," Sembrin agreed with a smile, then blew her a kiss before leaving the room. Bensia was so lovable when she asked something of him, and that trait always made him want to please her. But at the moment there were other, currently more important matters to think about . . .

The man called Rolver waited for Sembrin in the small study. Rolver was tall and heavy, with a bearded face that proclaimed he hadn't a brain in his head. Rolver's favorite way of finding things out was to pretend he was drunk and in a sullen, private mood. Then he would stand around listening while those who were talking ignored him. In point of fact Rolver drank very little, and what information he brought was always completely accurate.

"I was surprised to get that note from you, Lord Sembrin," Rolver said once Sembrin had settled himself behind the room's desk. "In truth, I never expected to hear from you or see you again."

"Let's hope that the peasants now in charge of this city feel the same way," Sembrin returned dryly. "When they finally learn how wrong they were, it will hopefully be too late—for them. Tell me what I need to know about what's happening in this city."

"It's hard to decide where to begin," Rolver answered as he scratched at his beard with one finger. "People still aren't over celebrating the arrest of every noble that could be found—no offense intended. Most of those arrested are already on their way to Astinda, and the rest are scheduled to be sent at any time."

"We won't bother about any of *those* people," Sembrin interrupted with a wave of his hand. "If they'd been worth anything, they would never have stayed where they *could* be arrested. I'd be interested in hearing about any of my peers who slipped the net, but the rest are a dead issue. What about the troubles the new administration is having? There must be quite a few of those."

"There were at one point, but the new leaders are handling them one at a time," Rolver said, apparently choosing his words carefully. "At first a lot of people thought they could take advantage while everyone was busy celebrating being free, but that idea didn't get them very far. A lot of those Highs and strong Middles who were in the army in Astinda have been patrolling the streets, and anyone caught trying something illegal gets arrested. Afterward they never try the same thing again."

"Now, that's a good point," Sembrin said, leaning forward with interest. "The new administration has a guard force made up of people who are different from the average man in the city. It shouldn't be hard to make them look a *lot* different, and then to suggest that the next ones they go after will be honest citizens who have done nothing wrong. After all, who would be able to stand up to them?"

"I don't think that line will get you anywhere," Rolver said, an odd expression on his face. "A lot of people have been taking those talent training classes, and once they finished a lot of them joined the new guard force. *They* now do the actual patrolling, and link up with each other and with the Highs. If there's any trouble it gets handled really fast, and the guard force is so effective that people aren't afraid to walk the streets alone even at night."

"That's not good," Sembrin said with a frown, leaning back again as he reluctantly gave up that line of attack. "What about those training classes? They should be taking the strongest talents first, which ought to make for hard feelings among everyone else. And how much of a dead end is the training once it's been given? Almost everyone must be going back to their old positions after believing they would have something new and wonderful to do."

"The training classes are taking first whoever signs up first," Rolver supplied, his face behind the beard neutral again. "Now there are even more classes, because they're using everyone strong enough from the first classes to teach in the new classes. And those who are really strong or who have a special side to their talent are being hired by the government, usually for jobs that make the little man's life easier. Like they've opened free clinics all over the city, staffed by Earth magic healers that *they* pay. Poor folks don't have to just live with being sick or hurt anymore."

"This is really depressing," Sembrin said with a continuing frown after sipping at his tea. "Do you mean to say that *no one* is unhappy with the way things are now? What about the beggars and thieves and those peasants who are dirt poor? Surely there are malcontents among *that* lot."

"There aren't any more beggars, and what thieves are left are hiding out," Rolver said with a sigh. "The beggars and people who were dirt poor were all interviewed, and those that really wanted to work were given jobs they could handle. The ones who just wanted a free ride were told to get jobs within the week or to leave the city. Getting a job was a choice left up to *them*, but leaving wasn't. And once they left, they weren't allowed to come back unless they really had changed their minds. And I didn't say that there wasn't anyone who was unhappy with the way things are now."

"Ah, encouragement at last," Sembrin pounced, having no trouble noticing that the last of Rolver's words had been on the reluctant side. "Who are these malcontents, and why are they unhappy?"

"There's a small group of people who expected to be important in the new government," Rolver said slowly, again as if he chose his words carefully. "They came forward once the new Seated Blending took over, and tried to arrange things so that they would be really important and control access to the Blending. Somehow the new Blending found out about their plans and didn't let it happen. Now they badmouth everything going on, but the only ones who listen are the sort who are never happy with anything no matter *how* good it is."

"But those particular malcontents ought to know precisely what needs to be done to disenchant many others," Sembrin mused, his lips now curled into a smile of satisfaction. "Can you provide a list of names, and where those people might be found?"

"I'm afraid I don't know any of their names, and they tend to move around a lot," Rolver said, and this time there was no hesitation behind the words. "I'll be glad to look around a bit more carefully, and then come back with the list."

"Yes, I definitely want you to do that," Sembrin said after putting aside his teacup and getting to his feet. "I'll arrange for one of my men to pay you, and that man will be your contact. You and he can arrange for a place where you can meet, as I would prefer that you don't return here unless it becomes absolutely necessary. I'll be back in a moment."

Rolver nodded his agreement as Sembrin passed, and then Sembrin was out of the room and looking around. One of the guardsmen on duty wasn't far away, and Sembrin walked over to the man rather than calling the guardsman to him.

"I'm afraid that my visitor isn't one I ever want to see again," Sembrin murmured to the guardsman. "He'll expect to be paid by you when you take him outside, so make sure that he's given something both solid and sharp. You understand what I'm saying?"

"You're sayin' you want me to make a body," the man concluded flatly and quietly. "You care where that body ends up bein' buried?"

"Not in the least," Sembrin answered, pleased with the man's response. Rolver had once been a very effective agent, but now the man was clearly a convert to the new regime. Sembrin had decided that letting the man live would be a mistake of vast proportions, as Rolver had obviously decided to learn what he could of Sembrin's plans before betraying him to the new "leaders." Now that betrayal would never come about, at least not through Rolver's efforts.

It took only a moment before Rolver was led away by the guardsman, ostensibly to be paid in silver. Instead the man would be paid in steel, and the problem of his loyalties would be settled with finality. Now all Sembrin had to do was find someone to locate those malcontents, assuming they were real.

But there had to be malcontents *somewhere*, and he was determined to find them. Sembrin smiled as he headed for the stairs to tell Bensia what he'd learned. He'd put the best face on the lack of true information, and hopefully the lovely dear would never notice. He was very much in the mood to relax—as soon as he took care of the matter of those servants, of course . . .

And he'd discovered earlier that Rimen Howser was gone from his room, possibly even from the house. Now where could *that* man have disappeared to?

Driffin Codsent hurried through the house he'd been brought to by his guide, automatically noticing and listing every precious object he passed. He had no real designs on those objects, not anymore, but the habit was a hard one to break.

"I'm glad you got here so fast, Driff," Oplis Henden said as Driffin was led into a sitting room almost the size of the warehouse Driffin still lived in. And now people knew him by his real name, although his changing names on them had done no more than raised an eyebrow or two. "My people are fairly strong Earth magic users, but none of them has the talent for healing that you do."

Driffin no longer felt like blushing when Oplis Henden spoke about his talent for healing. Oplis was the one who had recruited him for the clinic in his part of the city and also as an instructor for one of the new classes. Driffin had been in that class when he'd been sent for, and he hadn't wasted any time answering the summons. Oplis Henden was a High talent in Air magic who was also a member of one of the Blendings left in charge of the city, and the man didn't believe in wasting people's time.

"We've been able to keep him alive, but it's been a struggle," Oplis said as he gestured to the old man lying on the floor of the room. "That knife wound in his back should have killed him, and none of my people know why it didn't."

"Some of us have a stronger tie to life than others," Driffin muttered as he crouched beside the man on the floor, immediately beginning to look him over. "And this one looks like he has what to live for."

Driffin was referring to the man's clothing, which was obviously expensive despite its rumpled condition. But then awareness of everything but the man's health—or lack thereof—left Driffin, and he sank down into the process of pre-healing.

The man was now being kept alive only through the efforts of the Earth magic users in the room. The knife that had caused all the damage had somehow missed most of the man's vital organs, but one lung had been nicked and there was a lot of bleeding on the inside of the body. Driffin first stopped the bleeding and encouraged the body to begin making more blood, and then he turned his attention to the man's lung. The tear wasn't difficult to repair and the lung was able to function again, and after a last look around Driffin withdrew his attention.

"I've repaired the most serious damage, but it's going to be a while before this man is out of danger," Driffin said to Oplis as he straightened again. "He lost a very large amount of blood, and although I've set his body to replacing that loss he'll be very weak for some time. Do you have any idea who he is, or what he's doing in this house?"

"I'm not quite sure *who* he is, exactly, but I'm fairly certain I know *what* he is," Oplis answered with a mirthless smile. "Those clothes he's wearing tell me the man is a noble, and what he's probably doing here is hiding out. It was just his bad luck—or good luck, as it happens—that we came here today to gather up the house's valuables before someone breaks in and walks off with them. There are still a lot of projects that will need gold to get started, and these furnishings can be sold to give us that gold."

"Remind me to thank this particular noble once he's conscious again," Driffin said dryly, coming close to regretting having healed the man. The nobles in Driffin's life had never brought anything but pain and misery, and Driffin had always been more than ready to return the favor in kind. But healing was what he did now, no matter *who* the victim might have been . . .

"When this particular noble is conscious again, I have a number of questions to ask him," Oplis countered with a sound of faint amusement. "One of the first will be about the identity of the Spirit magic user who worked him over. My Blending brother in Spirit magic tells me that the man was so full of buried commands that it was a wonder he could remember to walk upright. If there's someone around who's strong enough—and mean enough—to do that, we want to know who it is."

"And I wish you luck in finding them fast," Driffin said as he glanced around. "The last thing we need around here are more manipulators, even if their victims are no one but nobles. They could decide to change targets at any time . . . Do you need me for anything else, Op? I have a class waiting for me to get back, and afterward I'm scheduled to try my hand at something new."

"Something new?" Oplis echoed, curiosity suddenly showing in the man's eyes. "Don't you have enough on your plate with teaching, keeping an eye open for other healers, and working in the clinic? What else are they making you take on?"

"No one is *making* me do it, Op," Driffin answered with a smile of amusement for his mentor's protective and almost outraged attitude. "It's a different kind of healing I want to try, working with someone strong in Spirit magic. Too many people are hurt in their minds rather than in their bodies, and it might be possible to repair the damage there as well. But I don't think I can do it alone, so I found a volunteer to try the experiment with me."

"Is that a real volunteer, or a volunteered volunteer?" Oplis asked, joining Driffin's amusement. "I don't know, but I think I may have created a monster. You'll let me know how the experiment goes? If it works, I can almost guarantee that you'll have earned a bonus in gold. Will you still talk to me once you become the richest man in the city? And when are you going to look into joining a Blending of your own?"

"Give me a break, Op," Driffin protested, not about to be cornered about the Blending question. "I'll look into other matters in my spare time, once I find a way to *have* spare time. And I'm not doing any of this for the gold, something you ought to know."

"I do know it, which is why *I'll* take care of getting you that gold," Oplis returned with a grin. "People who work for the common good need to be rewarded, so they'll be able to afford to *continue* working for the common good. We don't want you waking up one day and deciding that you wasted your life working for the benefit of others. You'll also have been working for your own benefit, yours and your family's. Or don't you plan to *have* a family?"

"Make sure your people are very careful when they move that man out of here," Driffin said, his family plans another topic he refused to discuss in public. "Have an Earth magic user standing by, to revive the man if moving him does damage. And next time I hope we meet under more pleasant circumstances."

And with that Driffin headed out of the room again, giving Oplis no chance to delay him even longer. He'd have to finish with his class before he could go on to the experiment, but then . . .

∞

THIRTY-ONE

∞

Kail Engreath lay on his pallet in the large shed, listening to the others around him sleep. Surprisingly, the sounds of exhaustion seemed to be gone, and after only one day of complete rest. Or maybe the lack of exhaustion wasn't that surprising. They'd all been hardened on their journey from Gan Garee to wherever this was in Astinda. They hadn't been brought to a city, but to a fairly large town not far from the area of devastation.

"Good morning," a very soft voice said from the pallet to Kail's left. "And I believe that *is* morning I see beginning through the window. Do you think we'll have another day to do nothing but laze around?"

"I seriously doubt that we will," Kail answered just as softly, turning to his left so that he might speak more easily to Renton Frosh. "There's a lot of work to be done before the land we traveled through lives again, and I can't see the Astindans waiting any longer than absolutely necessary to get started."

"Have you noticed that we're still in the same group they formed after we buried those first poor people?" Renton asked, his expression more serious than usual. "I've been wondering what that means, assuming it means anything of significance. Maybe I'm seeing a situation that doesn't exist except for pure chance."

"Actually, I think there *is* some sort of significance," Kail said, feeling his own frown of thought. "We were all assigned work on the trip here, but no one of our group was given the really nasty kind of thing to do. I think they gave us a chance to sort ourselves out that first time, and now they're making everyone live with what they chose."

"And those who chose to be uncaring and important are paying for their lack of compassion," Renton said with a nod. "My father always insisted that my softness would get me into real trouble someday. Compassion wasn't a trait that was well looked upon among our peers."

"Survival of the coldest," Kail muttered, still disturbed by his own memories. "Yes, my father felt the same and said so often enough, especially to me. I wonder if either of them has changed his mind by now."

"You've got to be joking," Renton scoffed with a small and mirthless laugh. "My father 'used the iron in his backbone' to climb over any noble who tried to get in his way to the top. Do you really think he'd waste a single thought on Astindan peasants?"

Kail was about to point out that Renton's father—and his own—weren't likely to be given any other choice, but their conversation was interrupted. An Astindan man came into the shed and rang a small bell, and everyone was immediately awake.

"It's time to begin the day," the Astindan said in the neutral voice they all seemed to use to their prisoners. "As soon as you're ready you'll be given breakfast, and then you'll be issued your assignments."

There was a mutter or two as everyone climbed out of their blankets, but the Astindan had already disappeared. There was no need for anyone to stand over the prisoners and bully them into motion, not when they had no choice but to obey. This time, though, Kail spent no time at all thinking about unfairness. Breakfast sounded good, and he wasn't tired enough to want to spend another day doing nothing but lying around. Today, he suspected, boredom would *not* be a problem.

Renton stopped to stretch once he was on his feet, and Kail couldn't help but notice how trim his friend looked. Renton had been pudgy for all the years Kail had known him, but the forced exercise and changed diet had done wonders. And little Belvis Drean, the man who had been so incensed over the treatment he'd been receiving . . . The man was still small, but no longer soft and overweight and always complaining. Kail couldn't remember a single word of complaint coming from Drean since the day they'd buried those poor murdered people.

"You're looking in top form, old son," Renton commented as they joined everyone else in filing out of the shed. "You weren't doing badly before, but now even your muscles have muscles. And believe you me, every lady in the place has noticed."

"A lot of good that does me here," Kail muttered, but it was still an effort not to show his embarrassment. The women among them *did* seem to pay him a lot of attention, but even if privacy had been available, he couldn't imagine himself returning the interest. Most of the women were older than he, and even those that weren't reminded him too much of his mother. Kail's mother had always had enough charm for three women, and too often had expended it on men other than his father.

Renton chuckled as they moved outside and joined the lines of people waiting for their turn at the facilities. Everyone knew it wasn't possible to dawdle and waste time, but standing on line in the morning made you forget that. It might be a good idea if they were awakened in shifts, Kail decided, and he would have to find a chance to suggest that to the Astindans. They seemed to have as little experience in handling prisoners as he and the others had with being prisoners.

By the time everyone had used the facilities and washed a bit before getting into the very plain clothing they'd been given the day before, their breakfast was ready. A thick cereal grain had been prepared along with slabs of bread and butter and gallons of tea, and there was even honey available for those who liked their cereal sweetened.

Some of the older prisoners had been given the job of preparing the food and then handing it out, and Kail couldn't help feeling grim amusement as he accepted his portions. He couldn't remember the name of the man serving him, but the former noble had been one of Kail's father's cronies. Fury filled the man's eyes as he was forced to perform such menial work, and for his social inferiors at that. As far as Kail was concerned, there were few better people it could have happened to.

"I believe I'm actually beginning to enjoy myself here," Renton murmured as they left the food line to find someplace to sit and eat. "That man you were glaring at once turned me down for a position in the government that my father wanted me to take. I struck him as being much too common for a noble, and he suggested that I consider manual labor in place of a position of importance."

"He never lowered himself to the point of actually speaking to *me*," Kail responded with a satisfied smile. "I was always much too unimportant for him to notice. I wonder if we'll come across our fathers at some time in the same way. I can't decide if I like the idea or not."

"Yes, I understand what you mean," Renton said as they claimed a bit of grass among the rest of their shedmates. "I would love to see my father's comedown in life, but some part of me is convinced that if I did I would pay dearly for the sight. I doubt if I'll ever get over being terrified of the man."

Kail gave most of his attention to the breakfast he'd been waiting to dig into, but one section of his mind insisted on repeating over and over what Renton had said. *Terrified of the man, terrified of the man*, echoed and rang in his head until Kail had to face the idea squarely. Yes, it would be fair to say that he, too, had been terrified of his father, and it was perfectly possible that nothing had changed.

But it was also possible that a lot had changed. Kail took a bite of his bread, savoring the taste of butter after much too long a time without it, and chewed over his thoughts as he chewed the bread. Kail hadn't been sure if it was his father's personality that had cowed him, or the man's power and position. Kail's future and his very life had been at his father's mercy, but that was no longer true.

"I think I *am* getting over being terrified of the man," Kail said to Renton after a long moment. "I may be a prisoner here in Astinda, but I'm less of a prisoner than I was at home. What happens to me here depends on *me*, not on the whim of a man who was never denied anything he ever wanted. I wouldn't have believed it was possible, but I'm beginning to think that being taken captive might be the luckiest thing to ever happen to me."

"I'll reserve opinion until we see what we're expected to do," Renton answered after swallowing some of his own bread. "But as far as being less of a prisoner is concerned, I really do have to agree. I may be forced to obey orders here, but our captors don't also make me feel like a total inferior and failure."

And that was the major difference, Kail thought as he continued to eat. Not being made to feel like a failure. It might be worth what had happened to them, but as Renton said, that remained to be seen. They still didn't know what would be expected of them as a day's work . . .

But once everyone was through eating, they found out. The group Kail and Renton were a part of was called together by two Astindan men, and as was becoming usual, the older man spoke.

"You people here will work with the others sent out, but not precisely in the same way," the man informed them. "The contaminants must be removed from the soil before it can be made viable again, and much of that labor will be done by hand. You will each be assigned a group of people to do that labor, and when necessary you will join their efforts. At all other times you will coordinate and supervise their efforts, making the most efficient use of your resources and time. Does anyone have a question about what I've said so far?"

Kail's brows had risen and he wasn't alone in that reaction, but he had no questions. Nor, it seemed, did anyone else in the group.

"Good," the Astindan said after looking around. "You'll now be taken to where you'll work, and more detailed assignments will be given out there. Everyone in your groups should be making the same effort, but there may be one or two who don't. If you happen to find one of that sort in your group, you aren't to permit them to continue with slacking off. If you aren't able to administer discipline yourself, you're to ask an overseer to do it for you. Now you may follow my associate."

His associate was the younger man, who lost no time in turning and heading for a large, open wagon. Kail and the others all followed and climbed into the conveyance, and once the wagon was moving Kail turned to Renton.

"Ren, how would it be possible for anyone to slack off?" he asked, surprised that the possibility had been mentioned. "We've all been given the same orders about obeying, haven't we?"

"Yes, but different talents react to those orders in different ways," Renton answered in a murmur. "I, for instance, have Spirit magic, and I have to admit that I've found I needn't obey *everything* I'm told to do with the same single-mindedness you others are showing. Do you hate me terribly for that?"

"I'll think about it and let you know," Kail responded with a faint smile. "In the meanwhile, continue to be smart and don't tell anyone else. They might not have to think about what their reaction should be."

Renton nodded his agreement, and they lapsed into silence. After a moment's reflection Kail discovered that he was glad not to have Ren's resistance to the orders. If he'd had a choice about obeying, he might well have gotten himself into trouble rather than into a supervisory position. A supervisory position. He smiled at the thought of that for the rest of the ride. What a really bizarre joke . . .

Once they reached the area where they would work, Kail discovered that there was nothing left to smile about. The day was cool but should have been a fairly pretty one, and would have been if not for the decimated landscape. The barren soil had obviously been poisoned, and what trees still stood looked like they were about to fall over. Some of the land had simply been burned, but the rest . . .

"All right, form a group, please," the younger Astindan they'd followed to the wagon said. He now stood at the tailgate, after having ridden to the area with the wagon's driver. Everyone left the conveyance without delay, and once they all stood on the ground the young man led them toward the place where a large number of other people waited.

"There will be twenty workers for each of you to supervise," the young man said to the group in general without turning to look at them. "Each group will be responsible for clearing a set amount of ground, and your people will continue to work until their part of the job is done. If you allow your people to falter, you could still be here working after everyone else has gone back to the barracks. Don't forget to rotate workers for the harder jobs, so as not to wear out certain people while the others are left untroubled. After your workers are assigned to you, take them over to where you'll be issued tools and such."

The young man gestured to a place beyond the large group of waiting people, then turned to point at one of *their* group. The man he pointed to stepped forward, and twenty people were counted out from the larger group. None of the twenty looked happy, but they still produced nothing of an argument as they followed the man who would supervise them.

It soon became Kail's turn to have a work force picked out for him. After the twentieth had joined the rest, Kail led the way to the spot where shovels and rakes and wheelbarrows were being given out. Strong Earth magic users might have been able to do the job with less work, but the strong Earth magic users were busy elsewhere.

"How does it feel to betray your own kind?" a voice asked from beside Kail once they'd left the Astindan behind. "You must be really proud of yourself."

The woman who had spoken showed a definite sneer

mixed in with the haughtiness that hadn't yet left her. She wasn't a very young woman, but neither was she terribly old.

"Betray my own kind?" Kail echoed with a snort of ridicule. "You've got to be kidding. My former 'own kind' specialized in betrayal, turning it into what they considered a fine art. That's probably why you mistook this situation for betrayal, because that's all you know about. I'm following orders just like everyone else around here, and pretending to be disappointed in me won't buy you a thing. My father has the exclusive license for being disappointed in me."

The woman sniffed her dismissal as she looked away, but Kail recognized defeat when he saw it. She couldn't make him consume himself with guilt and she couldn't force him to defer to her, so she turned her back on the confrontation she'd started to keep people from noticing that she'd lost. A glance at the rest of his group showed Kail that she was fooling no one but herself. The others were too miserably unhappy to be fooled.

Four of Kail's people were given wheelbarrows, and of the remaining sixteen, eight were given shovels and eight rakes. An Astindan then pointed out a large pile of wooden crates as the place where the loaded wheelbarrows were to be emptied. After that another Astindan showed them where they were going to work, and they were left alone. Their assigned area looked to be a mile square from where Kail stood, and probably looked even larger to the people of his group.

Kail established four smaller units of two people with shovels, two with rakes, and one with a wheelbarrow. He then took his units out to the farthest reach of their assigned territory and started them working there. It made sense to have the wheelbarrows travel the longest distance while the people behind them were freshest, but no one seemed to appreciate the consideration. They muttered when he set them to digging and raking, and most of them looked scandalized.

The day wore on very slowly. Kail started out regretting

that he hadn't taken a shovel for himself, but it became more and more obvious that he wouldn't have had the chance to use a shovel or any other tool. He had to move constantly from unit to unit, keeping his workers from taking endless rest breaks, from going through the motions without accomplishing anything, from bickering among themselves. They did have to obey his orders just as they all had to obey the Astindans, but they had been left a lot of latitude in *how* they obeyed.

After the first hour, Kail had the shovel people and the rake people swap tools, and the worker who had given him the least amount of trouble was appointed to the wheelbarrow. The former nobles hated the idea of actually extending themselves, but the lure of being assigned to the wheelbarrow was too great. A number of the workers decided that *they* wanted the chance to stand around while everyone else worked, so a bit more got done during the second hour.

They were only a few minutes into the third hour when Kail saw someone approaching. It was a woman pushing a small cart of some kind, and when she finally reached him, she wiped at the sweat on her brow with one forearm.

"Water delivery," she announced to Kail in a tone that sounded downright merry. "Would you rather have everyone come here to the barrel, or would you like me to push it from work group to work group?"

"Why don't you take it to the first group on the left," Kail suggested with a smile he couldn't hold back. "After they take their drinks, the wheelbarrow person can push the cart to the next group over, and so on until everyone has had a drink. That way you can have a minute or two to rest."

"I accept your offer with thanks," the woman said with an answering smile. "I'll be right back."

She pushed the cart to the first group on the left, and while they were busy getting themselves drinks she walked back to Kail.

"You're the first supervisor so far today to let his workers drink first," the woman informed him with what looked like approval. "I'm glad to see there's *someone* around capable of caring."

"It was one of my most terrible failings back in the city I come from," Kail answered, finding the woman incredibly attractive. She wore the same cheap clothing they all did and looked hot and sweaty, but there was something about her . . ."And I'm equally as glad to see that there's at least one citizen of Astinda who knows how to smile. I'll grant there isn't much to smile *about*, but people should keep in practice so they don't forget how."

"But I'm not an Astindan," the woman returned, now looking surprised. "I'm from Gan Garee just like everyone else, but I think of myself as being freed rather than captured. My husband was an absolute beast, and when he mentioned taking my son away from me so that I'd have nothing to distract my attention from *him*, I tried to run away. My own parents betrayed where I was, and his people had caught me and were taking me back when the Astindans started to round everyone up. They saved both *my* life and my son's, and I'm happy to do whatever I can to repay the debt."

"I used to think I was the only member of the so-called nobility who would have preferred to be born to a peasant family," Kail said, speaking the admission aloud for the first time in his life. "Peasant parents might have been just as bad as my noble family, but at least I would have had the chance that they might *not* be as bad. Then I discovered that there were more of us who were miserable than the official stance would admit."

"If the only way you can stay in power is by being totally ruthless, you have to make sure that your heirs are the same," the woman pointed out. "If you don't, then whatever you've managed to accumulate will be lost by the next generation. I just don't happen to value *things* so much that I'll do anything to keep them."

"Neither do I," Kail agreed, finding it hard to look at anything but this woman in front of him. "But if the only way you can stay in power is by being totally ruthless, then you're incompetent and don't *deserve* that power. By the way, I'm Kail Engreath."

"And I'm Asri Tempeth," the woman returned, smiling again as she held out her hand. "It's nice to meet you, Kail Engreath. I hope we'll see each other again."

As Kail took her hand, he realized that the last of his four units had finished getting their drinks. That meant Asri had to leave for the next group of workers, and Kail regretted that he couldn't do something to delay her. He used one of the metal cups hanging on the side of the water barrel to get his own drink, and then watched as Asri walked away. After a moment or two she turned to wave, and once Kail waved back he had to return his attention to his workers.

But that didn't mean he couldn't think about her. It was almost guaranteed that she would be around again in a few hours, and Kail found himself looking forward to the time with an eagerness no prisoner should have had . . .

Wilant Gorl, Fire magic user and a member of the Blending that temporarily ran the Gandistran empire, stood looking down at the old man who lay unconscious in the bed. He stared silently for quite some time, and only the arrival of Oplis Henden, his Blendingmate with Air magic, distracted his attention.

"How's he doing?" Oplis asked as he joined Wilant at the bed. "And is the rumor true that you now know who he is?"

"I'm told he's getting stronger even though he isn't conscious yet," Wilant answered with a sigh. "And yes, we do know who he is. We found one of the former servants of the nobility who knew every high ranking member by sight, so there's no mistake. He was the High Lord Embisson Ruhl."

"But that's who we were warned about!" Oplis exclaimed in surprise, turning to look at Wilant. "He's supposed to be really dangerous and ready to start trouble, not half dead from a knife wound."

"I'm tempted to think he ran into one of the nastier

thieves we missed, but that's not very likely," Wilant said with a shake of his head. "It's just about guaranteed that he didn't come to Gan Garee alone, but he must have had a falling out with at least one of his companions. Once he's conscious we can find out all about it, but until then we stay in the dark. While whoever did this to him runs around putting their plans into action."

"I don't like the sound of that," Oplis stated, just as though he thought Wilant might be responsible for the situation. "We're still in the middle of rearranging things in this city, so we're vulnerable to a blindside attack. Isn't there anything we can do to prepare a defense in advance?"

"How do you prepare a defense when you don't know what there is to defend against?" Wilant countered. "If we go out blind and start to push people around in an effort to learn what we can, we'll just be helping our enemies. There are enough unhappy people in this city now. The last thing we want to do is add to the number."

"The only ones who don't like the changes are those who are afraid they can't keep up," Oplis said, disturbance in his tone. "And the people who think they were just about to become members of the nobility. And the ones who wanted to start their own nobility, but were kept from doing it. And the ones who have always thought they ought to be important . . . We have a serious problem here."

"Tell me about it," Wilant grumbled, running a hand through his hair. "I should have had myself locked away before I let us agree to stand in for Jovvi, Lorand, and the rest. While they're off enjoying their ride through the countryside, we're stuck here like targets on a board. Anyone who wants to come after us knows just where to find us."

"You know, there was a brief point in time when I considered those six crazy for saying they would stay Seated only for a year," Oplis commented with his own sigh. "I thought that anyone who gave up that kind of power before they had to was out of his or her mind, but now that I've had a taste of 'ruling' I never want another. With all the boring things rulers have to cope with, I have almost no time to do what I most enjoy—forcing people into happy, productive lives they can't find on their own. So what are we going to do?"

"We'll have to talk to our Blendingmates, but I don't think there's much we *can* do," Wilant said as he finally turned away from the unmoving body in the bed. "We have Ruhl here in the palace, and I mean to keep him under constant guard until we can talk to him. I've already sent word to the former servants of the nobility to keep an eye out for any of their onetime employers, and I've notified the patrols to be on the alert for unexpected troublemakers—even though I haven't yet figured out how you can expect the unexpected. Do *you* have any suggestions?"

"One or two," Oplis said slowly, obviously having thought about it. "Some of the people I've been working with have . . . contacts to those who live on the shady side of the law. If I tell them what's happening, they'll pass the word and let us know if they come across something more than ordinarily wrong. And aren't we scheduled to start putting together the first Blendings from the people who have completed the training classes?"

"Yes, we'll be working with the first of the new Blendings tomorrow," Wilant answered with a frown. "What have you got in mind?"

"Once those people manage to Blend, why don't we assign them the exercise of sending their entity through different parts of the city?" Oplis's gaze was more inward than studying the man he spoke to, so he missed seeing Wilant's brows rise. "It's hard to hide things from a Blending entity, and that way we won't be the ones who are invading everyone's 'privacy.' "

"I like that," Wilant said with a distracted nod, now leading the way to the door. "I like it quite a lot. And now that we've rounded up most of the people following that renegade Guild man Holdis Ayl, we'll have the other Blendings join in teaching people how to Blend."

"It's too bad we didn't catch up with Ayl himself, but maybe we can put his name on the list," Oplis suggested as he followed along. "As long as the new Blendings are looking, they can look for everyone we want."

"The ones *I* want most are our esteemed colleagues, back from their vacation in the country," Wilant said. "The instant I see them I'm out of here, whether or not the rest of you come with me."

"Come with you?" Oplis said with a snort of ridicule. "That will be me racing out ahead of you, accompanied by the rest of our Blendingmates. We don't really blame you for getting us into this, but not one of us wants to stay a minute longer than necessary."

Wilant nodded with a wry smile, knowing that Oplis wasn't exaggerating. He—and most of the others—had been more than eager to "stand in" for the empire's rulers, but that was before they'd had the actual experience. So many itty bitty details that had to be taken care of, so many headaches that had to be solved rather than ignored . . .

As Wilant led the way up the hall to the meeting room where he and Oplis were scheduled to join the others, one fact stood out very clearly in his mind. In a year's time, when the current Seated Blending oversaw the competitions the people had been promised, he and his Blendingmates would *not* be among those who competed. Let some other fools with more strength than sense get stuck with the job . . .

THIRTY-TWO

"Antrie, the Gandistrans are here," Frode announced as soon as he walked into the house. "My people are still in the process of getting them all settled into the inn, but they *have* arrived. And they have more attendants than we were expecting."

"Attendants?" Antrie echoed, pausing after getting to her feet. "Is that what *they* call the people with them? Can the others be servants?"

"The Gandistrans don't seem to be calling them anything, and I'm told the people don't act like servants," Frode answered, showing a frown. "My man called them attendants for want of a better word, but from his description I think that some of them are acting like guards."

"Well, they'd be foolish coming here *without* guards, wouldn't you say?" Antrie suggested, immediately feeling better. "How many of them are there altogether? Twenty? As many as thirty?"

"Ah, the actual number seems to be one hundred and thirty-eight," Frode said with a bit of hesitation, watching her closely for a reaction. "You're surprised that they brought so many of their people with them, I can see, but I'm told that the leaders of the group are going out of their way to be pleasant and calm. I'm also told that their major Spirit magic user is stronger than anyone my people have ever come across."

"I think we'd better find out about the rest of their major talents as soon as possible," Antrie responded, her good mood long gone. "And for the moment we'd better keep what we learn about them to ourselves. The rest of the assembly was very disturbed to have it pointed out that their Blending is composed of all High talents. As nervous as my peers have become because of that, we don't want to give them anything else to worry about."

"Especially not when the new arrivals are to be presented to them tomorrow," Frode agreed with a thoughtful nod. "I'll make sure my people report only to me, and otherwise keep their mouths closed. Is there anything else you need done?"

"I'd just like to make triply sure that these people are well-protected," Antrie said, looking around for the bell to summon a runner. "I'll let Cleemor Gardan know that our visitors have arrived, and possibly he'll think of something I've overlooked. I'm much too nervous to be certain I've covered everything."

"Stop worrying, the meeting will go perfectly," Frode said firmly, his hands taking hers. "I'll make sure that nothing goes wrong, and if something bad does happen you can blame it on me and fire me. If those people were looking for an excuse to start a war, what was done to their army would be excuse enough."

"Yes, you're right of course," Antrie said with a smile as she moved closer to the delightful man. "Our visitors don't want war any more than we do, so we have to be as honest with them as possible. And we have to warn them that some of our people will be playing politics rather than being honest. If we let them know what to expect, they shouldn't get too upset if—when—something happens."

"That's the idea," Frode said with an approving smile of his own, hugging her briefly before stepping back. "We both have things to do, so I'll be on my way now. If I don't make it back tonight, I'll see you for certain tomorrow."

Antrie nodded and exchanged a quick kiss with him, and then he strode to the door and was gone. She stood quietly for a moment trying to hang onto the pleasant mood his presence always produced in her, but it was no use. The demands of the moment intruded to cover all pleasant thoughts, sending her back to looking for the bell to summon a runner.

"I don't know about the rest of you, but *I* certainly enjoyed that breakfast," Lorand said as I finished the last of the tea in my cup. "Now I just hope I can say the same for the rest of our time here."

"After that nice long visit to their bath house last night, I'm a new and patient woman," I said. "I'm even willing to admit that their hospitality so far has been perfect. Treatment like that either means they want to be friendly, or that whatever attack they have planned is supposed to come as a shock. But I'm willing to wait to find out which it will be."

"That *is* a patient attitude, at least for you," Vallant teased with a grin, his amusement increasing when I stuck my tongue out at him. "But they're waitin' with those carriages to take us into the city, so we really ought to get goin'."

"While our link groups stay here, just relaxing together," Jovvi commented as we began to get to our feet. I wasn't the only one who smiled at her because of the comment, but my smile was probably the nastiest. We'd done some experimenting while on the road, and had discovered that we could even reach the link groups from the two Blendings following us about four hours back. Reaching our own link groups from inside the city shouldn't be quite that difficult—assuming we needed them.

"Good morning, Exalted Ones," a man said with a bow when we walked out of the inn, the same man who had greeted us on the road. "Your carriages are ready, and our assembly is eagerly awaiting your visit."

There were six large carriages waiting, possibly because we'd been told that some of our "attendants" could accompany us. Vallant smiled when he saw the array, but he also shook his head.

"We won't be needin' so many carriages," he told our temporary host in his most pleasant tone of voice. "Our associates will be stayin' here today, restin' up after our long trip. With only the six of us goin', two carriages ought to do. And why are you callin' us 'Exalted Ones'?"

"That's the term of respect used for members of our assembly," the man responded despite his surprise. "Is there a different term you would prefer that I use? And are you certain that you require the presence of none of your . . . associates?"

"We still don't want your people thinkin' that we're here to invade or attack," Vallant pointed out pleasantly while the rest of us just smiled. "Shall we get started now?"

"Yes, of course," the man muttered, obviously disconcerted by all the friendliness we kept showing. Not to mention our lack of nervousness. The six of us were going into their city alone, and that had to be an indication of self-confidence the man would find frightening. Hopefully the people who sent him would get the message even more clearly and would decide on the better part of valor.

We were conducted—with more bowing—to the first two carriages in line, and we split up in the way we'd already decided on. Jovvi, Lorand, and Rion took the first carriage, while Vallant, Naran, and I took the second. Our still-nameless guide and host got into the first carriage, and another man joined us in ours. This second man was also one of those who had met us on the road, which meant that he was also a High in Spirit magic. The smile I sent him had a lot of amusement in it, which made his answering smile a bit uncertain.

The carriages moved off, and it wasn't long before we were rolling through the gates of the city. There were men standing around on the inside of those gates, but rather than being in uniform they were simply wearing some kind of armband. Either the citizens of Gracely were too cheap to supply their guardsmen with uniforms, or they were extreme in their dislike of anything that smacked of the military mindset. That didn't mean they weren't militaristic, of course, only that they didn't want to look like it.

The buildings we passed were ordinary at first, but once we got farther away from the gates the neighborhoods began to improve. Those lovely buildings we'd gotten a glimpse of became more plentiful, with carved stone facings and decorations of resin. The wood they used also looked to be coated with something that made it gleam, or else they made a habit of polishing the outsides of their buildings. Whichever, it still made for a pretty sight.

After a few minutes of riding on the nicely paved street, our carriages began to slow. We were heading for a large building that was stone, slate, and brick, with shiny wood embellishments around the windows and a wide lawn in front. The first carriage turned into the drive that made an upside-down U around the lawn, and our own carriage followed.

"This is where our assembly meets," our previously silent guide said suddenly. "All members of the assembly will be here to greet you."

"That's nice," I said while Vallant studied the building we were approaching. "All your Exalted Ones gathering to greet *us*. Will it just be them, or will the rest of your nobles be there as well?"

"Oh, we don't have any nobles in our empire," the man answered at once. "Every High talent is free to try to become an Exalted One, and every strong Middle talent works to become a member of one of their Blendings. Now that your own empire has gotten rid of its nobles, you'll probably start to do the same."

"We've already started to reorganize," I said after exchanging a quick glance with Vallant and Naran. "Not having nobles around makes everything *so* much easier."

The man nodded his agreement with a smile, pleased that he'd shown how current he was with our situation at home. Of course he'd also shown that Gracely was keeping close tabs on what went on in Gandistra, and had also told us something about the leadership of his country that we hadn't known.

It had sounded as though each Gracely Blending had only one High talent in it, which was definitely odd. I wondered why they would do it that way, but couldn't spend too much time on the question. Our carriage pulled up behind that of the others, and then it was time to get out. Once we were all on the walk and had gotten back together, a woman accompanied by two men came forward to approach us.

"Welcome, my friends, welcome to Liandia," the woman said with a smile that looked to be real. She was smaller than Jovvi, Naran, and me, but didn't seem to be diffident or overly shy. "I'm Antrie Lorimon, and this is Cleemor Gardan. Cleemor and I are both members of the assembly, and this other gentleman is Frode Mismin, our liaison man. With your permission, we'll take you inside and introduce you to the rest of the assembly."

"Thank you for greeting us so warmly," Jovvi said to the woman with a smile of her own. "I really must say that we've been treated beautifully by your people, and we're very grateful for the kind attention. Our trip here was rather long and tiring."

"We knew it would be, and that's one of the reasons

why we made arrangements for you at the gate inn," Antrie Lorimon responded, this time directly to Jovvi. "Stopping there is more convenient for weary travelers, as it saves them from having to find an inn inside the city before they can rest. Please, if you'll follow us inside, we've arranged to have refreshments waiting."

The invitation part of the woman's speech was directed toward all of us, and she gestured gracefully with one arm before turning. The two men, one huskier and older than the other, stepped aside to let us precede them, and that's when it happened. Without warning we were suddenly under attack, and not just by a single talent.

The petite Antrie Lorimon cried out as a blaze of flame extended toward her, but it never got to singe even a single hair on her head. My talent spread out to cover and protect everyone in the area, and then I had the time to look around for whoever was responsible for the attack with Fire magic.

And those attackers weren't hard to locate. Three men stood together in the crowd of onlookers gathered near the building, and they'd managed a lame sort of partial linking. But even with their abilities enhanced, they couldn't have been much more than ordinary Middles, if that. It took only a moment to burn all the clothing and hair off them and set them in a ring of fire, marking them for anyone official who would be interested.

During that time, my Blendingmates hadn't been idle. Three other men struggled with globes of water surrounding their heads, another three lay on the ground fast asleep, and three more rolled around gasping as if they couldn't breathe. A last three crouched down and huddled into themselves as though terrified of something, and that seemed to account for everyone.

"Do you think there are any more attackers hangin' around?" Vallant asked a shaken Antrie Lorimon as he continued to examine the people in the rest of the crowd. "If there are, we can round them up and put them in with the ones we've already taken down. And if you have guardsmen handy, we could use them right about now."

"Oh, yes, of course," Lorimon said at once, obviously

still rattled but just as obviously not about to let that stop her. "Frode, please summon your people at once."

"I should never have ordered them to wait for my signal," the man called Frode Mismin muttered, heavy self-disgust in the words. "And they should have used a little initiative . . ."

Instead of pursuing his complaints, the man put his fingers in his mouth and whistled. A moment later a large number of men pushed their way through the crowd, and when Mismin gestured all around, the newcomers separated to go to the various captives.

"Your pardon, Exalted One, but my men need that fire ring doused if they're to get to the fools inside," Mismin said diffidently, drawing my attention, then he spoke to my Blendingmates as well. "And if the rest of you Exalted Ones would also release the men you hold . . ."

The man was nothing if not brisk and competent, but he couldn't quite look directly at Jovvi. That told me he had Spirit magic, and his reaction to her talent level was at least as strong as the men who had met us on the road.

"I can't believe how strong that Air magic user is," Lorimon murmured, apparently speaking to the other man, who now stood beside her. "Cleemor, have *you* ever come across anyone that strong?"

"Not likely, but I'm certainly glad I came across it this time," the man Gardan answered her in the same murmur. "If they all *weren't* that strong, we'd have a serious problem right about now."

"We have a serious problem anyway," Lorimon returned, her expression the next thing to bleak. "How are we supposed to make them believe we had nothing to do with this attack? In their place, I would believe nothing I heard from the strangers I found myself in the midst of."

"Well, that seems to be that," Jovvi said in a bright and friendly voice as she moved closer to our two remaining guides. "Do you have to put up with this sort of thing very often?"

"Please, you must let us apologize for this monstrous outrage," Lorimon began, her expression just as hopeless as her earlier words had been. "We honestly had nothing to do with—"

"Now, now, it's all right," Jovvi interrupted to soothe her, putting one hand to the woman's arm. "We're well aware of the fact that you were completely appalled by the attack, which you wouldn't have been if you'd had anything to do with it. Do you by any chance have an idea about who *might* be responsible?"

"Not at the moment, but you can be sure that that will quickly change," Lorimon answered, relief and anger now mixed in her tone. "We thought everyone would understand how important friendly relations between our empires would be, but someone seems to have missed the point. And I'd like to say how grateful I am for *your* understanding. In your place I doubt if I would be as reasonable."

"You don't have to rely on reason when you're able to know the truth when you see it," Lorand put in as he stopped near Jovvi. "Surely your own Spirit and Earth magic users can do the same?"

"Of course they can," Lorimon answered with a small laugh aimed at herself. "I was so shaken by the attack that I never stopped to think about it. Do let's go inside now, and we'll see if we can make up for the inconvenience you were put to. If the assembly isn't completely open to any terms of treaty you'd care to put forward, I'll know the reason why."

The small woman looked and sounded very fierce as she said that last, but it seemed to be a fierceness based on personal power rather than nothing but pique. As I followed along with the others, I felt tempted to pity whoever it was that she decided was guilty . . .

Zirdon Tal stood in the shadows inside the assembly building, gleefully anticipating the attack that was about to take place. That little slug Syant had arranged all the details of the attack, but fate's luck had added the presence of Lorimon and Gardan. If they were damaged or even killed during the attack Zirdon might feel a small bit of regret, but nothing major. He wanted Lorimon and Gardan to live on and suffer for a while, but being finally rid of them would have its own compensations.

The newcomers left their carriages, spoke a few words with Lorimon, and then began to follow the woman toward the building. That was when the attack was supposed to begin, and it certainly did. Zirdon was only able to follow the Fire magic users, and their linked strength was mildly impressive. Together they were as strong as most High talents, and they ought to be able to do quite a bit of damage—

"No!" Zirdon choked out as the attack began—and was stopped almost immediately. "That isn't possible!"

"What isn't possible?" Syant asked from the deeper shadow he stood in. Zirdon had had the little slug disguised with extra hair and a beard, and the less-than-adequate diet the small man had been on at the shelter had added to the disguise by slimming him down. Coupled with the rags the slug now wore, Zirdon had thought that no one who'd known Syant should be able to recognize him if they happened to get a glimpse.

"The strength of that woman isn't possible!" Zirdon answered, the soft words sounding choked in his own ears. "Her talent is the strongest I've ever come across, and she handled those attackers of yours almost effortlessly! And the rest of them are being handled just as easily. Is this your idea of being effective?"

"This attack wasn't meant to succeed," Syant answered, the calm and patience he was being forced to show immediately grating on Zirdon. "In order to launch a proper attack against someone or something, you need to know just what it is you're going up against. I sacrificed a few useless men to gain the knowledge I need, and the next time I strike the results will be completely different."

"Why didn't you *tell* me this attack wasn't meant to succeed?" Zirdon demanded in a hiss, turning on the fool. "Didn't it occur to you that I'd want to *know* something like that?"

"You told me to take care of the matter and not bother you with the details," Syant pointed out in that same mindless, unexcited way. "Have you decided to change that order? If so, the details of the next attempt will be—"

"Not now, you fool!" Zirdon hissed, wishing he could shout instead. "I have to get to my place in the assembly hall as quickly as possible, and pretend to be as surprised by the attack as everyone else. But as soon as you've taken care of the next phases of the plan, you're to go to our meeting place and wait for me. I'll have questions to ask, and I expect full answers to all of them."

"Of course," the slug answered with that grating calm. "And the next phase of the plan should please you. The entire assembly will be thrown into complete disarray, and then the final phases will come into play."

"Yes, yes, whatever," Zirdon muttered, then hurriedly left the slug and made his way to the assembly hall. He'd find out all the details of the plan from Syant later, to be certain he wasn't surprised again. He should have known better than to leave the idiot Syant unsupervised, but he did have his own responsibilities, after all. And with Syant under his Blending's control, what could the foolish little man do other than obey?

Jovvi followed the woman Antrie Lorimon into the large room where a good number of people waited, her Blendingmates around and behind her. Lorimon's agitation had now settled down, but would have flared again if she'd had Jovvi's talent. It had been perfectly clear that the woman and her companions had been completely surprised by the attack, but that didn't necessarily mean they'd had nothing to do with it. Rion had told everyone privately that Lorimon and Gardan were protected by shells of hardened air, so they hadn't been in any danger during the attack. That meant they might have been surprised only by the timing of the attack, not by the action itself . . .

"My friends, these are our honored guests from Gandistra," Gardan rather than Lorimon announced as soon as they reached the center of the circle of seats. "They came here in good faith without even the smallest of guard escorts, and someone attacked them on our very doorstep.

That affront must be investigated at once, and the guilty caught and punished."

Exclamations of shock and outrage sounded from all over the room, but other emotions hid beneath the vocal outbursts. There were fifteen individual seats in the inner circle, the two belonging to Lorimon and Gardan the only ones empty. Some of the remaining thirteen men and women felt fear at the announcement, and a few were touched by disappointment. Apparently those few would have been happier if the visitors to their empire had to be shipped home in pieces.

"There are only two other women besides Lorimon in this assembly," Tamma murmured as the noise continued. "And it's Gardan who's breaking the news, not his female companion. It looks like the empire of Gracely is just like our own empire when it comes to letting women help run things."

"Yes, I'd say that one of the things bothering many of them is that fully half of us are women," Jovvi murmured back in answer. "They would have been happier if most if not all of us were men."

"I'm crushed," Tamma murmured, showing a hint of that very nasty smile she'd developed. "I may even go home and cry."

Various members of the assembly had stood to denounce the attack and whoever might be responsible for it, and most of the rest seemed compelled to follow their example. They apparently thought that speaking out would establish their innocence, but Jovvi found the procedure tiring. It would have been nice to have a hot cup of tea, but the refreshments mentioned were nowhere in sight.

"I have a question to put to our . . . honored guests," a voice rumbled out, and Jovvi looked up to see that a large, bulky man with dark hair and light eyes had risen from his place. He also hadn't been one of those doing the denouncing, so Jovvi listened with interest.

"I should think that all questions can be deferred until we get to the bottom of the most major problem before us,"

Gardan said, apparently trying to put the man off. "We need to find out—"

"Yes, yes, we do need to find out who was behind the attack, but that doesn't mean we can't do anything else," the bulky man interrupted to say. "I want to know why their Earth magic user is still touching the power. Surely he doesn't think he and his friends aren't safe *here*."

"We've noticed that most of your people don't touch the power except from time to time," Lorand answered before Gardan could lodge another protest. "For ourselves, the people in our empire have been denied the use of their various talents so long that we keep a constant touch on the power to show that we're no longer slaves. Worrying about whether or not we're safe has nothing to do with it."

"I can tell that you're speaking the truth as far as you've gone," the bulky man said to Lorand, his stare suggesting deep study. "What I can't tell is if there's anything you're *not* saying. How in the name of chaos did you manage to grow so strong, man?"

Lorand hesitated in answering the bald question, but Jovvi didn't get the chance to help him out of the corner. Just as she was about to speak, a number of ragged, obviously exhausted men stumbled into the room.

"Help, Exalted Ones, help!" the man in the lead called out, fear and pain in his voice. "There are invaders, attackers, and our people are being killed!"

If there was confusion earlier, pure pandemonium broke out now. The five men who had burst in were helped to seats quickly vacated by assembly members, and Lorand joined those people who were obviously Earth magic users in seeing to the newcomers' wounds. And they were *all* wounded, some so severely that it was a miracle they'd been able to stay on their feet. Jovvi wasted no time in joining her own talent to those Spirit magic users who worked to ease the men's pain, and after some minutes of effort it was possible to ask questions.

"Who are you, and where do you come from?" Gardan asked the man who had spoken. The man sat with eyes

closed and breath coming unevenly, but he roused enough
to respond.

"I'm Dislin Marne, governor of Eastgate," the man said
in a strengthless whisper. "I have no idea where those monsters hail from, but their ships suddenly appeared on the
horizon across the ocean. It disturbed us that there were so
many of them, but we had enough High talents in the city
to defend us if it came to that. It did come to that, but our
High talents weren't able to do anything. The invaders
landed hundreds, thousands, of men and attacked the city,
and we weren't able to stop them."

"Then what you need are Blendings," Gardan said, a
grim set to his jaw. "Four or five should do it, and we'll
decide right now on who's to go. We—"

"No, no, you still don't understand," the man Marne interrupted, looking as though he wanted to cry. "If you send
any Blendings, they'll be overrun just the way our High
talents were. Those monsters . . . they butchered our people,
men, women, and children alike, and we couldn't do a thing
to stop them. It . . . isn't possible to touch them with talent,
it just isn't possible."

Jovvi felt the shock flaring around the room, an emotion
she shared completely. Gracely was being invaded by people who couldn't be touched with talent? But *that* was what
wasn't possible, not the use of talent. *Everything* could be
touched, nothing else made sense. The man had to be
wrong . . .

But what if he wasn't wrong? What if Gracely fell to the
attackers? The next ones to be made victim would be the
people of *her* home, and hundreds if not thousands would
die before anyone in Gan Garee became aware of the problem. But even if they did become aware, if the man was
right there would be nothing anyone could *do* . . .

Get ready for

EosCon IV

The original publisher-sponsored, online, realtime science fiction and fantasy convention

January 6, 2001

Meet your favorite authors online as they discuss their work, their worlds, and their wonder.

(Hey, it's the first sf/f convention of the <u>real</u> new millennium!)

www.eosbooks.com